THE ALIEN MACHINES MOVED TO PROTECT HAFNER

"We're leaving, Meredith—call your people off." Dunlop hauled Hafner to his feet.

As he gazed at the six Gorgon's Heads standing motionlessly between them and the Great Wall, Hafner had the eerie feeling he was seeing a new level of programming being brought into play. With their tentacles poised like angry rattlesnakes, they seemed unnaturally alert, sensing the tension and danger and preparing to do something about it. Dunlop's soldiers clicked their rifles onto full automatic.

"Take it easy," Dunlop snapped, pushing Hafner ahead of him. "As long as we've got the doc here they won't touch us."

"Hell with *that*," someone behind Dunlop muttered. "Meredith! I'm accepting your deal!"

Dunlop swung around, brought his pistol to bear. "Back in ranks, you!" the major snarled—and Hafner leaped for the Gorgon's Heads.

He'd covered half the distance when he was deafened by what sounded like a small bomb. Where Dunlop had been standing, a charred figure now lay. . . .

Books by Timothy Zahn

BAEN BOOKS

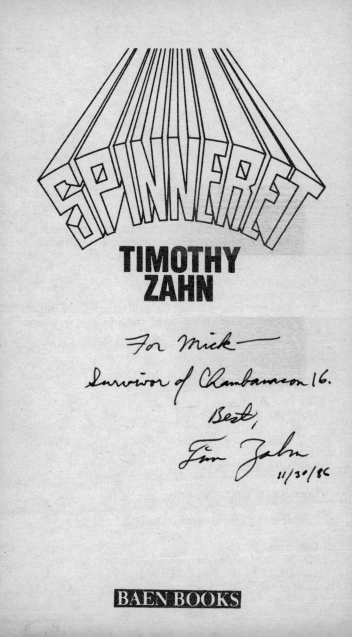

SPINNERET

TIMOTHY ZAHN

For Mick—
Survivor of Chambanacon 16.
Best,
Tim Zahn
11/30/86

BAEN BOOKS

SPINNERET

Copyright © 1985 by Timothy Zahn

A Baen Book

Baen Publishing Enterprises
260 Fifth Avenue
New York, N.Y. 10001

First Baen printing, November 1986

ISBN: 0-671-65598-1

Cover art by Vincent Di Fate

Printed in the United States of America

Distributed by
SIMON & SCHUSTER
TRADE PUBLISHING GROUP
1230 Avenue of the Americas
New York, N.Y. 10020

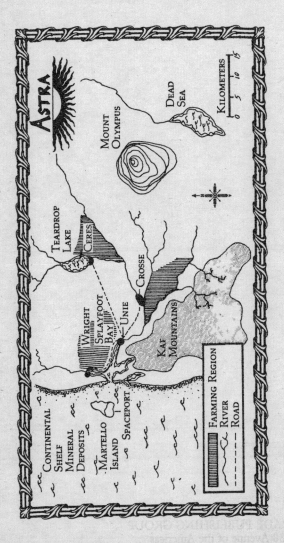

ASTRA

MOUNT
OLYMPUS

DEAD
SEA

KILOMETERS
0   5   10   15

TEARDROP
LAKE

CERES

CROSSE

WRIGHT

SPLAYFOOT
BAY

UNIE

KAF
MOUNTAINS

CONTINENTAL
SHELF
MINERAL
DEPOSITS

MARTELLO
ISLAND

SPACEPORT

FARMING REGION
RIVER
ROAD

Prologue

His only regret, Captain Carl Stewart thought as he stood on the bridge of America's first starship, was that there was no bottle of champagne available to smash against the U.S.S. *Aurora*'s side.

The ceremony would have been impractical, of course, even if the State Department had cleared it. In the airless cold of space, the bottle would have required special preparation to keep it from either freezing solid or exploding prematurely, and that kind of reinforcement might easily have kept it from breaking properly and on cue. With the launching ceremony being beamed live to the entire planet—and the 2016 elections barely ten months away—no one wanted to risk that kind of fiasco. Still, the sea and its traditions ran four generations deep in Stewart's blood, and it seemed wrong somehow to leave home without a proper christening.

The drone from the TV monitor stopped. Stewart brought his attention back to the screen in time to see President Allerton lay a hand on the switch by his podium. "Stand ready," he ordered, watching the image. An unnecessary command; the *Aurora*'s crew had been ready for hours.

". . . and with all of our hopes, prayers, and dreams riding with you, we send you forth to search out the new frontier; to find new worlds, new opportunities, new solutions; to reinvigorate and challenge the human race again to greatness. Godspeed, *Aurora*." With a final flourish heavenward, Allerton threw the switch—

And five thousand kilometers above him, the spotlights attached to the workframe scaffolding blazed with light, providing the TV cameras with their first clear view of the *Aurora*.

Stewart gave the dramatic moment a count of five, and then nodded to his helmsman. "Ease her out, Mr. Bailey," he ordered. "Mind you don't wing the *Pathfinder* on the way."

Bailey grinned. "Aye, sir," he said. Slowly, moving on its cold-nitrogen docking jets, the *Aurora* left the workframe's snug confines. It passed well clear of the *Pathfinder*'s workframe—Stewart noticed peripherally their nearly completed sister ship flashing its running lights in salute—and drifted off toward the barely visible horizon of the dark world rolling beneath them. "Lot of lights showing down there," Reger, the navigator, commented.

"Lot of people down there to use them," Stewart grunted. And the scientists with their fancy telescopes and theories had better be right, he added silently to himself; there had better *be* more planets out there for the *Aurora* to find.

"Clear for shift," Bailey announced, looking over at Stewart. "Course vector less than five-second deviation."

"Acknowledged," Stewart nodded, putting his fears for Earth's survival out of his mind. "Make it good for the cameras, Mr. Bailey: *shift!*"

And with a flash of sheet-lightning discharge through every viewport and vision sensor, the stars vanished into the absolute black of hyperspace. Next stop, Alpha Centauri.

Mankind was on its way.

*   *   *

"It certainly has every reason to be Earthlike," astrophysicist Hashimoto commented, his stubby fingers dancing lithely over the readout screen. "Position should give reasonable temperature, size is within a few percent of Earth's, and we're getting a strong oxygen reading even at this distance."

Stewart nodded, refusing to get his hopes up too high. In the six systems *Aurora* had so far visited, there'd already been one false alarm. "We'll continue on course; that should get us close enough for better readings. If a landing seems warranted—"

"Captain!" Bailey barked, his voice tight and a half octave above normal. "Something on the screen—moving fast!"

Stewart spun around in his chair . . . and froze. Coming out from behind the crescent of their target planet was a slowly moving star. Seconds later it was joined by a second . . . and a third.

Spacecraft!

"I'll be damned," Hashimoto gasped.

Stewart found his tongue. "*Shift,* Bailey. To hell with alignment—we can get back on course later."

"Wait a second," Hashimoto said—but with a flash the planet and moving stars vanished. "Captain!"

"As you were, *Mr.* Hashimoto," Stewart snapped, leaning on the title to remind the scientist of his temporary military position. "My orders are explicit on this point: in case of contact with nonhumans, I am to run if at all possible."

"But an *alien race*." Hashimoto was clearly in no mood to back down. "Think of the opportunities, the—"

"The *Aurora* is equipped for neither battle nor negotiation," Stewart interrupted him. "The diplomats can follow us once we've made our report; I hardly think the aliens will disappear in the next two months. I suggest you start analyzing the data we picked up and see if you can figure out just how Earthlike that planet really was. We'll want to know how interested the aliens are likely to be in *our* real estate before we make contact again."

Hashimoto's glare slipped into a thoughtful grimace; nodding, he left the bridge.

Stewart turned back to the gentle light of the displays, silently mouthing a word he'd once heard a Marine drill sergeant use. So life *did* exist out here . . . and if it existed so close to Sol, it must be pretty common, to boot. Perhaps a whole interstellar federation was sitting virtually on mankind's doorstep—a cosmic club whose members could finally give humanity the answers it so desperately needed.

It wasn't until much later that the other possible consequence of the "cosmic club" occurred to him.

The hiss of the landing jets died into a ringing silence in Captain Lawrence Radford's ears. Popping the release on his harness, he carefully rose to his feet, feeling awkward after three weeks of the *Pathfinder*'s zero-gee. "Start prelaunch check," he ordered the shuttle's pilot. "And get the atmosphere tester going, too."

"Yes, sir."

Stepping around his chair, Radford made his way to the airlock door, where the rest of the landing party was assembling. "Looks beautiful, Captain," Lieutenant Sherman smiled, reaching up to fasten Radford's helmet to his suit neck. "With all that green out there, it *has* to be running on chlorophyll."

"We'll find out soon enough." Carefully, refusing to rush, Radford completed his pre-EVA suit check. Then, giving the rest of the team a thumbs-up gesture, he stepped into the airlock. A ninety-second eternity later, the outer door snicked open . . . and Captain Radford of the U.S.S. *Pathfinder* stepped out onto mankind's first colony world.

He'd thought a lot about this moment, and he was ready. "In the name of—" He stopped short, the words dying in his throat.

"Captain?" Sherman's voice asked tentatively.

"All outside cameras on," Radford ordered quietly, wondering if the words would be audible over the thunder of his heart. The alien who had risen from the waist-high grass fifteen meters away was holding an oddly shaped metal device . . . and if it wasn't pointed directly at Radford, it wasn't off by very much.

"Uh-oh," someone muttered. "Captain—we're surrounded."

"Acknowledged," Radford said. "Kyle, are you getting all this?"

"Perfectly," the clipped voice of the *Pathfinder*'s first officer said. "We're on full alert; no sign of spacecraft up here."

"Yet," Radford said tensely. The aliens—he could see four more, now, in backup array behind the first one—were definitely wearing clothing of some sort, and the devices they held were identical enough to have been mass produced. No primitives, these—and the fact that the *Pathfinder* had spotted no traces of widespread civilization from orbit strongly suggested the aliens were themselves visitors here. "All right. I'm going to try backing into the airlock. We'll lift as soon as I'm aboard. Kyle, get the ship ready to shift."

"We'll be ready by the time you're back."

"Make sure you're ready before that," Radford said, "because if any alien spacecraft appear, you're to take off immediately. We're expendable; the information you've got isn't."

"Yes, sir." Kyle didn't sound very happy with the situation.

Radford wasn't especially thrilled with it either; but as it happened, the necessity for heroic self-sacrifice never arose. The aliens watched impassively as Radford eased back through the door; the shuttle regained orbit without anything like fighter aircraft appearing; and all screens were still clear as the *Pathfinder* shifted into hyperspace.

"Damn rotten luck," Kyle growled as they reviewed the films of the aliens later. "The place was absolutely perfect."

"We don't know that for sure," Radford reminded him. "Anyway, finding out man isn't alone in the universe is at least as important as finding new planets to colonize."

"*If* they're friendly, you mean."

"If they're not, at least they don't know where we came

from." Radford touched the rewind control. "Cheer up, Kyle—chances are good we'll find something else before we head home. And even if we don't, either the *Aurora* or the *Celeritas* is almost certain to."

"Maybe."

"Beautiful." Mario Civardi smiled at the planet centered in the telescope display. "Simply beautiful."

Captain Curt Korczak suppressed his own smile at the Italian's exuberance, which echoed his own, more private feelings. The European Space Agency had taken a lot of knocks for the delays that had enabled the Americans to launch their two ships first; but the *Celeritas* had just paid back the skeptics, with interest. A brand-new world, where mankind could start over again with a clean slate. No pollution, no acid rain, no overpopulation, no nationalistic posturing. It was almost like getting into Eden again.

"Captain!" the man at the radar shouted suddenly. "Something approaching from astern—"

The main vision screen flashed with light as something with a fiery tail shot over the *Celeritas* and vanished far ahead. "What the *hell*!" First Officer Blake gasped. "That was a bloody *missile*."

"Backtrack it," Korczak snapped. "I want to know where it came from."

"Got it, sir. Bearing down on us from—"

The chair slammed hard into Korczak's spine and a dull roar rattled his teeth. "Shift, Civardi!" he managed. "Get us out of here!"

And, for a miracle, the equipment worked. Safe in the blackness of hyperspace, the *Celeritas* limped toward home.

"I don't believe it." President John Kennedy Allerton shook his head, laying down the report. "Fifteen reasonably Earthlike worlds, and *every* one already occupied?"

General James Klein shrugged. "I agree it's pretty hard to

swallow, but the *Pathfinder*'s films can't be argued with." He hesitated. "I've also heard that the ESA's *Celeritas* showed signs of damage when it got back early this morning, so I'd guess they ran into them, too."

Allerton pursed his lips tightly. "If that's true we'll want an immediate meeting to compare notes. Probably better bring the Soviets and Chinese in on it, too. An alien race hemming us in on all sides isn't something we can afford to play politics with. I suppose we should tell the UN, too."

Admiral Davis Hamill snorted. "The Russians won't believe a word of it, at least not until they get their own firsthand data, and Chinese security is so lax these days that if we tell *them*, we might as well broadcast it to the Islamic Confederation and the Africans. I can just hear what *they'd* say."

Allerton smiled faintly. "You take the tirades at the UN too seriously, Dave. The Third World may think we're the cause of all their problems, but there's really no way they can blame Project Homestead's failure on us."

"They can blame us for alerting the aliens that we're here, though," Klein pointed out.

"Oh, come on—they surely already know we're here. They *surround* us, for heaven's sake. If they wanted to fight they would've moved in years ago."

"What about the *Celeritas*?" Klein objected.

"What about the *Pathfinder*? The aliens let *them* go."

Klein's rejoinder was lost in the simultaneous buzz of all three men's phones. Twisting his wrist to point the directional speaker at his face, Allerton clicked the switch. "Allerton."

"Situation room," a tense voice answered. "Sir, we've picked up a flash of light from a point near Mars orbit. We think it's a star ship . . . except that the flash was red, not blue-white."

Allerton looked up to meet Klein's and Hamill's hardening expressions. The shift flash represented wasted energy . . . and the lower-energy red burst meant the newcomer had a drive far more advanced than anything on Earth. "Full military alert," the President ordered quietly. "Worldwide. Prepare for possible invasion. I'll be down there shortly to take charge."

He signed off. The two military men, still talking into their own phones, were already heading for the door. Thumbing the White House operator, Allerton got to his feet and followed. "Get me the Kremlin, Chinese Premier Sing, and UN Secretary-General Saleh—conference call, scramble, and rush it."

The long star ship drifted delicately into high Earth orbit shortly afterward, stifling the Soviets' official disbelief and touching off near-panic all across the globe. But the end of the world didn't come on the anticipated schedule. Instead, the alien briefly blanketed the airline radio frequencies with a message, in passable English, requesting a conversation with Earth's leadership.

Considering the norm of international politics, the response to that call was remarkably swift.

". . . We welcome you on behalf of the Security Council, the United Nations, and the entire Earth. We look forward to the mutual exchange of knowledge and culture, and to a growth of true friendship between our peoples."

Secretary-General Hammad Ali Saleh sat down in his chair at the head of the semicircular table and reached thankfully for the water glass at his elbow. He hadn't been this nervous in thirty-five years, not since the Iran-Iraq border wars of the eighties. Then, he'd been a young Yemeni volunteer recognizing on an emotional level that the shells dropping out of the sky could kill him very dead. Now, his position was uncomfortably similar. No one knew why the alien wanted to talk to mankind's leaders, but the *Celeritas*'s experience suggested the answer might not be a pleasant one. Certainly the superpowers thought so; all three had voted in favor of letting the UN take the hot seat. Point man, stalking horse . . . the expendable ones. Sipping his ice water carefully, Saleh consciously relaxed his jaw and waited.

"The Ctencri greet you in response," the voice came

abruptly. "It is ever an honor to welcome a new people into space. Your race has advanced greatly in the eight hundred years since you were last studied. It is hoped that we may find a solid base for trade and mutual profit."

Something in Saleh's chest seemed to loosen up slightly. Trade and profit were business, not political, terms. Was this, then, merely a trading expedition? Saleh couldn't decide whether he would feel relieved or annoyed if the Ctencri government had indeed left their first contact with Earth to the aliens' version of AT&T.

Whoever it was out there, though, he had one very important point to clear up right away. "We would certainly be interested in discussing trade possibilities," Saleh said. "However, we have several questions we would like to ask first. Foremost among them is why your ships fired on one of our unarmed probes."

There was a short pause. "The question is meaningless. The defense units of Hreshtra-cten did not use force. Your lander was allowed to leave peaceably."

"You're referring to the incident with the *Pathfinder*," the American delegate spoke up from halfway around the table. "The *Celeritas* was in a different solar system when it was attacked."

"Only one ship entered Ctencri territory," the alien said. "The other presumably breached another people's region."

Saleh blinked. *Two* alien races . . . and both within ten light-years? The American President had implied it was a single race that surrounded Earth, not two or more. Honest mistake or deliberate deception? "Perhaps you can help us contact the other . . . people," he said, fighting to get back on balance again. "Or at least assure them we weren't attempting an attack on their territory. We seek only to find new worlds—unoccupied worlds, of course—that we may peacefully colonize."

"That will be impossible."

"Why? Don't you have communication with them?"

"Pardon; you misunderstand. We will certainly aid you in

contacting the other peoples. It is your seeking of worlds to colonize which is impossible."

Saleh frowned, his stomach tightening up again. "I don't understand."

"All suitable worlds are already occupied."

There was a moment of dead silence. "Occupied by whom?" the British delegate demanded.

"Many by their indigenous peoples," the Ctencri said. "Such worlds are closed to outside contact, as was yours until now. The remainder are occupied or claimed by space-going people such as ourselves."

"How many space-going races *are* there?" Saleh asked.

"The Ctencri have direct contact with nine others. The existence of seventeen more is known secondhand. We believe there to be many others."

The Russians didn't believe it, of course. Neither, to a lesser extent, did the Americans and the Europeans. The star ships were sent out again, in new directions. And again. And again.

Eventually, they were all convinced.

"So this is it," Saleh said, leaning back in his chair and gazing out the window at the lights of New York. They were glowing brightly, as usual, and the Yemeni felt his usual twinge of anger. The work at Oak Ridge and Princeton in the last century had guaranteed that the United States, at least, would not starve for energy for a long time to come . . . but the rest of the world still waited for the promised sharing of that technology.

Someone cleared his throat, and Saleh shifted his attention back to the five heads of state he'd invited to this meeting. "This makes no sense at all," Japanese Prime Minister Nagata said, laying down a copy of the report. "An Earth-type world complete with water and a breathable atmosphere and *no metals*? That's absurd."

"I only know what the Ctencri said," Saleh said, shrugging.

"It's *because* the planet hasn't got any metals that we've even got a chance at it—otherwise the Rooshrike would have found a use for the place long ago."

"Could this be some sort of elaborate trap?" Premier Sing of the People's Republic asked. "I understand the Rooshrike are the ones who fired on the *Celeritas*."

"According to the Ctencri, the Rooshrike simply act impulsively at times," Saleh told him. "Apparently, they jumped to the wrong conclusion when the *Celeritas* didn't give the proper identification signals. I've been assured that's all straightened out now."

"Less likely a trap than a swindle," Russia's Liadov rumbled. "How much would the Rooshrike and the Ctencri want for this worthless lump of mud?"

"Nothing humans can live on is completely worthless," President Allerton said mildly, a soft gleam in his eye.

The Russian snorted.

"The cost actually isn't that bad," Saleh said. "It would come out to eighty million dollars' worth of certain relatively rare elements—the list of acceptable purity levels is on the last page. For that we would get a hundred-year lease with renewal option." He paused. "Which brings us to the reason I've asked you here tonight. The rental fee would only be the tip of the iceberg if we intend to actually do anything with this world. Homes would have to be built, crops planted, industries started, colonists screened and trained—it would be a tremendous project."

"And so you've come to us for money," British Prime Minister Smythe-Walker put in dryly.

"Yes," Saleh nodded without shame. "The UN budget can't support something like this, let alone organize everything—we simply haven't the funds or manpower. We would have to contract out parts of the operation, which would take even more money. So before I even bring this up to the Security Council and General Assembly, I need to know whether or not the money will be forthcoming from those who *can* afford it."

"Why bother?" Liadov shrugged. "You ask a great deal for the privilege of flying the UN flag on a world with less economic value even than Venus. You would do better to fund expeditions to the Jovian moons."

"You overstate the case somewhat," Sing said, "but you are essentially correct. This world does not seem worth its cost."

"Crops won't grow without traces of metal in the soil, for starters," Nagata put in. "All food would need to be imported. And what could they export in exchange?"

"Other minerals," Allerton said, still skimming the report. "One of the continents appears to be ringed with underwater mineral deposits."

"What, silicates and such?" Smythe-Walker shook his head. "Sorry, John, but it's hard to imagine any rock formations worth carting up a gravity well and across forty light-years of space And there's still the thing with food, unless you want to add a few tons of iron and manganese silicates to the soil before you plant."

"Why not?" Allerton countered. "It's not as impractical as you make it sound."

"No—but it *is* expensive." Smythe-Walker looked at Saleh. "I'm sorry, but I don't believe His Majesty's government will be able to guarantee any support for such a project."

"Has it occurred to you—to any of you," Allerton added, glancing around the table, "that this whole thing *might* be some sort of test? That our willingness to take on what seems to be a hopeless task may be how all those aliens out there judge our spirit and ingenuity?"

"More likely testing our intelligence," Nagata murmured.

"I have an idea," Liadov spoke up. "As Mr. Allerton seems to be the only one of us interested in demonstrating mankind's resolve to our new neighbors—and as he is so fond of invoking Yankee ingenuity as the solution to all our problems—I suggest we give the United States a UN mandate to develop and administer this world. With a certain amount of UN support, of course."

For a long moment Allerton stared hard into the Russian's impassive face, and Saleh held his breath. He'd been in the vanguard of the Islamic Confederation's vocal attacks on the Americans' Homestead Project, but such political necessities hadn't kept him from secretly hoping the search for new worlds would bear fruit. A new frontier—whether intended as a private preserve for the rich or not—would give hope to all those who felt themselves trapped into ancient patterns without the possibility of escape. Four years ago he'd dreamed of a UN that could build its own ship to fly with the Canadians' newly discovered star drive; two years later he'd finally admitted defeat. Rhetoric and Third World support were no substitutes for money, and the West was ever more selfish these days with their wealth. But if Liadov's goading succeeded . . .

"All right," Allerton said abruptly. "If I can get Congress to approve, we'll do it. *And*"—he leveled a finger at Liadov—"we'll do it *well*."

The next day the matter was brought before the General Assembly, which endorsed the mandate by a 148 to 13 vote. A month later the U.S. Senate followed suit, and the world newly christened Astra became the center of perhaps the biggest project the Army Corps of Engineers had ever undertaken.

Eleven months after that, the first colonists arrived.

Chapter 1

From orbit Astra resembled nothing so much as a giant mudball on which someone had thoughtlessly spilled a bucket or two of pale blue paint. Both of the continental land masses were as dead-dull-bland as anything Colonel Lloyd Meredith had ever seen. No reds, certainly no greens; just the occasional blue of a lake or a line of white-capped mountains. Even the continental-shelf mineral deposits upon which the planet's future industry depended so heavily came out as a blue-washed white. "I wish we'd brought some paint," he commented to the man beside him.

Captain Radford snorted mildly. "You'll get used to it," he said. "I think you'll find you've got bigger problems down there than lack of decent scenery."

"No doubt," Meredith conceded. Radford had been ferrying workers and equipment back and forth for nearly a year now and undoubtedly knew more about the place than Meredith, who'd spent that same period up to his zygomatic arch in organizational details for the permanent colony. "Are we anywhere near the settlement? My map-reading courses never included looking at the terrain from this height."

"We're just coming up on it now." Radford indicated the western edge of the continent below. "You see that sort of four-fingered bay, with the big island just off it? That's the place. Right near the mineral deposits, with several feeding rivers for fresh water and the sheltered areas of the bay for fish breeding. The main military base and landing facilities are on the island; the towns are on the bay or within a dozen kilometers of it."

"Um." Meredith's eyes traced the line of mountains arcing into the bay from the southeast, shifted to a solitary shadow fifty kilometers or so due east of the settlement. "What about that volcano?"

"You mean Olympus? No sweat—the thing's been dormant for centuries."

"Yes, that's what the preliminary report said. Anybody done a more careful check of it since then?"

"I don't know. You've got your own geologists, though, don't you? I'm sure they can put your mind at ease."

Meredith pursed his lips momentarily at the other's faintly patronizing tone. A lot of the colonel's colleagues thought him overly cautious on the subject of volcanos . . . but then, none of them had seen firsthand the aftermath of the '88 Izalco eruption that had killed four hundred people in El Salvador. "I'm sure they can," he told Radford evenly. "All right. How soon can we launch shuttles and start getting this crowd down?"

"Any time you and the crowd are ready," Radford said. "As far as I'm concerned, the sooner the better."

Meredith nodded understanding; there'd been a lot of tension aboard ship the past three weeks. "They'll calm down once they've got room to move again."

"I hope so—for your sake." Keying his intercom, Radford began issuing orders.

Seen from ground level, Astra's color scheme wasn't marked-ly improved; but Dr. Peter Hafner didn't especially care. He'd studied all the photos and read all the soil analyses, but there was nothing that could compare to seeing the rocks close up and personally handling them. Leaning over the hovercraft rail, he gazed at the low cliffs flanking the narrow entrance to Splayfoot Bay, eyes tracing the subtle variations in hue and wondering about their composition. For the moment, speculation was all he could do; the extreme scarcity of metallic elements in Astra's crust opened the way for compounds never before suspected, let alone seen. He could hardly wait to begin work on them.

The hovercraft cleared the bay's entrance and headed toward the easternmost of the three main arms. Hafner caught a glimpse of a settlement up in the northern branch, but it was too far away for him to pick out any details. A few minutes later the craft entered the eastern arm, and Hafner saw that there was another collection of buildings at its far end. The majority seemed to be built along the lines of rowhouses, though there were a few larger ones that probably served as community or storage facilities. The construction material was obvious: some sort of adobe, probably baked in slabs for faster construction. Undoubtedly efficient, given the lack of wood, but the drab result was pretty grim.

Beside him, two Hispanic-looking men were also squinting at the town ahead. From the tone of their muttered Spanish, Hafner decided they were similarly unimpressed by its appearance. He wondered if anyone had thought to bring along any house paint, decided regretfully that such a consideration would rank low on military priority lists.

For the moment, though, the clothing of the people milling about added color to the scene. A small crowd was gathered near the dock, where one of the other hovercraft was still unloading. Hafner's craft slid into position on the opposite side of the welded metal pier, and the scientist joined the rest of the colonists streaming ashore.

The crowd turned out to be the queue for a sort of open-air check-in station the military had set up. Hafner took his place at the end of one of the lines, thankful that the Army had had the sense to give the colonists some time in the open after the cramped conditions aboard ship.

The sun was directly overhead—noon of a twenty-seven-hour day—and now that the mountain foothills blocked the stiff ocean breeze, the air was beginning to warm up. Hafner slipped off his jacket, wondering idly how good the meteorologists' seasonal predictions really were. Astra's smaller axial tilt should give milder temperature swings than those of Hafner's native Pennsylvania, but with barely a year's worth of data to go on, the planet's climate was far from established. Certainly it seemed hotter now than the early spring this part of Astra was supposed to be in at the moment, and if this wasn't just a temporary heat wave even the tough hybrid crop strains they'd brought with them might be in trouble. He hoped the experts had taken such possibilities into account.

Finally, it was his turn at the front of the line. "Name?" the sweating lieutenant asked, not bothering to look up from his portable terminal.

"Peter Hafner. I'm a geologist with Dr. Patterson's group—"

The terminal spat out a small card. "Hafner, Peter Andrew; 1897-22-6618; science/professional." The soldier handed Hafner the card. "House number 127 here in Unie; maps are posted in the courtyard over there; meal and orientation meeting times are on the bulletin board beside the maps. Questions will be answered at the meeting tonight; emergency questions can be handled at the admin complex. Next!"

Well, at least they've got things organized, Hafner thought as he headed toward the knot of people around the bulletin board. For a moment he considered finding the admin complex and seeing if they would tell him where Patterson would be living. But they were probably up to their necks in work over there, and there was no point making a nuisance of himself any sooner than necessary. The meeting tonight would be soon enough to find Patterson and discuss the work schedule; until then, he would do well to put a leash and choke collar on his eagerness. A quick look at his new quarters and a long walk around Unie should do him for today. In fact, if his luggage had been delivered to his house yet, he'd even have his sample boxes and a handful of reagents to take with him.

Smiling, he picked up his pace. Perhaps the afternoon wouldn't be a total waste, after all.

The stars were shining like frozen sparks overhead as the Ceres town meeting broke up, their brilliance seemingly unaffected by the handful of lights that defined where the streets were alleged to be. Cristobal Perez walked slowly toward the house he shared with two other men, the work orders they'd passed out in the meeting crinkling in his pocket as he moved.

A footstep scrunched the gravel behind him: someone overtaking. Turning, he caught a glimpse of the other's face. "Matro," he nodded in greeting. "How do you like your new home so far? A true land of opportunity, *sí*?"

Matro Rodriguez snarled an old Nahuatl curse Perez had often heard him use. "Farming. *Farming!* We came all this way just to be put to work in fields like migrants?"

"I told you not to expect too much," Perez said with a shrug. "If you'd ever been in the Army, you would know that *all* recruiters lie through their teeth."

"We might as well *be* in the Army. Or haven't you looked at the list of rules yet?"

"I looked at it. What did you expect—that we would be the new Pilgrims here, get to do anything we want?"

Rodriguez didn't seem to be listening. "Did you notice how practically everyone in Ceres is Hispanic? And how they've got us three to a house? I was behind one of the middle-class science types in line this afternoon—*he* got a house all to himself in Unie."

"Well, at least *we've* got our own lake."

"I'm overjoyed," Rodriguez said sourly. "The Anglos'll probably sit around it while we dig irrigation ditches to the fields."

"You're getting yourself worked up for nothing. All right, so they're treating us like peons—now. But there are a lot more colonists than there are soldiers, and I don't suppose the Anglos will be thrilled by Army rules for long either. As long as we stick together we can make this place what they promised us it would be.''

Rodriguez gave him a hard look. "You were always a pretty good talker, weren't you? I noticed you didn't say any of this at the meeting when they ordered us into the fields.''

"Of course not—we've *all* got to eat, haven't we? But the time will come, Matro, and when it does *we'll* be the ones bargaining from strength. Trust me.''

The other snorted. "Sure. But I won't believe it until it happens. *Buenas noches.*'' Lengthening his stride, he disappeared into the gloom.

Perez watched him go, feeling his lip curl slightly. He and Rodriguez had been friends since their high school days in Texas, and he'd yet to see the other use his head while his mouth and fists were still operable. Chances were good he'd go off half-cocked this time, too, and get himself in a lot of trouble. If that happened . . . well, Perez would just have to do what he could to help. It was a pain, but Rodriguez was people, and Perez could hardly claim to be out to save the world if he weren't out to save people, too.

Lost in conversation and musings, he'd overshot his turnoff. Retracing his steps, he headed down the dimly lit lane toward his new home, hoping his roommates weren't planning to stay up late talking. As in all farming communities, Ceres's day was going to start early.

Pulling the sheet up to her chin, Carmen Olivero turned off her light with a tired sigh. *Only one day on Astra*, she thought wryly, *and already I'm a week behind. A new record.* By all rights, she knew, she ought to still be at the Unie admin complex, where the rest of the organizational staff was busy with final duty rosters and equipment/supply check-in. The latter work had been done once, of course, when the ships were being loaded, but it all had to be done over to check for breakage and such during the voyage. But Colonel Meredith had left specific orders for her group to be available at 0700, and she knew better than to scrimp on sleep if she wanted to be at least halfway competent at her job. Especially after undergoing this new space-age equivalent of jet lag.

She closed her eyes, but her mind seemed to still be in high gear. Inventory lists and storage assignments hovered in front of her eyes, threatening her with an avalanche of paper. She'd been doing this sort of work for fifteen years now, but nothing in her experience had prepared her for the sheer complexity of this job. Ten thousand colonists and military people required a *lot* of supplies, and aside from water the local environment provided practically zilch. And it was a long, long way to Earth for anything they ran out of.

She fought it for ten minutes before finally tossing back the sheet and padding barefoot to the kitchen. The individual food supplies hadn't yet been distributed to the various houses, but the plumbing and microwave worked and she always carried a few packets of instant hot chocolate in her personal luggage. A few minutes later she was sitting by the kitchen window with the steaming mug, listening to the faint voices and machinery sounds from the direction of the docks. *I wonder when I'll start missing Fort Dix,* she wondered. Not that the base or even the rest of Jersey had held that great an attraction for her; but after a lifetime of periodic uprootings, she knew full well that the pangs of homesickness would eventually come. In her Army brat days the agony had sometimes seemed to be more than she could handle, enhanced as it was by the loss of school and friends; now, at the ripe old age of thirty-six, she knew the reaction would be no more than a dull haze over her life for a few days. Still, it was never much fun. *One of these days,* she told herself, sipping cautiously, *I'm going to have to give up this nonsense and settle down somewhere for good. Maybe when we've got Astra on its feet . . . or when we throw in the towel and all go home. Whichever comes first.*

Somehow, neither option seemed all that thrilling at the

moment. *Never get philosophical at two in the morning,* she thought, quoting Number Twelve of her personal list of rules, and dismissed the subject. Draining her cup, she rinsed it out and put it into the sink, hoping in passing that her new roommate wouldn't turn out to be a cleanliness fanatic. Back in bed, she found her brain had cut back to idle—far enough down for her usual sleep routine to be effective. Snuggling up to her pillow, she closed her eyes. *Sufficient unto the day are the troubles thereof,* she quoted to herself, and turned loose the future to handle its own affairs.

Two minutes later she was fast asleep.

Chapter 2

". . . and here are the inventory lists from Crosse," Major Thomas Brown said, laying one last thickness of printout on Colonel Meredith's desk. "Everything's out of the *Aurora* now, and the *Pathfinder*'s last load is on its way down. Most of the stuff waiting to be sorted is bulk food, clothing, and fertilizer."

Meredith nodded, glancing over the first page of the printout. His eyeballs ached their continual reminder that three hours of sleep was inadequate for a man his age. "How's the landing strip holding out?" he asked.

"Pretty well, actually. Those repulsers the Ctencri sell are pretty hot, but because the shuttles use a smaller chunk of runway for both land and lift there's actually less overall wear and tear on the permcrete. It'll need some patching, of course, but we've got three weeks before the *Celeritas* arrives on its supply run."

"Good. Do we have enough room to let the flyers lift?"

"Oh, sure. They don't need much more than their own length if you crank the repulsers up full."

"I know, but I'd rather not run them any higher than

necessary. You never know what the half-life of a chunk of technology is going to be."

"The Ctencri numbers—"

"Were provided by the Ctencri equivalent of a sales rep. Need I say more?"

Brown harumphed. "Well, they should still have no trouble. It's mostly the center of the runway that's torn up, and the flyers can easily fit on either side."

"Fine." Meredith raised his wrist phone and keyed a number.

"Martello hangar; Greenburg," the device responded.

"Colonel Meredith. Have the flyers been checked out yet?"

"Two are ready to go, sir. The third'll be another hour or so."

"Okay. Have the first two teams head out—alert the tower to monitor and record all data."

"Yes, sir."

Meredith disconnected and returned his attention to Brown. "Planting get started on schedule?"

"Mostly. The fields at Crosse were still too low in zinc and manganese this morning, and Dr. Haversham ordered another layer of fertilizer laid down. His guess was that the rivers bordering the fields cause a faster than normal ground water exchange that siphons off the extra minerals. Or something like that."

"Great. Well, if that's the worst goof the engineers made when they laid out this place, I guess we can live with it."

"At least we've *got* the fertilizer to spare." Brown was looking curious. "You expecting to find Captain Kidd's treasure or something hidden in the hinterlands?"

"What? Oh—the flyers? No, I just thought we should do some low-level surveys of the territory around the settlement."

Brown shrugged. "We've got cartography-quality photos for about a hundred kilometers around us. What more are we likely to need?"

There was a faint whistling noise, and Meredith looked out the window in time to see the two sleek flyers shoot by and head east toward the cone of Mt. Olympus in the distance. He'd fought the budgeteers tooth and claw to get a half dozen of the Ctencri-built craft assigned to Astra, and considered himself fortunate they'd only whittled the number down to three. Though primarily for blue-sky use—their plasma jets utilized atmospheric oxygen in burning the fuel to preplasma temperatures—the flyers were equipped with a self-contained oxygen supply that enabled them to reach low orbit, which meant they could serve as extra shuttles in an emergency. "Suppose," he said to Brown, "that there are colonies of spores or something out there, dormant now but ready to grow if and when the soil's metal content should jump—say, if one of those asteroids circling a million kilometers away comes down. Some of our fertilizer's bound to be blown off the fields, and if it starts something growing I want to have some 'before' pictures available."

Brown whistled under his breath. "I never thought about that," he admitted. "I guess that's why I'm in charge of runways and spaceports. Straightforward stuff."

"Actually, I can't take credit for the idea, either—it was the biology people who came up with it. When you think about it, the situation's analogous to desert ecology, except that here it's trace metals instead of water that's missing." Meredith paused as the faint sound of a sonic boom wafted in through the window. "Sounds like that last shuttle's coming in."

Brown hauled himself to his feet. "Yeah. I'd better take a quick look at how the unloading's going and hurry all the hovercraft back to Martello. If your terminals are on-line by the time we've got the inventory list I'll send it through; otherwise, I'll bring you a hard copy later."

"Fine. Make damn sure we've got everything before you let the *Aurora* leave."

"Right." Brown saluted and was gone.

Picking up the top printout, Meredith turned to the last page and scanned the loss/breakage list. Not too bad: a small amount of laboratory glassware broken and several bags of the metal-enriched fertilizer split. One item made him grimace—one of the broken dishes was a critical part of the apparatus for combining the fish ova and sperm they'd brought to Astra. There were spares, of course, but not enough to satisfy either Meredith or the scientists. *Idiots,* he thought harshly. *They give me a job to do, and then make sure I've got the absolute minimum I need to do it with.* Which wasn't entirely fair, he knew. President Allerton was a hundred percent solid behind the colony and always had been; but it was a handful of shortsighted congressmen who held Astra's umbilical. They obviously considered the whole thing a UN plot to drain the United States of manpower and resources and had adjusted the colony's budget accordingly.

Laying the printout aside, Meredith picked up the next one from the pile. The months of logic, persuasion, and arm-bending were behind him now, and there was nothing more to do but get Astra running just as fast and as well as he possibly could. Uncle Sam's honor—not to mention his own chance of ever making brigadier general—was on the line here. The scoffers *would* be proved wrong.

And with that settled once again in his mind, he got to work.

It was just over an hour later when his phone buzzed with bad news. "Flyer Two has gone down, Colonel," a tense-sounding lieutenant reported. "Somewhere south-southwest of Mt. Olympus, we think."

Meredith felt a shiver go up his back. Near the volcano? He threw a quick look out the window as he headed across the room, but there was no sign of any smoke rising from the distant cone. "What happened?" he asked, throwing open the door and hand-signaling his aide to get the car.

"We're not sure, sir. We got just a fragment of something about the repulsers going crazy, and then they were cut off."

Damn unreliable alien technology. "Are any of the normal planes in service yet?"

"One of them is, sir."

"Put a medical team aboard and get it in the air. Have them

pick me up east of Unie—they can land on the Unie-Crosse road. Where's Flyer One?"

"Heading toward Olympus, sir. It was over the Kaf Mountains south of here when Two went down."

"Cancel that. Have One return to base immediately."

"Yes, sir." The phone went dead for a few seconds: the lieutenant on another line. "The Cessna's being wheeled out now, Colonel. They'll be leaving in five minutes or less."

Lieutenant Andrews already had the car running as Meredith slid inside. "Good. We'll be waiting a couple hundred meters outside town. Let me know immediately if Two makes any response."

The medical team, it turned out, was unnecessary. Both of the flyer's crewmen were already dead.

Meredith walked carefully over the crash site, his stomach sore with the ache of tight muscles. The flyer had gouged a furrow perhaps a hundred meters long, scattering pieces of itself along the entire length, before coming to rest as a mangled pile of metal and plastic. The crewmen, similarly mangled, were discovered still in their cockpit.

It was midafternoon before the crash specialists finished their survey and returned to Martello Base. "Near as we can tell, Colonel, all the repulsers just seemed to quit at once," the captain in charge of the team told Meredith. "We'll know more when the electronics people finish with the stuff we brought back."

Meredith nodded, gazing past the man as the Cessna was wheeled back into the hangar. He'd come here with the medical men and bodies earlier in the day, knowing he would simply be in the way at the crash site and hoping he could get some work done while the experts sifted through the rubble. The tactic had been only half successful; his mind had understandably refused to concentrate on inventories. "Any ideas as to why the repulsers should do that?"

"None, sir. I'd go so far as to say it *should* be impossible. They run off of three completely independent systems."

"The radar showed they were going pretty slow when it happened. If just the underside repulsers went out, would they have had time to switch to forward motion?"

"They should have—they were high enough and that maneuver's programmed into the on-board. And if they *had* tried that and simply not made it up to speed in time, they would have hit a lot harder than they did." The captain shook his head.

"All right," Meredith said after a moment. "Get busy on that analysis; I'm grounding the other two flyers until you find out what went wrong."

"Yes, sir. I'm . . . sorry, Colonel." Saluting, the captain strode off toward the hangar.

I'm sorry, too, Meredith thought as he turned and trudged toward the docks. Their first full day on Astra, and already he'd lost two men. *That's really showing the scoffers, Meredith. For an encore, maybe I could shoot myself in the foot.*

Three of the five hovercraft were bobbing gently beside the dock; Meredith passed them up in favor of a small motorboat. Casting off, he headed at half throttle toward the narrow entrance to Splayfoot Bay. By now the death certificates would be waiting on his terminal at Unie, and his stomach tightened anew at the thought of filling them out. He'd never been able to stoically accept death in his commands, not even as a line officer in the Honduras conflict where he'd faced it every other day. His years of desk riding, he was now discovering, hadn't made him any better at seeing human beings as faceless numbers. *Damn the Ctencri, anyway,* he thought, twisting the tiller hard as he steered around a half-submerged rock. *If it turns out to be a manufacturing fault, I'll twist their silly crests together.*

He was just turning into the five-kilometer-long inlet leading to Unie when his phone buzzed. "Meredith," he answered.

"Colonel, this is Major Dunlop," the caller said, his voice

barely audible over the engine noise. "I think we've got a riot brewing here in Ceres."

Meredith cut back the throttle. "Explain."

"About a hundred of the Hispanic field workers have gathered in front of the admin building and are yelling something about better housing and recreation facilities. I've got my men in riot-control position, but I haven't got nearly enough of them if things turn ugly. Can you possibly send me another thirty or so troops?"

"Have you tried talking to them?" Meredith countered.

"Sir, if I open the door, they're likely to pour in before we can stop them."

Meredith grimaced, but the reply was not unexpected. Dunlop was a competent administrator, but the finer points of diplomacy and compromise were far beyond him. Spraying the crowd with stunner fire would be much more his style, and that was the last thing Meredith needed right now. "All right, then, just stay put," he told the other. "I'm a few minutes out from Unie; I'll have a team waiting and we'll drive up there as soon as I get in. Do *not* attempt riot procedures unless there is an *immediate* threat to life or safety—got that?"

"Got it, sir. I recommend you hurry with those reinforcements."

"Noted. Out."

Almost savagely, Meredith yanked the throttle back to full power. *Reinforcements, my eye*, he thought as the boat leaped forward. What Dunlop needed was a negotiating team—and that was precisely what he was going to get. Preferably one whose members spoke at least halfway fluent Spanish. *First the flyer crash, and now this. Murphy's Law is really riding high today.*

Raising his phone, he keyed for Lieutenant Andrews and began giving orders.

"Three to an apartment, we got—sometimes even *four*," Matro Rodriguez's bullfrog voice bellowed out, clearly audible

even over the other shouts and the loud background muttering of
the crowd. Standing to one side, Cristobal Perez alternately
gave his attention to the mob and to the squat adobe building
they faced. The building's windows were empty of official
faces, but Perez knew they were watching. Sooner or later they
would decide they'd been under siege long enough and do
something about it. *Idiots,* he thought, his eyes flicking back to
the crowd, watching as some of the men began waving clenched
fists over their heads. *All they're going to do is get the major's
back up and force him to take action.* They had as yet no real
economic power and certainly no political power. All they had
was numbers and the threat of violence, and that only worked if
those in authority were hesitant about shooting. The soldiers,
Perez knew, would be under no such handicap.

A flicker from one of the dark windows caught Perez's eye:
someone moving up to what could only be firing position.
Cursing under his breath, Perez stepped forward, heading for
the front of the crowd. He'd hoped Dunlop would hold off a
while longer, give the mob time to blow off their steam and
maybe leave peacefully. But moving troops to the windows
could only mean he'd decided to have it out right now.

Nobody seemed to notice Perez as he strode to Rodriguez's
side directly opposite the admin building's door; only a few
looked quizzically at him as he raised his hand for quiet.
"Friends!" he called . . . but his voice didn't have anything
like Rodriguez's carrying power. He was inhaling for a second
try when, as if by delayed action, an expectant hush swept up
the hubbub.

Turning, he found himself practically nose to nose with Major
Dunlop.

The major opened his mouth to speak—but Perez had always
been fast on the uptake and managed to beat Dunlop to the
verbal draw. "Good afternoon, Major," he said, managing to
put both respect and righteous displeasure into his voice.
"We would like to have some words with you about the conditions—"

"*All right,* you lazy troublemakers," Dunlop bellowed without even looking at Perez, "you've got exactly thirty seconds to clear out of here and get back to your jobs. After that you'll wish you had. Now *move!*"

His answer was a cloudburst of angry shouts and a sudden surging forth of the mob. "Wait a minute!" Perez shouted—but his voice blended with all the others and was lost . . . and an instant later his body jerked with agony and numbness and the world tilted crazily and went dark.

Chapter 3

"Is this," Meredith asked icily, "your idea of staying put?"

Standing with the stiffness of a sentry at the admin building door, the marks of dragged bodies still visible in the dust around him, Dunlop nevertheless wasn't giving an inch. "I went out to talk as you suggested, Colonel. The mob moved forward, and my men opened fire in my defense. Frankly, sir, I don't see the problem. We only had to stun a few of them before the rest dispersed, and they'll think twice about starting trouble now."

" 'The problem,' as you call it, we'll discuss later," Meredith said, working hard to keep the fury out of his voice. He had no desire to tear Dunlop apart in front of junior officers, but that resolve was fading fast. "Now, where's this person you arrested and what makes you think he was one of the leaders?"

"His name is Cristobal Perez, one of the field workers. He was in the front of the mob and led the move forward."

"I want to talk to him."

"If you'd like—but I can tell you right now he's not very cooperative. We're holding him in one of the offices in back."

"All right." Meredith glanced once more at the scuffle marks on the ground and gestured Andrews to his side. "I want you

31

and the others to locate and get statements from all the soldiers who were involved in this. Make it clear we aren't out for scalps, just information. When you finish with them, look up any civilian witnesses or participants and repeat."

"Yes, sir," the aide nodded. "Do you want any of the Spanish speakers to stay with you?"

"Probably should. Who's best?"

"Carmen Olivero," Andrews said, gesturing to the attractive woman standing quietly among the uniformed men. The only one among them in civilian dress . . . on a hunch, Meredith nodded.

"Miss Olivero, come with me. Let's go, Major."

Dunlop led them inside and down a couple of corridors to a door flanked by two stunner-carrying soldiers. The guards came to attention; without bothering to knock, Dunlop opened the door and went in.

Cristobal Perez was stretched out on his back on the floor in front of the desk, a wadded-up jacket serving as makeshift pillow. About twenty-five or twenty-six, Meredith automatically estimated, his face already showing the first signs of a lifetime out under the sun. His eyes, which had been shut, opened briefly to survey the newcomers and then closed again. "I don't suppose you brought a doctor this time," he said tiredly.

"All you need is rest," Dunlop told him. "The effects'll wear off in another hour or so. On your feet now—Colonel Meredith has some questions."

"Colonel Meredith, eh?" Perez made no move to get up, but his eyes opened again, shifting from Meredith to Carmen and back. "You always let men in your command fire on unarmed civilians, Colonel?"

"Be thankful they were only using stunners," Meredith countered, watching the other's face closely. "Other mob control methods are just as uncomfortable and usually take longer to go away."

A flash of anger swept Perez's face at the word *mob*; but instead of the verbal explosion Meredith had expected, the

Hispanic seemed to withdraw behind a stony mask. "You obviously haven't been shot by one of the damn things," he said, closing his eyes again.

"No. But I *have* been shot with real bullets. How about telling me what happened out there?"

"My word against Dunlop's? No, thanks—my breath's too valuable to waste just now."

Meredith pursed his lips. "If you tell the truth—"

"Look, Colonel, I was in the Army a couple of years," Perez interrupted. "I know how military people stick together. You just go ahead and figure out my sentence and we can skip the show of impartiality."

"Perez—" Dunlop began.

"No, it's all right, Major," Meredith cut his subordinate off, mentally berating his own carelessness. His deliberately tactless choice of words had forced a reaction out of Perez, all right, but driving the other into silence was a result he hadn't counted on. A strategic withdrawal was in order. "Perez, whenever you're ready to talk, just let me know." He opened the door and left, Dunlop and Carmen behind him.

"I told you he wasn't very cooperative," Dunlop commented as the three of them stopped a few meters down the hall.

"Uh-huh. What sort of charges have you filed against him?"

"Incitement, congregation with felony intent—a couple other minor charges. Object lesson stuff, mostly."

"I want them dropped. Miss Olivero—"

"*All* of them?" Dunlop looked nonplussed.

"That's right. What's the problem?—If my investigation indicates he's guilty of something, we can always charge him later. It isn't like he can skip town or something. Miss Olivero, I want you to go back in there and talk to Perez."

Carmen turned wide eyes on him. "*Me*, Colonel? But *I* don't know anything about interrogation methods."

"I don't want you to interrogate him, just to talk with him awhile," Meredith explained patiently. "Find out what exactly his complaints are, for starters. Let him know we're not out to scapegoat him or anyone else. You're a civilian; maybe he'll be more open with you.''

Carmen's lip twitched, but she nodded. "All right. I'll . . . try.'' Stepping back to the guards, she took a deep breath, tapped once on the door, and went in.

"Keep an ear out for trouble," Dunlop advised the soldiers quietly.

"There won't be any," Meredith told him. "Let's go, Major—we have a *lot* to talk about.''

Perez's first surprise was that someone was coming in so soon after the colonel's party had left; his second surprise was that the visitor bothered to knock. Prying his eyelids up against his fatigue, he watched the woman close the door behind her and stand with her back to it. For a moment there was silence as they eyed each other. "How do you feel?" she said at last.

"Tired, mainly," he answered, wondering idly about her background. From looks alone she could be fresh from Guadalajara, but her speech was definitely middle-class American. Second generation, perhaps, whose parents had become respectable before the flood of illegal refugees from the 2011 Mexican collapse had made "Hispanic" a curse-word again? "Most of the pain's gone.''

She nodded. "Good. Uh—my name's Carmen Olivero.''

"Honored. Meredith send you in to wring a confession from me?''

Some of her nervousness seemed to vanish, to be replaced by coolness. "Hardly. The colonel has gone with Major Dunlop to get the charges against you dropped. He asked me to find out what your complaints are—assuming you want them addressed, that is, and aren't just using them as an excuse to riot.''

"We *weren't rioting*!" he snapped, the outburst intensifying the pain behind his eyeballs. "We wanted to complain about the lousy conditions in Ceres and the damn soldiers fired on us.'' He stopped abruptly as she took a half step backward, her hand reaching for the door knob. *Good job, Perez,* he berated himself silently. *You wanted a sympathetic ear, and now you're trying to bite it off.* "You say he's dropping the charges?" he asked in a more reasonable tone.

She regarded him uncertainly, her hand on the knob. "That's what he said."

"Very kind of him." Moved by an obscure feeling, Perez forced himself to a more dignified sitting position, sliding back so that he could lean against the wall. "I'm sorry I blew up a minute ago. I've never been wild about pain." He waved to the desk chair. "Please sit down?"

She hesitated only a second before stepping to the chair and sinking a bit tentatively into it. "So . . . what is it you don't like about this place?"

He snorted. "The list would fill a disk," he said. "As far as I'm concerned it would have made more sense to colonize the South Sahara. I've never understood why the UN wanted to pour so much money and effort into Astra in the first place."

"If you felt like that, why did you sign up?"

"*I* volunteered because many of my people were coming. Many of *them,* on the other hand, didn't truly volunteer."

Her eyes widened momentarily, then settled into cool disbelief. "You have any proof of this?"

He shook his head. "Nothing that would be seen as such. And don't misunderstand me: I'm not saying they were kidnapped and loaded aboard trucks for the training center. The pressure was much more subtle than that—portrayal of Astra as a new beginning, the land of opportunity and freedom that the U.S. had turned out not to be, plus the implication that life would be getting harder if not enough of us volunteered. We were painted a rosy picture—can you blame us for being unhappy with the housing and working conditions we've been put into here?"

"This is a brand-new world. Did you expect to find hotels and theaters waiting for you?"

"I expected exactly what is here—a continuation of the social injustices I was already tired of."

"Everybody's had to make sacrifices—"

"But some aren't making nearly as many as others," he shot back. "Are the scientists living three and four to a house? The soldiers? How many Anglos are going out in the fields tomorrow, planting crops by hand because the extra machinery is still packed into their crates?"

"All right, then," she said after a short silence. "Assume for the moment that you're right. What do you suggest be done?"

"For now, a sincere commitment to improve conditions in Ceres would probably be enough. We're not stupid—we know you can't build new houses overnight. If you could get us another couple of hologames for the rec center, that would be a nice gesture." Perez paused as a flicker of surprise crossed Carmen's face. *Probably expected some wildly impractical scheme for turning Ceres into Little Mexico*, he thought. *Well, enjoy it while you can, because here comes the bite.* "And I think Major Dunlop has proved he has no real feeling for the people here. He should be transferred and someone else put in charge."

Carmen's pleased/surprised expression vanished. "Oh, you think that, do you?" she asked coolly. "Do you want to suggest a replacement while you're at it?"

"Not necessarily. But why are you suddenly so hostile? I thought United States citizens had the right to choose their own leaders."

"Don't play word games," she snorted. "You know perfectly well that you gave up certain rights when you volunteered for this trip."

"Perhaps," he shrugged, locking eyes with her. "But having spent time in the Army myself, I can tell you that people grow tired of military rule very quickly. I think that Colonel Meredith would be wise to consider what he'll do when that happens."

Her face darkened still further, but before she could speak, the door was opened and one of the guards peered in. "Olivero? Colonel Meredith's ready for you."

"All right." Carmen stood up—with more than a trace of

relief, Perez thought—and went to the door. There, she paused and looked back. "I'll tell the colonel what you said. But no promises."

The door closed behind her. Wincing with the effort, Perez eased himself back to the floor. Closing his eyes, he replayed the conversation and Carmen's facial expressions as best he could. *Still on the side of the middle-class conservatives,* he decided, *but not close-minded, either. Obviously has some influence with the colonel. . . .*

He was still sorting out the possibilities when the soldiers came to turn him loose.

The drive back to Unie was long, dusty, and quiet. Meredith kept his eyes on the patch of lighted road ahead of them, his brooding silence stifling all other conversation in the car. Which was fine with him: most of the team's reports could wait until they were officially filed onto the computer, and the single exception could wait until they reached the privacy of his office.

The lights in the admin complex were still burning when Andrews pulled the car to a stop in front of it—one more reminder that there were a war's worth of details still waiting to be handled. "Your reports are due by oh-nine-hundred tomorrow," Meredith told the group as he opened his door and climbed out. "Miss Olivero, come with me; the rest of you are dismissed."

The colonel led the way down deserted hallways and into his outer office—and because it was the last thing he expected at that hour, he was three steps into the room before his eyes registered the visitor waiting there for him.

He stopped abruptly, combat senses flaring with the surprise; but the other showed no signs of hostility as he scrambled to his feet. "Colonel Meredith?" he asked, his casual stance and tone immediately tagging him a civilian.

"Yes," Meredith acknowledged. "You?"

"Dr. Peter Hafner—I'm a geologist with Dr. Patterson's group. Sorry about the hour, but your secretary said I could wait until you got in."

"No problem," Meredith assured him, making a mental note to set up new guidelines on such things. "What can I do for you?"

"Well, sir, I've been trying to arrange for a flyer and pilot to run me out to Mt. Olympus, but everyone I've talked to says the flyers have been grounded."

"You haven't heard about the crash?" Meredith asked sourly.

"Yes, sir, I have; and I'm sorry about the loss of its crew. But everything I've heard indicates the accident was a fluke, some aberration of the plasma itself and not an actual equipment malfunction—"

"Whoa. An aberration caused by *what*?"

"Maybe a rogue solar flare or something—*I* don't know. The point is it's very unlikely the other flyers would run into the same problem."

"Unlikely's not good enough," Meredith said, shaking his head. "Until we have a better idea of what went wrong you'll just have to make do with cars or the Cessnas."

"Neither of which will be of much use," Hafner sighed. "I understand your concern, Colonel, but please recognize I'm not talking about some abstract search for knowledge here. Astra has *got* to have some metal *somewhere*, and if it's not in the crust it must be deeper down. If volcanos like Olympus show any evidence at all of metal content in their rocks, it'll offer a reasonable alternative to the asteroid mining you have planned."

Meredith held up a hand. "Doctor, it's late and I've had a very hard day. If you'll file a formal request with Martello Base, you'll be put on the list for whenever the flyers are put back into service. Until then, I repeat, the cars and planes are all we have." A footstep behind him made him turn: Andrews, back from returning their car to the pool. "Now, if you'll excuse us," he added, "Lieutenant Andrews will escort you out. Good night, Doctor."

Hafner grimaced slightly, but had the sense not to argue. "Good night, Colonel. Thank you for your time."

The geologist left, followed closely by Andrews. Unlocking his office door, Meredith ushered in Carmen and waved her to a seat. "Now," he said, sinking into his desk chair, "tell me about Perez."

He listened in silence for the few minutes it took to recount her conversation with Dunlop's alleged riot leader. "He seemed pretty sincere, Colonel," she said when she had finished.

"I'm sure he did," Meredith nodded. "Whether he was or not is another story. A massive plot to press-gang Hispanics is a bit hard to swallow."

"I know." She paused. "There *do* seem to be a lot of Hispanics here, though."

Meredith shrugged. "The climate here approximates the Southwest, and we needed people experienced in farming sandy soils. That focuses on the area where Hispanics are already concentrated, so what's the big deal?"

Carmen shifted uncomfortably. "Yes, sir. But even if nothing . . . unfair . . . has occurred, there's still that perception. I was thinking on the way back . . . perhaps you could set up something like a city council in each of the towns. Not with any real power," she added quickly, correctly interpreting his expression. "It would be more of an advisory sort of body, a clearinghouse for complaints and suggestions."

"We already have channels like that set up," he reminded her.

"Yes, but . . ." She pursed her lips. "It's all organized along military lines. The civilians may not feel comfortable with that; I know it took *me* a while to get used to military procedure and I was *raised* in an Army home."

"What you're suggesting is that I give them the illusion of democracy without the substance." Meredith shook his head. "It'd be more trouble than it's worth. You'd add top-heaviness to the administrative sector, inject a battalion-worth of unnecessary political maneuvering and infighting, and generally use up man-hours for no net gain."

"The gain would rest in smoother cooperation between civilians and military," she countered.

"Technically speaking, Miss Olivero, there *are* no civilians on Astra. Everyone is under military rule and law, and if some of them don't like it, I'm sorry. They'll get used to it in time." He glanced at his watch. "I'd better let you go; it's getting late. I'll want a formal report from you for the file, but there's no particular rush."

"Yes, sir." She recognized the dismissal and stood up, but then hesitated. "Colonel? What are you going to do about Major Dunlop?"

"Whatever I do, it won't be because of Perez's veiled threats," Meredith told her shortly.

She swallowed. "Yes, sir. Good night, Colonel."

"Good night."

He gazed at the closed door for several seconds after she was gone, wondering what exactly he'd done to deserve such a day. Then, with a sigh, he turned to his computer terminal and flicked it on. The screen lit up but remained blank; apparently the underground light-pipe network was still generating problems. Cursing under his breath, he turned the machine off and buzzed for Andrews.

"Yes, sir?" the aide said as he entered.

"I hate to do this to you, Lieutenant, but I've got a couple of projects I want started right away, and I'm just too dog-tired to hunt up a working terminal."

"That's all right, Colonel," Andrews said, pulling out a notebook and sitting down. "I'm fine." He looked it, too, though Meredith knew for a fact that the other hadn't had any more sleep lately than he had.

"Okay. First off, I want every scrap of information we've got on Cristobal Perez. Not just his colonist file; check to see if any military, educational, or employment records came to Astra with us. Second, I want farm equipment assembly bumped a couple of levels up on the priority charts—and for the time being have some of the planting equipment in Crosse shifted up to Ceres. The farmers in Crosse are sitting on their hands now anyway."

He paused. Andrews finished writing and nodded. "Anything else?"

"Yes." Meredith hesitated, then plunged ahead. "I want you to work up a list of possible replacements for CO at Ceres."

Andrews looked up in obvious surprise. "You're transferring Major Dunlop?"

"I don't know. I haven't yet made up my mind."

Andrews toyed with his pen. "The major's pretty popular with his men," he said obliquely. "He has a reputation for sticking up for the common soldier, making sure they get all the rights and privileges they have coming."

"I know," Meredith nodded. "But that 'us versus them' mentality is exactly what's going to lose him the support and confidence of the civilians in Ceres. We can't afford unnecessary friction."

"I understand that, Colonel. But . . . you know it's going to look like you're giving in to pressure."

"Of course it is—and I hate the signal that'll send. If Dunlop hadn't fired from the hip like he did I'd back him all the way; but as it is I either look like a coward or someone whose orders can be ignored with impunity. Either way, I give someone the wrong idea." He shrugged. "If you can come up with a better idea I'll be glad to listen."

"Yes, sir." Andrews stood up and put away his notebook, and for just a second a smile twitched at his lips. "I'll see what I can come up with in that department. In the meantime, I'll get busy on these other things."

"Appreciate it, Andrews. Good night."

It was a walk of only a couple hundred meters to his quarters, but Meredith doubted he had the strength left for even such a short trip. Fortunately, someone had had the foresight to install a cot in a back corner of his office. Flipping off the lights, he stripped to his underwear and stretched out under the light blanket. For a minute or two he watched the pattern of light and shadow on the windowshade, trying to come up with some other solution for the Dunlop/Ceres problem. But no answer came, and he quickly gave up the attempt. *Maybe in the morning,* was his final thought, *things will be clearer.*

Chapter 4

With her fifteen years of Army experience, Carmen had left Meredith's office with the depressing certainty that it would take days for the colonel to take any action on the problems she had discussed with him—and that it would be *weeks* before she saw any of the results. It was therefore a pleasant shock when she arrived at her desk the next morning and found the shifting of extra farm machinery to Ceres already underway. A fast scan of the priority listing showed none of her coworkers had yet taken the job of organizing the assembly of spare farm equipment; keying that job onto her terminal, she set to work.

It was routine data manipulation—a simple matter of locating the equipment and necessary tools from the computer's listings and then shuffling work schedules for the right number of qualified mechanics—and as she tapped keys, her mind drifted back to the previous day and her conversations with Perez and Meredith.

She hadn't worked under Meredith for long, and aside from a brief interview when she'd been accepted for the colony, her personal knowledge of him was limited to the Ceres trip. Still, military bases had their fair share of gossip, and the stories she'd heard about the colonel had invariably painted him as honest and fair, which made his quick dismissal of Perez's allegations seem out of character. True, he was under a lot of pressure—and, admittedly, *she* wasn't convinced Perez had a case either—but it still seemed like an investigation was in order. As for Dunlop's dismissal, she couldn't make up her mind which way she hoped Meredith would decide.

In one corner of the terminal screen a yellow light blinked on. Startled, Carmen looked at what she'd just typed, realized with mild annoyance that in her reverie she'd tried to shift a worker who was already on a higher priority job. She blanked the command, the yellow light disappearing as she did so. Keying for the next page, she resumed scanning the job assignments.

One thing she *was* sure of, though, was that part of her responsibility to Astra was to do her bit to lower tensions and friction . . . and to that end she was determined to push her town council idea as hard as she could. Meredith's scorn notwithstanding, it seemed to her the simplest way to make the civilians feel more at home. Besides which, if the colony survived it would eventually shift to civilian government anyway, and having such a setup already in place would undoubtedly ease the transition.

Without warning, a red-bordered rectangle appeared in the middle of her screen, the words TOP PRIORITY MESSAGE flashing above it. Frowning, Carmen watched as words began filling the box . . . and felt her eyebrows climbing her forehead as she read them.

ATTENTION: ALL PERSONNEL: SATELLITE ARRAY HAS DETECTED ROOSHRIKE SPACECRAFT APPROACHING ASTRA. NO HOSTILITIES—REPEAT, NO HOSTILITIES—ARE EXPECTED, BUT ALL MILITARY PERSONNEL ARE TO REMAIN ALERT. LEGAL/ORGANIZATIONAL STAFF WILL IMMEDIATELY PREPARE LISTING OF KNOWN ROOSHRIKE CUSTOMS AND RITUALS FOR TRANSMISSION TO COLONEL MEREDITH'S OFFICE.

Carmen read the message twice before blanking it from her screen. "Hell in a Stealth," someone behind her muttered. The astonished chatter was just starting when Carmen's superior cut it off.

"All right, all right; delete the noise," she growled from her own terminal. "Smith, Hanson—start a Legal File search; Barratino, you check military records; Eldridge, start a general search for anything that's gotten buried in odd corners. Olivero, you organize and format everything as it comes in."

The room fell silent, except for the steady sleet-on-a-window sound of computer keys. *What rotten luck*, Carmen thought as she waited for the data flow to begin. *Stuck in a little room twenty kilometers from the landing field when I could be out there catching my first glimpse of a real live alien.*

Though come to think of it, perhaps it wasn't such bad luck, after all. The Rooshrike *had* contacted humans once before . . . and *that* time they'd opened fire.

The Rooshrike attack on the *Celeritas* was also on Meredith's mind as he watched the shiny dot driving over the ocean toward Martello Base, the feeling of being a massive sitting duck adding stiffness to his back as he sat in the lead vehicle of the five-car welcoming committee. The chances that this was a sneak attack were small—after all, over half of Astra's rental fee had yet to be paid—but business logic had only minimal effect on Meredith's combat reflexes. Trying to pretend that the sweat collecting on his forehead was due solely to the warm day, he squinted into the bright blue of the sky and waited.

Radar had already shown that the ship was considerably larger than the shuttles Martello's landing strip had been designed for, but the Rooshrike pilot had assured Meredith that that wouldn't be a problem, and as the arrowhead-shaped craft made its final descent, the colonel saw why. Unlike the largely horizontal approach used by American shuttles, the Rooshrike's was predominantly vertical, reminding Meredith momentarily of the old single-use space capsules. He winced, recalling the helplessness of those ancient craft; but at nearly the same instant the image vanished as white spears of repulser fire erupted from beneath the ship. Even at their supposedly safe distance Meredith distinctly felt the heat wave of that ignition, and with a silent prayer for the runway's permcrete, he watched the alien touch down. A minute later, he ordered the motorcade forward.

The Rooshrike ship had deployed a debarkation ramp by the time the humans reached the area. The ramp, designed to bypass the hottest sections of permcrete, was considerably shorter than the ones the Ctencri who'd landed on Earth had used, and Meredith decided the description of the Rooshrike as hot-planet aliens hadn't been overstating the case.

The Rooshrike itself, when it appeared, wasn't particularly impressive; but then, as Lieutenant Andrews would comment later, there wasn't a lot even aliens could do with basic spacesuit design. Apart from the oddly shaped face just barely visible through the dark visor, the creature descending the ramp might almost have been a slightly misproportioned human.

It came alone. Taking the cue, Meredith left the cars and went forward, moving as close to the ramp as he could stand. The alien reached the end of the ramp and stopped expectantly.

Meredith cleared his throat. "I greet you," he called to the alien, "and welcome you to Astra. I am Colonel Lloyd Meredith; I speak for my people."

There was a barely discernible pause as the Rooshrike's translator caught up, and then the alien stepped off the ramp and started forward. Meredith started breathing again; apparently he'd gotten the formal greeting right.

Or else the Rooshrike was being tolerant with the new race.

The alien stopped a couple of meters in front of Meredith. "I greet you in turn," it said, its voice hitting the same slight mispronunciations Meredith had heard from the Ctencri translator computers on Earth. "I am Beaeki; I speak for my people."

"We're pleased to have you here," Meredith told him, easing back a few centimeters. The alien's spacesuit was noticeably hot; Meredith wondered what the internal temperature was. "I regret we cannot offer proper accommodations for your stay, but our information concerning your environmental needs is incomplete."

"I will not require accommodations; my visit will be brief. And your lack of complete information is per our instructions to the Ctencri."

Not much for the odd polite lie, Meredith thought. *That'll be a welcome change.* "I see. Would you care to explain why? After all, we're neighbors now, and either of us might someday crash a ship in the other's territory."

"Your argument is unidirectional. Should a Rooshrike ship be distressed in this system a rescue team from the inner planet would provide aid."

"You have a colony in this system?" Meredith asked carefully. The Ctencri hadn't mentioned *that*.

"A mining base only; the surface is too dry for practical colonization. The base is adequately defended against attack, however."

Meredith let the implication pass without comment; a stiff denial that Astra had any militaristic intentions might be misconstrued. "I see. May I ask how long you intend to stay here? I would like to give you a tour of our colony and the facilities we are setting up to mine the mineral deposits near here." A sudden thought struck him. "I take it you referred to liquid sulfur when you spoke of your mining base being too dry. Our analysis indicates that sulfur is the third most common element in our soil. Perhaps when we get our mining and separating equipment going you'd be interested in purchasing some of the sulfur from us."

There was a long pause—so long, in fact, that Meredith wondered if the translator had hit a snag somewhere. He was trying to come up with a complete rephrasing when Beaeki spoke. "Forgive our breach of understanding," he said, slipping his hands momentarily behind his back. "I am named Beaeki nul Dies na. We did not realize you were of equal status with your home planet. We assumed you were a vassal world, or possibly a detention center. We apologize."

"It's all right," Meredith assured him. *Now what brought that on?* he wondered. *The business about selling them our sulfur?* He wished desperately the Ctencri had given them a little more data on Rooshrike psychology. "Human political and organizational structures can be pretty hard even for humans to understand, let alone outsiders. I take it the Ctencri didn't tell you very much about us?"

"The Ctencri do not give information away free. We ascertained you would be no military threat to us, even if you were outcasts, but could afford no more."

"Mm. The Ctencri charge too much, you think?"

"The Ctencri are usurers," the Rooshrike said flatly. "They perhaps appear generous to you at this time because you are newly contacted and they do not yet know what they want from you. But you will learn, as we did, that their only interests are building their own power and influence."

"Well, we have a long history of that ourselves. Once we find our feet the Ctencri may find us harder to fleece than they expect." Meredith suddenly remembered his duties as host, and gestured back toward the cars. "May I offer you that look around now? I'm sure the Ctencri didn't tell you what we had planned for Astra—and we don't charge for the tour."

"I will accept." If Beaeki had caught the attempt at humor he gave no sign of it. "I would prefer we use my vehicle, though. If you have no objection."

Meredith shrugged, trying hard not to read anything sinister into the suggestion. "No objections at all. Whenever you're ready."

It took only a few minutes to offload the vehicle, a sort of cross between a hovercraft and a powerboat with stubby outriggers; but once he and Beaeki were inside, Meredith understood the alien's reluctance to rough it in Astra's more primitive cars. The passenger compartment was large, comfortable, and whisper-quiet, with a climate control Beaeki had thoughtfully set to match the outside air temperature. The ground effect cushion, which seemed both more powerful and less dust-making than those of the military ground-effect vehicles Meredith was used to, handled even boulder-sized obstacles with ease. Meredith's escort, confined as they were to cars and the water-only hovercraft, had a hard time keeping up, but Meredith wasn't overly concerned. Beaeki didn't seem bothered by the possible breach of protocol, and as their conversation was being monitored via Meredith's phone, the colonel didn't feel nervous when out of sight of his men.

What he *did* feel was surprise. Beaeki, he'd judged, was only mildly interested in what the humans were building on Astra, and he'd accordingly been thinking along the lines of a half-hour trip to Unie and back. But the Rooshrike, with no trace of his earlier official coolness, asked question after question, and before he knew it Meredith had launched them on a grand tour.

They began at the continental shelf due east of Martello Island, where the mysterious mineral deposits lay clearly visible a few meters beneath the water. Crossing the narrow strip of land that separated the ocean from the northernmost finger of Splayfoot Bay, they came to the village of Wright, where the mined minerals would eventually be separated and purified. The road from there to Unie bordered both the bay and the Wright-Unie farming area, and Meredith spent several minutes talking about the special fertilization being used. He broke off the monologue when Beaeki explained that his race had little interest in plant cultivation; on Rooshrike worlds, with solar energy up to thirty times more abundant than on Earth, keeping the flora cut back was more of a problem than persuading it to grow. The fish nurseries near Unie were far more to his interest, inducing him even to stop the vehicle and get out. Squatting by the offshore mesh pens, whose tops barely cleared the surface of the water, he peered into the depths as Meredith described how the metal-rich runoff from the Crosse fields would be carried by the river to the bay, where it would presumably allow the growth of algae and more complex plants to which the penned fish would have access.

"You go to great lengths for such a useless world," Beaeki commented as they headed toward Ceres.

"It may be the only other one we ever have," Meredith said sourly, "if the Ctencri are to be believed. Besides, we humans are very big on challenges."

They made a fast circuit of Ceres—where, thankfully, the workers were sticking to business today—looked at Teardrop Lake, and then headed south to Crosse, at the junction of whose rivers a second fish nursery was located.

And through it all, Meredith learned a great deal about the Rooshrike.

They were a young race, relatively speaking, technologically anywhere from eighty to three hundred years behind the other starfaring races of the region. As junior members of the six-nation trading association, they had chafed somewhat under the perceived condescension of the older races, particularly that of the Ctencri, and while they had rapidly built an empire of twenty colonies and bases, they had always had the feeling none of the others really took them seriously. Though Beaeki never actually said so, Meredith got the distinct impression the Rooshrike were relieved that the beings from Earth were taking their former place at the bottom of the pecking order.

"Nice that at least no one's all *that* much more advanced technologically than all the others," Meredith noted at one point. "Still seems sort of odd, though, considering all the time that's been available for life to develop in."

"An accident of nature," Beaeki said, gazing out the side window as he drove. "Approximately one hundred forty million years ago a supernova saturated this part of space with enhanced cosmic radiation, resulting in rapid mutation of disease organisms, destruction of high-atmosphere protective regions, and direct large-creature destruction via tissue damage. Those peoples capable of survival lost nearly all technology; the few who survived are more primitive now than even your people."

"I would have thought some of their knowledge would have survived with them."

"But the material base did not. Too much of their metal was already in forms too difficult for a primitive technology to extract."

Meredith swallowed. Metal again; metal, and lack of same. Just what his low-flying morale needed to hear about.

"Other more advanced races are reputed to exist," Beaeki continued. "But they are far away and few have seen them. They show as little interest in us as we do in the non-space-going peoples within this region."

"Um." *Probably*, Meredith thought, *just as well*.

He probed for information about the other nearby races, too, but here he had somewhat less success. Whether Beaeki simply wasn't interested in talking about their trading partners or whether the Rooshrike had learned the folly of giving away useful information for free Meredith didn't know. Still, he managed to get the races' names and general locations and, in a couple of instances, a brief physical description. Of those, the most interesting was that of the Poms, sea-going creatures that sounded something like dolphins equipped with manipulative tentacles. Meredith had often heard that a mechanical culture was impossible without fire, but Beaeki wouldn't say what the Poms had discovered as a substitute.

"That's something else that seems odd about this whole setup," Meredith commented. The tour over, Beaeki had brought his vehicle back to the ship and set it down expertly beneath its davits. "You said the edge of the Poms' territory is only a couple of light-years away. Since you're only interested in hot, Mercury-type worlds and the Poms live in liquid water, why haven't your two empires interpenetrated? Surely each of you has planets the other could use; it seems a perfectly reasonable deal for both sides."

"You will learn that there are only two things of value in an interstellar community: information and resources," Beaeki said as they left the vehicle and walked around to the ship's entry ramp. "All the solid bodies in a nation's territory, whether useful for colonization or not, can be exploited for mineral wealth and are thus guarded carefully."

"I would think asteroid mining would be cheaper than hauling cargo out of a planet's gravity well, though," Meredith suggested.

"Certainly. But asteroid belts are rare."

"Oh." A stray fact clicked in Meredith's mind: the Ctencri mission to Earth had rather offhandedly brought up the subject of mining rights. He would have to send back a warning with the next ship to watch out for a possible swindle. "As I recall, our lease includes the rights to this system's asteroids."

"Correct. But you may be disappointed. The belt is curiously deficient in the high-density, heavy-metal asteroids which are most profitable for mining."

Meredith grimaced. How much of the eighty million dollars, he wondered, had gone for those mining rights? "You people seem to have learned the principles of cutthroat business without much trouble."

"The Ctencri are good teachers; but their lessons have been expensive."

"Thanks for the warning. We humans are supposed to be pretty good businessmen ourselves."

"Perhaps." Beaeki paused at the edge of the ramp and made a sweeping gesture across the torso of his spacesuit. "If you would be interested in buying metal from us, our refinery here may be able to supply small amounts."

"We would certainly be interested in discussing the matter," Meredith nodded. "And *you* should consider buying the sulphur and other minerals we will soon be producing."

"I will pass your offer to the proper reviewers. Farewell."

Turning, the Rooshrike walked up the ramp and disappeared back into his ship. Meredith's escort, which had parked a respectful fifty meters back, drove forward to pick him up, and within half a minute they were speeding toward the control tower and the safety of distance. They needn't have worried; Beaeki waited until they were well clear before withdrawing the ramp and starting the plasma compression cycle.

The launch, a few minutes later, was more spectacular than even the landing had been. The ship drifted almost leisurely upward at first, its repulsers muted in obvious consideration for the permcrete; but at a hundred meters the white spears abruptly became a pillar of fire, and the ship shot up like a fly off a table. Five seconds later the drive repulsers added forward motion; a minute after that it was lost to sight past the hazy cone of Mt. Olympus to the east.

Seated next to Meredith in the car, Lieutenant Andrews let out a low whistle. "Either the Rooshrike have one hell of a technology," he commented, "or else the repulsers the Ctencri sold us are about five generations behind state of the art."

"Probably both." Meredith felt drained, as if he'd just spent the morning before a hostile congressional committee. "Well, I guess that's our taste of diplomacy for the week. Let's get back to work, shall we?"

Chapter 5

Beaeki's departure coincided with the beginning of over a week of relative quiet on Astra, a breather that allowed Meredith to finally get the colony back on some sort of schedule. Whether it was the small concessions he'd thrown to the militants in Ceres or whether the adjustment to Astra's twenty-seven-hour day had simply worn everyone out, he didn't know. Whatever the reason, though, he was grateful.

News from other fronts was somewhat less encouraging. The fields at Crosse had finally been enriched enough for planting to begin, but they were still losing metals too fast. Proposals for countermeasures began to clog Meredith's desk, and he had to pull two of Major Brown's engineers off construction work to do cost/practicality studies on all of them. The offshore mining had begun, but it was quickly becoming evident that unless the Rooshrike could be induced to buy some of the final products, the whole scheme was going to be a gigantic waste of money. Given the lackluster support the UN was giving the colony already, a failure of its one potential money-making project might induce them to simply throw in the towel. To Meredith that would be nearly equivalent to losing a war, a scenario of national dishonor that he had no desire to preside over. But if there were any other way for the colony to help support itself, neither he nor any of the scientists he'd put the problem to had been able to find it.

The only real bright spot amidst the gloom was that by the end of the week the two remaining flyers were back in the air again. The techs at Martello had finally concluded that Hafner's earlier guess was correct, that some outside electric field in exact resonance with the repulser confinement fields had allowed the plasma to leak out. *Where* such a field could possibly have come from was a question no one could answer; but as the flyers continued to crisscross the area without the slightest hint of trouble, even Meredith was finally able to hear their characteristic whistle overhead without wincing.

And on the tenth day the quiet was shattered.

"Now you listen to me, Major: you will *stay put*. Is that clear? No sweeps, no stunner spray; *nothing*."

Sitting in Meredith's office, Carmen waited for the colonel to finish his conversation, her fury at Cristobal Perez a churning knot in her stomach. *Yes*, the colonel's phone had an unlisted number, and *yes*, her office was just down the hall from his—but Perez still should have called the listed duty officer number instead of putting her in the middle of something that wasn't any of her business.

"Not unless they start breaking more than windows," Meredith growled into his phone. "Just go back to observing and keep me informed, okay? . . . Right; out." Muttering a curse, the colonel flipped off his phone. "Idiot," he growled, shaking his head. "The planet's practically *made* of silicon and he's worried about a few windows." Looking back at Carmen he almost visibly shifted gears. "Right, now. You were saying you had a message from Perez?"

"Yes, Colonel." Gritting her teeth, she plunged in. "Mr. Perez called me a few minutes ago with a couple of suggestions—"

"You mean demands, don't you?" Meredith interrupted.

"I don't know, sir. They *did* sound more like suggestions to me."

Meredith dismissed the point with a grunt. "All right. Let's hear them and be done with it."

"First of all, he again says that Major Dunlop should be relieved of command in Ceres." The list was short, and Carmen ran through it as quickly and precisely as she could. When she was finished, Meredith grunted again.

"As it happens, I'm still considering what to do with Major Dunlop," he said. "Relieving him of command is one possibility, but I'm not going to be rushed in my decision—certainly not by some transplanted professional troublemaker."

Carmen frowned. "Sir?"

"Oh, you didn't know? Your friend Perez is one of the new breed of college-educated Hispanic Rights activists crowding the landscape these days. Sort of a newcomer to the field, but damn good at it—has one of those golden oratory styles that turns crowds and liberal media inside out. I don't know who the iron-head was who approved him for Astra, but I intend to get him *dis*approved and sent back to Arizona as soon as I can."

"I see." Perez's presence here was starting to make sense— perhaps on more than one level. "Colonel . . . have you given any more thought to the idea of setting up a citizen advisory council? I think it might ease the tension if you announced—"

"Miss Olivero." Meredith's voice was soft and excruciatingly patient. "The farm work in Crosse is three days behind schedule, work on Martello's landing field is being interrupted while Major Brown tries to figure out whether we should be building defenses against that Rooshrike mining group two planets over, and about thirty percent of my troops are currently tied up with civil peacekeeping duty. I'll tell you just once more: *we cannot spare the man-hours a farce like that would cost.* Is that clear?"

"Yes, sir," she said between rigid lips.

"Good. You can tell Perez you delivered his message—and the next time he has something to say, he can write me a note. Dismissed."

Silently, Carmen got to her feet and left the room, resisting the urge to slam the door behind her. Of *course* an advisory council would use up time—but so did civil unrest. In the long run the good such councils did nearly always outweighed their costs; she'd seen the studies that proved it. Why wouldn't the colonel at least give the idea a fair hearing? Was he simply allergic to civilian politics, like so many other career officers she'd known? Or—

Or was it because she was a Hispanic?

"Excuse me, miss?"

She came to an abrupt halt and focused for the first time on the man who had stepped between her and the outer office door. "Yes, ah—?" she said, trying to figure out where she'd seen him before.

"I'm Dr. Peter Hafner," he identified himself. "Geologist. I saw you with Colonel Meredith the second night here, when I came to ask about the grounded flyers."

The memory clicked. "Yes, of course. You wanted to study Mt. Olympus."

"Right. Well, I've been trying to see the colonel about getting one of them—they're back in service, but I'm way down on the list."

Carmen shot a glance at Meredith's secretary, caught the other's look of strained patience. She'd once worked as a secretary herself. . . . "Tell you what," she said to Hafner. "Let's go to the lounge and you can tell me why a car or plane won't do. Maybe we can work out something."

"Well . . ." Hafner's eyes flicked behind her to Meredith's door. "Okay."

He didn't wait for them to reach the lounge, but launched into his spiel before they were even out the door. "Let me remind you first of all why an examination of Olympus is so important. For whatever mysterious reason, there appears to be little or no metal content anywhere in the first five hundred meters of Astra's crust, if the Rooshrike data can be trusted. A volcano like Olympus gives us a sampling of the deeper magma—and if that layer should turn out to be metal-rich, it would give us an indication of where the weak points are for drilling."

He paused for breath, enabling Carmen to get a word in. "Yes, I remember all this from the last time. You haven't said yet why you specifically need a flyer."

"A car doesn't have the room I'd need to carry a coring tube and driver—the tube breaks down into sections, but they're almost five meters long. I don't know if a Cessna can carry them, but even if it can I wouldn't be able to land as far up the volcano cone as I'd need to. I need VTOL, and that means a flyer."

They'd reached the lounge now, little more really than a widening of the hall with a few chairs and low tables. Three junior officers sat around one of the tables, deep in conversation; Carmen steered Hafner to the table farthest from them and sat down. The geologist took a seat opposite her, an expectant look on his face. "First of all," she told him, "I'm not really in a position to do much about this. I'm technically a civilian, and don't fit anywhere into the chain of command."

He waved the disclaimer away. "You clearly have the colonel's ear, though. That's more important to me now than any silly ranking scheme."

First Perez, Carmen thought, *and now him. What on Earth am I doing that makes me look so authoritative?*

"Besides," Hafner continued, "civilians like you I can talk to. I sometimes think military procedure was set up specifically to confuse and intimidate those of us outside the secret club."

Somewhere in the back of Carmen's mind a light flashed on. "You're having trouble adjusting to Army rules?" she asked casually.

Hafner let his breath out in a *whuff.* "I've had less trouble with the L.A. city government. That's why I've been haunting

Colonel Meredith's office, in fact—I can't seem to find the right way to go through channels.''

"I know how you feel," she nodded. "It took me the better part of six months to figure my own way around." She paused. "As a matter of fact, that whole problem's been on my mind lately. What would you think of us organizing a sort of citizen's advisory council to act as—oh, complaint clearinghouse and general go-between with the military?"

"Sounds great," Hafner said. He cocked his head slightly. "Though . . . that 'us' wasn't specifically you and me, was it?"

She laughed. "No, I'm not roping you in as cochair or anything. Actually, I'm afraid the colonel hasn't gone for the idea yet; he thinks it would take up valuable man-hours."

Hafner grunted. "If it simplified communication, it would pay for itself in the long run." He leaned back slightly, a knowing smile playing at the corners of his mouth. "So. I gather you want me to make the same suggestion to him, using my scientific authority or whatever?"

"More or less." She found herself mildly impressed that he'd caught on so fast. "You don't need to fake an independent brainstorm, though. All I want is for you to get as many of the other scientists and technical people as you can to support the idea. You're the real VIPs here, and the colonel knows it."

"And once you've got his permission to go ahead?"

She hesitated only a second. "When the colonel authorizes the council, I'll get you one of the flyers."

"It's a deal," Hafner said promptly, getting to his feet. "If you'll excuse me, then, I'll go find myself a soapbox and get busy." Whistling something nineties-sounding, he disappeared down the hall.

Carmen stayed where she was another minute before starting back toward her office. What Meredith would think of all this she couldn't guess, but with any sort of backing from the scientific community, he should find it impossible to refuse at least a trial run. And once set up, the council *would* be worthwhile—she knew it.

And then life on Astra might settle down a bit . . . and she would have to finagle a flyer for Hafner. But that was all right; she'd manage it.

Somehow.

Chapter 6

"... and the elections will be exactly two weeks from today, terms to be six months each." Meredith glared over the top of the computer screen, and Carmen felt the room chill down a degree or two. "Will that be satisfactory?"

"Yes, sir," she said promptly. A longer preelection period would have been nice, but as long as the council was strictly advisory it didn't much matter whether or not the best people got on it. "Thank you for giving this a chance, sir. I know you won't be sorry."

Meredith leaned back in his chair and gave her a long, measuring look. "It's a pity you never actually joined the service, Olivero. You have the type of self-confidence that makes for the kind of officer COs either love or can't wait to transfer."

Carmen swallowed and said nothing.

"But I like to think of myself as open-minded," Meredith continued. He reached forward and typed for a moment on his terminal. "So I'm going to give that optimism a real test. As of right now, *you* are in complete charge of this council: its organization, election, procedures—everything. Your file lists an impressive paralegal background, so this should be right up your alley. It'll all be done in your off-duty time, of course."

Carmen stiffened, but she knew she should have expected something like this. She'd backed the colonel into a corner and he was getting his revenge. "I understand, sir," she said.

"Good. Now, since your organizational department conveniently keeps track of Astra's progress versus the original projected schedule, we know that—after two weeks—we're about five days behind, overall. If we ever drop to *ten* days behind, your council will be summarily disbanded—no arguments or appeals. If, on the other hand, we ever get *ahead* of schedule, you can come to me and we'll discuss whether to relieve you of the extra council duty or else cut back your official work load. Fair enough?"

"Very fair, Colonel," she said, both surprised and pleased. He *was* being reasonable about this, after all. "Thank you, sir."

His mouth quirked in a wry smile. "Just remember this warm glow when you're trying to function on four hours of sleep a night. Dismissed."

Not surprisingly, Dr. Hafner was waiting for her in the outer office. "Well?" he asked, getting to his feet.

"All set," she said. "He took the package pretty much as I'd presented it."

"Great." Hafner opened the door and they walked together into the hall. "So . . . when do I get my flyer?"

"How are you on early mornings and long days?"

"Haven't had anything else in years."

"Okay. Have all your stuff out at Martello Base by oh-four-hundred tomorrow. Can the two of us load it by ourselves?"

"We can if we've got access to a forklift." He gave her a quizzical look. "You're coming too?"

"I pretty well have to, since I'll be flying the thing."

Hafner stopped short. *"You?"*

"Sure. The Army gave a bunch of us a crash training course right after the *Celeritas* got shot at and they thought we might be heading into a war. I'm not very experienced, but I *am* qualified, and flyers are actually simpler to handle than normal aircraft. More automatic systems, for one thing."

"I've heard that." Hafner still looked unhappy. "Uh . . . look, I don't doubt that you're capable—"

"And if we *don't* do it this way, you'll just have to wait your normal turn," Carmen put in calmly, "because I can't shift around both a flyer *and* a regular pilot without flashing red lights all over my boss's board."

Hafner considered for a second, gave in with a wry smile. "Well, since you put it that way, I accept. See you at four."

The notice, stuck prominently to the Ceres bulletin board, was surprising in and of itself; but to Perez, its coauthorizing signature was even more unexpected. So Carmen Olivero *had* gone and gotten herself involved. He'd hoped his nudges would do some good, but he hadn't expected anything this fast. *You see, Carmen?* he silently addressed her signature. *Underneath all that cultural armor you're just like the rest of us. Hispanic blood does not thin with distance.*

He read the notice again, more carefully this time. Meredith, at least, was sticking to expected form. The council was clearly being designed as a cardboard cutout, with a slightly louder voice but no more power than any ten citizens had right now. But that was all right . . . because eventually it would change.

Turning, Perez strolled toward the rec center, where other workers would be gathering after a long day in the fields. Ceres's fifteen hundred civilians would have two representatives on the new council . . . and one of those, Perez had decided, would be him.

Chapter 7

Astra's sun was peeking over the eastern horizon as Carmen eased open the throttle to send the flyer drifting smoothly into the air. Hafner kept his eyes on the handful of displays and meters as she shifted from vertical to horizontal flight, but if the maneuver was in any way a tricky one, it wasn't apparent. On the contrary; the more he watched, the more it seemed that a bare handful of the dozens of controls were all she needed to guide the craft. He wondered what the others did, but their glowing labels were more confusing than informative. Eventually, he broke down and asked her.

"Most of those are used only when the flyer is in its spacecraft mode," Carmen told him, raising her voice over the low rumble of the repulsers.

"Ah." At least they wouldn't be needing *that* capability today, Hafner thought.

"Have you decided yet where you'll want me to land?" Carmen asked.

"If we have the time, perhaps we can circle the cone first. I need to find a good area to sample."

She nodded and for a few minutes neither of them spoke.

Looking out his window, Hafner let his eyes drift over the landscape. Just south of their path Unie was a collection of tannish blocks set on slightly darker tannish ground. Much farther to the south the white-edged peaks of the Kaf Mountain range provided only a slight contrast of coloration; and most of *that*, he knew, was due to shadows and other basically optical effects. No ferric red, no cupric green—the whole territory had all the washed-out blandness of a Hawaiian hotel beach. His eyes drifted ahead to Crosse . . . and narrowed a bit. "Carmen," he called, "can you slow down just this side of Crosse?"

She glanced curiously at him. "Sure. Anything wrong?"

"I think I can see the outline of a shallow circular depression between the river and the Unie-Crosse road. I want a better look at it."

"What is it, a dead volcano or something?" Carmen asked, shifting the flyer's course toward the area he'd indicated.

"More likely an old meteor crater," he said, peering down. "A little higher, please . . . yes . . . yes, damn it. That's what it is, all right. Too circular to be anything else. Thanks; we can go now."

The flyer tilted slightly to her side and he saw her take a quick look for herself before resuming their horizontal flight. "You sound annoyed," she ventured. "Are you worried about meteors hitting us?"

"Yes, but not the way you're thinking." He waved toward her window. "Teardrop Lake over by Ceres. If you look at it on satellite photos you can see that it's a circular depression that's been eroded by the rivers entering and leaving. The Dead Sea southeast of Olympus is the same thing plus what appear to be fault-line appendages. Even Splayfoot Bay shows a deep area in the center that's basically circular. This planet has been literally *pelted* with rocks over maybe the last half million years—not surprising when you consider how close we are to the asteroid belt here. *So where's all the metal those meteorites brought down with them?*"

Watching her, he noted with approval the furrowing of her

forehead. At least she recognized the paradox there; some he'd talked to hadn't even made it that far. "Well . . . could the Rooshrike survey data be wrong?"

"That's the most likely explanation," Hafner nodded. "The problem is that we've done our own spot checks since then. Our equipment doesn't have their half-kilometer range, but the chunk of rock that dug out Splayfoot Bay ought to have left *some* of itself scattered through the topsoil."

"Then maybe the asteroids that hit were just as metal-poor as Astra," she suggested. "If the whole system formed from the same cloud of dust . . . no. Doesn't work, does it?"

"Not when we know the Rooshrike are mining metals on the first planet," Hafner agreed. "Besides which, some of the smaller asteroids were analyzed by the original survey team and turned out to have a reasonable metal content. No, whatever happened here happened only to Astra."

They rode in silence for the next few minutes. Ahead, the hazy cone of Mt. Olympus gradually became sharper, the low angle of sunlight showing first the gross and finally the fine structure of its surface. Hafner watched with undivided interest, eyes probing for clues as to the type of lava that had formed it. The steepness of the cone suggested viscous lava flows, which on Earth would mean a predominance of andesitic rock. On the other hand, he could see little evidence of the surface characteristics that usually accompanied that type of lava. Still, if the volcano had been dormant for a long time, erosion would have altered many of the visual reference points. As with everything else in geology, there was ultimately no substitute for physically digging out the rocks and analyzing them.

"What about some weird process that breaks the metal down?" Carmen spoke up abruptly. "A nuclear fission sort of thing. Maybe it's some organism's way of producing energy."

"Chemical energy is a lot safer to work with," Hafner grunted. An interesting idea . . . but the flaw was easy to find. "Besides, that would only get rid of elements in the bottom half of the periodic table. Sodium is far too light a metal to fizz, but Astra hasn't got any of it, either."

"Oh. *Wait* a minute." She threw him a puzzled look. "No sodium either? But I thought Astra's ocean was salty."

"Not really. There's a fair assortment of stuff dissolved in it, but none of it strictly qualifies as salt. A salt, you see, is formed by replacing the hydrogen atom in an acid by a metal, as in hydrochloric acid to sodium chloride. Without metals, the acids remain as is or make bonds with oxygen or silicon." He shook his head. "We're sitting on a genuine treasure trove of strange chemistry here. Compounds that wouldn't last five seconds on Earth are just lying around waiting to be examined. I think we're up to eighteen brand-new carbon compounds alone since we've landed."

"Anything valuable?"

"You mean in terms of sending to Earth? So far, no. But we haven't even scratched the surface. We'll find *something* useful here—I'm sure of it."

"I hope you're right." She paused. "All right, I'm starting a clockwise circuit of Olympus. Pick your spot this time around, because I've got to get the flyer back soon."

"Right." A metallic glitter a few kilometers south of the cone caught Hafner's eye; but even as he opened his mouth to shout the discovery he realized what it was. Even with the incredible scarcity of metal, no one had yet found it worthwhile to come out here and scrape up all the tiny fragments of steel and magnesium scattered across the landscape by the ill-fated Flyer Two. Shivering, he resolutely turned his eyes back to the volcano.

He found the spot he was looking for in less than half a circuit: a small lump halfway up the slope that might indicate an old pipe vent. "There," he told Carmen, pointing. "It's at least a ten-degree slope, though—can this thing handle that?"

"Easily," she told him. The dull background roar changed pitch as she switched back to vertical thrusters. Three minutes later they were down.

Hafner's core-sampling equipment, while bulky, was not very heavy, and it took only fifteen minutes to unload it from the flyer and move it out of range of the repulsers. "Now you sure you're going to be all right?" Carmen asked as he dropped the last load of bracing bars onto his pile.

"I'll be fine," he assured her. "It's not like this is my first time on an all-day expedition, you know. I know what I'm doing."

"Fine. Okay, then, I'll be back to pick you up around twenty hundred. 'Bye."

It was closer to twenty-one hundred by the time she returned, but the delay didn't especially matter to Hafner. With all his samples taken, he had nothing to do for the moment but sit on the ground and brood . . . and brooding he could do anywhere.

"Zilch," he told Carmen as the flyer lifted off. "Not a single bit of metal in any of the half-dozen samples I ran."

"So that means Astra's magma is metal-free, too?" she asked.

"I don't know. Maybe I just got anomalous samples. The rock looked more heat-treated than actually melted—and, no, I don't know what could account for that. Say, would you take me the rest of the way around before we head back? I might as well look for a second test site while we're here."

The flyer tilted slightly as she complied. "I'm afraid it'll probably be a month or so before you'll be able to get back—I don't think I'd better pull this trick again."

He grunted. "Unless the borings show something promising it'll be a good stretch longer than that."

For a moment he studied the ground in silence. Directly ahead the blue water of the Dead Sea glinted in the fading sunlight; a couple of kilometers to the west of it he again saw the wreckage of Flyer Two. To his immediate right Olympus sat profiled against the multicolored western sky, and he noticed for the first time that the southern slope of the volcano seemed climbable, a bit of information he filed away for future reference. As the flyer continued its slow circle, the Dead Sea began to disappear from his view. He glanced one final time at it . . . and frowned. "Carmen, take us back to the east, would you? There's something funny in the Dead Sea."

"What is it?" Carmen asked as the flyer banked to the left.

"I'll let you know in a minute."

Seconds later they leveled out, bringing the Dead Sea into Hafner's view again. "Look down there," he told her. "The Sea's northwestern shore. See it?"

"You mean that white stuff? Looks like the offshore mineral deposits near the colony."

"Right. Like its namesake, our Dead Sea hasn't got any outlets, so minerals collect there. As the water evaporates, some of them are left to encrust the shoreline. But why only on the northwestern side?"

"Well . . . why do the offshore deposits only show up near Splayfoot Bay?" she countered.

"Presumably they're just more visible there because the continental shelf has a very gradual slope," he said, with waning enthusiasm. "You're right; it's probably something like that. Let's go on home—I think I've had it for one day." *A fast dinner and right to bed,* he told himself firmly. *For once, the samples can wait till tomorrow.*

An hour later he was at the lab, eating a sandwich at his desk as the analyzers chugged industriously away. The results, when they finally came, were painfully predictable: no metal, of any sort, in any of the borings.

Chapter 8

". . . and un*less* the military leaders become more responsive to the people, there will *never* be the close cooperation and mutual respect that distinguishes a people from a mere assemblage of individuals." Perez paused for a smattering of applause, led by the other four Hispanics on the Council.

Grimacing, Meredith slapped the video player's Off switch, blanking the screen as Perez's image began speaking again. "Quite the demagogue, isn't he?" the colonel commented.

Carmen looked as uncomfortable as her image on the tape had. "There's very little I can do," she told Meredith. "He *is* a duly elected representative, and I think it's obvious he speaks for the other Hispanic councillors, as well."

Beside her, Major Brown cleared his throat. "It seems to me, Colonel, that all these thinly veiled demands for Council authority could be construed as incitement to disaffection. Maybe we could get him sent back to Earth on that basis."

"I doubt it," Meredith shook his head. "It's becoming rather clear that he was shipped here specifically to get him out of the Arizona authorities' hair."

"The hell," Brown growled. "What are we running here, Devil's Island West?"

"Not yet. But almost certainly someone's been thinking along those lines. Or hadn't you noticed the odd mixture of highly skilled scientific people and low-to-moderately-skilled Hispanic laborers?"

"You didn't find that significant a month ago," Carmen put in quietly.

Meredith looked at her. "No, I didn't," he agreed. "I've had time to think about it since then. It's pretty clear that, at least as of our departure date, Congress hadn't really decided whether or not it really wanted us to succeed. At least a dozen senators thought the UN was playing us for fools, putting just enough international support in to keep the U.S. from simply cutting its losses by pulling out. An even bigger group was sort of behind us but busy arranging cover for their own tails for whenever we eventually failed. *Somewhere* in all that hostility someone surely ran the numbers and realized that Astra doesn't cost much more per person than a maximum-security prison—and if we get any reasonable agriculture going that price tag will come down." He paused, taking a moment to get out of what had been referred to as his preachy mode. "You'll forgive my slight bitterness toward Congress, Olivero, but it should be clear now why Perez's high democratic goals have *got* to be cooled down. I don't want us to be ordered home on the grounds that we're spending too much time rioting to accomplish anything, and I *don't* want anyone to start thinking how nice it would be if all troublemakers could be put this far away from the voters. You understand?"

"Yes, sir," she said, nodding. "I'll talk to Perez, see what I can do."

"I'd appreciate it. Thank you for dropping the tape by—I'll have it returned after I've finished with it. Dismissed."

She stood to go, and as she did so Brown's phone beeped. "Yes?" the major answered. ". . . *What*?" He looked at Meredith, a look of disbelief on his face. "Martello Base says all the tools in the flyer hangar are gone—along with the shelves they were stored on."

Meredith keyed his own phone into the connection. "Meredith here. Put a guard on the docks immediately."

"Already done, Colonel," the duty officer reported. "We've started a full search and are checking to see if anything else is missing."

"Good. Major Brown and I will be right there. Keep us informed." He broke the connection and headed for the door.

Brown was already halfway there. "Why would anyone bother with the shelves? They'd have to disassemble them to even get them out the door."

Meredith suddenly noticed that Carmen was still in the room, standing with one hand on the knob. "Get back to your computer," he ordered her. "Call up a description list of the tools stored in that hangar and put it out on the military net under a theft alert."

"Yes, sir." She frowned. "I don't like this, Colonel. It doesn't sound like a normal robbery to me."

"We'll find out soon enough. For now, just get that alert out."

It was only a two-minute car ride to Unie's docks; but even before the colonel, Brown, and Andrews arrived there, Carmen's hunch was proved correct as new and increasingly bizarre reports began to flood in. In Ceres, a tractor lost its harrow—somehow—while working on a new section of field. In Wright, a bulldozer sank out of sight in ground that wasn't even remotely swampy, leaving only various hoses and glass parts to mark the spot where it'd been. The rattled operator had had to be sedated, as had two of the five workers who had lost their shovel blades in an attempt to locate the vehicle. And Martello called back to report that shelving all over the base was missing, as were large numbers of tools. Spare parts, in cardboard and plastic boxes, were left in piles where the shelves had been.

Andrews was the first one to actually come out and say it. "It's the metal," he said as they piled out of the car and jogged to the nearest motorboat. "It's all disappearing into the ground."

"That's impossible," Brown said, without conviction.

"Of course it is," Meredith snapped as he stepped off the dock into the boat's stern and swiveled the motor to drop the propeller shaft into the water. "But it's happening, isn't it?"

Andrews threw off the bow rope and gave them a hefty push toward deep water. Simultaneously, Meredith hit the starter and they were off.

For about two seconds. Then, abruptly, the motor's roar became an anguished squeal that echoed in Meredith's ears even after he slapped the throttle back down. Cursing, he reached for the starter again . . . but halfway there he changed his mind and instead swiveled the motor back out of the water.

From the waterline down, the shaft had simply vanished.

Meredith looked up to find both Andrews and Brown staring at the ruined motor. Finally, Andrews shifted his gaze to Meredith and cleared his throat. "I guess whatever's stealing our metal works underwater, too."

There was nothing even Brown could say after that. In silence the men unshipped the boat's oars—plastic ones, fortunately—and headed back to shore.

The chaos lasted three hours more, and Meredith considered it a tribute to his officers and men that the colony remained as orderly as it did. Pockets of panic among the civilians were quickly defused by a combination of authoritative orders and up-to-the-minute information. One unexpected plus was that no one's life seemed to be in immediate danger; a series of quick tests on the plants and fish indicated that living tissue was not subject to the general metal loss, and Meredith was able to broadcast assurances that standing on furniture was unnecessary. The few people who went into hysterics anyway because they had touched the ground were bundled off to their local infirmaries, where they could be kept away from their already edgy neighbors while the doctors calmed them down. For a while, Meredith had teams of soldiers searching for equipment that might be salvaged, but soon gave the effort up. Metal not directly in contact with Astra's surface was untouched and apparently untouchable; for everything else, it was already far too late.

As it seemed to be, in fact, for Astra as a whole. When the phenomenon finally ceased, it left behind a ruined colony.

It was nearly sunset before the final list came through. Scanning the pages of close-spaced computer print, Meredith felt a numbness settle in over his mind. Tools, heavy equipment, assorted spare parts—nearly a half-million dollars' worth, not counting transportation from Earth. Exhaling heavily, he looked up at the four senior officers grouped around his desk. "Suggestions, gentlemen?"

Major Craig Barner laid aside his copy of the printout. "Speaking only for myself and the Crosse contingent, I think we can recover," he said. "As long as it doesn't happen again, we should be able to replace our losses. I see that plasticized undercoating on the boats seemed an effective counter; perhaps we can coat all our vehicles with it. Certainly we can learn not to leave smaller items lying on the ground; I taught my brother to do *that* when he was five."

"And the next time it happens, maybe it'll just pull harder—maybe hard enough to pull the metals out of *us*." Major Dunlop looked around the room. "Any idea how fast you'd die if that happened?"

"So you want to pull out?" Major Gregory asked. Meredith studied the other's face carefully, wondering where he stood. Gregory never liked committing himself early to a course of action, but his town of Wright had suffered even more losses than Martello had.

"Pull out, hell," Dunlop snorted. "I think we ought to teach those responsible a painful lesson."

"'Those responsible'?" Brown frowned. "Do I take it you're blaming the Rooshrike?"

"Who else? We weren't even settled before they were down here snooping around and probably scattering micro-who-knows-whatsies all over the place."

"Why would the Rooshrike do something like that?" Barner asked. "They're getting *paid* to let us stay here."

"Who knows how their minds work?" Dunlop shrugged. "Maybe this is their version of hologames."

Barner snorted. "That's absurd—"

"Rooshrike guilt or lack of it is not at issue," Meredith said, interrupting what could have become a lively discussion. "Let's leave the impotent sound and fury to the UN, all right? The *only* question here is whether or not we use the five days till the *Aurora* arrives to pack up the colony." A beep from his terminal signaled incoming data. Turning to it, he scanned the report as it filled the screen. It was as bad as he'd expected. Tight-lipped, he pressed for hard copy and handed the single sheet to Barner. "Soil analysis report from Dr. Haversham," he told the group quietly.

Barner muttered something vulger and passed the sheet on. "I never thought of that," he admitted, looking at Meredith. "That changes things, doesn't it?"

Meredith nodded, waiting silently as the others read the report. Every bit of the metal enrichment they'd added so carefully to Astra's fields had vanished.

"So what happens now?" Brown asked after a minute.

"Well, the crops are still alive, but unless we add more fertilizer right away they won't last very long. We've *got* the fertilizer, so that's not an immediate problem. But it'll essentially wipe out our next year's allotment, which means we'll have to go hat in hand to Congress to ask for more."

There was another short silence. "It seems to me," Gregory said at last, "that we ought to get some feedback from the troops and civilians before we make any final decision."

"I agree," Barner nodded. "Why don't we set up town meetings for tomorrow evening? That should give the short-lived emotional response time to pass. Get some idea as to their feelings, then meet together afterward to compare notes."

"Sounds reasonable," Meredith said. "Objections or other comments?"

"Only that we might as well refertilize the crops, in that case," Brown suggested. "If we decide to leave we wouldn't drag the stuff back to Earth, anyway."

Meredith nodded. "I'll have the work orders logged on tonight. I guess that's it, gentlemen; you'd better get back and see to your commands."

They filed out. Picking up the missing-item list again, Meredith began going through it more carefully, noting especially those entries the computer had marked as irreplaceable. But he'd barely started when Andrews, waiting in the outer office, interrupted with an unwelcome announcement. "Colonel, Cristobal Perez is here to see you. Council business, he says."

Meredith grimaced. "He always does. All right, I suppose you might as well send him in."

"Yes, sir. Uh—Miss Olivero and Dr. Peter Hafner are also here; they've been waiting about a half hour."

Hafner? Oh, yes—the scientist who'd helped ram through the Council setup. Probably all three were there to make the same complaints. "Send the whole batch of them in," he sighed. "It'll probably save time."

"Yes, sir."

He'd rather expected Perez to stomp in blazing with righteous indignation, and was disappointed only in degree. The Hispanic was mad, all right, but had toned down his expression and posture to something reasonably short of impolite. Carmen and Hafner, by contrast, seemed more thoughtful than anything else. Meredith considered greeting them first, just to annoy Perez; but the latter's open hand slamming down on his desk effectively removed that option.

"Colonel Meredith," he said with cold formality, "you are

holding without reason eight Hispanics from Ceres and Crosse. I demand they be released at once.''

Meredith returned his gaze steadily. "The Hispanics you refer to went hysterical earlier today and are undergoing standard post-trauma treatment—along with a handful of Anglos, if that makes you feel less picked on."

"So those who attempt to alert the populace to your ineptness are drugged and locked away. Is that your idea of responsible command?"

Meredith shook his head tiredly. "What the hell are you trying for, Perez? You can't make a ploy like that go anywhere—everybody on Astra knows those people had to be calmed down. In half the cases, their neighbors called *us*."

"I am trying for nothing but justice and competent leadership," Perez said. "This incident has demonstrated beyond a doubt the Army's inability to defend the people and property of Astra against attack. We received no warning, no useful instruction—"

"And I suppose you and your Council would have done better?"

"If we were given the authority we deserve—"

"I doubt if anyone could have done anything," Hafner interrupted. "I'd guess that what happened here today has happened several times in the past hundred thousand years."

Meredith and Perez both looked at him, Perez as if seeing him for the first time. "What's that supposed to mean?" the Hispanic demanded.

"Just what it sounded like," Hafner replied. "Something's been leeching metals out of Astra's crust since at least before the Kaf Mountains were formed."

Meredith shifted his attention to Carmen, cocked an eyebrow questioningly. "I thought you should hear Dr. Hafner's theory as soon as possible," she said. "It makes a lot of sense, and I was afraid it would be bounced by someone if he sent it through channels."

Meredith nodded and leaned back in his chair. Listening to all this would at the very least buy him some time to figure out what to do with Perez. "All right, Doctor, let's hear it. For starters, how do the Kaf Mountains figure in?"

"If you examine the rocks there, you find out two interesting things: the mountains were formed recently, geologically speaking; and they were formed *after* the metals were removed from the crust."

"Who said there ever *were* metals on Astra?" Perez interrupted. "You're arguing your conclusion."

Hafner gave him an irritated look. "This isn't a freshman logic class. I'm describing what turns out to be a self-consistent scenario."

"You're welcome to leave if you're not interested," Meredith offered. The Hispanic sent him an angry glare; Meredith ignored it and looked back at the geologist. "Why couldn't they have formed earlier?"

"Because most of the rocks in Terran mountains involve reasonably high percentages of metals—aluminum, iron, and sodium in particular—and if you suddenly pulled all those atoms out you'd completely destroy the structural strength. I haven't had a chance yet to study the satellite photos, but I'd bet we'll find evidence of collapsed mountains ranges now that we know to look for them. The Kafs, on the other hand, are composed almost entirely of christobalite—silicon dioxide—and moissanite, a silicon-carbon mineral. In other words, they're made of the strongest rocks available *after* the metal was gone."

"I see." This was starting to make altogether too much sense, and Meredith didn't like that at all. "You said it had happened several times . . . ?"

Hafner nodded. "Some of the meteor craters have been formed more recently than that, and they almost certainly brought metals in with them. The fact that those metals were gone before the Rooshrike surveyed Astra means this happened at least one more time."

"You keep saying the metal is 'gone,'" Perez said. "Gone

where? The center of the planet? And more importantly, *how?* I don't know much chemistry, but I *do* know yanking iron atoms out of a solid hammer ought to be impossible."

"Agreed," Hafner shrugged. "So should getting those atoms to slide through the soil. *I* don't know how it was done, either; but I *might* know where to look for the answers."

Meredith straightened up in his seat, belatedly touching his terminal's *audio record* button. "The Rooshrike base?"

"No, I'm pretty sure they aren't involved in any of this. The source of the effect is on Astra . . . and I *think* it's a localized source, as well." He hesitated. "I suppose I should explain my reasoning on that one. Basically, I'm assuming this leeching effect singles out metals because of their electrical conductivity, which probably implies the mechanism is electromagnetic in origin. Anyway, it occurred to me that ions dissolved in water also act somewhat like conductors, and that whatever force draws the metal atoms might draw those ions, too."

Meredith had a sudden flash of insight. "The offshore mineral deposits. Right?"

Hafner blinked in obvious surprise. "That's exactly right, Colonel. When the ions reach shore and come out of solution, their conductivity disappears and they don't go any farther into the ground."

Meredith tapped some computer keys, and seconds later had a map of the offshore deposits. "So the reason only this continent is bordered by the desposits is that the metal is being drawn and deposited *here*?"

Perez snorted. "A great theory. With twenty-five million square kilometers to search for this alleged El Dorado, it would be years before you could be proved wrong. Except that we already *know* the metals aren't here."

"Not necessarily," Meredith countered. "All we really *know* is that they have to be deeper than the Rooshrike's half-kilometer range. And as for finding them, that much metal should be a gigantic mascon. A properly positioned geosat could pinpoint it in days—" He broke off at Hafner's look of strained patience. "Or do you have an easier way, Doctor?"

"I think so." Hafner leaned over the desk, touched the coastline on both sides of Splayfoot Bay. "The deposits are closest to the surface along here, which indicates to me that the El Dorado, as Mr. Perez calls it, is somewhere to the east and relatively close to us here. However"—he shifted his finger— "when Carmen and I flew over the Dead Sea last month, we found very similar deposits—but on the *northwest* shoreline."

There was only one logical conclusion, and Meredith reached it without trouble. "Mt. Olympus. The volcano."

Hafner nodded solemnly. "Mt. Olympus—except that it's *not* a volcano. The rocks don't show the characteristics of lava flow, and the overall shape doesn't fit with the viscosity of the samples I took." He hesitated, but only for a second. "Colonel, I realize all this sounds pretty unbelievable, and I'm painfully aware there are a lot of questions I haven't got even half-baked answers for yet. But what happened today can't be explained by any science I know of—"

"You want to take an expedition to Olympus for a closer look?" Meredith interjected mildly.

"Yes, sir. And the sooner the better."

The colonel shifted his attention to Carmen. "I take it you've already checked out the logistics?"

She reddened a bit. "Almost everything Dr. Hafner would need seems to be available, sir," she said. "I haven't logged any orders yet, of course, but all it would really involve would be pulling one of the flyers off survey work and three or four mountain-trained soldiers from routine duty."

"A pilot?"

"I thought I'd do that myself. All the pilots are technically due for downtime, anyway."

"Um. Actually, Doctor, your theory sounds a lot more believable than anything else I've heard this afternoon. When do you want to leave?"

"Just a minute, Colonel," Perez cut in before Hafner could

speak. "I don't know whether you two cooked up this bafflegab smokescreen together or whether it was a solo effort, but it is *not* going to get you out of answering my charges of mismanagement."

Behind Perez, Hafner took a half step forward. "Unless you have a couple of advanced degrees I don't know about, I'd suggest you keep blanket assessments to yourself," he told the Hispanic shortly. "*I* know what I'm talking about, and I doubt very much that you do."

"And as to your ridiculous charges—" Meredith began.

"Why don't you come with us tomorrow, Cris?" Carmen interrupted suddenly.

All three men looked at her. "To Olympus?" Perez frowned. His eyes flicked to each of the others, as if looking for a trap. "Why?"

"Why not? It would give you the chance to see Peter test his theories. You could be sort of an unofficial observer for the Council."

"The Council doesn't need any observers there—unofficial or not," Meredith growled.

Perez sent a tight smile in the colonel's direction. "Your point is well taken, Miss Olivero," he said, bowing his head briefly. "I accept. With the doctor's permission, naturally."

Carmen shifted her eyes to Hafner. "Peter?"

Hafner's expression was that of a man facing a tax audit, but he shrugged fractionally. "As long as he stays out of the way," he said. "We're leaving before sunrise, though—I want to be ready to start climbing as soon as it's light enough."

Perez's smile this time had a trace of bitterness to it. "Those of us who work the fields are used to rising early."

"Um." Hafner's irritation seemed to soften a bit. "Well, be at Martello by four o'clock. Colonel, thank you for your time and permission on this. I hope we'll have some answers for you when we get back." He took Carmen's arm and together they left the office.

"You're invited out, too," Meredith told Perez.

"Of course." The Hispanic walked to the door, paused with his hand on the knob. "But this matter is *not* settled, Colonel. Miss Olivero's efforts to sidetrack me have merely postponed the inevitable." Turning, he wrenched open the door and strode through it.

Deliver me from demagogues. With a sigh, Meredith let himself sag from the straight-backed military posture he'd adopted for Perez's benefit. Once, he'd thought this command would be the sure way to that long-awaited general's star; later, as the survey reports came in, his optimism had waned, replaced by grim determination. After today—

After today, he'd be lucky to keep his eagles. Or his butt.

But until the scapegoat-hunters in Congress got to him, he was still in charge; and neither hell, high water, Perez, nor Astra itself was going to change that.

Picking up the missing-items printout again, he began making a list for the *Aurora* to take back to Earth.

Chapter 9

The early morning air was relatively cool, but nothing, Perez decided, compared to the chill in the flyer's cockpit as the expedition burned through the sky toward Olympus. Carmen's scientist friend—Hafner—clearly still considered Perez an unnecessary bit of luggage, and had rather pointedly taken the copilot's seat, leaving Perez to rattle around in back with the three soldiers and Hafner's assistant. Perez hadn't argued; he'd simply folded out the emergency jumpseat behind Carmen's station and settled in, ignoring Hafner's order to find a safer seat. The view was lousy, and as his presence seemed to put a damper on Hafner's talkativeness he didn't learn anything useful. But he'd long since learned that distinction was a vital ingredient of power, and for that reason alone he would willingly have put up with the jumpseat. Actually, he found the situation rather amusing as well.

Still, it was probably a good thing the trip was short.

The eastern sky was glowing but the sun not yet up when they landed south of Olympus's cone. The climbing equipment, Perez noted with secret relief, was the kind suited to straightforward trips up easy slopes—apparently the more advanced rock-climbing skills weren't going to be needed here. Whatever else Hafner might be, he *was* a decent organizer: ten minutes after landing, their route pointed out to them on map and terrain and the equipment distributed, they began to climb.

And five minutes later, they had their first casualty.

"How does it feel?" Hafner asked as he carefully removed Carmen's left boot and felt the skin below.

"About like a twisted ankle always feels," she snorted, tight-lipped with pain and anger. "*Damn.* Of all the stupid times to fall over my own feet."

"Better now than later," Hafner countered. "It'll be easier to get you down to the flyer from here."

"I'll be all right." She struggled to her feet and eased some weight onto her left foot. She managed not to wince, but she didn't leave the weight there long, either.

"Uh-uh." Hafner shook his head. "Nothing seems broken, but you're not going to be walking on that foot for a while, let alone climbing mountains." His eyes swept the group; settled briefly on Perez, then moved to one of the soldiers. "Sadowski, help Miss Olivero back to the flyer and stay with her."

"Yes, sir." The man stepped forward and put his arm around her waist.

Reluctantly, Carmen shifted her grip from Hafner's arm to Sadowski's shoulder. "All right. But keep your radios on, okay? I want to hear what you're doing."

"Sure," Hafner nodded. He waited until the two of them had taken a few steps downslope before turning and starting up again.

They climbed for another half hour in relative silence, most of the conversation between Hafner and his assistant, Al Nichols. The technical jargon was annoyingly cryptic, but Perez got the impression they were making a catalog of anomalies to be found on and about the volcano. Apparently, Hafner's contention that Olympus was something other than it seemed was still open to debate. A sliver of sunlight broke the horizon, and with the official coming of day Perez felt his step lightening, raising his spirits along with it. A southerly wind began whispering at his back, as if Astra had noticed the tiny band and was offering her help. At this rate they'd be at the summit in no time—

He almost bumped into Hafner as the geologist abruptly stopped. "What's up?" he asked, his growing contentment changing to irritation at the near-collision.

Hafner turned, and the look on his face made Perez's eyes narrow. "What's wrong?"

"Don't you feel it?" Hafner shot glances at the other three, now grouped around them. "Don't any of you feel it? We're *light*—we're *too light*."

"We *are* climbing a mountain—" Perez began.

"Al—stopwatch," Hafner cut him off. He dug a heavy-looking hammer from his pack and was holding it in front of him and a few centimeters above his head by the time Nichols had the watch ready. "This is just about two meters up; Astra's gravity is about three percent under Earth's"—he tapped his wrist calculator—"so it should take about point six five seconds. Ready; on one: three, two, *one*."

Perez had never paid much attention to things like this; but even to him the hammer's fall looked somehow wrong. Nichols's slightly choked report merely confirmed it: "Point eight two."

Someone swore gently. "Try it again," Hafner said. "Three, two, *one*."

This time it took point eight five second to hit the ground.

"You must have calculated wrong," one of the soldiers suggested.

"No," Nichols said. His eyes were darting everywhere, squinting when he faced south into the wind. "No, I checked his numbers. For it to take point eight second to fall, it'd have to start three meters up. We're *not* making an error that big."

"Broken stopwatch, then," the soldier persisted.

"Or maybe the wind is affecting it," Perez offered. "It's been picking up for the last few minutes."

Whatever the revelation was, it hit Hafner and Nichols simultaneously. "Damn," Hafner breathed. "We'd better try it again, Al—and then get the hell out of here."

He dropped the tool again; it hit the ground point eight nine second later.

"All right, everyone; down the mountain," Hafner ordered, his voice sharp with apprehension. "*Move.*"

They moved. Perez hadn't realized just how strong the wind had become until he started pushing through it, and it scared him more than the falling hammer had. "What's going on?" he yelled over the gale in his ears.

"The gravity around here is decreasing," Hafner shouted back, his words barely audible. "Maybe even goes to zero someplace upslope. All the air's shooting up the mountain and out into space!"

Perez's heart skipped a beat. "But that's impossible."

"So is a planet that eats shelves and bulldozers," Hafner retorted. "Save your breath for running."

Swallowing, Perez tried to increase his speed. *This can't be happening!* he thought wildly—but he knew full well that that was nothing but emotional wish-making. He could *feel* the bounce in his feet now, the extra time it took to come down from a running step. And—whether an effect of the wind in his face or not—it was getting harder to breathe.

At his hip his radio buzzed. Fumbling it out, he thumbed up the volume and pressed it against his ear.

It was Carmen, calling on their general frequency. "—*down* the mountain; repeat, the wind here is coming *down* the mountain, not *up*." There was a moment of silence. "Peter, did you copy? I said—"

"I heard you," Hafner's voice cut in, his panting just barely audible. "It doesn't make sense—wait a minute. Everybody; hold it a minute. *Hold it!*"

They came to a disorganized stop, crouching down against the wind. "Who's got a good throwing arm?" Hafner called.

"Wilson? Here—take this." He handed one of the soldiers his hammer. "Now throw it—as far as you can—toward the flyer."

Wilson straightened, braced himself momentarily against the wind, and threw. The hammer arced into the air toward the distant silvery shape below; reached its peak and started to fall—

And slammed straight down with blinding speed, disappearing into the ground where it landed. Even through the gale Perez heard the *crack* of its impact. "What—?"

"Forward again—carefully," Hafner ordered, his voice grim. "Don't get too close to the hammer. Carmen, get this and get it right; I may not have time to repeat. There's a zone of high-gravity surrounding us—I don't know how wide—that's got us trapped in here. We're losing air fast. Whatever we've got here must be pretty important for a defense this wild to be set up around it."

"Peter, listen to me." Carmen's voice sounded odd in Perez's ears. The first sign of asphyxiation? "I can bring the flyer in there and pick you up. Just hold on another few minutes."

"No! The way the hammer fell—must be a hundred gees or more in there. You'd never make it."

The group had stumbled to within sight of the hammer-dug hole now, and the hurricane wind had cut back to a stiff breeze. Perez's mind felt somehow sluggish, and it took him several seconds to realize that that was bad: less wind implied less air. Beside him, Hafner stooped and picked up a pebble. He lofted it ahead of them; it slammed to the ground a millimeter from the late hammer. "Everyone on the ground . . . right here," the geologist ordered, breathing heavily. "There may be some . . . air leakage from . . . other side. No moving, no . . . talking. Save your strength."

Perez dropped awkwardly to the ground, positioning himself with his feet pointing upslope. Directly above him the sky was markedly darker than it had any right to be. Against it, Olympus's cone looked unreal, the side not directly sunlit almost black. Beneath him, the ground seemed to vibrate, and he almost laughed. An *earthquake* on top of everything else? Madre *Astra, you work much too hard just to kill a few poor humans.*

The thought faded. Closing his eyes, Perez listened to the breeze and waited for the end to come.

"Peter! Cris! Anyone!" Without taking her eyes off the group lying motionless on the ground, Carmen slapped the radio selector switch. "No response, Colonel. I don't know whether they're dead or just unconscious, but I can't wait any longer. I'm going in."

"Take it easy," Meredith's voice came back, soothing on top, combat-ready underneath. "Flyer Three is scrambling now—"

"No time, sir," Carmen interrupted. "Cross your fingers."

Without waiting for a reply, she kicked the underside repulsers to life and eased on the main engines. Hovering a meter or two off the ground, the flyer swung around and drifted cautiously up the mountain toward the trapped expedition.

It was a nerve-wracking trip, caught as she was between the need for haste and the need for caution. She had no idea where the near edge of the high-gee ring was, and if she hit it too fast she could easily lose control and ram the flyer all the way in. Licking dry lips, she kept going, peripherally aware of Sadowski sitting tensely in the seat beside her. The others were ten meters away now . . . seven . . . four . . . the hole the hammer had made was visible—

With a snap of sheared connectors and the boom of a sledge-hammered oil drum the flyer's nose slammed to the ground. Carmen shoved on the throttle, but even as she cut the drive the nose flipped up again, overshooting level by a meter or so. For that instant the underside repulsers were aiming slightly forward, giving the flyer a small backward thrust. By the time they'd leveled out once more they were three or four meters from the high-gee field, leaving behind a very flat piece of metal to mark the place.

"Nice flying, Miss Olivero," Sadowski said tightly. "I hope whatever we lost there wasn't vital."

"Me, too," Carmen agreed, the first glimmering of real hope stirring in her. The high-gee ring was no more than a meter wide—an impassable barrier for a human being, but perhaps not for what she had in mind. Taking a deep breath, she swung the flyer around and backed into the field.

They were moving faster this time, and hit the ground with a correspondingly louder crash. Ignoring the groans and snaps of tortured metal and plastic, Carmen ran the thruster limit all the way up and waited tensely for the automatic leveler to raise the tail off the ground. The usual background rumble rose to a scream, and she felt her hands curling into fists. The repulser units themselves could handle enormous temperatures, but it was doubtful the designers had expected the flyer to be flat on the ground at the time. She envisioned the underside plates buckling with the heat, perhaps melting or even boiling away—

And with a barely perceptible lurch the tail came off the ground.

Carmen was ready. The flyer's nose jets spat at full thrust, pushing the craft backward. Two meters were all they could manage before the underside temp monitors hit critical and shut down the repulsers, bringing the craft back down with a bone-jarring crunch. But two meters was enough. Flipping to "spacecraft" mode, Carmen shut down all fuel to the main engines, killed the preheating ignition system—and the monitors that might otherwise prevent her from doing this—and slammed the throttle to full power.

And with nothing to hinder or react with it, the flyer's compressed oxygen supply began pouring through the main repulser units, spraying directly toward the motionless figures beyond the barrier.

"They're moving!" Sadowski, pressed against the side window, turned back to face her, a wide grin plastered across his face. "They're okay."

Carmen closed her eyes briefly and let out a shuddering

breath. Reaching down, she put the throttle back to half and popped the door beside her. "I'm going out for a look. Let me know when the O_2 level hits point three—that screen over there."

Hopping down carefully, she limped around the curve of the flyer, making certain to stay well back of the high-gee field. Beyond it, the five men were sitting up now, looking dazed but otherwise all right. She started to wave; but even as she raised her arm Hafner suddenly clutched Nichols's shoulder and pointed toward Olympus. Carmen raised her own eyes—and gasped.

Glittering like spun silver in the sunlight, a filament was shooting skyward from the volcano's crater. She was just in time to see the leading end vanish into the blueness above, and for an instant the strand seemed motionless, conjuring the image of Astra hanging from an impossibly thin skyhook. Then the other end of the thread left the volcano, and she realized with a fresh jolt just how fast the thread was moving. Escape velocity for sure; perhaps much more.

She was still standing there, staring upward, when the steady wind blowing in her face abruptly died, nearly toppling her onto her face. Recovering, she looked down at the others. As if on cue they turned back to her as well; and after a moment of uncertainty, Perez picked up a stone and lobbed it in her direction. It landed at her feet without any detectable deviation, and a minute later they were all standing together by the flyer.

"Are you all right?" she asked, her eyes flicking to each in turn.

"We're fine," Hafner nodded. He had a bemused look on his face, as if wondering whether any of it had really happened. Carmen could sympathize; with gravity back to normal and that mysterious thread long out of sight, she could almost imagine the whole thing had been a dream or mass hallucination.

Until, that is, she got a close look at the flyer's crumpled tail section.

Chapter 10

"The shuttle's matched orbits with the cable now," Captain Stewart reported. "It should be just a few more minutes."

Listening in from a few million kilometers away, Meredith swallowed hard against his frustration. He'd desperately wanted to be on the scene when rendezvous was made, and the fuel-efficiency arguments which had prevented the *Aurora* from stopping first for passengers weren't the least bit comforting. Whatever that cable was, it was an Astran discovery, and he didn't like the feeling that Stewart was cutting them out of things.

Brown, sitting beside Meredith in Martello's communications center, seemed to feel the same way. "We're still not getting the picture you promised," he told Stewart. "You want to get someone on that, Captain?"

"So far, there's nothing to see," Stewart replied. "Even the shuttle's cameras still only show occasional glints. We'll tie you in when they go EVA for the material tests."

"Do that," Meredith said. "In the meantime, have you refined your dimension estimates any?"

"Not really. We still make it about six centimeters in diameter and something over two kilometers long. When we can get a piece of it to work on we'll get density and composition, but I'll bet you the *Aurora* we've got your missing metal right here."

"Yeah. Well, there's just one problem with that." Tapping computer keys, Meredith called up a list of numbers. "Our best estimate right now is that we lost about forty-seven hundred kilograms' worth, including all the stuff in the fertilizer. If the cable's the density of iron, say, it shouldn't be more than a tenth that length. So where'd the rest of the mass come from?"

"No idea," Stewart admitted. "Maybe the chemical analysis will give us a clue." He paused. "Okay, they're exiting the lock now. Here we go."

In front of Meredith the screen came to life. To one side of the camera was the bulk of the shuttle, from which a spacesuited man equipped with a maneuvering pack was emerging. On the other side of the picture, the cable was just barely visible. A second figure joined the first, and for several minutes they jockeyed around the cable taking pictures. As Meredith had half expected, there was no more detail to the cable's surface at close range than had been visible farther out.

"That should be enough," Stewart said at last. "Try the cutters now—stay near the end."

"Roger." The first astro had unclipped a set of what looked to Meredith like a mechanized lobster claw. Moving forward, he set the blades against the cable—and suddenly swore. "Damn! It's *stuck*!"

"What do you mean, stuck?"

"As in glued to the cable, Captain. I barely touched it, and now I can't . . . I can't even get it loose running the motor in reverse."

Meredith exchanged a quick glance with Brown. "Maybe you can still cut it," he suggested into the mike. "Or at least cut enough groove to give us its hardness."

"Yes, sir." A pause. "I'm trying, sir, but nothing's happening."

"That's impossible," Stewart cut in. "I've seen those cutters handle ten-centimeter tungsten plate without—"

"Look out!" one of the astros shouted, and Meredith flinched in automatic reaction as the men on the screen jerked back.

"You all right?" Stewart asked sharply.

"Yes, sir," the rattled answer came. "We've just lost the cutters. The motor burned out—scattered small bits of itself all over the place. Uh . . . I can't even see a scratch underneath the blades."

For a long moment there was nothing but the hum of the radio's carrier. "I see," Stewart said at last. "Well . . . does the reflectivity read low enough to try using a laser on it?"

"Just a second, sir. . . . We could try the UV, I suppose; the reflectivity seems to increase with wavelength. But I'm not at all sure it'll do any better than the cutters did."

"Try it anyway," Meredith instructed. "You can at least get a heat capacity estimate that way."

It took a minute to get the laser ready, and two or three more to position the infrared sensors that would measure the cable's temperature. "Here goes, sir. Laser's going . . . reflection about thirty-eight percent—that seems low for a metal—"

"Temperature's starting up slowly," the second astro put in. "Up to . . . what the *hell*?"

"What?" Stewart snapped.

"The temp just . . . *dropped*, Captain; dropped like a stone all the way down to . . . well, to a few degrees absolute."

"Superconductor," Brown murmured, sounding awed.

"That's impossible," the astro retorted. "The reading was well above superconductor temperatures when it dropped."

Stewart ordered several more tests run, but each one simply added another mystery to the growing list. A portable wire-tester was hopelessly inadequate for measuring tensile strength—the cable didn't even stretch, let alone break. A standard metal detector gave no reading even a few centimeters away from the cable, but a direct measurement of resistivity showed that, under sufficiently high voltages, the material became a superconductor of electricity. And possibly the oddest discovery of all came when one of the astros accidentally brushed the cable and stuck fast. In attempting to cut him loose, his partner found that the "glue" had somehow penetrated several centimeters *into* the spacesuit fabric, rendering that section nearly as unbreakable as the cable itself. In the end they had to cut a gaping hole around the affected material, leaving the astro to do a decompressed reentry to the shuttle.

"I don't know about you," Meredith told Stewart when the two astros were back inside, "but I'm ready to call it a day. It's obvious we're not going to find out anything more with the equipment you've got out there. I think we're going to have to bring the cable back here."

"As in Astran orbit, you mean?"

"As in groundside."

There was a long pause. "And how, may I ask, do you intend to land two kilometers of heavy cable?" Stewart asked. "Without endangering one of my shuttles, that is?"

Meredith looked at Brown, gestured toward the mike. "We've been studying the problem ever since the cable was discovered," Brown told the captain. "Given the length and stickiness, I think it would be most reasonable to wrap it around itself, pretzel fashion, and tow it into near orbit. Once there, you could put a remote booster and some parachutes on it and send it on down. There are lots of open areas we could drop it in—north of Wright might be good, since a lot of our heavier equipment is up there."

"Out of the question," Stewart said. "We'll tow it back to Astran orbit, but that's where it's going to stay. Bring it down and you'll never see it again under the layer of dirt it'll collect."

"And then you'll run off and report all of this to the Pentagon, right?" Meredith asked.

"In a few days, yes. Why?—Were you planning to keep it secret?"

"No. But once you're gone, what's to keep someone else—

the Rooshrike, perhaps—from towing the cable back *out* of orbit?"

There was another long silence. "Do they know about the cable?" Stewart asked.

"I haven't the foggiest. You want to take that chance?"

"Damn." Stewart let out an audible breath. "Major Brown, let's hear those numbers you said you'd worked out."

In the end, with a maximum of difficulty and a minimum of actual damage, they brought the cable down.

Chapter 11

It was known colloquially as the "silent room" because it was the only place in the White House proper that was absolutely guaranteed against all forms of audio, electronic, or laser-scan eavesdropping. Today, President Allerton reflected, it was even more silent than usual. There were none of the normal mutterings or whispered discussions among the assembled advisors, Cabinet officials, and military men; just the soft sounds of pages turning. Generally speaking, their faces made up for the lack of vocal expression.

Allerton gave them plenty of time before clearing his throat. "Well. Comments?"

General Klein got in first with the obvious one. "Unbelievable. Simply unbelievable. Something on Astra *made* this thing?"

National Security Advisor Thomas Morley was staring into space. "I trust you realize, Mr. President, how self-contradictory this report looks. A supersticky metal that doesn't show up on metal detectors? And stronger than graphite-boron sandwich but only four-fifths as dense as water?"

"I assure you, Mr. Morley," Captain Stewart said quietly,

"that I was present while the cable was being tested. I don't understand any of it either, but the numbers *are* accurate."

"Wasn't implying they weren't," Morley said. "I was just anticipating what others are going to say when we release this."

"Why release it at all?" Admiral Hamill rumbled. "It was discovered by American citizens on an American colony—that makes it American property."

"Except that we're technically running it under a UN mandate," Allerton reminded him.

Hamill's snort concisely gave his own views on that.

"I think Tom's right, sir," Secretary of State Joshua Purvis spoke up. "We've complained all along that the UN should be footing more of Astra's bill. Someone's bound to accuse us of making up this cable and this—this planet-sized spinneret for the sole purpose of stirring up interest and funding. And so far there doesn't appear to be any way to bring a section of the cable back here to show."

"Why do we have to show them anything?" Hamill persisted. "If you think we have to tell the UN, all right; but if they don't want to believe it that's *their* problem. I hope they don't, in fact, because that'll leave us free to send *our* experts out to study the thing."

On that point, at least, everyone was agreed, and the rest of the meeting was devoted to deciding on the procedure for recruiting the necessary scientists and getting them to Astra as quickly and quietly as possible. Afterward, Allerton put through scrambled phone calls to the British, Japanese, Soviet, and Chinese heads of state, whose reactions combined fascination and thinly veiled disbelief in about the proportions Allerton had expected. And lastly, he made a call to UN Secretary-General Saleh.

Saleh was silent for a long moment after Allerton had finished, his face almost expressionless as his eyes probed Allerton's own. "You would not," he said at last, "insult me by creating such a ridiculous lie. What are your thoughts about this—did you call it *Spinneret*?"

Allerton shrugged. "Nothing I've heard the Ctencri say has even hinted at this type of technology. Particularly the gravity control the Spinneret exhibited—if the Ctencri or anyone else in the area had something like that they ought to at least be using it to launch spaceships."

"You can surely assume the Rooshrike had no inkling it was on Astra, also," Saleh ruminated. "Unless they had tried already to locate it and hoped we could do so for them . . . no. That makes no sense."

"I agree. Almost certainly this is completely unknown, at least in this part of space. And it's going to drastically change mankind's position in the interstellar trading community."

Saleh smiled sardonically. "As well as that of the U.S. in *this* community, of course." The smile faded. "I imagine your mandate will have to be reconsidered."

"I don't see why," Allerton said, keeping his voice steady. He'd known the Astran Mandate would quickly be altered—if not scrapped altogether—but had hoped disbelief in the report would slow the process. "We haven't broken any of the conditions of the agreement."

"Don't act naive. We both understand the politics involved . . . and how those politics have now changed."

"Certainly. But if those nations—and groups of nations— who thought Astra was an amusing albatross to hang around our neck think they can vote themselves a large piece of the pie we've discovered, they'd better check the fine print. The mandate can't be changed without Security Council approval, and last I checked we still had a veto there."

"Legally, of course, you're correct," Saleh conceded. "But I'll warn you that you'll face a great deal of worldwide public condemnation if you attempt to keep Astra's discoveries for yourself."

Allerton leaned back in his chair and favored Saleh with a faint smile. "Actually, Mr. Saleh, I think in a case like this I'd be perfectly willing to tell world opinion to go take a walk in hard vacuum. For once the United States is not going to back down from a perfectly legal *and* reasonable position just because someone else doesn't like it."

Saleh's face was still calm, but there was a glint in his eye. "I understand your feelings, perhaps better than you think. But I warn you against biting off more than you can chew. Remember that all contact with the Ctencri is still by way of the UN, including trade both ways. We have more teeth now than at any time in our history . . . and I know of quite a few nations that would welcome the opportunity to test those teeth."

"Well, you tell them to go ahead and try it," Allerton said. "I think that as of right now we have a few new teeth ourselves. Good-bye, Mr. Saleh; I'll have a copy of this report sent over to you by secure messenger."

He broke the connection. *I probably shouldn't have told him off like that,* he thought, a bit guiltily. Saleh wasn't so bad, even if he *was* spokesman for the biggest unlanced boil in history. But every time a UN vote went down, he got a thousand irate letters demanding he do something, and up to now he'd always had to choke down the national pride and pretend he was above such petty politics.

And he was damned if it hadn't felt good to let it out at last.

Still. . . . Activating the phone again, he keyed for the Secretary of State. "Josh, have you gotten anywhere yet with the Ctencri on direct trade?"

"Nowhere at all. They still insist all goods in either direction go through the UN Secretariat. I don't know whether they're pushing for a one-world government or just generally like sticking with their first contact in a new market."

"Whichever it is, we can't let it continue," Allerton told him. "Step up the pressure. I want a trade pipeline that's free of UN control as soon as possible."

"I understand, sir. We'll do our best."

Saleh's office was also classified a silent room; but unlike that at the White House, his had played host on numerous occasions to Ctencri representatives . . . and Ctencri surveillance equipment was on a par with the rest of their technology.

The pulse reader went black, and First Trader Sen sat quietly for the moment it took his mind to process the information from visual short-term memory. Unbelievable. Utterly. An unsuspected alien technology—and on Rooshrike Parkh-3, of all unlikely places. An irony of first magnitude . . . but an equally great opportunity. For once the Ctencri policy of patiently taking new races by the ears and pointing them toward interstellar trade had brought in something more useful than a few paltry *troid*-weights of metals.

Turning to his recorder, the First Trader grunted it on and began outlining his campaign. Other races—the M'zarchs, for obvious example—would, in such a position, probably attempt to gain control of this Spinneret through threats or open violence. The Ctencri weren't incapable of such actions themselves, but experience had showed there were better ways. In this case, it would be a simple matter to inveigle for themselves the position of agent for the Humans, handling the sale and leasing of their new technology for them. Not only would the commissions bring immediate profits, but the simple act of handling all out-system contacts would continue to keep the Humans isolated from the other races and thus increase their dependence on the Ctencri. It was an old, old technique, but surprisingly effective for all that.

So first: all Ctencri contacts and surveillance on Earth would be immediately tightened. The Humans' tangled political system was still murky enough to defy predictive analysis, and pressure might be needed at any of a hundred points on a moment's notice. Second: the home world would be notified. There was a small bit of personal hazard in that, of course— they might decide to replace him with someone else and he would thus lose the chance to see the campaign through to completion. But even if that happened, his name and financial position were still secure. The discovery and project initiation were his, and his percentage of the final profits was fixed. If he were replaced and his successor muffed it, he would be paid out of the bungler's personal holdings.

And third: potential buyers had to know the product existed. A notice, sent free to each of the other races, describing the cable and perhaps a bit about the Spinneret—curious name!—itself. Not too much of the latter, though. If the metal-leeching and gravity-control aspects of the device weren't exaggerated they represented a truly awesome potential, and it would be best not to tempt any of the more violent races overmuch. The delicate political structure of the trading community was bound to shift somewhat with this discovery; the First Trader had no interest whatsoever in bringing the whole thing crashing down. Wartime trading wasn't nearly as profitable as it was often portrayed.

Dialing up a vial of *semarin*—not really the brain stimulator it was reputed to be, but a pleasant scent nonetheless—he took several sniffs and began composing the data release.

It was something of a truism among those who knew them that the M'zarchs never talked when they could be taking direct action instead; but even with such a base line the meeting of the High Command was abnormally short.

"No question," the Senior Commander declared. "We attack."

There were grunts of agreement around the tableless room—tableless so that none of the assembled Clan Commanders could secretly draw a weapon. "We will need to penetrate both Rooshrike and Pom territory," one of the others pointed out.

Another hissed depreciatingly. "It will not take a fleet to annex this world. A quarter-wing could bypass Rooshrike detectors with ease."

"The Poms will not be fooled."

"Poms do not engage alien craft unless they perceive a threat to themselves," the Senior Commander said. "Our course through their territory will be open and clear of worlds and bases."

The first speaker covered his eyes briefly with the backs of his hands. "I do not object; I merely caution. The subtleties of alien minds are still new to me."

"Do not grovel," the Senior Commander admonished sharply. "Coward's Advocate carries rights as well as duties. No one may challenge you for what you say—but you must not then leave that role."

A startled expression passed over the other's face, replaced quickly by dismay, and the Senior Commander permitted himself a moment of satisfied amusement. Coward's Advocate was always the hardest Command position to fill, but it was usually possible to trap newcomers into it in precisely the way he had just done. By the time the new Coward's Advocate had built his clan's power to the point where he could withstand any challenges his role might retroactively bring him, there was bound to be someone else the duty could be maneuvered onto.

The moment passed, and it was back to business. "You and you," he said, gesturing to the two most powerful Clan Commanders. "One warship each. You—" he indicated a third—"a heavy troop carrier. Each clan to provide a company/minor. Rendezvous at Kylisz Outpost in ten days; assault launch in eleven. Question?" He looked at the new Coward's Advocate, but the latter remained silent. "Then we are dismissed."

Chapter 12

Dr. Simon Chang had a round face, an almost equally round body, and a naturally sunny countenance that had somehow managed to survive the boring three-week trip from Earth. He didn't look much like a materials scientist—at least not to Meredith—but the way he gazed at the Gordian knot tangle of cable spoke louder than even the credentials he'd brought with him. "Magnificent!" was his first comment.

Meredith had to agree. Though much of the cable had acquired a heavy layer of dust, a six-meter length near one end had wound up in a nearly vertical position, its own weight having since bent it into a shiny quarter-circle. At the very tip were the remnants of the cords that had once connected to a reentry parachute; arrayed along the length were various clamps and sensors, all held solidly in place by the cable's own glue. "I hope you and your people can hold on to that enthusiasm," he told Chang. "The cable is proving a *very* tough nut to crack."

"I don't doubt it." Chang tore his eyes away long enough to glance around the warehouse-sized shelter that had been erected around the landing site. "But we've brought a good deal of specialized equipment with us. What have you learned so far?"

Meredith beckoned to a harried-looking officer. "Captain Witzany, Corps of Engineers," the colonel introduced him. "His people are the closest thing to materials specialists we have. Captain, tell Dr. Chang what you've got."

"Very little, I'm afraid." Witzany gestured to something that looked like a giant vise. "We know now that its tensile strength beats that of a graphite-epoxy bar by at least a factor of three, but that was the limit of our jury-rig. The glue—or whatever— doesn't seem to bond appreciably to liquids or gasses, but it really *does* extend a few centimeters into any solid material that contacts it."

"Does the effect begin before contact is made?"

"No, sir. It's not like a magnet starting to attract iron, if that's what you mean."

Chang nodded thoughtfully. "Have you learned anything more about its electrical properties? The preliminary report was rather self-contradictory."

"That's the cable's fault, not ours," Witzany replied. "It's a very all-or-nothing sort of material: either insulates or superconducts, but nothing in between. Based on that, we're guessing that if we ever *do* break it, it'll snap without stretching first."

"*When* we break it," Chang corrected mildly. "Have you done any tests on the emission spectrum when you heat it? I know it becomes superconducting, but the heat has to come out *somewhere*."

"We did that, sir—it took three days of continuous heating to get it hot enough, but we managed it. The spectrum centers mainly in the red and infrared, of course."

"That should be good enough." Chang looked at Meredith. "From that we should be able to get some idea as to its composition."

"I wish you luck, Doctor," Meredith said. "I don't believe Captain Witzany's team has been able to match up any significant section of the spectrum with known elements or compounds."

Chang waved that aside. "I think my library will be adequate to the task. I'd like two clear copies of the spectrum and some computer time as soon as possible."

Something sour flickered for a moment in Witzany's eyes. "Yes, sir," he said. "I'll be happy to give you any assistance you need—"

"Won't be necessary, thanks," Chang told him. "My staff and I can handle things from now on. Just give us all the data you've got and then you'll be free to return to your other duties."

This time the look in Witzany's eyes lasted long enough for Meredith to identify it. After sweating over the cable for a month and a half it was suddenly and casually being taken away from him, and he didn't like that at all.

Neither, Meredith suddenly realized, did he. Astra was finally getting the official attention it deserved—but in a way, it served mainly to remind him of the lukewarm support they'd been given up until now.

Witzany nodded toward Meredith. "Colonel Meredith has classified all our reports. I'll need his written authorization before I can turn them over to you."

"Don't be absurd, Captain—I have both Congressional and Joint Chiefs clearance to examine anything on Astra I want to."

"Of course, Doctor," Meredith interjected. "It's just a formality, but a necessary one. It'll just take a few minutes."

"Colonel—"

Meredith cut off Chang's protest with an upraised hand as his phone buzzed. "Excuse me," he said, and answered it.

It was Major Brown at Martello. "Colonel, we've got a Rooshrike spacecraft approaching. Says he's Beaeki nul Dies na—the one who visited right after we arrived—and that he wants to land and talk with you."

Meredith felt his eyes narrowing. "About what?"

"I don't know. But he's being *very* polite."

Meredith focused on Chang. "Can you put me through to the *Pathfinder* on a tight beam? I want Captain Radford."

"Just a minute, sir."

Chang took a step toward Meredith. "Is anything wrong?"

"I don't know yet," the colonel told him shortly.

There was a crackle and Radford's voice came from the phone. "Radford here. What's up, Colonel?"

"Had anyone on Earth leaked news of our cable before you left?" Meredith asked. "Specifically, had they leaked it to the Ctencri or the other aliens?"

"As far as I know, it was still a dead-dark secret," Radford said slowly. "Why would you think . . . the Rooshrike ship?"

"Yeah. I find the timing highly suspicious, given they've been ignoring Astra entirely for the past three months."

There was a short silence. "I thought the idea of bringing the cable down there was to keep anyone from trying to filch it."

"It was." Meredith let his breath out in a hiss, tapped a button on his phone. "Brown?"

"Yes, Colonel?"

"I want you to patch me through to the Rooshrike. You and Captain Radford are to listen in and make recordings of the conversation. Got it?"

"Yes, sir."

"Give me a second to set up the tamper-proof recorder," Radford added.

Meredith was suddenly aware that all activity and conversation in the cable shelter had ceased. Chang was looking slightly befuddled; but Witzany and his assistants had nothing of uncertainty in their expressions. They knew something was up.

The phone beeped. "You're through, Colonel; go ahead," Brown told him.

Meredith brought the phone a bit closer to his mouth. "This is Colonel Lloyd Meredith. I'd like to speak to Beaeki nul Dies na."

"I am Beaeki nul Dies na," the response came immediately. "I speak for my people."

"Uh, yes—I also speak for my people. I'd like to know the purpose of your visit."

"I wish to discuss trade with you."

"I see. Trade for our sulfur, I presume?"

"You need not seek to deceive," Beaeki said. "I offer you free information as a sign of sincerity: we know of the advanced technology which you have discovered and of the cable it has produced. We wish to purchase a length of the cable for examination; depending upon its properties we may be interested in trading for usable quantities of it."

Meredith stared at the phone for two heartbeats, his thoughts racing. "How did you find out about the cable?" he asked, more to gain time than anything else.

"We obtained the information from the Ctencri, who intend to act as agents for Earth in future sales. My people feel a more mutually equitable arrangement may be possible by trading directly with you."

"I see." So Earth had made a deal with the Ctencri without even bothering to tell him . . . or had the Ctencri set up the whole thing unilaterally? Or, for that matter, were the Rooshrike making the Ctencri connection up in hopes of pushing Astra into a hasty and ill-considered contract? Meredith hesitated, knowing that to appear indecisive might be the worst thing he could do, and wishing like hell he had a little more information. "As far as selling you a piece of the cable, I'm afraid I cannot permit that at present. However, we *will* sell you the data we have collected, either now or in a few days when our new test equipment has been set up."

Beaeki's answer might have helped Meredith figure out what was going on; but as it happened, the Rooshrike was never given time to reply. "Colonel, we're picking up another ship," Brown cut into the conversation, his voice tense: "Just shifted into the system—we caught the flash. About one point four million kilometers and coming toward Astra."

"Colonel, we just picked up a second flash," Radford announced. "—Make that a second *and* third."

"Confirmed," Brown said.

"Are those yours, Beaeki?" Meredith asked sharply.

"No," the alien replied. "It is possible a trade delegation from another people—"

"I doubt that seriously," Radford cut him off. "Trade delegations aren't likely to arrive in flanking maneuvers."

Flanking maneuvers. Uh-oh. "If those aren't yours I suggest you get out of here fast," Meredith said.

The Rooshrike didn't answer; but suddenly the phone erupted with a low whistle. "There he goes," Radford reported. "Like a bat with afterburners . . . there—he's shifted. Intruders still coming."

"Major? Try to raise them."

"Right." There was a long pause. "No answer. Either they ignore all the supposedly standard frequencies or else they haven't got a translator that handles English. Or they don't want to talk."

"I don't think there's any real doubt as to which it is," Meredith said quietly. "I think we'd better prepare for an invasion."

"Agreed," Radford said, his voice icily calm. "The *Pathfinder*'s at your disposal, Colonel."

"Thanks, but I don't know what you can possibly do except get yourselves blown out of the sky. I suggest you pull back— *way* back—and wait to see what happens. If they threaten you directly, you'd better run for it."

"I unfortunately agree. All right. Pulling back now and going to communications silence. Good luck to you."

"Thanks. Brown?"

"Sir?"

"Red alert, all units. You might as well make it a general announcement; the civilians are in this with the rest of us and might as well have as much time as possible to prepare."

"Yes, sir. Announcement going to all centers now. Deployment orders?"

Meredith paused for thought, and as he did so noticed for the first time that the others in the room had quietly gathered into a semicircle behind Witzany and Chang. To a man, they all wore the same expression: scared and edgy, but with a spring-steel resolve beneath it all. He'd seen that expression only once before, on Egyptian villagers preparing to defend their village against the Libyan war machine rolling toward it. It was a shock; he hadn't realized that in just three months his men could start thinking of Astra as home.

Or, for that matter, that he himself could.

"Squad-level dispersal," he told Brown. "It doesn't make any sense to try and hold Martello or the admin buildings. We'll split into guerrilla-size groups and try hit-and-run tactics once whoever-they-are have landed."

"Not much cover for that."

"I know, but if we stand and fight they can wipe us out from the sky. As many men as possible should head for the Kaf Mountains or the hills near Teardrop Lake. Someone should take the flyers into the Kafs, too."

"What about the cable, Colonel?" Witzany asked.

"Leave it," Meredith said. "If that's all they want, they can take it and go."

"What?" Chang exploded. "Colonel, that cable is priceless—"

"What's priceless is the machinery that made it," Meredith cut him off. "And I'm betting that's what they're really after."

"Colonel," Brown spoke up. "Orders are out, but we've got a glitch re the flyers—one of them is at Olympus with Hafner's group."

"Damn." Hafner's daily attempts to locate the cable-making machinery had become so routine that Meredith had clean forgotten them. "Better have them stay put."

"Right. Flyer One is heading for the mountains now."

Meredith mentally crossed his fingers—Flyer One hadn't been up since limping back to base from its encounter with that high-gee field—and then put the matter out of his mind. Valuable as the flyer was, it held just two lives in its grip—two out of the nearly ten thousand Meredith was responsible for.

"All right. I'm heading back to Unie; I'll pick up coordination from you when I get there."

He had just passed Wright and hit real road once again when the inevitable ultimatum came. "They won't identify themselves," Brown relayed tensely, "but they order us to halt all aircraft and ground vehicles and to assemble outside our buildings."

"Any 'or else' come with that?"

"Not explicitly, but it seems pretty self-evident."

"Yeah. How's the evacuation going?"

"Slowly. The civilians just aren't moving fast enough."

Meredith swore under his breath. "Are the invaders close enough to spot car traffic yet?"

"Depends mainly on whether they know where to look, I'd say. One of the ships is already below geosync; the others are hanging back. So far they're ignoring the *Pathfinder*."

"Um. All right. Tell the aliens that until we have their identity and full intentions your commander refuses to knuckle under. Use as much slang as you can—out-of-date slang, if you know any. That plus having to run their messages through you may buy us a little more time."

"Right. Even so, I don't think we'll be able to get everyone out of the towns. Permission to set up defensive positions?"

"I suppose we'd better. The admin buildings are probably your best bet—you can use fertilizer sacks in lieu of sandbags."

"Already thought of that. Do you want to set up deployment now or wait until you're back in Unie with secure lines?"

Meredith hesitated. He very much wanted to handle that personally, but he had few illusions as to how long they could stall the enemy. "You'd better do that yourself," he told Brown. "Give the local commanders autonomy, consistent with the goal of defensive holding action. Use the computer net as much as possible—they'll at least have to work hard to tap into that."

"Yes, sir. I'll funnel the final plans through to your office; I think we can keep them confused up there until then."

Meredith wasn't at all convinced of that; but whether through confusion or a simple desire to take a good, long look at the landscape, the invaders *did* hold off long enough for the colonel to reach Unie. He was in his office, skimming through Andrews's hastily prepared defensive setup, when Brown informed him the close-orbiting ship had launched two craft. Bare minutes later a low rumble became audible, growing quickly to a sonic-boom crash as one of the craft shot directly overhead, heading east. Through his window, Meredith watched it brake to a midair halt on its repulsers and settle to the ground somewhere between Unie and Crosse. He tensed, waiting for the sound of gunfire . . . but for the moment, at least, there was just a watchful silence.

So here we go, Meredith thought, reseating himself at his desk. *The Battle for Astra has begun. I wonder what our chances are.*

But that line of thought was unprofitable. Flipping on his phone, he began checking to see which of his communications lines were still open.

Chapter 13

"They're rolling out some kind of flyers now—bigger than ours," Hafner announced, adjusting the focus on his binoculars a bit. "Looks like they've got four of them. The rest of the troops are still fanning out toward Crosse and Unie."

Standing beside him, Carmen shaded her eyes with one hand as she peered off to the west; the other hand, pressed to her side, was clenched into a fist. Two-thirds of the way up Olympus's south face, Hafner's expedition had found themselves in a grandstand seat for the alien ships' landing—but for Carmen, at least, the ability to see but not to help was an almost suffocating combination. *I should be down there,* she thought over and over. *I should be helping run tactical programming. I take off one day to run Peter up here and the whole world falls apart.* "Shouldn't we call and warn them about the flyers?" she asked Hafner.

Binoculars still at his eyes, he shook his head. "I'm sure both Colonel Meredith and Major Barner have scouts within sight of that ship. No, if we radio anything now we'll just advertise our presence here. I'd rather save that for something really important."

"But we can't just sit here twiddling our thumbs," one of the others objected. "Isn't there something we can do with *our* flyer? A bombing run, evacuation—anything?"

"If you can whip together some bombs out of moissanite rock, be my guest," Hafner said tartly. "And as for evacuation, you wouldn't get half a kilometer before you'd have all four of those things on your back. . . ."

He trailed off. "An idea?" Carmen asked.

"Maybe." He lowered the glasses and frowned off toward the south. "Do you remember the spot where the other flyer crashed, our first day here?"

"Flyer Two? Um . . . I've got a rough idea."

"They never did find an actual cause for it, did they?"

"Not that I know of. Why?"

"Well," he said slowly, "we know now that this mountain has some incredible collection of machinery underneath it. Could it be that the fields in the flyer's repulsers triggered a— oh, I don't know; a resonance or feedback type of reaction in something underground?"

She thought about that a long moment. "I suppose it's *possible*," she conceded. "But I don't know what good that would do us. Besides, it seems to me we've flown over that spot ourselves, so whatever happened must have been a one-shot event."

Hafner was still gazing south. "Perhaps. . . ." Abruptly, he took a deep breath and turned back to the west. "At any rate, that gives us an idea of the scale involved here. The aliens won't be able to just pack everything up in a suitcase and take off with it."

"Un-huh." *But that's not what he was thinking,* she told herself, studying his profile suspiciously. *He's got something else in mind. What?*

But for the moment, at least, he didn't seem inclined to talk about it. Swallowing her curiosity, Carmen turned her thoughts back to the drama unfolding to the west, wishing she were there.

Meredith had rather hoped the alien commander would use the communicator's vision attachment, but wasn't overly surprised when the screen remained blank. Though off-planet radio was being thoroughly jammed he'd seen enough of the aliens to know they preferred to err on the side of caution. Of course, concealing their identity could also mean they were planning to keep their victims alive. It was a thought worth holding.

"I'm sorry, Commander," he said, for the fourth time in half that many minutes, "but many of my people do not carry personal phones. I simply cannot whisk them back to their digs on a second's notice." A note from Major Gregory in Wright appeared across his computer screen: the second landing craft had set down in the fields just east of Wright and was disgorging spacesuited troops at an alarming rate. Preliminary estimates—

The alien's reply cut into his reading. "You seek to slow me with dialect variants, but such tactics are pointless. I do not intend to harm your people unless absolutely necessary. I similarly do not intend to allow them free movement. If necessary I can use infrared and composition sensors from low orbit to locate them individually. You have one planetary rotation to return them to their towns. After that they will be considered as challengers to my rule and dealt with accordingly."

Meredith's throat felt very dry as he swallowed. He had no idea how accurate the aliens' sensors actually were, but he doubted any of his troops could burrow underground deeply enough in twenty-seven hours to escape them. *I should have started building defenses as soon as we realized the size of what we had here*, he berated himself dully. *But, damn it all, this trading association is supposed to be politically stable*.

"Commander, I await your decision," the alien said.

"Yes. Uh . . . what guarantees do you offer for the safety of my people?"

The other began to speak . . . but Meredith never heard the answer. A short message from Major Barner appeared on his screen, grabbing his full attention:

FORWARD SPOTTERS REPORT ALIEN LANDING CRAFT
RESTING ON METAL REPEAT METAL LANDING SKIDS.

Meredith stared at the screen, his mind racing. Barner's implied suggestion was obvious . . . but how did the major expect Meredith to put it into effect? No one knew how the thing had been triggered the first time, and there was certainly no time to experiment now. He would have to gamble, and hope Astra was on their side for once.

The alien stopped talking and Meredith licked his lips. "Very well," he said. "If you will lift your jamming, I'll broadcast instructions to as many of my people as I can."

"The jamming has ceased."

With fingers that trembled only slightly, Meredith keyed in all the broadcast channels available, not forgetting the phone systems. "This is Colonel Meredith," he announced. "To avoid unnecessary killing, I'm ordering all units to surrender to our unexpected guests. As a gesture of good faith, all fertilizer bags being used for shelter are to be *immediately* slit open and their contents dumped onto the ground. Repeat, all fertilizer to be dumped onto the ground immediately."

"You did not give instructions for assembling in towns," the alien said as Meredith shut down the transmitters.

"That'll keep," the colonel told him. Surely they couldn't know *too* much about humans. "When we undertake an act of good faith, we are duty-bound to complete it before other activities may be started."

He waited tensely, but the alien remained silent. *Nothing to do now but wait,* he told himself, wiping ineffectually at the perspiration on his face. *If it doesn't work we'll have to surrender. If it does . . . they'll probably start shooting.*

"You heard the order, soldier," Major Barner said, nodding to the bewildered sergeant at his command-post barricade. "Start slicing. And be sure and spread the fertilizer evenly over the ground."

"Yes, sir." The man still didn't look happy, but the order he barked to his squad was forceful enough. Holstering their pistols, they produced trench knives and got to work on the thick plastic.

Raising his binoculars, Barner focused on the top of the alien lander, all he could see of it with Crosse's buildings in the way. If this worked, it should start at any time. . . .

It took Carmen nearly a minute of straining before the intervening kilometers of air calmed enough for her to glimpse the underside of the distant landing craft; but once she had seen it she had no doubts left. "Landing skids," she told Al Nichols, who had moved up beside her. "No rubber wheels. Almost certainly bare steel or something equally vulnerable." Lowering the glasses, she offered them to him.

"So *that's* what the fertilizer business is all about." Nichols hung the binoculars around his neck. "Meredith thinks extra metal on the ground will trigger the leech effect. Should work."

"*If* metal concentration is what causes it to start up," Carmen reminded him. She glanced around the mountainside, eyes flicking over the expedition members huddling together as they gazed westward.

Hafner was missing.

She thought about it for a moment as she double-checked the group; but there really was only one place he could reasonably be. Leaving Nichols, she headed downslope toward their flyer.

Hafner was in the pilot's seat when she arrived, forehead furrowed with concentration as he studied the controls. "Going somewhere?" she asked, sitting down beside him.

He glanced up, then returned to his study. "Be a friend, Carmen, and show me how to start this thing up," he said. "Then get out of here."

For a moment she stared at his profile. Then, deliberately, she reached over and flipped the switch that transferred control to her half of the board. "Where are we going?" she asked, snapping her flying harness around her.

"You can't come," he growled, trying to reach past her to the switch. "I'm serious, Carmen; this is too risky. Give me back the controls and disappear."

"Tell me what you're planning first."

"Oh, for—" He ran his right hand through his hair. "Look, it's obvious what Colonel Meredith is trying, but I don't think the fertilizer alone will do the trick. We've got to get more metal into the ground as fast as possible."

Her stomach knotted. "You're going to crash the flyer?"

"Are you crazy?" He was aghast. "I'm not *that* desperate. I'm going to try and get the aliens to crash one of *theirs*."

"Oh. Well, that's different. For that you'll need a decent pilot." Flipping the ignition, she fired the underside repulsers, their low roar not quite covering Hafner's yelp. "No argument!" she shouted as the flyer lifted. "Colonel Meredith can give me orders, Peter, but you can't. Besides, you know perfectly well I'm right. Now, where to?"

There was a short pause, but when he spoke the argument was gone from his voice. "North and maybe a little east. I want to draw one of those flyers the aliens unloaded and make him chase us."

Carmen nodded and cut in the main engines. Olympus dropped away behind them and she took a moment to check the radar screen. "You have some way in mind to keep them chasing and not shooting?"

"I hope so. But I'm not sure." He hesitated. "That's one reason I wanted to go alone."

Carmen nodded grimly, swallowing all the obvious comments. "Well, get your plan in gear . . . because here they come."

Hafner turned to look out his window. Carmen was on the wrong side to see, but the radar screen told her everything she needed to know. Two of the alien's four flyers were coming in fast, one at reasonably high altitude, the other almost skimming the ground. Turning back, Hafner slipped on his radio headset. "Is this thing on?" he asked.

She hit the right switch and one-handedly got her own headset on.

"—immediately," a flat translator voice greeted her. "Repeat: the unauthorized Ctencri flyer is to land immediately."

"If you have any interest in the cable we've discovered, you'd better not bother us," Hafner said, his voice betraying none of the uncertainties of a minute ago. "We have in our possession delicate equipment vital to the operation of the machinery. So just pull back and let us go our way." Without waiting for a reply, he reached over and shut off the transmitter. "All right," he said to Carmen, "double back and head southwest toward the spot where Flyer Two crashed."

"Mind letting me in on the secret?" she asked as she put the craft into a right turn.

"No secret, just a hunch. As you pointed out earlier we've flown over that area several times before . . . but Flyer Two was heading due *south* when it failed, and I'm pretty sure we've never passed by going anywhere near that direction."

Carmen thought it over for a long minute. It wasn't impossible, she realized; something like a long underground solenoid or antenna could conceivably provide that kind of directional dependence. But it could just have easily have been a one-shot event. "I hope you're right," she said aloud, wishing she'd known all this when there was still a chance of talkı. ۱im out of it. "So what do you want me to do, run an S-curve ٤r the region and assume our pursuers will follow a straight north-south path?"

"Exactly. I'm hoping they'll be smart enough to realize that if they just stay with us we'll eventually run out of fuel and have to land. That may keep their trigger fingers steady long enough—*yipe*!"

Carmen twitched violently, the flyer's automatic systems smoothing out the effect on their motion. Bare meters away, flanking them on both sides, the alien flyers had suddenly appeared. Close up, she realized for the first time just how big they really were.

"Carmen!" Hafner's cry was half agonized expletive, half bewildered question.

"I don't *know*," she shook her head, feeling her own nerve sliding away. "Twenty seconds ago they were fifteen kilometers away—I never even saw them move." She broke off, forcing her mind back to the task at hand. *For all their superior equipment,* she told herself firmly, *we know something they don't.* But how to use that knowledge, now that their opponents would be watching their every move?

She thought of a way. Maybe.

"Take a deep breath, Peter," she ordered, "and brace yourself. Here goes nothing."

Ahead, Olympus was sweeping toward them like an inverted tornado. Pulling back on the stick, Carmen shoved the throttle to full power, sending the flyer arcing toward the clouds. The alien craft matched the maneuver without the slightest trouble that she could detect; matched it again when she turned the flyer to point due south. Olympus's cone flashed past, far beneath and to her right. Somewhere along here Flyer Two had lost all power—

Gritting her teeth, she shut down the repulsers.

The sudden silence seemed to roar in her ears. She spared a quick glance to the side, found Hafner tight-lipped but with the look of understanding in his eyes. Giving her full attention to flaps and elevons, she tried to remember every scrap she'd ever learned about gliding. The review, unfortunately, didn't take long.

"Any idea what our range is like this?" Hafner asked, his voice studiously casual.

"None." She tried to match his tone, but her performance wasn't nearly as good as his. "We were still climbing when I cut power and we're just leveling out now. It all depends on the glide characteristics of this thing, and I have no idea what those are. I think we'll be past the crash site before we have to restart the engines, but I don't know how much farther than that we'll get."

Hafner turned and gazed out the window. "Staying right with us, aren't they? I wonder how we'll be able to tell if—hey! He's dropping below us a bit."

Carmen shot a glance out her side. "This one, too." Could it have happened already? Without so much as a flash of light or crackle of radio static to mark the event? "Hang on," she told Hafner. "We're going to gamble."

Pulling back on the stick, she brought the flyer's nose up sharply, killing their forward momentum in a standard stall maneuver. If the aliens still had power, they would have no trouble staying with her . . . and with most of their speed gone, she would have no choice but to give up and abort the whole plan—

"They're still going down!" Hafner called, his fist slamming excitedly onto the edge of the control board. "They're gliding, too. *We did it!*"

Carmen's reply was a long exhalation of a breath she hadn't realized she was holding. Pulling out of the stall, she sent them into a lazy starboard turn. Only when they were heading west did she risk starting the engines again. They caught at once, and as she started them back toward Olympus she flipped on the radio once more. "Attention, invaders," she said. "Your aircraft, which we ordered to back off, have been dealt with. If you value your lives you will leave Astra immediately." Switching off, she gave Hafner a tight smile. "If nothing else, that should confuse them."

But Hafner was still staring out the window. "Carmen, can you take us back toward where the aliens just went down? I'm not sure, but I think it's started."

It had indeed started.

Unnoticeably at first, of course. Aboard the huge M'zarch landing craft the only indication was a slight vibration, unexplained but not especially worrisome; the troops outside, their attention turned outward, never noticed as the skids melted silently into the ground. The giant ships sank down to rest on their bellies and continued further . . . and by the time the *hull-breach* alarms began their clanging, it was too late. The underside repulsers, already being eaten away, could not be fired.

For many aboard the ships it was too late in another sense as well. Trapped inside their attack-resistant rooms, their minds and reflexes slowed by shock, they found themselves inexorably crushed to death as ceilings were brought down by disintegrating walls and combat armor dissolved into the sandy ground like spun sugar in water. And since these were precisely the people who were considered too valuable to risk outside, the ground troops suddenly found themselves on their own, without senior officers, tacticians, or clan liaisons . . . or heavy weapon support, intersquad and long-range communications, or defensive sensor cover.

"We have destroyed your landing craft," the Human commander's flat voice came from the translator at the High

Command's Chosen's elbow. "You will order your troops to abandon their weapons and surrender or they will likewise be destroyed."

The Chosen's fingers twitched with reaction. It was *impossible*—M'zarch armored landers couldn't be neutralized so quickly by anything short of nuclear weapons. But neutralized they had been, and the troop carrier's own sensors had picked up no sign of a nuclear blast. Had the alien Spinneret technology included weaponry? If so, it was more vital than ever that the M'zarch people gain control of this world.

The S'tarm Clan Liaison behind him might have been listening to his soul. "You must not let such technology exist outside M'zarch possession," he said.

The Chosen controlled his temper. "I am listening for suggestions as to strategy," he said, directing his words to all the clan liaisons and High Command officers on the bridge. "I have one-way communication with my ground troops; I can order them to attack and even direct their actions, though at low efficiency. But it is not reasonable to assume the Humans will not use their weapon against the troops if an attack is ordered."

"It is the purpose of troops to give their lives to advance M'zarch holdings—" someone began.

"It is *not* their use to be wasted for no purpose," the Chosen shot back. "Or do you believe their armor can withstand this weapon long enough to accomplish any practical objective?"

"You hold yet one landing craft in reserve," the Chief Tactician murmured, thinking aloud as tacticians were supposed to. "But without more information you cannot expect to add effective countermeasures to its equipment. It is also impossible to predict the weapon's range."

It took most of the clan liaisons a moment to catch the full implications of that. "Impossible!" the S'tarm snorted. "Surely this ship is beyond danger, and if not, the warships certainly are. We still hold the threat of total annihilation over the Humans."

Again the Chosen held his tongue. If the S'tarm continued such stupid comments one of the Command officers would eventually challenge the fool and save him the trouble. One *never* made threats one was unwilling to carry out, and wanton destruction of such a prize as this would draw the perpetrator death for both himself and his entire clan.

"Threats of destruction against the planet are useless," the Chief Tactician said, dismissing the S'tarm's suggestion with a gesture that was just short enough of contempt to avoid drawing a challenge. "However, you may be able to realistically make such threats against their spacecraft."

The words were barely out of his mouth when the three-tone alert twitter rendered them moot. "Chosen," the Defense Officer called over the alarm, "we've picked up the shift mark of six vessels, on intercept vectors. By configuration . . . Rooshrike corvet-class warships."

The Chosen made an acknowledging sign, the sound of crumpling status loud in his soul. To have failed in such a task would topple him back to the low echelons from which he had so laborously risen . . . but to have failed *and* to have thrown away lives for nothing would be worse. His own two warships could easily handle six corvets, but that would be only the leading edge of the wave, and he had neither the ability nor the desire to challenge the entire Rooshrike military. "Steersman," he called to the pilot, "raise us to geosync orbit. Speaker: inform the Humans my ground forces will surrender if they will then be permitted to leave the planet. Broadcast like instructions on the troops' local frequency. Then order my warships to stand ready to submit to the approaching Rooshrike force."

"You are surrendering?"

The Chosen turned back to face the S'tarm. "Yes," he ground out between clenched teeth. "You object?"

"Yes! The glory of the M'zarch people—"

It wasn't precisely a formal challenge, but the Chosen was

fairly certain the S'tarm got the point sometime before he caromed off the far bulkhead, his chest already bruising from the blow. The Chosen waited, hands ready for combat, but the other—perhaps recognizing that zero-gee fighting was too far outside his experience—slunk off the bridge instead. *At least,* the Chosen thought, *I won't have him under my eyelids for the return trip.*

Of course, upon their return he would no longer be the Chosen either. Perhaps then the S'tarm would take vengeance.

It didn't matter that much. For the Chosen, life as he knew it was already over.

Chapter 14

It wasn't until nearly sundown the next day that the observers Meredith had stationed at the foot of Mt. Olympus reported the gravity beginning its high/low divergence; and the ocean was cutting almost dead center across the sun as the new cable was catapulted from the volcano's cone.

"First sunrise, now sunset," Hafner nodded as Andrews relayed the news to Meredith. "Must be designed to fire the cable into Astra's own orbit, more or less. Probably makes pickup a lot easier, especially if a bunch of them drift into the Lagrange points."

"Um," Meredith nodded. "Though at this point I'd say pickup was already the simplest part of the whole operation."

Hafner gave him a wry smile. "Or in other words, our progress out at Olympus has been less than remarkable."

"Still no sign of an entrance?"

"None. However the crater opens up to let the cable out, it doesn't seem designed to let people in."

"Maybe you're just overlooking it," Meredith said with a shrug. "Three hundred square meters of cone floor plus a hundred more of interior wall around it is a pretty good-sized area to hide a secret entrance in."

"Except that I don't think it was designed to be especially *hidden,* and service doors usually are set up to be at least visible."

"What do you mean, 'not hidden'?" Andrews spoke up. "It's disguised to look like a volcano, isn't it?"

"I'm starting to think the form is accidental," Hafner replied. "The short piece of cylinder inside the cone is relatively smooth—made of something like the cable material, I think, minus the stickum—and the outer surface really doesn't look like igneous rock. The more I think about it, the more I'm convinced that the Spinners—"

"Spinners?" Meredith frowned.

"Oh, that's the hypothetical race that built the whole thing," Hafner explained, looking a bit sheepish. "Dr. Chang's team calls the apparatus the Spinneret, you know, and the other just came naturally. Anyway, I'm convinced the Spinners just piled up the stuff they'd dug out in making their underground factory, and that heat from the central shaft gradually fused the loose stone into its present form."

"Yes—this underground work area," Meredith said, finally getting to the topic he'd called Hafner in to discuss in the first place. "In the report you and Miss Olivero filed this morning you state that you'd like permission to search the area around the Dead Sea for the entrance. Isn't that going just a bit far afield? We're talking some ten kilometers, *minimum,* between the Sea and the volcano cone."

Hafner shrugged. "The spot where the M'zarch flyers lost their repulsers was nearly that far from the cone."

"But at least a kilometer west of the Sea."

"True. But unless the Spinners went to the trouble to put in a stage elevator in the middle of nowhere, the only convenient place to put an entrance is among the hills bordering the Sea."

Across the desk, Andrews held his phone up and murmured something. Eyes and half his attention on his aide, Meredith said, "You have to understand, Doctor, that while I appreciate the need to learn more about this—ah, Spinneret, I also don't have the resources to spare for the kind of long, drawn-out search you're requesting. We've again lost every bit of metal fertilization and are going to have to either harvest prematurely or lay down more fertilizer. The latter would have to be done immediately and mostly by hand—" He broke off as Andrews looked back up. "Well?"

"Colonel, the *Pathfinder* reports two Rooshrike ships have left orbit and are moving to intercept the cable."

Meredith nodded slowly, thinking. It was immediately obvious that he could either like it or lump it, that the chances of the *Pathfinder* interfering with the Rooshrike retrieval were essentially zero. Anyway, with the departure of the M'zarch ground troops still underway, it wouldn't be a good time to antagonize the cavalry who'd come to Astra's rescue. "Have Radford inform the Rooshrike that we're giving them the cable in return for their timely help and all that—he can figure out how to phrase it."

"Yes, sir."

Meredith turned back to Hafner, half expecting an argument. But the scientist nodded agreement. "Good idea. They'll see through it, of course, but it shows them we understand politics. Incidentally, did the first cable disappear when the leecher went on?"

"No, it didn't seem to be bothered."

"Um. Well . . . Am I to take it, then, that I'm not getting any more men to help with my search?"

Meredith spread his hands. "We've got to do something about those crops immediately, as I said. After that's taken care of we're going to be building some giant plastic-lined window-box contraptions to see if those could be a possible long-term defense against the leecher. And all of that's on top of all of our other work. I can assign you a car and a *reasonable* amount of digging gear, but that's all. You can take it or leave it."

Hafner shrugged. "I'll take it, of course. But I have to say,

Colonel, that you seem pretty indifferent toward what is clearly an incredibly valuable find."

"Then you haven't been paying attention," Meredith said, some of his annoyance creeping into his voice. "If I didn't care about it you and your fellow scientists would have spent the last two months working in fields or on construction crews instead of poking around Olympus. I'm not stupid, Doctor; I understand what we've got here. But the survival of the people comes *first*. The *Aurora* will be here in a week or two, and Radford said it should be bringing all the extra supplies we asked for. If he's right—if the Hill's penny pinchers haven't cut out half of it—then things may loosen up a bit. But I'll believe it when I see it."

"I understand." Hafner got to his feet. "It occurs to me, though, that the problem with the crops might be most simply handled by finding the Spinneret's controls and turning the leecher *off*."

With that he left. Sighing, Meredith looked at Andrews. "I could get very sick of having scientists under my command," he told the other, shaking his head. "Every one of them suffers from tunnel vision."

Andrews shrugged. "Actually, that last didn't seem like such a bad idea to me, sir. Assuming we'd be able to turn the leecher back on again if we wanted to, of course."

"Which is by no means guaranteed. But even if we find something as dead simple as an on-off switch . . ." Meredith grimaced. "No telling what kind of ground-monitoring equipment the Rooshrike have up there. Or the M'zarch, for that matter—and we don't *know* they'll be leaving as soon as their troops are all aboard."

"And you think that when we find the entrance to the Spinneret," Andrews said slowly, "they'll know about it, too. Is that what the delaying tactic is all about?"

"Mainly. We really *don't* have any extra manpower, but some of the projects could be put off without major trouble. But for the moment I think we'd do better to stall."

There was a short pause. "I hope you're not expecting the Pentagon to rush lots of defensive weaponry to us," Andrews said. "Even if Congress didn't debate the issues for six months, they'll practically have to invent the kind of material we'd need."

"I know—space war weapons that do fine against spy satellites would be pretty useless against M'zarch cruisers. No, I'm counting on the people who already have the weapons."

"The Rooshrike?"

"And the Poms and Orspham and Whissst," Meredith said, nodding. "Tell me, what would you do as President if the Spinneret had been discovered in, say, Upper Volta and you heard that the Chinese had made a grab for it?"

"Send two squadrons of F-26's for their use and offer them anything else they wanted," Andrews said promptly. "So you want to stall long enough for all the aliens in the area to hear about the M'zarch attack?"

"Bull's-eye. I suspect the Rooshrike may spread the word on their own; if not, we'll send a message to the Ctencri trading group at Earth and let *them* do it."

Andrews nodded slowly. "Three weeks one-way for the *Pathfinder*. Any idea how fast Rooshrike ships are?"

"No, but we already know the Ctencri scrimped on the technology they sold us way back when. I'm going to guess— oh, a month at most for the other aliens to get ships here for close-range analysis of the situation. Until then we'll have to hope the Rooshrike can hold off any other bargain hunters."

"And that the Rooshrike themselves don't get ideas."

Meredith grimaced. "There's that, too."

"A truly great joke," the young Whist said, snapping his ripper claw with a gesture of extreme pleasure.

"A great joke, indeed," the older Whist facing him on the viewscreen agreed. "Second only to the finding of the Spinneret itself."

"True. And the M'zarch are normally such humorless people."

"We should send a representative to Rooshrike space to see this thing."

The young Whist pondered a moment. "But such an action will have no humor at all to it," he said, touching a control with his leftmost antenna. Above his compatriot's face a map appeared, accompanied by a list of numbers. "The predictor calculates an eighty-nine fraction that the Whissst will take such an action."

"I understand your reluctance, my scion. But you must learn the fact that not all one's actions may be humorous. In this case it is more profitable to have a representative available to observe than to extract a joke from the situation. Besides"—the older Whist twitched his antennae—"who knows what jokes the Spinneret has yet to offer?"

"True. I would rather take humorous action when dealing with offworlders, but I accept your logic. I will place my calls."

"Good." The screen blanked.

The young Whist wasted no time in keying the first number onto the screen, but even so the monitor informed him there would be a slight delay. Small wonder, with each of his same-year brothers trying to call their assigned less-year kin, each of whom would call five others . . . and likely other families had received the word and were engaged in similar operations. The pyramid was undoubtedly an efficient way to pass news, but there was no humor whatsoever in its practical application: the lines *always* jammed.

Still. . . . Gazing at the map, the young Whist brightened. Even if the Whissst *were* expected to go to Astra, the ships could trace a curve past Rooshrike space and come in from the same direction as the Orspham. A small joke, to be sure; but small was better than nothing.

The line cleared and the summons tone sounded. Settling his claws in the proper posture for greeting a less-year brother, he waited for the other to answer.

* * *

On the Pom home world the news went out as a rippling series of sonar waves, amplified at thousands of strategic points along their journey until they reached every reef and wavetop of the mighty ocean. To assemble the people took far longer, even with the speed and tirelessness Poms prided themselves on. The discussion could have been held more simply, of course, via either the sonic amplifiers or the emergency ELF radio equipment. But from time immemorial a Gathering had been the required form for dealing with major issues . . . and a threat to Pom borders definitely qualified as a major issue.

"It is *not* a threat to us," the Prime Male insisted, swimming a convoluted path among the assembled Poms as he assessed popular agreement with his point of view. "We need not act. The Humans and their Spinneret are the object of interest. Pom territory is not threatened."

"Is it not?" the Prime Female countered from her own path. "What of the possible violation of Pom space by aliens? Astra is approachable only through Rooshrike or Pom space, and the Rooshrike are well known as fierce and jealous warriors within their own borders. Will not invaders thus choose to travel Pom space instead?"

"Space is free," the Prime Male insisted. "We have no indication Pom worlds or ships would be threatened."

"See the opportunity for advancement," the Second Female suggested, her path interweaving that of the Prime Female to indicate their basic agreement. "The Spinneret cable has many potential uses, as do the other technologies involved. To purchase from the Humans will undoubtedly prove easier than to purchase from a successful invader."

"To strengthen our border defense thus serves our interests twice," the Prime Female added.

"It is interstellar politics," the Prime Male said. "No concern to Poms."

The discussion lasted nearly a day, but at the end of it over half of the assembled Poms were swimming intertwining paths with the Prime Female. The voting finished, the Gathering was dispersed, and the Prime Male relayed their decision to the messenger ship circling high above the waves.

Within a few days the ships began to gather at the border, sealing off Pom space as had never before been done in peacetime.

From that direction, at least, the Spinneret would be safe from invasion.

For the Orspham there was no disagreement whatsoever. The M'zarch had tried to take Astra, and the Orspham would do all they could to make sure there would be no further attempts along such lines. A diplomatic mission would be sent immediately to the Humans' home world to offer defensive military assistance; a military force would wait just outside Rooshrike space for permission from both Humans and Rooshrike to proceed to Astra.

It wasn't simply the traditional rivalry that prompted such a response. Even the Orspham recognized the M'zarch nose for valuables; and if the M'zarch thought the Spinneret worth risking war with the Rooshrike over, it must be very valuable indeed. Until the Orspham had ascertained the full extent and particulars of this value, it was merely good sense to keep the planet out of M'zarch hands.

The Orspham might be slow, but they weren't stupid.

Of all the races in the area, it was the Ctencri who perhaps saw clearest the full implications of both the M'zarch attempt and its failure.

Mentally replaying the Rooshrike report, First Trader Sen held a *semarin* vial to his nostrils. *A technical act of war,* he thought miserably. *And repulsed by the Humans through direct use of the Spinneret technology. Military use, right from word one.*

It wasn't exactly an unexpected development—all technology *could* be adapted to warfare, after all. But now the military applications would be uppermost in everyone's minds, and that would complicate sales efforts tremendously. Demand would certainly go up, as no one would want to be caught without weapons or defenses others already possessed. But balancing that would be the climate of tension the Ctencri would have to work in.

And, of course, there was always the uncomfortable possibility that a race with genuine interstellar capabilities would gain total control of the technology. For the Humans to be given adequate defenses without simultaneously providing them with offensive capabilities was going to be a sticky problem, particularly as the Humans couldn't be allowed to suspect they were being treated like rash cubs.

Well. The first thing that would be needed would be faster communication between Earth and her colony. It was strict policy to keep the more advanced star drives away from younger races, but with some maneuvering the plans could "accidentally" fall into Human hands. . . . No. No, it would be both faster and safer to simply provide them a pair of unarmed courier ships with sealed drives. As free gifts, the First Trader decided; a gesture of goodwill that would subtly put them into Ctencri debt.

The *semarin* vial was empty, the volatile perfume having apparently evaporated several minutes ago without Sen noticing. Tossing the vial toward the recycler opening, he hummed on the intercom and ordered Secretary-General Saleh to be contacted.

It was an odd feeling, a detached part of Saleh's mind noticed, to be at the same time greatly relieved and absolutely furious. *The M'zarch will pay for this*, he thought blackly. *By all that is holy, they will pay.*

With a supreme effort, he choked down his rage, bleeding it off to a half-unconscious pool where it could simmer until the time for vengeance was ripe. He thought in silence for several minutes; then, picking up his phone, he punched President Allerton's secure number.

"I've just received a message from the Ctencri, Mr. President," he said, dispensing entirely with the usual social pleasantries. "A force of M'zarch soldiers has tried to overrun Astra."

Allerton's eyes narrowed, but he remained silent as Saleh recounted the incident. "Did Trader Sen say whether the Rooshrike were going to remain on guard over Astra?" he asked when the Secretary-General had finished.

"According to him, they'll stay there as long as we want them to. But I don't expect they're doing it for free."

"Um. You suppose their fee will involve some of the Spinneret technology?"

"Possibly. But that's not the point. No man or group of men can claim possession of land they cannot defend. We have been shamefully negligent in this area, and it is by the grace of God alone that we have a second chance."

"What are you suggesting we do?" Allerton asked calmly. *Too* calmly, in Saleh's opinion. Where was that warmongering, saber-rattling American belligerence when you truly needed it?

"I'm suggesting we get some real weapons to Astra immediately," he ground out. "Anti-aircraft missiles, certainly; equipment for ground warfare, probably. And we'll need to arm our ships, too—"

"Who's going to pay for all this?"

For nearly a second Saleh completely lost his voice. "Have you perhaps forgotten those are *your people* out there?" he snapped when he found his tongue again.

"So you want *us* to foot the bill for these useless weapons," Allerton nodded. "That's about what I expected."

"*Useless?*"

"You don't seriously think anything we can make will be effective against the kind of military technology we'd be up against, do you? Our only chance would be to buy state-of-the-art weaponry from the Ctencri—and I doubt seriously they would sell that to us."

Saleh stared at Allerton's image, again forcing his temper down. "All right, then. If we *can* find a supplier of such weaponry, will you help pay for it?"

"Possibly," Allerton said. "It depends partly on who would have control of the weapons and how you would guarantee they wouldn't show up later in various national arsenals."

"We—the United Nations—would retain control, naturally."

"That's a little vague. Do you mean the Security Council, the General Assembly, or just the Secretariat?"

Saleh favored him with a long, cool gaze. "You don't trust us, do you?"

"As you've so often pointed out, Mr. Saleh, all Ctencri contacts run through the UN. Given the anti-West invective that seems to be a staple of Assembly speeches, I think I have a right to be concerned when you start talking about hasty weapons deals."

"Yet you are offended when I suggest the benefits of Astra and the Spinneret should be more evenly distributed."

"That's a different situation entirely, and you know it."

"Of course I do. But world opinion is seldom so rational." He paused. "So I'm giving you advance warning as to my plans. One: I'm going to make public the full details of the Spinneret's discovery and capabilities tomorrow morning, along with the Ctencri report of the M'zarch attack. At the same time I'm going to introduce a resolution in the Security Council that the UN take over the operation and defense of Astra."

"The United States will veto any such action," Allerton cut in sharply.

"So you've told me. And two: I'm going to authorize the formation of an international scientific task force to study the Spinneret and its cable. They will be transported to Astra aboard one of the new courier space ships the Ctencri have generously offered us—ships that will make the one-way trip in approximately four days."

He had the satisfaction of seeing Allerton's expression twitch at that. "So. Faster ships," the President said slowly. "Well, if you're expecting a communications advantage like that to shake us off Astra, you're going to be disappointed. What Astra needs most is a stable source of supplies, and I doubt your little couriers are going to have anything near the capacity of our ships."

"True. But who knows? In a month you may be leasing those ships to us—because I assure you, Mr. President, that the Spinneret will not remain long under the domination of you or any other single nation. It is the property of *all* mankind, and I intend to make that status both explicit and legal. I suggest *you* decide just how graciously you will bow to the inevitable. Good day, sir."

Allerton was still staring blackly at the camera when Saleh cut off the connection.

Chapter 15

Meredith had guessed the political ripples of the M'zarch attack would take a month to return to Astra; but in fact the ships started arriving barely ten days after the incident. Three warships from the Orspham Empire were first, hulking monstrosities that completely dwarfed the Rooshrike corvets which escorted them in from the border. The Whissst arrived a few days later, their ships much smaller and reminding Meredith of nothing so much as large, steel-plated pretzels. The Ctencri sent no warships, but the flying warehouse they brought was a gadgeteer's delight, judging by the catalogue they transmitted groundside. As each race arrived Meredith did his best to send properly courteous greetings, and to gratefully acknowledge their offers of assistance and defense without actually accepting any of them.

"I feel like an Exxon heir at a gold diggers' convention," he grumbled to Major Barner one afternoon in the latter's Crosse office. He seemed to be spending a lot of time in people's offices lately; the thought of all the radio monitors overhead had made him increasingly leery of the phone for anything but the most innocuous conversations. "You can practically hear dollar signs dropping every time one of them calls down."

"Except with the Orspham," Barner noted. "They seem more interested in finding a M'zarch ship to shoot up. Have you figured out yet what you're going to do about all of them?"

Meredith grimaced. "Not yet. It's obvious we're going to need *some* protection, if only to keep the M'zarch from taking another crack at us. The only problem is making sure the guards we pick don't decide at some point that robbery would pay better." He shook his head. "Never mind that for now. We can afford to string them along for a while longer. Did you really want me here to discuss the harvesting, or is this more from Hafner's people?"

"The latter." Barner unfolded a map and indicated the new areas of crosshatching. "They've eliminated three more hills and most of the ridge that overhangs that end of the Dead Sea."

"Um. Still using that sonic echoing gadget Brown's people cobbled together?"

"And hoping slabs of cable material don't play games with sound waves as well as electric fields, yes. So far nothing that looks like a cavity has shown up."

"Have they talked to Dr. Chang's team about that? I don't know if they've done any sonic studies on the cable, but they should be able to rig up something."

"Probably could." Barner hesitated. "I don't really think Hafner's people want Chang in on this, though."

"The hell with what they *want*," Meredith growled. "We've got a set of experts here and we're going to use them. What does Hafner think this is, some new version of keep-away?"

"I don't think Dr. Hafner cares that much, himself. But some of his people—well, *resent* the way Chang just came in and took over up at the cable site."

For an instant Meredith remembered how Captain Witzany had reacted to that same event. "This whole place better start remembering that Astra is a territory of the United States, not some free and independent country. You'll send a messenger to

Chang this afternoon to ask about the cable's sonic characteristics." He caught the objection in Barner's eyes and mentally backed up a step. "You don't have to tell him why we want the information, though."

"That'll help." Barner pushed the map to one side, replacing it with a sheaf of photo enlargements. "Dr. Hafner also took an extensive set of photos of the area and suggested we try shape analysis on the hills. I think it might be worth a try."

"Yeah." Meredith picked up the top photo, glanced at the one beneath it. "Unfortunately, it would mean putting all this on the computer, and I'm still not sure I want to risk that."

Barner shrugged. "I'll admit my knowledge of computers is limited, but it seems to me that if you tore out the entire remote-access system the thing should be secure enough. No one's going to eavesdrop on buried fiberop cables from thirty thousand kilometers, and the machine itself should be adequately shielded."

"'Should be' is about as far as I get, too. Given our truly abysmal ignorance of the local state of the art in such things, it's not very reassuring." The colonel dropped the photo back onto the stack. "You might as well put all these into your booby-proofed file. I'm going to have to get back to Unie—some sort of silly resolution Carmen Olivero told me the council was taking up this afternoon. Keep me informed on Hafner's progress."

"Yes, sir."

Heading back outside, Meredith paused beside his car and peered for a moment toward the south. Two harvesters were visible in the fields, working to bring in the meager crop. Nearly thirty percent of the plants had died under the shock of having their trace metals twice yanked out of their soil. *I hope the* Celeritas *is bringing plenty of extra food,* he thought, climbing behind the wheel and starting the car. *And lots of spare fuel, too.*

The last speech—Perez's, as usual—was already in progress when Meredith finally showed up, choosing a chair by the door instead of joining the others at the table. Carmen shot a brief look of annoyance his direction and then returned her attention to Perez and the other faces around the table. The outcome, unfortunately, was no longer really in doubt. From previous speeches and the accompanying applause, it was clear that at least six of the ten councillors were strongly in favor of Perez's resolution, and of the four remaining only two were definitely against. She'd hoped to at least get a tie situation, where she would have the deciding vote, but it was obviously not going to happen.

Perez sat down, and Carmen waited for the applause to run its course. "Further comments?" she asked. "Then we'll proceed directly to a vote. All in favor . . . ?"

The tally was a solid seven to three. Suppressing a grimace, Carmen turned to Meredith. "Colonel, the Council of Astra calls on you to issue an order barring all but Astran citizens from approach or examination of Mt. Olympus, the cable lying north of Wright, and all alien technology and artifacts that may be subsequently uncovered. Specifically, this order is to include both those members of Dr. Chang's group already on Astra and the various alien representatives currently in this solar system."

"Request denied," Meredith said briskly. "Any other business you want me here for?"

A ripple of displeasure went around the table, and Carmen braced herself for the inevitable outburst. But Perez kept his poise.

"I'm afraid you don't understand, Colonel," he said calmly. "This is one resolution you're not going to simply sweep away into a corner somewhere. We've done our homework on this one: I have petitions signed by seventy-two percent of the inhabitants of Ceres that support this resolution, and other councillors have similar proofs of support from their districts. The Spinneret belongs to Astra, Colonel, and neither you nor the faceless bureaucrats in Washington are going to take it away from us."

Meredith regarded him coolly. "You have a remarkably poor

memory for certain facts of life, Perez, such as those dealing with your citizenship and my authority here. I'm at perfect liberty to ignore anything you or your seventy-two percent have to say—and if you get rude about it I can toss the lot of you into detention."

Perez didn't bat an eye. "It wouldn't be nearly as neat and tidy as you make it sound. If you don't throw Chang's group out immediately, I can guarantee there will be rioting—and *this* time I won't be trying to hold anyone back."

Meredith didn't move or change expression, but suddenly Carmen had the uncomfortable feeling that perhaps Perez had pushed the colonel a shade too far. "In such a case, Mr. Perez," Meredith said, his voice deadly, "neither would I."

"Of course," Perez said. "And you would win . . . but only temporarily. Because signs of civil strife down here could very possibly persuade one or more of the aliens out there that we needed some strong, neutral hand on us—strictly for our own good, of course—and take the appropriate action."

The room was very quiet. Meredith never flinched or broke eye contact with Perez, but Carmen sensed his frosty silence was a simple lack of any answer to that. After a few seconds Perez pulled a thick folder from the stack of papers in front of him and added to it a copy of the Council's resolution. Standing, he stepped over to Meredith and offered him the bundle. "I think you'll find, Colonel," he said, "that above all else we *must* present a united front if we're going to survive here."

Tight-lipped, Meredith got to his feet and accepted the papers. "We'll see," he said shortly. With a single glance at Carmen he turned and left the room.

Carmen licked her lips. "This meeting is adjourned," she said, banging her makeshift gavel with rather more force than necessary and immediately turning her full attention to loading her briefcase. The others took the hint and began packing their own paraphernalia without protest and with a minimum of quiet conversation. She waited until the last sounds of footsteps were cut off by the closing door before permitting her chosen expletive to come out.

"Agreed. And I apologize."

She looked up, startled, to find Perez sitting quietly in the chair Meredith had recently vacated. "I thought you'd slithered out with the others," she snarled.

He shrugged. "I wanted to make sure you were all right. And that you understood why I'm doing what I am."

"I'm fine," she bit out, getting to her feet. "And you don't need to explain the finer points of blackmail technique to me, thank you."

She tried to step past him, but he rose and took her arm, and before she knew it he had steered her back to the table and seated her again. "You're angry because you don't agree with my methods," he said, sitting down next to her. "But I'm afraid it's a simple fact of history that the only way a ruling class is ever persuaded to share power is through violence—either actual or threatened."

"So why don't you just go ahead and ally yourself with one of those aliens out there and do the job right?" she said bitterly.

He sighed. "I'd hoped you would grow to understand what I stand for better than that. Don't you see?—I'm not trying to exchange one inequity for another. Astra can be this century's version of the Americas, a place where people can come to escape the foolish rigidity of Earth politics. But that can't happen as long as we're simply a transplanted chunk of the U.S."

"And what are you going to feed all these tired, huddling masses when they get here?" she shot back. "We can't even grow enough to feed the ten thousand people we've got."

"We can feed them anything they want—up to and including imported caviar. Or haven't you considered what our Spinneret cables might sell for?"

She shook her head. "Your ideas of marketing show the same shallow thinking your politics do. If the cable turns out to be really useful it's not going to be ours much longer, not with all those warships circling overhead."

"We can handle them," he assured her. "Playing big powers off against each other is a skill the Third World is well acquainted with."

She laughed, a short, derisive bark. "Oh, terrific. You scramble to get us free of American politics and instead turn us into a transplanted Yugoslavia spending all of our energy juggling the local superpowers. What a *great* improvement."

She had the satisfaction of seeing him struggle to fight down his own anger. "The position the Spinneret has put us in isn't my fault, Carmen. I don't like it better than you do, but sitting around wishing things were different won't change anything." He paused. "I'm sorry, though, that you can't slough off that middle-class upbringing long enough to see things from the point of view of the less fortunate. I see I've been wasting my time with you."

So all of it *had* been deliberate. She'd wondered about that, ever since his message to Meredith through her had started this whole Council mess. "You flatter yourself," she said, again getting to her feet. "It's you and your methods, not any sort of upbringing, that's soured me on your planned utopia."

"Carmen—"

She shrugged off his hand. "And as long as you've got all the answers, consider what all your huddling masses are going to do for a living once they get here. Or are you just going to distribute the Spinneret income evenly and let people sit around all day like overgrown parasites? If that's your idea of a satisfying existence, you're more foolish than I thought." With that she turned and strode out of the room, slamming the door behind her.

She was outside the building and halfway back to the admin complex before her anger cleared enough for her to think straight again. She slowed down, looking at the dull adobe buildings around her as she walked. After living in modern military bases, Astra had always seemed almost like a throwback to the 1800s to her . . . but never until now had she noticed its complete vulnerability, both to external and internal attack. *What,* she thought miserably, *am I going to do?*

On one level the question was trivial; on another, impossible. She would certainly go and see Colonel Meredith immediately, offering whatever assistance she could to block Perez's power grab. How that end could be accomplished, though, was another matter entirely.

The quiet burp of a distant sonic boom penetrated her thoughts, and she looked westward in time to see a shuttle drop toward Martello Base. An alien delegation? It could be nothing else; it would still be a couple of weeks before any kind of reaction to the M'zarch attack could arrive from Earth. Quickening her step, Carmen changed direction to head for Unie's docks. The colonel would almost certainly have gone to the base to greet the visitors, and she saw no particular point in sitting around his office until he came back. Besides, which—it suddenly occurred to her—as moderator of the Council her visible support of Meredith in any discussions might help short-circuit Perez's scheme to promote disunity.

The armed guard waiting at the docks was a surprising but welcome addition to the scenery; apparently, Meredith was taking Perez's threats seriously. Carmen half expected to be denied access to the boats, but her military ID proved acceptable, and soon she was guiding a roaring motorboat up Splayfoot Bay toward Martello.

There were ten of them in all, and the names on their identification papers were as prestigious as any on the UNESCO listing. They sat quietly, for the most part, some of them gazing out the window at the Martello landing area or the hills of the mainland to the east.

The four UN officials accompanying them had equally prominent names, but not anything like the scientists' patience as Meredith went through their credentials one by one. Possibly, he thought, they felt insulted that he'd chosen to meet them in

Major Brown's office instead of ferrying them to Unie and his own. Perhaps he should have; the trip would've given him that much more time to think.

Finally, he could stall no longer. "I must say, first of all, that Astra is honored by your presence," he said to the scientists as he returned their papers. "Under other circumstances you would be most welcome . . . but I'm very much afraid you may have made this trip for nothing."

"Would you care to explain, Colonel?" Ashur Msuya said, his voice cold. Meredith had never before met the man, but his virulent anti-West oratory had for years been one of the main rallying points for what little unity the African Bloc was ever able to muster. He'd been merely the head of the Mozambique delegation when Meredith had left for Astra, but his credentials were now identifying him as Assistant Undersecretary for Trusteeship and Non-Self-Governing Territories—a change in position Meredith found more than a little suspicious.

"It's actually rather simple, Mr. Msuya," the colonel said, turning slightly to face the other. "I've been given command of Astra—all of Astra—by the United States government, and there's no legal way I can relinquish that authority to you or anyone else without direct orders from my superiors or from President Allerton."

Msuya smiled thinly. "Yes, I rather expected you to quote regulations of one sort or another. However, Astra is United Nations territory, and we don't need the Pentagon's permission to withdraw the mandate your government has given. If you insist on being legalistic, I can also argue that the Spinneret and its cable are alien devices not really part of Astra at all, and that your mandate does not include them. Either way, we wind up in control of the Spinneret."

"Mr. Msuya, again I say that without orders I can't simply take your word for that—and all these papers still boil down to being your word. Now, if our regular supply ship brings me such orders, that'll be a different matter. But until that happens . . ." He shook his head.

One of the scientists cleared his throat. "Suppose your ship doesn't say anything one way or the other?"

"Then I'll send a message back with her captain describing your mission and requesting instructions. The round trip would take about six weeks, I'm afraid."

"Our ship could bring you a response in eight days," Msuya pointed out. "It's an advanced craft—one of two the Ctencri have given the UN."

"Interesting. How much is Saleh paying for them?"

"They were free gifts."

Sure they were, Meredith thought. "Of course," he said aloud. "But I'd prefer using American ships for any such messages."

Msuya leaned back in his seat and regarded Meredith coolly. "In other words, you choose to stall. All right, have it your way. I trust you'll at least be willing to find accommodations for the scientific team down here while they work on the cable. I and my delegation can stay aboard our ship if you'd prefer."

And here was where the organic fertilizer was going to hit the fan, Meredith thought with a sinking feeling. He had no intention of letting a group of foreign nationals get at the Spinneret cable, UN instructions or no. "I would be honored to host these distinguished ladies and gentlemen," he said, "but as for examining the cable, I'm afraid that won't be possible."

"Colonel Meredith." With deliberate movements Msuya rose from his chair and stepped up to the edge of the desk. "It's clear you don't care that your career is being endangered by your uncooperative attitude; I presume that if I had an armed force of troops available you would be equally contemptuous of your life. But I tell you right now: you are now endangering your entire country. We know you have U.S. scientists here studying the cable; failure to grant equal access to us will raise serious questions as to American intentions. It could easily lead to an immediate embargo of all alien goods and technologies to both you and the U.S.—and I assure you that the embargo will be an airtight one."

He paused for breath, and Meredith moved into the gap. "I understand your concerns," he said, "but I can assure *you* we have no intention of withholding information on the cable from anyone." He shifted slightly in his chair, wondering what he was going to say next; and as he did so the paper in his coat pocket crinkled. A gift from heaven, and he grabbed it with both hands. "But I think you've jumped to a false conclusion. It's not a matter of American versus UN scientists; the fact is that *all* non-Astrans are going to be barred from the cable, at least for now." Pulling out the copy of the Council resolution Perez had given him, he handed it over.

Msuya scanned it, his frown heavy with suspicion. "What is this *Council* fabrication? Astra's supposed to be under military rule."

"Americans are very democratically inclined people," Meredith shrugged. "The Council was set up shortly after our arrival to act in an advisory capacity."

"Then this resolution has no legal force behind it." Msuya tossed the paper back onto the desk.

"It has the force of public opinion," Meredith told him. "In America we consider that important."

One of the scientists cleared her throat. "You say *all* non-Astrans have been ordered away from the cable, Colonel?"

Meredith saw the trap. "I was about to issue the orders to Dr. Chang's team when I was notified your delegation was arriving. The Council's resolution was passed less than an hour ago."

"Perhaps we should give you a few minutes now to do that, then," she replied.

There wasn't really any way out of it. Raising his phone, he keyed for Andrews, waiting outside in Brown's outer office. "Lieutenant, I want you to go up to the cable site and have Dr. Chang's people brought back here. Pull copies of all their data, too. Then get in touch with Captain Witzany and put him back in charge of all cable testing."

One of Andrews's best qualities was his ability to accept even strange orders without question. "Yes, sir. I presume the scientists are to come whether they want to or not?"

"Correct. If they have any complaints, tell them it'll all be explained when they get here."

"Yes, sir. Uh, Miss Olivero is here, Colonel, and seems anxious to see you."

Chair of the Council. . . . It was a chance, Meredith realized, to add credibility to his position. Provided Carmen was smart enough to pick up on what he was doing. "Please ask her to come in," he told Andrews.

The door opened, and Carmen stepped inside, her face set in a decidedly neutral expression. Meredith wished fleetingly he knew how much, if anything, Andrews had told her about their guests. "Carmen Olivero, current chair of the Council of Astra," the colonel introduced her, rising to his feet. "This is Mr. Msuya of the UN Secretariat; I've just had to inform him of the Council's decision to forbid non-Astrans from direct access to the Spinneret cable."

For a long moment he thought she was going to bring down the whole house of cards. Her eyes, which had been sweeping the group, cut abruptly back to him, widening in surprise. But only for a moment. "I see," she said. "Well. I'm glad you decided not to bother appealing the resolution; with a seven-to-three margin it would've been useless, anyway." She focused on Msuya. "Were you expecting to take over the cable studies, sir?"

"The cable is UN property," he told her coldly. Turning back to Meredith, he added, "I don't know what you expect to gain by this charade, Colonel, but rest assured that no one in this room is in the slightest taken in. You're going to bring in the American scientists, make a big show of taking them off the project—and the minute we're gone they'll be back at work."

"I'm sorry you think me so underhanded," Meredith said, matching the other's tone. It was time he showed some irritation at all this verbal abuse. "You and Dr. Chang can compare notes on my character on the trip back to Earth; I'm sure he'll have one or two things to add by then."

Msuya blinked, and for the first time a hint of uncertainty showed through his animosity. "What do you mean?"

"Well, we cetainly can't afford to feed any extra people here," Meredith said calmly. "I just assumed you wouldn't mind giving them a lift home. It *is* only a four-day trip, you said?"

Msuya took a deep breath, turned back to gaze at Carmen, still standing just inside the door. "So your civilian Council presumes to dictate to an authorized military commander, does it? What do you think the U.S. Congress is going to say when it hears about this? Or the Pentagon? I expect they would appoint a new commander rather quickly."

Meredith held his breath . . . but Carmen had clearly figured out what was going on. "I don't see that the Pentagon or anyone else has any cause to complain. Your average military base isn't ninety percent civilian, either, and I can vouch for the fact that the Council has made the colony run smoother." She fixed Msuya with a steely glaze. "As I recall, that *is* what the UN mandate called for: to establish and maintain a viable settlement on the world Astra; to choose, equip, and train such personnel as may be deemed necessary and sufficient—"

She rattled off the whole General Purpose section from memory, and when she was finished, even Msuya looked grudgingly impressed. "I see you at least put someone with legal experience in charge of your Council," he said, turning back to face Meredith. "But you're digging yourself into a hole where you will literally starve to death. You can throw us off Astra *now*, yes, but how long will you survive when the UN cuts off all food and supply shipments to you? How long could you hold out if the Security Council voted to send a military force to deal with your blatant disobedience?"

Meredith couldn't help it; he laughed out loud. "A *military force*? Have you *seen* the collection of warships riding around us out there? Damn thing looks like a three-dimensional traffic jam—and every one of them ready to jump at the slightest suggestion that we're being invaded. I suggest you bear that in mind when you start talking about military action."

For a moment the two men stood there, gazes locked. Meredith waited long enough for the tension in the room to get good and thick. Then, dropping his eyes to Brown's computer console, he keyed for a status report. "Your shuttle has been refueled and will be ready to lift in about an hour. Before you leave, I'll ask Major Brown to give you a tour of the Martello Base facilities."

"This is outrageous!" one of the scientists snorted. "Mr. Msuya—are you going to let him just throw us out?"

Msuya's eyes were still boring into Meredith's face. "For the moment, Doctor, there is little else I can do. But that condition is temporary. Very temporary."

Meredith phoned for Brown and endured the minute of stony silence it took the major to arrive. He half expected Msuya to hurl some final threat as Brown led them out, but the undersecretary passed up the chance for last-minute dramatics. Carmen started to follow the group; Meredith signaled her to remain. The door closed and she let out a long, sighing breath. "You shouldn't have laughed at him, Colonel," she said.

Suddenly weary, Meredith sat down again behind the desk. "I know, but that particular threat was *so* ridiculous. Not that it matters, really—Msuya couldn't possibly get madder than he already is." He shook his head. "What did you want to see me about? Andrews seemed to think it was important."

She smiled lopsidedly. "Actually, I came here to offer whatever help I could to head off Perez's power play. I see I was a little late."

"Not at all—both your timing and assessment of the situation were perfect."

"I meant—never mind."

"You meant you missed the episode where I switched sides?"

She flushed. "Well . . . yes. I was a little . . . surprised by that."

"Yeah. My own fault, too—I should've expected the UN to try a direct takeover and been better prepared. They moved a lot faster than I thought they could."

There was a moment of silence. "What happens now?" Carmen asked. "Are you really sending Dr. Chang home?"

"I have no choice. You saw Msuya's expression—he's just itching for a chance to come down like a Marine battalion on either Astra or the U.S. Throwing everyone off Astra like this should get the U.S. off the immediate hook, though there'll now be pressure on the President to replace me. I hope he understands what I'm doing and can stall them."

"What if he can't? I have to tell you, Colonel, that legally you're on very soft ground. Council or no, you're still the one who's ultimately responsible for everything that happens on Astra . . . and the UN *would* be well within their rights to cut off our supplies."

"Um." Meredith stared out the window for a moment. Like the courier ship still in orbit, the UN delegation's shuttle was clearly of alien design—another "gift" from the Ctencri, no doubt. Meredith had never been as opposed to the UN as some of his colleagues were, but this business of the organization being sole contact for alien trade was beginning to look ominous. It was putting far too much power into the hands of the Secretariat, and he wondered fleetingly whether Msuya's presence here had been a play by that body alone. He'd offered no evidence of a Security Council vote, after all, and such a vote should be necessary for any altering of the Astran Mandate. Unless the U.S. had capitulated before the threat of economic sanctions and had voted with the majority. . . .

"All right," Meredith said abruptly. "As the saying goes, two can play this game." He keyed his phone for the base communications center. "Put a call through to the nearest Rooshrike ship," he instructed the officer on duty. "Tell them I'd like a talk with Beaeki nul Dies na at his convenience." He got an acknowledgment and looked back at Carmen. "Is there anyone in your department who's ever handled trade negotiations?"

Frowning, Carmen leaned across the desk and started tapping computer keys. "I think Ruth Eldridge might have. . . . No, that was a labor dispute." She pressed more keys, but the screen remained blank. "Nothing like that in anyone's file, sir," she said.

"Damn. Well . . . how about you? You want to help me open up trade with the Rooshrike?"

She looked up at him, jaw dropping open. "*Me*? Why?"

"Why not? Common sense and a fast mind are at least as important as experience in something like this. Besides, as head of the Council you'll lend an air of legitimacy that may keep Perez's crowd off my neck."

"But—Colonel, don't you think you're giving me just a little too much extracurricular work?"

He smiled in spite of himself. "Oddly put, but you have a point. All right; as of right now you're relieved of all your normal duties. I'll get you a priority number for materials and personnel by tonight or tomorrow morning, but try to use it sparingly."

"I understand." She sighed. "Oh, all right; I'll do it. What exactly do you want from the Rooshrike?"

"Ultimately, our own private channel to both U.S. and alien markets, one the UN can't shut off. Priorities right now are foodstuffs, heavy equipment—well, it's the same list that's on the computer. All the stuff we lost to the Spinneret's leecher."

"How about weapons?"

"None." His lip twitched at her expression. "Yes, I know I'm a military man and that we've already been attacked once. But our best chance of survival right now is to look and act as harmless as possible. Remember, the warships upstairs know even less about the Spinneret than we do—and they *don't* know we aren't in actual control of the thing. I've already had to deflect two or three veiled questions about the 'weapon' we used against the M'zarch landers, at least one of which concerned the thing's range. The minute we start looking militant I think they'd come to a pretty quick agreement on joint action."

"I suppose so," she agreed reluctantly. "I just don't like feeling so vulnerable."

"Neither do I, but for now it can't be helped."

She shrugged, as if dismissing the matter. "All right. Now, how are we proposing to pay the Rooshrike for whatever they get us?"

Meredith took a deep breath. He hated to do this, but could see no alternative. "We'll pay them—and any other race with which we do business—in lengths of Spinneret cable. The value per meter will be assessed later, once we've completed our tests on its material properties."

Carmen's dark eyes held his. "You're going to let the aliens buy the cable, just like that? Suppose one of them figures out what it's made of or how the glue works or something?"

"I don't think that's likely to be a problem," he returned dryly. "And even if they do, I doubt it'll hurt our profits any. If Dr. Hafner's right, the Spinners' factory could be the size of a small city, and I can't see the Rooshrike or Ctencri throwing one together overnight." He paused, but she still looked troubled. "You disagree?" he prompted.

"What about Earth? Are you going to give the UN or U.S. some cables free, or make them pay for it like everyone else?"

Meredith shook his head. "I don't know yet how we're going to handle them. My first inclination is to pay off the costs of the colony and then treat Earth as just another customer . . . but since the U.S.'ll get the lion's share of cable that way, it's bound to cause a major stink at the UN. And this damn six-week communications lag doesn't help any—we could spark off a war and never even know about it until it was all over." He scowled toward the computer screen. "Let's add a couple of those fast courier ships to the Christmas list you're making. If the UN can get advanced drives, we ought to be able to, too."

"Yes, sir." She hesitated. "Colonel . . . before I came

here I was talking to Cris Perez. He's also starting to talk about selling Spinneret cable."

"Oh? I would've thought tawdry mercentile matters beneath him."

She flushed. "He's less interested in profits than he is in making Astra an escape hatch for Earth's poor. He sees the Spinneret as the cornucopia that'll make that possible."

"He would," Meredith grumbled. "Perez is a grade-ten idealist."

"Perhaps," she said noncommittally. "But you're now talking about a similar course of action . . . and either way I'm worried about what we'll do here with a sudden influx of wealth. I'd hate to see all of us sit back and loaf while the Spinneret pays the bills for us."

Meredith rubbed his chin. "I doubt that it'll come to that extreme. The cable may be strong as hell, but what can you really *do* with something shaped like cosmic spaghetti?"

"I don't know. But the Spinners apparently did."

"Yeah." For a moment Meredith stared past Carmen. An entire planet-worth of metal . . . quintillions of tons of it . . . all made into six-centimeter cable? *Why?* "You'd better go back to your office and get busy with your preparations," he said, instinctively pulling back from what could only be futile speculation. "I'd like to get Beaeki's people down here tomorrow morning for a preliminary meeting."

She nodded and stood up. "I can be ready."

"Good. I'll let you know the time after I talk with the Rooshrike."

He glared at the desktop for a minute after she'd gone. So he and Perez were both thinking along the same lines for once, were they? An annoying thought, in some ways; but if handled properly it might enable him to take some of the wind out of the Hispanic's rhetoric. Even a brief respite would be helpful; between Perez, the UN, and the collection of alien ships overhead, Meredith was facing too many opponents as it was.

And speaking of opponents . . .

Hitching his chair closer to the terminal, the colonel keyed for the job file and began to type:

> SEARCH ALL AVAILABLE ALIEN LITERATURE FOR HISTORICAL RECORDS, LEGENDS, OR MYTHS RELATING TO OTHER RACES, GODLIKE BEINGS, ETC. EMPHASIS ON ROOSHRIKE AND POM TERRITORIES. FULL ANALYSIS REQUESTED, INCLUDING CORRELATIONS AND COMPOSITES WHERE POSSIBLE.

Know thy enemy, the ancient dictum went . . . and if the Spinners had left any other trace of their passage behind, Meredith wanted to know about it.

Chapter 16

The report was short and maddeningly uninformative, and Secretary-General Saleh slapped the last page onto his desk with a snort. "I don't suppose," he said sarcastically, "that you have any idea what these meetings with the Rooshrike are about?"

Ashur Msuya shook his head. Judging from his expression his own mood wasn't much better than Saleh's, but he knew better than to snap back at his superior. "Nothing positive. There's been nothing like a general announcement about changes in defense arrangements or anything. It's possible they're working on a trade agreement, but the shipments that the Rooshrike landed there could equally well have been in return for the cable they made off with after the M'zarch attack."

Saleh snorted. "Oh, it's a trade agreement, all right—Allerton is moving to open up an independent pipeline to the alien marketplace."

"Or Colonel Meredith is," Msuya offered, shaking his head. "I'm not really sure whose side Meredith is on these days."

"Forget your doubts. He's an American soldier on American-claimed soil. Any rifts that appear are purely for show."

"Perhaps. But either way I submit that it's high time the UN made a move to assert its rights on Astra."

"Your economic embargo of the colony, I presume?"

Msuya nodded. "Whatever agreement Meredith—or Allerton—is setting up, the Rooshrike can't deliver food that we don't let off the Earth."

"The Americans have their own starships—"

"Which now use Ctencri drives and are supplied from the ground by Ctencri shuttles. We can cut off the flow of spare parts and fuel cylinders any time we want. It would take months or longer for them to get their older shuttle fleet back in service."

Saleh pondered. He hadn't liked this idea much when Msuya first proposed it, and he didn't like it any better now. To deliberately put his hands to the throat of a colony he himself had helped set up . . . but, then, it undoubtedly wouldn't come to that. The Americans would back down before they'd let their people starve. "You're sure their own crops won't be adequate?"

"Positive. Even after harvest, crop yield analysis can be done very accurately."

"And if the Rooshrike open up a shipping route to Earth . . . ?" Saleh smiled and answered his own question. "We don't let them, of course. Earth is technically within Ctencri borders, and we could simply ask them to keep Rooshrike traders out. Very well; I'll put the matter before Allerton this afternoon, give him a chance to back off on his Rooshrike deal."

"Why bother? You'll just give him that much more time to prepare for the embargo."

"Because if we proceed with so drastic an action," Saleh said coldly, "I want the world community to have no doubt that it was fully justified."

And whether it actually was or not was almost incidental. That much, at least, every politician knew.

* * *

Secretary of State Joshua Purvis looked about as surprised as Allerton had ever seen him. "*What* Rooshrike treaties?" he asked.

Allerton shrugged helplessly. "I gather it's something Meredith has initiated on his own, for whatever reasons. We won't know for sure for at least another week, until the *Pathfinder* comes in. Possibly not even then."

"So what'd you tell the Lord High Secretary-General?"

"I tried to stall, of course—told him that I couldn't take any action or make any statements until I had Astra's own report on what was going on out there."

"He buy it?"

"Not really. He offered to fly a U.S. representative out in one of their new Ctencri ships to assess the situation and give any appropriate orders." Allerton paused, then picked up a piece of paper from in front of him and handed it across the desk. "Complicating matters, I'm sure, a Ctencri ship arrived only half an hour ago and delivered this to Saleh's people. I don't suppose it improved his patience any."

Purvis scanned the paper briefly. "This is, what, the results of the Rooshrike tests on their Spinneret cable? . . . Holy mullah." He looked at Allerton. "This *has* to be a misprint, John. A *billion* pounds per square inch?"

"Check the footnote—that's a *minimum* tensile strength. Apparently even the Rooshrike weren't able to break it."

"But a *billion pounds per square inch*?" Purvis fumbled with his calculator. "That means . . . one of those cables could lift over two million tons. That's half a fully loaded supertanker."

"And don't forget it's less dense even than water, let alone normal metals," Allerton pointed out. "Now remember that superglue coating and its unique superconducting properties, and consider that Saleh thinks we're trying to keep all of it for ourselves."

Purvis studied the paper for another few seconds, then put it back on the President's desk. "I think," he said quietly, "that we'd better figure out right away exactly what our policy position here is—and then make sure Meredith is operating in line with it." He hesitated. "Whether we're willing to go on being unpopular with the rest of the world because of Astra is your decision, of course. But I think that stand could use a little reevaluation."

"In other words, you think we should knuckle under to Saleh and just hand over Astra and the Spinneret to the UN?"

"I didn't say that." Purvis shrugged. "But an embargo of food to Astra would be hard if not disastrous for them, and it's only the tip of the iceberg as far as Saleh's options go. Legally, we may have some mandate rights to the Spinneret cable, but in practice as long as Saleh's got the Ctencri in his pocket he can keep us from getting a single strand of the stuff. In any real confrontation the *Aurora* and *Pathfinder* might as well be space-going tuna boats."

Allerton grimaced. "You think the Ctencri would give the UN *armed* ships?"

"Before the Spinneret came along they apparently wouldn't even give us advanced star drives; Saleh's now got two. I think the Ctencri see a chance to get in good with the official owners of Astra and are grabbing it. Who knows how far they're prepared to go to protect their investment?"

"Yeah." Allerton sighed. "Well, then, I suppose we'd better take Saleh up on his offer of a lift out to Astra. Try to straighten things out as quickly as possible."

"You want me to go?"

"No . . . no, I think I might just go myself." He smiled lopsidedly at Purvis's expression. "Come on, Josh—space travel's supposed to be as easy as crossing the Delaware these days. And a lot safer."

"Unless Saleh decides he'd like you put on indefinite hold," the other said bluntly. "In which case you could hardly give him a better opportunity."

Allerton waved the objection aside. "Saleh's neither strong

enough nor desperate enough to kidnap a head of state. Not yet, anyway."

"Maybe," Purvis said. "Maybe not."

"It's so nice to be invited here, for a change," Perez commented as he sank into the chair across from Meredith. "Usually I have to bully your secretary to let me in."

Meredith's expression remained studiously neutral, and Perez mentally crossed off the possibility that the colonel had a social chat in mind. "I understand," Meredith said, "that you're thinking about the possibilities of making some spending money off the Spinneret cable."

"That's right," Perez nodded. "And I understand you're actually going to do so."

The colonel's eyebrows rose fractionally. "Miss Olivero told you?"

"She confirmed what I'd already guessed. Was it supposed to be a secret?"

Meredith smiled sardonically. "Don't you wish. Secret deals by the corrupt military dictator—it would have been made to order for you."

"That's a little unfair, Colonel," Perez said, feeling his face warming. "I don't deliberately distort the truth—I just try and keep others from doing so."

"Of course." Meredith tapped computer keys and swiveled the screen toward his visitor. "Well, here's a little bit of truth for you—see what you think."

Perez leaned forward. *Preliminary Analysis of Alien Cable,* he read . . . and suddenly he knew what this was. "It's the Rooshrike test results, isn't it? Is this why you're keeping the trade deal quiet?"

"We've been keeping the *negotiations* quiet; no deals have been made yet. After all, we needed to know more about the cable in order to fix a fair price for it."

"You're going to use the Rooshrike's own numbers for that purpose?"

Meredith shrugged. "I know what you're thinking, but there's no real way around it. The Rooshrike have both better testing equipment and a better feel for what the cable would bring on the open market."

"Mm." Perez thought for a moment. "Perhaps if we offered them a small percentage of what we get from sales to other races . . . that might deter them from suggesting too low a price."

"As a matter of fact, Miss Olivero had already put that idea to the Rooshrike representatives. They seem agreeable to it."

"I see." *A woman of many talents,* Perez thought with mild surprise. He'd done a little trade negotiation himself some years back; just enough to know that he didn't care for it. Of course, Carmen had the distinct advantage of a seller's market to work with here. "What price range are you talking about?"

"Our current thought is to charge about forty million dollars per kilometer plus the two and a quarter tons of metal that go into a cable that long."

Perez whistled softly. "That seems rather expensive."

"It's less than twice the current price of gold," Meredith pointed out. "And a *lot* more valuable."

"For study, perhaps. But aside from building long suspension bridges I would think its uses limited."

"You would, would you?" Meredith leaned back in his chair and started ticking off fingers. "One: loop it back and forth—it's flexible enough—so that each segment lies next to the one before. The glue sticks the whole thing into what is essentially a flat plate; coat it on all sides to take up the rest of the glue and you have sixty square meters of impenetrable material. Put another cable on each corner and get yourself a strong crane and you've got a sling you could carry small mountains around with. Two: wind the cable into a helix and you have a superconducting solenoid—a million applications right there. Three: link some of the cables end to end and make a giant circle out in deep space. Attach a few of these in parallel and you've got the backbone for a wheel-shaped space station. Four:

wrap it around a thin metal shell—hell; make it cardboard or sausage skin, for that matter—and you've got a spaceship hull. Do I need to go on?"

"No, I get the idea," Perez said, impressed in spite of himself. Clearly, the colonel had done a lot of thinking about this—much more than Perez himself had. "I capitulate; buyers will soon be breaking the door down. So why did you ask me here today, since you've apparently got all the details worked out? To rubberstamp your decision?"

Meredith snorted. "Hardly. You keep forgetting that I don't need your permission to govern Astra as I see fit." He paused, and almost grudgingly went on, "What I called you here to talk about is what we're going to do when we start making money from all this."

Perez shifted in his seat. "Carmen was talking about that some time back. She seemed to think we'd become a world of parasites."

"You disagree?"

Perex locked eyes with him. "It's been my experience that, given a choice, people prefer to work for their living. No one on any form of welfare is truly happy to be there."

"Granted. All right, then, let's assume we want all the people who emigrate from Earth to have meaningful jobs here. What will they be doing?"

"What do you mean?" Perez asked, puzzled. "They'll be doing the same sort of things people do on Earth."

"Wrong," Meredith said quietly. "Or haven't you noticed the lack of minerals and useful farmland?"

Perez stared at him for a moment . . . and then it all clicked. "Manufacturing and agriculture will be gone. Is that it?"

Meredith nodded. "There'll be some of each, but nothing like the percentages in any economy on Earth. It just doesn't make any sense to ship in raw materials to work when we can just as easily bring in finished products."

"But surely there are similar setups on Earth," Perez

objected, searching his memory for a useful example. "How about—well, how about Monaco? It runs well enough with no minerals to speak of."

"Is that what you want for your huddled masses?" Meredith snorted. "To be servants and waitresses for tourists? Assuming we could even get tourists to come here, of course."

"No, of course not—"

"Put them all in government? Storekeeping? Selling insurance to each other? You're the one who wants to make this a paradise for the poor—tell me what they're going to do here."

"All right, the point is made." Perez got to his feet. "I agree the problem needs thought, but I'm sure we can come up with an answer. If you'll excuse me, then—"

"I'm not done yet," Meredith interrupted.

Perez considered leaving anyway, thought better of it, and sat down again. "I suppose you want my word that the Council won't press for new colonists until we've sorted all this out?"

"Not really—I credit you with better sense than that. No, this is about a different matter entirely." Meredith pursed his lips. "We need to work out some kind of security arrangement with all those warships out there. Miss Olivero thought you might have some suggestions on how we might do that without creating either paranoia or animosity among whoever we send home."

Perez blinked; it was about the last thing he would have expected the colonel to ask his advice on. "I take it you don't want the whole crowd to stay up there?"

"The Rooshrike don't. They're within an ace of kicking the whole raft of them out of the system and taking over all security duties themselves."

"Not a good idea—especially after you and Carmen have been holding secret meetings with them."

"That's what I told them," Meredith nodded. "We've talked them into giving us a week to come up with a better solution."

"Hm. Well . . . perhaps a lottery drawing or something would be seen as fair—" He broke off as Meredith's phone buzzed. The colonel answered, and Perez let his eyes and mind drift out the window and up into the cloudless sky. Six alien races, all of them jockeying for position to get at the Spinneret. He'd talked glibly to Carmen about playing them off against each other, but the more he thought about it, the trickier it sounded. What sort of psychologies were they dealing with, for starters? Could they even assume all the aliens saw profit and loss in the same way? Surely there was overlap of some kind—they all *did* trade together, after all. But for a prize as unique as the Spinneret any of them could easily suspend their normal business methods . . . to say nothing of their treaties or ethics—

"—wait there; do you understand? Do *not* attempt to—ah, continue until I arrive."

Perez's attention snapped back at the intensity in Meredith's voice. One glance at the colonel's expression told him instantly something was up. "Are we being attacked?" he stage-whispered.

Meredith waved irritably for silence. "I'll bring everything we'll need. You just stay put. Right." He broke the connection, punched another number. "Major Barner? Colonel Meredith. Green-seven-go; right away. Rendezvous with me west of target for directions . . . right. Out."

Meredith stood up, punching another number, and glanced at Perez. "We'll have to continue this conversation some other—"

"What is it?" Perez interrupted, stepping to block Meredith's path to the door.

"Dr. Hafner's team's uncovered a door in one of the hills near the Dead Sea. It may be the entrance to the Spinneret machinery." He moved his phone closer to his mouth. "Colonel Meredith. I want a flyer ready for me in fifteen minutes . . . no, thanks, I'll fly it myself. Thank you."

He dropped his arm to his side and made to go around Perez. "Let me go with you," Perez said, blocking his way again.

Meredith glared at him . . . then abruptly nodded. "All

right. But stay out of our way.'' Sidestepping the other, he disappeared through the door.

Perez followed, lengthening his own stride to catch up. *Maybe now,* he thought, *we'll finally find out what this whole Spinneret thing was for.*

Chapter 17

It seemed like forever before the flyer swooped in out of the west to settle down among the low hills, but Hafner knew it had actually been less than half an hour since his call. His four-man team had made good use of the time, though, uncovering enough of the double doors to get an idea as to how big they really were. In the silence that followed the flyer's landing, Hafner could hear the sound of approaching cars, and he wondered uneasily just how big a crowd Meredith was bringing. He debated heading out to the flyer to ask, decided not to waste the effort. Meredith and that pain Perez had emerged from the flyer; any questions could wait until they reached the doors.

As it turned out, everyone arrived at the same time: the two from the flyer plus six cars bursting at the seams with soldiers. "What's all this for?" Hafner demanded as the troops piled out and began taking up positions around the hill. Organizing things, Hafner saw, was Major Barner from Crosse.

"Security," Meredith said briefly, striding past the geologist and stopping in front of the doors.

Hafner joined him, trying to ignore the racket behind them. Moments like this should be celebrated with champagne, not machine gun emplacements. "We've been trying to enlarge the hole so that the doors will have room to open," he told the colonel. "You can see from that hinge over there that they swing outward."

"Um." Meredith ran his fingertips a few centimeters along the door. "Feels awfully smooth for something that's been buried this long."

"The Spinners seem to have built things to last," Perez commented, coming up behind them.

"Yeah." The colonel turned away and looked around. "Well, let's get them clear. Sergeant! Digging team, on the double!"

The caravan had come well equipped with shovels, and within two minutes a double handful of soldiers were making the dirt fly. It was relatively fast work, the crumbly ground offering little resistance; but had the doors been as tall as their five-meter combined width would have suggested, it would still have taken a good part of the day to uncover them. As it was, the doors proved to be just under four meters high, and the process took only an hour.

"Now what?" Perez asked when Meredith had taken as many pictures of the exposed doors as he seemed to feel was necessary.

The colonel deferred to Hafner. "Doctor? Can you suggest a way to get them open?"

"Well . . ." Hafner stepped to the hairline crack separating the twin panels and carefully prodded a raised design that spanned the doors at eye level. "This is the obvious candidate for lock or doorknob. The problem is . . . it doesn't seem to want to move in any direction."

Meredith joined him and tried it himself. "Mm. You think we've been deliberately locked out?"

"Hard to tell." Hafner stepped a few paces back and peered at the edges of the hill. "This particular mound looks like a simple case of particle accumulation—dust and sand collecting first on the lee side of an obstacle and slowly growing to cover the entire thing."

"You're saying the entrance wasn't deliberately concealed?" Perez asked.

"I don't think it was, no."

"Then chances are it's not deliberately locked, either," Perez concluded. "What do we try first: sledgehammer or dynamite?"

"Perhaps you'd prefer a small nuclear device," Hafner snapped. "It's faster and gives a much more satisfying boom."

"I wasn't suggesting we break down the doors," Perez replied mildly. "Obviously, anything that's lasted this many years isn't going to be bothered by a couple of blasting caps. I was thinking more of seeing if we could dislodge any sand that may have gotten into the latch mechanism."

"Oh." Hafner felt like an idiot.

"May be worth a try," Meredith grunted, squinting at the raised design. "Looks like a small crack between this thing and the doors that dust could've gone through."

"Let's try something a bit less drastic than dynamite first, though," Hafner said as the colonel started to signal one of the soldiers.

"Such as?"

"Hydrofluoric acid. We can squirt it into the crack or dribble it in from above. It should take care of any dust, and shouldn't affect the actual mechanism."

He regarded it as a small personal triumph when Meredith agreed.

It took only a few minutes for Hafner to retrieve the bottle of acid from his supplies and squirt a healthy dose of it behind the raised door design. He gave it time to get into any hidden crannies, then tried the lock again. This time it moved a millimeter or so upward. More acid, and a few careful taps with a prospector's pick, and the lock abruptly came free. Hafner swiveled it a hundred and eighty degrees around its left-hand door pivot point before it stuck again. . . .

And with a crunch like a steamroller on gravel, the doors slowly swung open.

"Get down!" Meredith snapped. Hafner, backing rapidly out

of range of the huge panels, was yanked down into a crouch by a nearby soldier. Behind the doors was a dark tunnel that seemed to angle downward. Nothing moved back there, at least not that Hafner could see from his angle, and for a moment he considered standing up and telling Meredith there was no danger. But the soldier still had a solid grip on his arm, and with a mental sigh he resigned himself to waiting.

He didn't notice the faint sound of a motor until it cut off into silence, leaving the doors standing parallel to each other like extensions of the tunnel's walls. From somewhere behind him a car-mounted searchlight probed the gloom, reflecting briefly off dull metal as it danced around.

"All right, everyone; at ease," Meredith called. The hand on his arm loosened, and Hafner stood up, turning to face the colonel. Only then did he see the double semicircle of soldiers behind him, their weapons only now shifting away from the tunnel mouth as they rose from prone and kneeling firing positions. *My Lord!* he thought, his hands starting to tremble. *What if the Spinners had left something behind to greet visitors? They would've cut it in half!*

"So. Even their doors still work," Meredith commented as he came to Hafner's side. "Smells sort of strange."

Skin crawling with the thought of the guns at his back, Hafner took a step nearer the tunnel and sniffed. "Probably just *very* stale air," he said. "I've opened caves on Earth that were a lot worse. We can do an analysis, though, if you'd like."

"Please." Meredith stepped to one of the doors and began studying the inside surface. Easing his way past the soldiers, Hafner went to get his air-test kit.

The smell was already dissipating by the time he was set up to begin, and a fast check showed that the air composition was indeed basically Astran normal. "Some trace things that look like metal oxides and a slightly higher concentration of radon gas are the only anomalies I get," he told Meredith. "There *could* be alien bacteria, I suppose; we don't have the equipment to test for organic contaminants."

"Given the rest of Astra, I don't think that's a real danger," Meredith countered dryly. "All right. Let's go see what all the Spinners left us." He gestured toward Major Barner and started back toward the cars.

"Just a moment, Colonel," Hafner stopped him. No telling how Meredith would take this, but Hafner's conscience demanded he bring it up. "How many of these soldiers were you planning to take in?"

Meredith cocked an eyebrow. "Three squads—that's thirty men. Don't worry; I'm sure they can handle anything we run up against."

"Exactly my point. They'll handle things, whether those things actually need handling or not."

The colonel frowned. "What?"

"I doubt very seriously if there's anything dangerous in there, provided we keep our hands off any equipment," Hafner said. "I'm more worried about someone shooting up something irreplaceable because it reflected a flashlight beam back at him."

"Come on, Doctor—my men aren't that trigger happy—"

"Furthermore, I think this is the right moment to set a precedent here." Hafner waved at the tunnel. "If we want the other races around us to treat the Spinneret as a peaceful manufacturing device, we've got to make it a *civilian* matter right from the start. You put soldiers inside here and everyone's going to jump to the wrong conclusion."

"You're oversimplifying," Meredith said, with obviously strained patience, "not to mention anthropomorphizing. At least two of the species out there don't seem to even *make* a distinction between military and civilians."

"Then let's do it for ourselves," Hafner insisted. "*We* make that distinction, and so do all the people back on Earth. In the UN, for instance."

Meredith gazed at him for a long moment, and Hafner wished he had some clue as to what the other was thinking. Certainly the geologist's personal leverage and influence were very near zero, a fact Meredith obviously knew as well as he did. His only chance was that the colonel might somehow glimpse the various political consequences involved here—consequences Hafner himself only dimly understood—and make his decision appropriately.

And apparently he did. "All right," Meredith said at last, his eyes flicking back toward the troops. "The military presence will be limited to Major Barner and myself. I trust you won't mind if I have a defensive perimeter set up out here?"

The last was definitely sarcasm, but Hafner didn't care. "No, that'll be fine."

"*Thank* you." Quickly, the colonel issued orders: he, Barner, Perez, Hafner, and Hafner's assistant, Nichols, would go inside for a fast look around. All would be equipped with emergency packs; Meredith and Barner would be armed as well with stunners and dual-clip pistols. There was some discussion as to whether or not to take a car inside, but the vehicle's ability to carry extra equipment eventually tipped the balance against the traditional military dislike for bunching up. In addition, Barner would wear a medium-range radio headset.

"We'll stay in continuous contact as long as possible," Meredith told the captain being left in charge of the Crosse contingent. "Don't worry if we fade out, though, because these walls will probably cut off the signal long before we get to the end of the road. If we're not back in four hours contact Major Brown at Martello for instructions and assistance." Climbing into the front passenger seat, the colonel glanced at the others: Barner, Perez, and Hafner squeezed together in back; Nichols at the wheel. "Everyone set? Okay, Nichols; slow and easy."

The young geologist eased the car into the tunnel and started forward. Hafner discovered he'd been right; the floor *did* angle a couple of degrees downward. He was leaning forward, eyes searching at the limits of the car's headlights, when the tunnel abruptly blazed with light.

Nichols slammed on the brakes, and Hafner heard the double click of two pistol safeties. For a moment there was a tense silence; but as Hafner's eyes adjusted to the light he saw that the tunnel was still empty.

"Automatic," Barner muttered. "We hit the Spinner version of a welcome mat and they turned the lights on for us."

"Yeah." Meredith seemed to take a deep breath. "Well. Nothing seems to be threatening us at the moment. Let's keep going."

Nichols got the car moving again, and Meredith craned his neck to look at Hafner. "Doctor, you quoted me a minimum time of a hundred thousand years once for how long the Spinneret has been operating. Does the length of time this entrance has been covered up correlate with that number?"

Hafner shrugged as best as he could, squeezed as he was between Perez and the right-hand door. "I really couldn't say for sure. We still know next to nothing about Astra's climatological patterns, let alone the erosion and compacting rates for many of the minerals here. I'd guess we're still talking in the tens to hundreds of thousands of years."

"Does it matter?" Perez put in. "It doesn't seem all that different to me whether a piece of equipment lasts a thousand years or a million."

"The difference—" Meredith broke off. "Never mind. Is that a door off to the left up there?"

It was indeed a door, one as tall as the outside entrance and nearly as wide. "Looks like it slides open instead of swinging," Barner commented as they climbed out of the car.

Hafner nodded; he'd already noted the lack of visible hinges and the way the door was set back instead of being flush with the tunnel wall. "If you all want to stand back, I'll see if that plate in the center works the same as the one outside did."

This time there was no sand gumming up the mechanism, and it took only a moment for Hafner to discover the eye-level design needed to be pushed in instead of rotated. As the door slid smoothly into the wall a set of interior lights came on, revealing a vast, empty-looking room.

"Looks like a high-school gymnasium," Perez commented as the others joined Hafner. "Floor markings and everything."

"You'd never play basketball here, though," Hafner muttered, eying the four-meter-high ceiling.

Nichols had taken a step into the room. "Boxes off in the corner, Dr. Hafner," he announced, pointing.

"Where?" Meredith asked, moving alongside. He still held his pistol loosely in his hand, Hafner noted with some uneasiness. ". . . Ah. Interesting." The colonel looked at the opposite side of the room, then back to the boxes. "Yes. See how they're not really arranged in rows? If the floor pattern's symmetric on both sides, it looks like they're set out along one of the French curves back there."

"Odd," Barner murmured. "Some sort of giant board game, you think?"

"Not necessarily," Meredith said. "It could just be their method of storing supplies."

"Seems like that would waste a lot of space," the major said.

"Even if you had them in rows you'd need room for ventilation and forklift maneuvering," Meredith pointed out. "And as for identification purposes, a row number plus pallet number is no simpler than a curve number plus distance along it. I understand in some parts of Japan they still use a similar system for addresses."

Hafner found himself staring at the elaborate floor pattern, trying to visualize a race that would rather think in curlicues than in straight lines. *Do the Rooshrike do things that way?* he wondered suddenly. *Might be worth finding out.*

"Should we open one of the crates up, see what's inside?" Nichols asked.

"Not now," Meredith said, turning back toward the car. "The follow-up teams can handle details like that."

They passed several more of the storeroom-type doors in the next two or three kilometers, Meredith vetoing any suggestion that they be examined for contents. "It's obvious that what we've found is a freight entrance and storage area. Interesting, but not nearly as important as the control room for the Spinneret machinery."

Perez spoke up. "Just out of curiosity, Colonel, what exactly do you propose to do if and when we learn how all this is done?"

Meredith turned halfway around to look at him. "For starters, I'd like to either shut down or drastically restrict the metal leecher—our attempts at agriculture are going to be limited to hydroponics if we can't do that. It might also answer some questions if we found out whether six-centimeter cables are all the Spinneret can produce, or whether we can make plates of the material as well. Why?—did you have some project of your own in mind?"

"I'm wondering about the basic science involved," Perez said. "Are you going to offer the gravity nullifier for sale, too, for instance?"

Nichols caught the key word before Hafner did. " 'Too'?" he put in before Meredith could answer. "What's going on? What are we selling?"

"We're putting Spinneret cable on the market," Meredith said—rather grudgingly, Hafner thought. "It's not a secret, exactly, but we weren't going to say anything to the rest of the colony until we'd settled with the Rooshrike on terms and prices."

"The Rooshrike?" Hafner frowned. "I thought the Ctencri handled all trade with Earth."

"They do," Meredith said. "That's one of the reasons we're going through the Rooshrike."

Hafner thought about that for a long moment, not liking any of the implications that came with it. Clearly, important things had been happening while he'd been occupied with digging up the Astran landscape; just as clearly, Meredith wasn't interested in giving out details. He wondered if Carmen knew what was going on, and made a mental note to get in touch with her as soon as possible.

"But as for the gravity nullifier and leecher," Meredith

continued, "that technology is staying on Astra. Period. Unless you have objections?"

"None at all," Perez answered. "Though I would actually go further and say we shouldn't even study the equipment too closely. The minute you begin to store such knowledge you invite its theft, and we can't afford to lose Astra's secrets."

"I expect Drs. Hafner and Nichols would take a somewhat dim view of that philosophy," Meredith ventured. "Or would the scientists here be happy working with a machine that's running on black magic?"

Hafner's inner ear signaled a change in direction. "We've leveled out," he announced, glad of an opportunity to short-circuit the argument. "I think I see a cross corridor up there, too."

"You do," Meredith confirmed, craning his neck to see the car's odometer. "About six kilometers from the end . . . puts us something like one to two hundred meters underground. Hm. Odd that the Rooshrike metal detectors didn't pick up the place; they're supposed to have a half-kilometer range."

"Maybe it's all made of the same stuff as the cable," Barner suggested. "That doesn't register well on detectors, remember."

"Won't work," Hafner said. "Cable metal's fine for structure and power cables, but the electronics have to use normal metal."

"Why?" Perez asked.

"You need both normally conducting metals and semiconductors for any kind of electronics," Hafner told him. "Cable metal either conducts perfectly or terribly. More likely the walls here shielded the electronics in some way."

They'd reached the cross corridor now, and on Meredith's orders Nichols brought the car to a stop. "Anything look interesting either direction?" the colonel asked, sending his own gaze back and forth.

"Looks like the hall just dead-ends at a single big door on this side," Barner reported.

Hafner leaned forward to look past Perez. Sure enough, it did . . . and suddenly he had an idea what they'd find behind that door. "Let's take a look," he suggested.

Meredith shot him an odd look over the front seat, but nodded. "If you think it's worth doing. Major, how's contact with the outside world holding up?"

"It's been fading steadily, but we've still got them."

"Warn them we'll be moving in and out of corridors from now on and likely only have erratic contact. All right, Nichols; drive us over there."

Hafner's hunch proved to be correct. Behind the door was another corridor, parallel to the entrance tunnel and with perhaps four times its cross-section. Mounted up off the floor, disappearing away to infinity in both directions, was a huge solenoid.

"A particle accelerator?" Nichols whispered as they stood and stared at the monster coil.

"Who knows?" Hafner shrugged. "All we know for certain is that it knocks out repulser plasmas."

Meredith muttered something; apparently, he hadn't made the connection. "You mean some sort of resonance effect with this thing is what wrecked our flyers?"

"Or with one of the pieces of equipment you can see hooked into the solenoid in places," Hafner said. "Must be a tremendous field inside the coil if the stuff that leaks out is that strong."

"Wonder what it's for," Barner said. "Any ideas?"

"Could be practically anything." Hafner shook his head. "This whole place is incredible. Why on Earth would anyone go to the trouble to build something like this?"

"Maybe it was their normal mining method," Perez suggested. "This is impressive, certainly, but so are off-shore oil rigs and the Exxon Tower."

"Then where's the rest of their civilization?" Nichols objected. "They should've left *some* other traces behind."

"After a hundred thousand years?"

"We find fossils older than that on Earth."

"Actually, the Spinners probably weren't native to this system," Meredith interjected. "Possibly not to this entire region of space. Let's get back to the car and move on."

"What's your evidence the Spinners were strangers here?" Perez asked when they were again driving down the main tunnel. "Lack of fossils hardly counts—nobody's really been looking for them."

"How about lack of other cable-material structures?" Meredith countered. "Not just here, but elsewhere in the system? Remember, the Rooshrike did a pretty complete survey of this place when they first ran across it. Besides, if they lived anywhere near here they ought to at least be hinted at in Rooshrike archaeology or legends."

"Maybe they are," Hafner said. "Stories of godlike creatures and all could be references to them."

"The computer doesn't think so. All the appropriate mythological figures are too similar to Rooshrike themselves to be aliens."

"But after several thousand retellings—"

"Hold it!" Barner barked, cutting Hafner off and causing Nichols to stomp on the brakes. "On the right, down the corridor we just passed—looked like a hole in the rock."

Nichols backed the car up the necessary few meters and turned off to the right. Hafner leaned forward, peering over Meredith's shoulder. Sure enough, where the metal walls and lights ended, the tunnel continued on. "You've got good eyes, Major," he commented.

"They're no better than yours," Barner replied, a bit tartly. "I just use mine, that's all."

Hafner reddened and shut up.

The corridor ended in what had once been a T junction with another hallway; the rough tunnel Barner had spotted led through the crossbar of the T, as if someone had planned to extend the corridor and never completed the job. "Sloppy work," Nichols commented, running his fingers over the rough stone within the hole. "Must've had their funding cut."

"I don't think so," Meredith said. "Note that the whole wall's been left open to the rock here, as if they'd *planned* to drill into it."

Hafner stepped back and looked down the hallway. "You're right—looks like another hole down there, just past that vertical support bar."

Meredith produced a flashlight from his pack and aimed it into the tunnel. "Goes pretty deep . . . well, well. Looks like there's something metallic back there." Shifting the light to his left hand, he ducked his head and stepped carefully into the passageway. "Everyone wait here and keep your eyes open. I'll be back in a minute."

It was more like five minutes before the colonel reappeared. "Well?" Perez demanded as Meredith put away his light.

"Hard to be sure, of course, with an alien design," Meredith said, "but the thing back there seems to be an automated digging machine."

"So they *were* extending this tunnel," Nichols said.

"Or else mining the rock for the nonmetallic elements the leecher doesn't get," Hafner suggested. "Maybe hauling the digger out would give us a clue."

"I wouldn't recommend that," Meredith said. "The thing's still active."

They all turned to face him. "It's *what*?" Hafner said, cocking an ear toward the tunnel.

"Oh, it's not actually running—there's a rock jammed between two of the track links. But there's something that looks like a display panel in the rear, and a half-dozen lights are still showing on it." Meredith brushed at the dust that had collected on his shoulders and headed back toward the car. "Come on; let's keep moving."

They returned to the main corridor and continued on inward, driving for the most part in silence. It shouldn't have been such a shock, Hafner told himself—they all knew, after all, that the main Spinneret machinery was still operational. Somehow, though, he'd always pictured the Spinneret as an essentially solid-state apparatus, barely surviving through the grace of multiple redundancies. For a small peripheral unit—and a *tunneling* machine, at that—to be in equally good shape was both awesome and just a little bit creepy.

The corridor made a thirty-degree angle to the left . . . and without warning, they were abruptly in a new world.

"Snafu on toast," Barner gasped, craning his neck to look up. "What the hell *is* this?"

Chapter 18

Like Barner, Hafner's eyes were drawn first upward, to the impossible blue sky overhead. Fluffy white clouds drifted visibly by, occasionally cutting across the shining yellow sun midway to zenith . . . it was nearly a minute before he could tear his gaze away and focus on the village scene around them.

His immediate impression was that they'd driven into a replica of Jerusalem's old city. White-walled, domed buildings squeezed closely together along narrow, winding streets, while in the near distance a decorative wall cut in front of a minaret-like tower. A closer look, though, showed him the myriad of architectural differences between these buildings and anything he'd ever seen on Earth. The shapes and positioning of the windows, the elaborate carvings on doors and archways, even the faint iridescence of the walls themselves all emphatically marked the place as *alien*.

Perez broke the spell first, with a murmured Spanish phrase that sounded simultaneously blasphemous and awe-struck. "This is impossible!" he whispered. "The sky—but we were a hundred meters underground!"

"It's artificial," Meredith said, and Hafner had to admire the confidence in the other's voice. The geologist had stared at the sky for an entire minute without finding any flaws in the simulation. It *was* a simulation, of course; it *had* to be. "Probably a hologram or something projected on a domed ceiling," Meredith continued. "Looks like the Spinners were settling in for a long stay here."

"But why underground?" Perez asked, clearly still shaken. "Why not on the surface where they could have *real* sunlight?"

"Probably wanted a place where they could burn their steaks in peace," Nichols said, sneezing violently. "Or can't you smell that mess?"

Hafner sniffed cautiously. He hadn't really noticed the odors drifting in on the breeze, but now that he was paying attention he discovered Nichols was right. A faint smell that indeed resembled burnt meat was dominant; but beneath it he could detect traces of jasmine, sulfur, and something like a cross between rusty iron and oregano. "Whoo-ee," he said. "Smells like someone burned down a kitchen pantry."

"Again, probably artificial." Meredith pointed to a bare patch of ground Hafner hadn't noticed. "I'd guess that used to be a garden or small park. You can see that whatever used to be there is long gone. Anything that could possibly have decayed did so centuries ago."

The wind died and began again from a slightly different direction, changing with equal subtlety the mixture of scents. Hafner glanced upward; the phantom cloud, too, had shifted direction. "Someone went to an awful lot of trouble to make the workers feel at home."

"Yeah." Meredith pointed toward the minaret in the distance. "Let's leave a marker at this entrance and head over toward that tower. I want a look at that wall, too."

Barner produced a fluorescent orange-and-pink stick-on from his pack and got out of the car. Peering ahead, Nichols sneezed again and shook his head. "I don't understand why they'd bother putting in any walls down here," he said to no one in particular. "What would they want to cut this place in two parts for?"

"It may be simply decorative," Perez suggested. "Or possibly it separates the laborers from the elite."

"Or," Meredith put in, "it could have had a genuine defensive purpose. And if so, we'd better find out fast what they were defending against." He glanced back as Barner climbed into the car, nodded to Nichols. "Let's go, Doctor. Take it *real* slow and easy."

It was, Perez decided, the ultimate ghost town, raising boyhood memories he'd have preferred to leave buried. Many of the buildings they drove past had open doors, and he found himself peering nervously into each one as they passed, half expecting some lone survivor of the mass exodus to charge out at them. Originally, he'd applauded Hafner's stand on military participation in this trip; now, he almost wished Meredith had brought those three squads along.

Hafner, at least, seemed to feel some of his same uneasiness. "Looks like they left in a hurry," the scientist murmured, gazing out his window. "A lot of doors and windows were left open."

"Why lock them?" Barner asked reasonably. "Unless they imported their own burglars, too—"

"They also left the Spinneret running," Hafner pointed out.

Barner shrugged. "You leave a fluorescent light on if you expect to be right back."

"Yeah," Meredith agreed. "So . . . why *didn't* they come back?" Tapping Nichols on the shoulder, he pointed ahead. "There; on the left—that wide spot in the road. Pull over there and let's take a look inside one of these houses."

Nichols did as instructed and they all piled out. The building by the parking space was larger than the ones immediately around it, with inset doors and an archway extending almost to the street. "I'm going inside," Meredith said in a low voice, drawing his pistol. "Major, you and the others stay here. Are we in contact with the outside at the moment?"

"No, sir," Barner replied. He, too, had drawn his pistol.

"You still at quarter-power setting?"

"Yes."

"All right. I don't expect to run into any trouble, but if you hear a shot and I don't check in within a ten-count, boost power all the way up and call for assistance. If the snoopers overhead hear . . . well, at that point we've probably got worse worries."

Barner nodded. "Understood. Good luck, Colonel."

"Thanks." Meredith stepped under the archway, pausing as Perez joined him. "What do *you* want?" he growled.

"I'm coming with you," Perez told him calmly. "If you think there's possible danger in there, two would have a better chance than one. And you have to admit I'm the most expendable man here."

Meredith snorted, but waved his pistol impatiently. "Oh, all right. But don't touch anything, and if I give you an order, you hop. Got it?"

"Got it."

The door had seemed closed from the street, but the leftmost of the twin panels turned out to actually be ajar. Meredith halted there, spending nearly a minute examining the entire area before easing it open. Motioning Perez to stay put, he stepped over the sill and disappeared off to the right. A moment later his beckoning hand appeared. Wondering belatedly if his curiosity hadn't perhaps gotten him in over his head, Perez gingerly stepped inside.

They were in a large room, lined on all sides with floor-to-ceiling shelves. Unrecognizable objects rested on some of them, uniformly coated with dust. Directly across from them a wider chest-high counter replaced one of the shelves, its surface showing more wear than Perez had noticed anywhere else. He pointed that out to Meredith, who nodded. "Yeah. I thought at first this whole place was built out of painted cable-type metal, but it's looking more like we've got some sort of ceramic here, maybe over cable-type metal frame." He glanced to either side, perhaps at the two closed doors exiting from the room, and then walked over to the counter. Trying to watch both doors at once, Perez followed.

"The floor looks a little more scuffed here," Meredith said. He touched the edge of the countertop experimentally, exerted some pressure—

And with a *crack*, a section several centimeters long disintegrated into a cloud of white dust.

Perez clamped his mouth hard over the exclamation that wanted out and backed hastily away as the cloud drifted toward him on the eddy breezes. Meredith had dropped into a crouch, pistol ready. Perez held his breath, listening, but he heard nothing.

"I was right," Meredith stage-whispered a moment later, straightening up and brushing the remnants of the ceramic off the dull metal edge beneath. "Cable metal, almost certainly."

"Uh-huh," Perez nodded. He glanced around the room. "You suppose this place was a store or something?"

"A store, or a fast-food restaurant or bar," Meredith murmured. "Maybe the Spinners liked to stand up while eating. Let's check out those other doors—and keep your voice down, huh?"

"What exactly are you worried about running into here, anyway?" Perez asked. The crumbling of the countertop had put his ghost town fears back into perspective, reminding him once more how old this place was. Even ghosts disappear after a few centuries.

"It occurs to me," Meredith replied, "that there's another possible reason the Spinners might not have worried about leaving their doors open: they may have had some very good antiburglar equipment."

"After all these years—"

"The digging machine was still functional."

Perez swallowed. "Right. Well . . . nothing's attacked us yet."

"Yet," Meredith echoed. "Let's check out those doors and then move on. I don't think we're really going to find anything in this part of town."

They were halfway across the room when Meredith's short-range radio beeped quietly. "Meredith," the colonel answered it. ". . . Where is it?"

Perez stepped to his side, close enough to hear Barner's voice. ". . . -dred meters away and closing. It's not terrifically fast, but it may be armed."

"Yeah. Pull back as quietly as you can; let's see if it's us the thing's after." Meredith moved to the front door, sent a quick glance outside. "Looks like the basic structure's cable metal," he said, stepping back again. "Perez: check out that door. See if it leads outside."

Perez broke his paralysis and tiptoed to the side door. Opening it, he found another room, much smaller than the first one but equipped with the same sparsely laden shelves. There were no doors, but one of the windows facing the street looked big enough to get through quickly. If *we can open it,* he added to himself, sidling along the wall to check. Keeping his head low, he reached up to try and find a latch . . . and as he did so, he got his first look at the machine bearing down on them.

It was as if someone had built a giant mechanical spider, fitted it with a turtle shell, and grafted a nest of snakes on top of the result. *A walking Gorgon's head,* Perez thought, suppressing a shudder . . . and it *was,* indeed, heading for their building. Across the street, he caught a glimpse of Barner and the others crouched beside one of the other houses.

"Perez!"

Perez jerked violently before his brain could register the fact that the stage whisper from behind him was Meredith's. "It's coming, Colonel," he breathed. "I can see it!"

"I know, but we've got at least a minute before it gets here. Does that window come open?"

Perez's hands remembered their task. "Uh . . . I think I feel the latch here . . . there. It moved about a quarter turn." He glanced cautiously out again. "I'd rather not try pushing it just yet."

Meredith was crouched beside him now, fingering the window himself. "Yeah . . . well, we'll just have to hope it's not stuck." He raised his radio. "Major, the minute it's inside here I want all of you in the car ready to take off. No covering fire unless it seems necessary; the last thing we want is to attract any more of them." He got an acknowledgment and slid the radio back into its pocket. "Wait here," he told Perez. "When I fire, shove the window open and get out. If it sticks, hit the floor and yell and I'll try an armor-piercer on it."

Perez nodded silently, and Meredith moved back across the room. Closing the door to a crack, he stood peering out, his pistol held tightly at the ready in a two-handed marksman's grip. Perez bit at his lip, staring at the gun and hoping the colonel hadn't wasted any of the six spots in his number-two clip on flare shells or something equally useless. *Though will even armor-piercers do anything against cable-metal?* he wondered suddenly. *A vulnerable spot—there* has *to be a vulnerable spot for him to hit—*

From the other room came the *clip-clip-clip* of metal feet. Perez caught his breath . . . and Meredith fired.

The blast of the shell was deafening in the enclosed space, its echoes almost drowning out the sounds of Meredith's next two shots. A snowstorm of ceramic dust erupted from the walls and ceiling as the building shook to the explosions. Perez threw one arm up to protect his eyes from the dust as he stood and shoved with his full weight against the window. It held an instant and then gave with a screech. Grabbing the edge, Perez vaulted through, banging his shoulder in the process and nearly losing his balance when he hit the ground. Meredith was right behind him, giving him a shove in the proper direction and shouting something he couldn't catch. Running full tilt, he got his eyes clear of dust and tears just in time to skid to a halt by the open car door and dive into the back seat beside Hafner. Meredith hit the front seat an instant later, and Perez was abruptly jammed into the cushions as Nichols stomped on the accelerator. The car jumped ahead, throwing Perez back and forth as Nichols fought to keep the car on the winding street.

"You all right?" Meredith asked.

"I think so." Perez fished out a handkerchief and wiped his eyes. There was a grunt from the other side of the car, and he looked up to see Barner slide awkwardly in through the window, where he'd apparently been sitting in rear-guard position.

"As far as I could tell it never fired a shot," he said, twisting to look out the back window.

"I'm not sure it wasn't for lack of trying," Meredith replied grimly. "At least two of those snakes were tracking me from the second it came through the door."

Barner grunted. "You get it?"

"Wasn't trying to. I was firing at its feet, trying to knock it over long enough for us to get out."

"Maybe all the dust helped, too." Barner turned back to face forward. "The local police force, you suppose?"

"Or else a burglar alarm," Hafner offered.

"Burglar alarms are usually set up in the individual house," Perez said, coughing ceramic dust.

"*Ours* are," Hafner said. "But the whole setup of this town seems pretty cozy by human—well, at least by Western culture standards. It's quite possible that a gregarious people like the Spinners would go with a centralized burglar-proofing system."

"A police force by any other name," Barner said, dismissing the distinction. "And the real question then is how many more of them are still functional."

The car hit a tight curve and fishtailed a bit getting around it. "I think you can slow down now, Nichols," Meredith said.

"Yeah. Okay." Nichols threw quick glances in all directions before somewhat reluctantly easing off on the gas. Perez stared hard at the geologist, wondering at how shaken the other seemed over the incident. Only gradually did it occur to him that he'd been too busy himself at the time to consider what the Gorgon's Head might have done. . . .

The unfamiliar architecture and geography of the Spinner cavern made distances deceptive, and it turned out that the wall was both farther and higher than it had looked from the tunnel entrance. Rising a good six meters above them, its surface an intricate pattern of subtle colors, it was as if a hundred rainbows had been caught and smashed together into the leading edge of a glacier. Meredith grimaced; the image was an oddly unsettling one.

"Well, Colonel?" Perez prodded from behind him. "Was it for defense or not?"

Meredith let his eyes rove the wall's length. No crenels or loopholes for gunners to shoot through, no towers or turrets, nor any indication the wall had ever had them. "If it was, it was an extremely passive system," he said. "Regardless, we've got to get through it. Anyone see anything that looked like a break or gateway on our way in?"

"I thought I saw a gap over to the left," Barner offered, frowning off in that direction. "But I can't find it now."

"Maybe the color pattern's hiding it," Meredith suggested. "Let's go take a look."

They piled into the car; and barely fifty meters away they found the tall, thin opening Barner had seen.

"Wouldn't have believed a simple hole could be that hard to see," Barner grunted, leaning through the gap for a quick look at the other side. "Well . . . it's a cinch we're not going to get the car through here, Colonel, but the tower looks to be only a ten-minute hike away."

Meredith motioned him aside and stepped through the opening himself. Unlike the other side, this part of the cavern was nearly devoid of structures. Those he could see looked less like houses than industrial or business buildings: long and low, with little of the decoration they'd seen on the domed homes behind them. *Or they could be the town cafeteria and rec centers*, he reminded himself. *All the vacant ground could have been gardens or a forest. In which case the tower would have been . . . what?*

The tower. It rose up from the ground perhaps half a kilometer away, looking rather like a cross between a church spire and an airport control tower. About fifty meters tall, he estimated, with what looked like wide windows halfway up and also near the top. A half-dozen flat-roofed buildings were clustered at its base. Service sheds or housing for the night shift, perhaps? Or were they the local dispatch points for little nasties like the one they'd already run into?

"We'll go on foot," he announced, stepping back to the group. "Major, get the rifles and four grenades out of the trunk. Dr. Hafner, go with him and bring back the Geiger counter that's under the front passenger seat."

Hafner's eyes widened a bit at mention of the extra weaponry, but he obeyed without argument. Meredith consulted his watch: they'd already used up over an hour of the four he'd allotted for his reconnaissance. The return trip should be faster, but that was still a lot of tower to explore in two hours. They'd have to make some guesses as to where the most interesting sections were likely to be.

Barner and Hafner returned with their loads. "Okay," Meredith said, slinging his Stoner 5.56 mm over his shoulder and hooking two of the rifle grenades onto his belt. "Stay in a loose formation and keep your eyes open."

The cluster of huts surrounding the tower base were not, as Meredith had assumed, physically connected to the structure, but were placed two or three meters away from its dull-metal wall.

"Interesting," Hafner said as they circled the tower in search of a door. "First structure we've come across in here that doesn't have that white ceramic coating."

"Would that make it a more recent building?" Perez suggested. "Put up near the end, when they didn't have time for cosmetic appearances?"

"Or else it's subject to vibrations," Meredith said, recalling the fragile ceramic in the village building. "I think I see a door around that side. Let's take a look."

Like the doors they'd seen elsewhere, this one was tall, slender, and elaborately carved. It was also unlocked, leading into a bare lobbylike area shaped like a small piece of pie with a bite taken out of the tip. The missing point contained a floor-to-ceiling cylinder. "The elevator, I'd guess," Barner said as he took one final look outside and closed the door behind them. "Shall we see if it's running?"

"We can," Meredith said reluctantly, "but we'd better not actually ride it. Let's see if the Spinners understood the concept of stairs."

It took several minutes, but eventually they discovered that pressing a wall design caused the whole cylinder to rotate, bringing an off-center and doorless opening into view. Stepping into the opening and turning to the right led into the elevator car proper, while a left-hand turn ended in the stairway Meredith had hoped to find. With the colonel in the lead, they started up.

Progress was slow, hampered as they were by both the relatively cramped quarters and by Meredith's insistence on slowly easing his weight onto each new step. Hafner muttered at least once that such exaggerated care was a waste of time with cable material structures, but Meredith ignored him. There was little conversation; faint hums and clicks were becoming audible from the areas around and above them, and no one seemed willing to drown them out with idle chatter.

Meredith took them to the very top of the stairway, hoping the most important equipment would be at that level. The inside release for the rotating cylinder, once located, worked perfectly. Holding his pistol ready, the colonel stepped through the short tunnel and into a garish sea of color.

For a moment he just stood there, his eyes and mind struggling furiously to adjust to the sight. *Give a small child a box of crayons and a detailed photo of a shuttle flight deck,* he thought, *and you might wind up with something like this.* The meter-wide semicircular ring that wrapped around the room beneath the windows was a familiar control board design; the panels set into it were decidedly not. Painted some of the brightest colors Meredith had ever seen, the panels had curved or even squiggled edges; some vaguely rectangular, but most not. For several seconds Meredith's brain tried anyway to classify them in terms of familiar polygons—squarish, trapezoidal, triangular—before finally giving up the exercise as pointless. The controls themselves—mostly black, but with occasional colored ones mixed in—were similarly arranged without regard for the concept of straight lines. None of the panels had exactly the same shape or layout, and some of the color juxtapositions were almost painful. *Make that a* color-blind *child,* he added.

The others were crowding out behind him now, muttering their own reactions to the visual assault. Of all of them, Hafner seemed the least affected, stepping over to the board with only a slight pause and peering down at it. "Well, at least the controls seem to be marked," he announced. "That's something."

Meredith joined him. Sure enough, there were small black marks to the left of each of the buttons and knobs, marks that looked like a cross between Chinese and Arabic. "Yeah, it really helps," he told Hafner dryly. He looked back at the wall that split this floor into halves, eyes searching for a doorway that would get them through to the other side. Two full-length cylinders, smaller versions of the elevator/stairway shaft that they flanked, were the obvious candidates.

"Sure looks like the place," Nichols commented, looking around the room. "Must be . . . oh, a good five to ten thousand separate controls in here. What else could anyone need that much stuff for?"

"Who knows what else they might have down here?" Perez countered, leaning carefully on a bare part of the control board to gaze out one of the windows. "One certainly gets a good view from here. Perhaps all this does is handle power or lighting for the village."

"Maybe whatever's in the other room will give us a clue," Meredith said, taking one last look at the odd Spinner lettering. *In a science fiction movie,* he thought, *the hero would take all of ten seconds to figure out an alien control board like this. Wish to hell we'd brought one of those geniuses along.*

"Colonel," Barner said, his tone getting Meredith's instant attention. The major was peering out another of the windows. "We've got company."

Meredith followed the other's pointing finger and felt his jaw tighten. Approaching the tower from different directions were eight mechanical creatures like the one that had chased them out of the village.

"Gorgon's Heads!" Perez hissed. "Colonel, we'd better get out of here."

Automatically, Meredith estimated distances and speeds. It would be a close race. "Right. Everybody down the stairs—fast." He turned, took a step, and abruptly halted as his legs froze beneath him.

"Bloodsucking hell," Barner murmured.

The two small cylinders flanking the stairway had rotated to their open positions. Standing inside were a matched set of Gorgon's Heads.

Chapter 19

For a long moment the only sound in the room was the thudding of Meredith's own heart. The Gorgon's Heads stayed where they were, as if frozen by the same shock that had immobilized the humans. Only the gentle waving of their snakelike tentacles showed they were still active.

Hell. Now *what do we do?* Meredith thought. The machines were barely five meters away—impossible to miss with either his pistol or rifle . . . but only if he had time to get one of the weapons lined up. An unarmed Gorgon's Head might be able to get to him before he could fire; an armed one could blow him off the map a lot faster. Run for it? Again, if they were unarmed one or two might make it back to the stairs. But *only* if they were unarmed . . . and there were still the reinforcements coming in at ground level to be dealt with.

"Shouldn't one of us be saying, 'Take me to your leader'?" Perez asked quietly.

"Shut up," Meredith snarled.

"No, Colonel, I'm serious," Perez said. "They haven't attacked us yet, or made any other movements that could be considered hostile. Maybe they recognize we're not Spinners and are waiting for us to open communications."

"Or maybe they're waiting for their friends downstairs to join us." Still . . . it might be worth trying. Bracing himself, Meredith took a step forward. One of the snakes on each Gorgon's Head seemed to track the movement, but otherwise there was no reaction. "I'm Colonel Lloyd Meredith; commanding the Earth colony on Astra," he said, keeping his volume level conversational. "We come in peace, seeking the creators of this cavern."

He paused, sweat trickling down his shirt collar. But again there was no response. "Any other suggestions?" he asked the others.

"Maybe you should try to get to the stairs," Barner offered. "I can't seem to get through with all this metal around, but you might be able to do so from outside."

"For all the good a rescue party fifteen kilometers away will do us," Nichols muttered.

"Let's dispense with the pessimism, shall we?" Meredith said tartly. But it *was* beginning to look like suicidal moves were about all they had left. "All right. Major, get ready to rip off that headset. The rest of you are to hit the dirt the second anything happens. Got it?" There were murmurs of quiet assent. "Okay. Here goes."

Carefully, Meredith slid his leading foot forward, his full attention on the silent machines flanking the exit. He brought the rear foot up, pausing before easing out the leading foot again. The door was a meter and a half away now. . . .

And without warning, the leftmost Gorgon's Head snapped one of its snakes out, the tentacle doubling in length to solidly grip Meredith's left wrist.

Afterward Meredith would remember hearing the clatter of Barner's rifle being brought to bear and a general cacophony of startled yelps; but for that one horrifying second there was nothing in the universe but his wrist and the cold metal suction grip fastened there.

There was no question of making a break for the stairs; every instinct in Meredith's body screamed for him to get the tentacle off *fast*. Throwing himself backward, he snapped his arm over his head—

And sprawled on his back at Perez's feet.

"What happened?" Barner snapped.

Meredith sat up, ignoring a momentary dizziness, and examined his arm. Completely whole, apparently functional, and without even a mark where the snake had gripped him. "It just . . . let go," he managed, not entirely believing it. "It—I guess it wasn't trying to hold me." He shifted his attention to the Gorgon's Head, which had withdrawn its tentacle again but had otherwise not reacted. Waiting? And for what?

"Could it have injected something into your wrist?" Hafner asked anxiously.

Meredith shook his head. *Waiting.* "No needle marks or inflammation—I already checked. And even with a hypospray you feel *something*." Cautiously, he got to his feet and again faced the Gorgon's Head. Natural fear fought natural curiosity . . . and for the moment the curiosity was stronger. "I'm going to try it again," he announced, amazed at the calm in his voice. Clenching his teeth, he started forward.

This time he stepped directly toward the Gorgon's Head, getting only a pace and a half before the same elongating tentacle snapped out. He managed to hold still as the metal again gripped his skin, his eyes on two other tentacles that arched over the machine like rattlesnakes preparing to strike. For five heartbeats nothing happened . . . and then the Gorgon's Head emitted a sound like a hiccup, and suddenly Meredith was surrounded by a cloud of smoke. He took an incautious breath and nearly choked. "It's all right," he gasped, to forestall any action from the others. "Just like being buried alive in spice teas." He sniffed again, but the cloud already seemed to have dissipated. Simultaneously, the Gorgon's Head withdrew its tentacle from his arm.

"Well?" Perez asked from behind him.

"Why are you asking *me*?' Meredith retorted. "I'm not in charge here."

"I wonder," Hafner said slowly. "Colonel . . . why don't you try going for the stairs again."

Meredith thought about it for a moment, then shrugged. "All right. Major, get ready with that headset."

Neither machine made the slightest move to interfere as he walked into the stairway entrance, nor did they react when Barner lobbed him the headset. "They seem to have lost interest in me," he commented as he put on the headset, temporarily out of reach of both Gorgon's Heads. "Let's hope the word's been spread to the rest of the gang."

"I'll be very surprised if it hasn't," Hafner said. "I think, Colonel, that you've been declared a friend."

Meredith paused. "You mean that puff of cinnamon smoke was my security clearance or something?"

"Either that or a confirmation signal that you were logged onto the computer. It may be that that tentacle was recording your scent or heartbeat or something."

"That's ridiculous," Meredith snorted. "I can't possibly smell anything like a Spinner."

"Maybe the data's been lost," Nichols suggested. "Maybe the Gorgon's Heads are trying to reestablish it, using you as a prototype."

"But—" Meredith closed his mouth. "Okay, let's put it to a real test, then. That other squad of Gorgon's Heads must be downstairs by now. If *they* don't give me any trouble, I'll concede you may be right."

He had to walk through the lobby and all the way around the base of the tower, but by the time he started up the stairs again he was convinced.

"I don't believe it," he puffed as he entered the control room. "Damn things acted like a bunch of pet poodles—took a sniff and then ignored me completely." He turned to Barner, motioned him forward. "Let's see if it'll accept you, too, Major."

It did; and in the end all five of them submitted to the Gorgon's Head's olfactory inspection. "I still don't understand it," Barner shook his head as the others cautiously tested their new immunity. "Why should their security system be the only thing that's fallen apart after all this time?"

"*And* fallen apart in just the right way to help us," Nichols added, gingerly touching one of the Gorgon's Heads' shells. "It could just as easily have decided to keep *everyone* out of the tower."

"It may not be nearly as providential as you think," Perez said. "You could explain it just as well by a single minor failure plus a breakdown in communications. Suppose, for instance, that there's supposed to be a lock or independent security scanner elsewhere in the building, and that system's broken down. Now, these Gorgon's Heads find us here; but since the other system shouldn't have let us in if we weren't allowed, we must *be* allowed. You see? And since the Gorgon's Heads don't have us on their VIP list, they hurry to remedy that gap in their memory."

"Clever idea," Hafner grunted. "But pretty stupid of the things."

Perez shrugged. "Oh, I don't know. I've used the same technique myself. Once you're actually inside a restricted place it's not too hard to stay there."

"Well, whatever the reason," Hafner shrugged, "being in the Gorgon's Heads' good graces will come in handy when the anthropologists get here. I don't suppose they'd like working with snakes looking over their shoulders."

Meredith frowned. "What anthropologists are these?"

"Should I have said linguists? The people who we're going to have to call in to translate all this." He waved over the control boards.

"Probably need computer experts, too," Nichols added. "Also mathematicians, materials specialists—"

"Hold it a second," Meredith cut him off. "Just where do you think we're going to find these people?"

Nichols blinked. "We got Dr. Chang and his group easily enough, didn't we? All we should have to do is send a list back with the next shuttle."

Meredith glanced at Perez, noted the sour look on his face. For obvious reasons, the colonel hadn't exactly advertised news of the Council's ultimatum and Chang's forced departure; it now appeared that no one else had given it much publicity, either. "As it happens, Doctor," he told Nichols, "Dr. Chang is no longer with us. He left because of a Council resolution barring non-Astrans from Spinneret facilities." He inclined his head toward Perez in a caricature of supplication. "Unless, of course, the Council would consider scrapping its edict."

Perez flushed; whether in anger or embarrassment Meredith couldn't tell. "The resolution was meant to protect Astra from having its only resource plundered by outsiders and being left then to rot or starve. That danger still exists."

"Aren't you being just a bit melodramatic?" Hafner grunted. "Not to mention living in the nineteenth century? We're not exactly native savages here, you know, who'll just sit around while the Spinneret is taken apart and shipped back to Earth."

"The secrets can still be stolen," Perez pointed out. "Besides, we don't need anyone else. The Ctencri have computer programs that can decipher an unknown language—they translated Earth's major languages in less than a week, I'm told."

"They also had some hundred thousand radio and TV channels as their database," Nichols pointed out. "All we've got are a bunch of control switches."

Perez still had a stonewall look on his face, but Meredith could tell he was weakening. "Well . . . if we kept the investigation team small—*and* international," he added, glancing at Meredith, "I suppose we could take adequate safeguards."

"Why international?" Barner asked suspiciously. "The U.S. has all the experts we could want."

"Let's not argue about that right now," Meredith interjected.

He didn't want to fight with Perez in front of Hafner and Nichols; the threats he might have to make on this one would best be delivered without witnesses around. "We'll figure out who to invite *after* we decide exactly what we need and *after* the Council decides whether or not to make trouble on the whole issue."

"In that case, maybe we ought to head back," Hafner shrugged. "I'm sure there's more to see around here, but we're not going to hit all of it in the time we've got left."

"Good point." Meredith stepped to the window and gazed out for a moment, scanning the cavern wall and fixing in his mind the direction of their marked exit tunnel. At least two more tunnel openings were visible, one of which ought to lead to the gravity equipment under the volcano cone. A complete mapping of this labyrinth would be an early priority, he decided, followed by a thorough examination of the tower and any other control areas they found. After that . . . repair the digging machine he'd found? Maybe. It would be instructive to see what part it was supposed to play in this ballet . . . and why its contribution hadn't been missed. "Yeah, you're right," he sighed, turning back. "There's too much here for one day. Come on; let's go home."

Chapter 20

The first napkin had been easy, but for some reason Carmen had to fold the second one four times before she finally got it right. Setting it down in the center of the plate, she stepped back to survey the result. *Terrible,* she decided, the perfectionist within her choosing that moment to surface and be offended. *Starburst napkin designs on Army-issue plates. Miss America at the shipyards. Oh, well. Peter probably won't even notice.*

That last, at least, was almost certainly true. Not that Hafner was uncultured; she would hardly enjoy having him around if he were. But the past weeks had been hectic ones for him, and the last four days had topped even that. It'd only been with great difficulty that she'd been able to draw him back to Unie long enough for this dinner.

Which brought up another issue entirely. She'd known Hafner for almost four months now, and while she appreciated him as a friend she had no feelings toward him that could remotely be considered romantic. So why had she missed his company so much while he was out poking around the Dead Sea? For that matter, why had she knocked herself out to make this evening something special? *Maybe I've simply forgotten what it's like to have a really good friend*, she thought—which was a rather depressing thought all by itself. *No doubt about it; I've got to settle down somewhere one of these days*.

There was a tap on the door, and she glanced at her watch with mild surprise. Hafner was seldom very late for appointments, but he usually wasn't this early, either. But no matter; things were adequately ready. Smiling, she opened the door.

"Hello, Carmen. May I come in?"

Her smile winked out. "Cris," she said, with a cold formality she hoped covered up her surprise. "As a matter of fact, I'm expecting someone else at the moment. So if you'll just—"

"Ah—Dr. Hafner, I presume," Perez nodded. "Don't worry, this will take only a minute." He moved forward . . . and somehow he was past her, strolling by the table settings with an appreciative nod.

Gritting her teeth, Carmen closed the door and stalked after him. "Contrary to popular opinion, I'm *not* on twenty-seven-hour duty here," she said icily. "So if you'd kindly restrict your calls to business hours—"

"Somewhere in the computer library is a copy of the *Scientific Directory*," he interrupted, turning to face her. "For reasons I won't go into it's been classified and hidden behind some security password. I'd like you to get me access to it."

Carmen took a deep breath. "In the first place, I'm not *about* to give you classified material without specific orders to the contrary. In the second place, you have an incredible gall to burst in on me without any better reason than *that*. I could have told you no over the phone."

He waited her out, and then lifted a finger. "In the first place, as you put it, there's absolutely nothing remotely classifiable in the *Directory*. Not only is it in half the libraries in North America and Europe, but I know for a fact it was accessible here a month ago. And in the second place—" He hesitated. "I don't want Meredith to know I talked to you."

She arched her eyebrows. "My, we *are* getting paranoid,

aren't we? What makes you think the colonel would *want* to record your calls, let alone is actually doing so?"

He smiled tightly. "Come on, Carmen, you know better than that. I'm the thorn in Meredith's flesh, the major obstacle to his dream of making Astra America's fifty-second state. He's going to suggest to the Astran scientists that a number of American experts be invited to help us decipher the Spinneret controls, and the only reason he's hidden the *Directory* is to keep me from counterproposing a more international group."

She thought about that for a moment. Perez was probably the last person in the world she was interested in doing favors for— he'd proved time and again to be a master pain to everyone around him. And yet . . . it *did* make sense to get the best people possible. The sooner they learned how to operate the Spinneret the better; and given the current situation in the Spinner cavern, there was precious little chance of any foreigner sneaking off on their own and stealing something. As for Meredith—well, if Perez had something devious in mind, the colonel had already proved he could take Perez's best attacks and use them to his own advantage.

And Peter was due at any minute.

"All right," she sighed. "Tomorrow morning I'll try to find your *Directory*. If I can get to it in ten minutes or less I'll copy it under 'Cris' on the general-access list. But I'm not going to waste any more time on it than that. Clear?"

"I'm very grateful," Perez smiled, inclining his head toward her as he headed for the door. "If you'll excuse me now, I must get back to Crosse; I'm on early-morning duty tomorrow. Good night, and thank you."

"Good *night*."

Closing the door firmly behind him, she leaned against it for a moment, working the irritation out of her system. Then, glancing at her watch, she headed to the kitchen to check on dinner.

She'd half expected Hafner to arrive as Perez was leaving, a confrontation that would probably have left a distinct damper on the evening. It was therefore with an odd sense of relief—odd, at least, for her—that she had to wait nearly ten minutes for Hafner's knock to finally come.

"Hi, Carmen," he greeted her with a tired-looking smile as she let him in. "Sorry I'm late."

"No problem," she assured him. "The lasagna just needs a twenty-second final heating and it'll be ready."

"Lasagna, eh? Pretty extravagant meal for a poor civil servant—getting this private apartment must have really gone to your head. The mozzarella alone probably cost a fortune in favors." He sat down at the table and peered admiringly at the folded napkin.

"Actually, it didn't, though I *am* anticipating things a bit." She set the micro and went to drain the vegetables. "The Rooshrike are going to start regular goods shipments from Earth as of Thursday, and I've made sure every other food package is heavy on these so-called luxury items."

"That'll be nice—I know it'll raise *my* morale a lot. You going to distribute it through normal military channels or set up special stores?"

"I don't know." The micro pinged and she carefully carried the steaming dish to the table. "I'd like to start moving toward a normal economic system, but Colonel Meredith thinks things are still too unstable for that. Anyway, I'm not sure a luxury food store is the way to start. It smacks too much of the foreign-currency-only places in Moscow."

"Yeah." Almost reluctantly, she thought, he unfolded his napkin. "I wish I'd had a bottle of wine to bring, but I don't have friends in high places like you do."

"Except Gorgon's Heads."

He smiled wryly. "And with friends like them—" Shaking his head, he dug into his food.

"Rough day, I gather?" Carmen asked, pouring them each some water.

"More just dead-dull boring," he shrugged. "I'm not even *doing* anything aside from sitting there keeping the Gorgon's

Heads quiet—it's everybody else that's photographing the control labels and computer-coding everything in sight. I never before realized how tiring it gets sitting around doing nothing."

"You *can* leave other people alone once they're in the tower, though, can't you?"

"Everywhere except the main control room. The top floor, I should say; we haven't actually proved it's the control room yet." He waved his fork. "But even in the other rooms no one can get to the stairs or elevators without one of us five escorting them. And heaven help anyone who tries leaving the tower itself. Davidson tried it once and nearly got strangled by one of those tentacles."

"Ouch. I don't suppose there's any way to persuade that guard circle to go patrol the village or something."

"I'm sure there is—just as I'm sure there's a way to induct more people into the Grand Order of Den Mothers, as Al Nichols calls it. We just haven't found it yet."

"Mm." Carmen shook her head. "I still don't understand exactly why you five were able to get special status but nobody else can. It seems—well, sort of capricious."

"Not really." Hafner finished off his lasagna and helped himself to another spatulaful. "Actually, if Perez's theory is right, the Gorgon's Head system is being quite self-consistent. The five of us had made it to the control room without being challenged by either one of their own units or by anything else, so as far as the Gorgon's Heads were concerned we must have been supervisors and had to be recorded as such. But now that they've set up a cordon around the tower nobody else *can* get up there alone, and so no one else gets to be a supervisor."

"Leaving you five as rotating tour guides." The entire setup still seemed pretty bizarre, but if she worked hard at it she could believe it made sense. *The Spinners* were *aliens, after all,* she reminded herself.

"Actually, we're more like three to three and a half," he said. "Colonel Meredith hardly ever comes by, and Perez and Major Barner together don't pull much more than a single shift. It almost makes me wish I hadn't supported the whole Council idea way back when—at least then Perez wouldn't always be pulling 'official business' on us and ducking out.''

"If there weren't any Council, Perez wouldn't have been there in the first place," Carmen pointed out. "It would've just been the other four of you.''

"Plus thirty soldiers, if I hadn't gotten all righteous about *that*," he grumbled. "Someday maybe I'll learn to keep my mouth shut.''

They ate in silence for a few minutes. The dining nook window faced west, and through it she could see that the lights of the admin complex were still ablaze. *Finishing up the details on our trade proposals?* she wondered. *Or still trying to figure out how to code the Spinner script? Probably both.* For a while she'd been resentful that no one had informed her when the Spinner tunnel was unearthed—by her reckoning she'd done more than her fair share for both the alien device and the people involved, and she'd deserved to share in some of the triumph, too. Now, though, she was just as glad she'd been somewhere else. She was already indispensable to too many projects.

"Penny for them."

She focused on Hafner again. "Sorry—just thinking about all the work we have to do to make Astra economically stable." She sighed. "And so much of it depends on how fast we can learn to control the Spinneret.''

Hafner pursed his lips and looked out the window himself. "Carmen . . . what are the races out there planning to do with the cable they buy from us? You have any ideas?''

She frowned. "No, not really.''

"It's not an idle question," he went on, almost as if he hadn't heard her. "The Spinners went to incredible lengths to build this place—someday soon I'll take you down to see their village, and I guarantee you'll be floored by it. But why did they do it? Suck an entire planet dry of its metals to make six-centimeter cables—what were they *using* the stuff for?''

"Any number of things," she shrugged. "We've worked up a

three-page list of possibilities ourselves, and we don't know half of what there is to know about the cable yet."

He shook his head. "You're missing my point. The buildings down there—the whole Spinneret, for that matter—everything's lasted a hundred thousand years. Why on Earth would *any* culture make something that lasts that long?"

She started to speak, then paused. It *wasn't* a trivial question. "Maybe they were building the ultimate city back on their home world or something. Maybe a tomb or memorial, like the pyramids or the Taj Mahal."

"Or maybe a cage for something very big and long-lived," he said quietly. "That's one of the possibilities that keep occurring to me."

She grimaced. "That one I'd rather not think about. Maybe—well, maybe they just lived a lot longer than we do. In terms of lifetimes, then, the cable may not seem exceptionally durable."

"Maybe." Hafner leaned back in his chair. "That list you mentioned—any overtly military uses on it?"

"I—" She frowned. "Now that you mention it, no, there aren't."

"The colonel's playing it cool," Hafner nodded heavily. "But I doubt that it's doing any good. None of the races out there are dumb enough or naive enough to have missed the warfare possibilities."

She nodded silently. It was a topic she and Meredith had never discussed openly, but from the very beginning it had fluttered like a vulture over the trade negotiations. Using that superconducting solenoid to throw missiles; wrapping a warship in unbreakable cable; hurling a giant tangler thread among an enemy's ships to glue them randomly together—practically every peaceful use had its darker flip side. "I don't suppose there's any way we can dictate how our clients use their cables, though," she said aloud. "I think that's one reason Colonel Meredith wants all the aliens to have equal access to the cables, to minimize any strategic advantages it might provide."

"It could still foul up the political balance, though, maybe in more subtle ways," Hafner said. "Suppose one of the empires out there is having internal dissent, a problem maybe that the central government could quickly crush with a cable-wrapped spaceship. That would free the government's resources and attention to be turned to its neighbors."

"What would you have us do, then?" Carmen growled, knowing full well that he wasn't attacking her personally, but still feeling compelled to defend her project. "Turn Astra over to the UN? Or pull out entirely and let the Rooshrike have it? Either way, the cable's going to be made and used by *someone*. The genie's *out*, Peter; you can't stuff it back in its bottle."

He held up his hands, palms outward. "Peace. I wasn't picking on you or your work—and as far as genies go, I did my fair share to pop the cork. I just . . . that's the other possibility that keeps coming back to me. Maybe the Spinners used the cable material for warfare, too. If the crew here was recalled to help fight and never made it back . . . well, that would explain why the Spinneret was left running."

She shuddered. "You *would* bring that up, wouldn't you?"

"Sorry." He shook his head. "Look, let's get off the whole subject, okay? I didn't bring any wine, but I *did* bring some music. Why don't you put it on while I clear the table, and then you can pick up the story of your life again. I think we'd made it through high school last time."

She forced a chuckle and accepted the cassette he handed her. "All right—but this time *you* start."

"If you insist," he said, stacking the plates. "But I warn you: I was a very dull person in college."

They both did their best, but it was clear the mood of the evening had been irreparably darkened, and Hafner left early.

Is this how it's going to be now? Carmen wondered as she undressed for bed an hour later, the book she'd tried reading abandoned for lack of concentration. *Is the Spinneret going to so dominate life here that we'll never be able to shut it out?*

Oh, don't be so dramatic, she chided herself. *You're tired, you're overworked, and you're feeling sorry for yourself. Ride it out, girl; at the very least, nothing more can happen to you until morning.*

But she was wrong.

It was still the dead of night when the insistent buzz of her phone dragged her out of a surrealistic melding of all the war movies she'd ever seen. "Hello?" she answered groggily, knocking the instrument into bed with her before she could get her fingers to close on it.

"Carmen? This is Colonel Meredith. How fast can you pull yourself together and get out to Martello?"

"Uh . . . half an hour, I suppose," she said, still not fully awake. "What's, uh, going on?"

"One of the UN's ships has just arrived in orbit and is sending a shuttle down," he told her. "Aboard are our old friend Ashur Msuya . . . and President Allerton."

"Allerton?" she asked unbelievingly, the last remnants of fog evaporating in a rush.

"That's what I said—and as the old line goes, I've got a bad feeling about this. Whatever they're up to, I want you there, both as Council head and chief trade negotiator."

"Yes, sir. Are you bringing anyone else in?"

"Just you and me and possibly Major Brown. Why?"

"Well . . . I don't know, Colonel, but it sounds to me like we're about to be delivered an ultimatum. Perhaps we ought to have a small delegation there, a delegation that would more completely represent the population."

There was a short pause. "The danger is that a group like that would display a complete *lack* of unity, which I presume is the exact opposite of your intent."

"True. But Msuya, at least, already knows about the Council and the fact that you listen to it. At least occasionally."

"That's why you're going to be there."

"Yes, sir . . . but I'm not in control of the Council. I can certainly back you up on anything you say, but if the Council as a whole doesn't agree we could have trouble later."

"In other words, you think I should invite Perez," Meredith said flatly.

Carmen swallowed. "Yes, sir. And maybe Dr. Hafner, too, as representative of the scientists."

The silence this time was longer. "I suppose you're right," he said at last, reluctantly. "In the short run we can afford squabbles in front of Msuya more than we can afford riots in front of the Rooshrike. In the long run . . . well, that'll have to take care of itself. All right, I'll give them a call. Be at the Martello conference room as soon as you can; the shuttle's due in under an hour, and I'd like time to confer with you first."

Carmen already had the phone strapped to her wrist and was pulling on her underwear. "Half an hour or less, sir."

"Good. By the way—any particular reason you suggested Perez and Hafner?"

"Yes, sir. Since they've seen the Spinner cavern, I thought they might have a clearer idea of what's at stake here. That might make a difference."

He grunted. "I hope you're right. See you soon."

Chapter 21

The conference room at Martello had been put together out of two offices and a small machine shop in anticipation of face-to-whatever meetings between Carmen and alien trade representatives. It was not yet even remotely plush, but the chairs were comfortable and the table had been polished to a high gloss. Standing stiffly behind his chair, Meredith glanced around the room once more, wishing they'd had more time to work on the place. A room adequate for meeting a Ctencri merchant seemed considerably less so for a talk with the Commander in Chief.

The far door opened and a young corporal stepped in, looking about as nervous as a soldier not actually under fire can look. "Colonel Meredith: may I present the President of the United States and Mr. Ashur Msuya of the United Nations." Flattening against the door, the corporal snapped a salute as Allerton and Msuya strode past him into the room.

Followed by four quiet men in dark suits, who spread inconspicuously along the back wall. *Secret Service?* Meredith wondered. *Or did Msuya decide to bring some muscle this time?* Hiding his worry, he threw Allerton a salute of his own. "Mr. President; Mr. Msuya: welcome to Astra. I'm sorry we haven't got a more elaborate ceremony for you, but we're a bit short of brass bands here."

Allerton smiled slightly at that; Msuya didn't. "That's quite all right," the President said. "We're actually here more on business, anyway."

So we're skipping even the pretense of a casual visit. Uh-oh. "I expected that was the case, sir," he said. He gestured to the three people flanking him. "Permit me then to introduce Dr. Peter Hafner, Civilian Council Head Carmen Olivero, and Councillor Cristobal Perez, whom I've asked to sit in on the meeting. If there are no objections, of course."

"There are," Msuya said. "Having civilians here serves no useful purpose. *You* are in command on Astra, Colonel, and I for one have no patience with this 'Civilian Council' smoke-screen."

Deliberately, Meredith turned to Allerton. "Mr. President?"

"Mr. Msuya is correct in that all responsibility for Astran activities must rest with you," Allerton said. "However, if you want to consider these people as *advisors,* I think we can accept their presence."

Msuya growled something under his breath, and for an instant he and Allerton locked eyes. Then, with a fractional shrug, he pulled a chair out from the table and sat down. *So,* Meredith thought as Allerton and and the Astrans followed suit, *Allerton hasn't completely knuckled under to UN pressure yet— or at least is willing to lock horns with Msuya on minor issues.* Tucking away the information for future reference, he looked at Allerton and waited for the other's move.

It wasn't long in coming. "Colonel, we've been hearing reports recently of what must be considered unusual policy decisions coming out of your office. Your refusal to allow Mr. Msuya's scientific team to study your Spinneret cable and your abrupt dismissal of Dr. Chang's group at that same time, your inability to provide Earth with cable samples for study, and your apparent efforts toward unauthorized trade agreements have all raised questions about your fitness to command. I'd like to hear what explanations, if any, you have for your actions."

A well-rehearsed speech, Meredith thought, keeping his eyes on the President. "Am I being court-martialed, sir?" he asked bluntly.

"Not in the usual sense, no. Neither your rank nor your record are in any danger. Only—as I said—your position on Astra."

"I see." Meredith glanced once at Msuya's poker face, thinking furiously. "As far as the scientific teams are concerned, I believe my jurisdiction includes the final decision on personnel joining the colony, even if their stay is to be temporary. As the Rooshrike had retrieved the second Spinneret cable and I had already obtained assurances that they would share their test results with us, it seemed redundant and a little ridiculous to waste time with the few boxfuls of equipment we had available."

"The time was ours to waste if we chose," Msuya put in with a mildness that seemed to shelter the promise of later fireworks. "Furthermore, as a commissioned UN group we were legally outside your command authority."

"Excuse me, Mr. Msuya, but I had no independent confirmation of that fact," Meredith countered. "As I explained then, such orders or authorizations had to come through the holder of the mandate, namely the United States government." He glanced at Carmen, got a small confirming nod. "Now, as to providing Earth with cable, we're perfectly willing to do so once we figure out the best way to move it through hyperspace."

"Free of charge?" Msuya asked.

"At the very least, we'll need to be supplied with the equivalent mass in other metals—all of our customers will need to do that much. As for the price . . . we haven't decided on such terms yet."

"I see nothing requiring any decisions," Msuya said. "Astra

is UN territory; we should not have to pay for what is already ours."

"Iowa is a state of the U.S.," Meredith shrugged, "but its farmers don't give their grain away free."

Msuya arched his eyebrows. "I believe I said Astra was UN territory, not part of the U.S. Unless there is some unilateral agreement here I'm unaware of?"

"No, of course not," Allerton said, throwing an annoyed look at Meredith. "Colonel Meredith was merely making an analogy."

And a damn stupid one, too, Meredith berated himself. Msuya had a strong enough case without having extra ammunition hand-delivered to him. At his left Hafner shifted in his chair, and on his far right Perez muttered something inaudible.

"I see," Msuya said, his tone making it clear the point was merely being postponed until later. "That of course leads directly into the whole question of trade agreements and your authority to make them. Do you deny you're offering UN property—namely Spinneret cable—for sale without proper authorization?"

Meredith took a deep breath—and Carmen stepped unexpectedly into the brief pause. "It seems to me, Mr. Msuya, that we've kept very strictly to our legal duties, which I'll point out include both development *and* defense of the Astran colony. We're currently being orbited by ships of six alien races, more than half of them fully equipped warships. Do you have any idea what they could do if they thought we wanted to keep all of the Spinneret's technology and cable production for ourselves?"

"You fought off the M'zarch attack well enough."

"Through a combination of our luck and their ignorance," Meredith said. "Miss Olivero is correct: the only way to keep our neighbors peaceful is to make sure they see immediate benefits for doing so."

"So you're saying these offers of cable are basically fraudulent?" Msuya asked.

"Absolutely not," Meredith said. "Or would you have the human race stuck with a reputation as swindlers?"

"In other words, the UN had better rubberstamp your deals or else."

He was pushing hard to get Meredith into a corner; and Meredith was starting to get tired of it. "If you reject them you'd better be prepared to explain why we, as what the Rooshrike call an equal-status colony, are not permitted to make local trade arrangements. You'd better also be prepared to start any diplomatic overtures back at square one, in that event."

"All right, then"—Msuya switched tracks smoothly—"as long as you've brought it up, what about this alleged trade agreement with the Rooshrike? Or were you unaware that the UN has an exclusive contract with the Ctencri?"

"If you'll recall, Mr. Msuya, you ended your last visit to Astra by threatening us with total embargo of food and supplies," Meredith reminded him. "You made it abundantly clear that we would starve. As Miss Olivero pointed out, I had an obligation to protect Astra. Opening up an independent supply line seems to me to come under that heading."

He had the satisfaction of seeing the other frown with surprise; apparently that wasn't a defense he'd expected. "You can't protect your colony against its *owners*," he growled at last. "That's a completely ridiculous argument."

"Perhaps," Meredith shrugged. "But I have yet to see any proof that these threats and orders are the genuine will of the UN. It could just as easily be that the Ctencri are threatening Earth with an embargo of its own unless the UN obeys its orders in this matter."

Msuya stared at him for a moment, his jaw working with either rage or frustration. Then, leaning back in his chair, he gave Meredith a cold smile. "You dance exceedingly well, Colonel, especially for a military man. Let's see if you can dance out of *this*." He waved a negligent hand toward Allerton. "Mr. President?"

Allerton had the look of a bad toothache on his face. But his voice was firm enough. "Colonel Meredith, as Commander in Chief of the United States Armed Forces, I order you to comply fully with any and all instructions Mr. Msuya may give you concerning the Spinneret equipment or cable."

Meredith pursed his lips, trying hard to think. "Has the U.S. mandate been rescinded, then?" he asked in an effort to gain time.

"No, you're still in command of the colony itself. It's only the Spinneret that the UN will be handling directly."

"I see." *So we've knuckled under to threats of embargo,* he thought bitterly. "Suppose I refuse?"

Allerton didn't bat an eye, "Then you'd be relieved of duties and brought back to the States aboard the UN ship."

Meredith nodded slowly. "Which means you brought my potential successor along with you. May I ask who he is?"

"You'll be replaced by General Benigno Sandoval of the People's Republic of the Philippines," Msuya spoke up. "And, yes, he is aboard the main ship."

A puppet for Msuya to work, Meredith guessed, given the mess the ten-year-old regime had made of the Philippine economy. *Either way, the UN is going to have the Spinneret now. Unless . . .*

At his left, Hafner stirred. "May I ask, Mr. Msuya, just what you'll do with the Spinneret if you're put in charge?"

Msuya's eyes hardened briefly at the *if.* "We'll be continuing your work, mainly: learning about the equipment and how to use it."

"With all this knowledge going exclusively to the UN, as opposed to all the world's governments?"

"Primarily. We couldn't risk the leak of sensitive material to the aliens."

"I see." Hafner paused. "And the cable, too, would be UN property, I suppose. How would it be distributed to countries who want to, say, build suspension bridges with it? Free, or would you charge for it?"

"I don't see that as any of your business," Msuya told him bluntly.

"Oh, but it is," Perez spoke up. "You see, whoever is giving the orders is going to need Dr. Hafner and myself to escort all of his workers into the Spinneret control room."

"Really." Msuya favored him with a patronizing smile. "Some local union regulation, I suppose?"

"No," Perez countered tartly. "More a matter of continued breathing."

Msuya snorted. "If you mean to threaten us—"

"Not at all. If you'll permit me, I'd like to explain about the things we call *Gorgon's Heads*." In a few crisp sentences Perez described the Spinners' security machines and the apparent misunderstanding that had given five of the Astrans free passage among them. By the time he finished, Msuya's amused look had vanished completely. "So you see," Perez concluded, "we couldn't in good conscience help you unless we were convinced your plans were the best possible for the common people of Earth."

Msuya studied him, his eyes flicking briefly to Meredith and Hafner as well. Meredith held his peace, trying to figure out what exactly Perez was angling for. A UN commitment to the expanded immigration the Hispanic wanted? Or was it something more basic—personal power in the new Astran regime, perhaps?

Msuya might have been reading his mind. "I think I can assure you, Mr. Perez—and you also, Dr. Hafner—that we'll take every step necessary to make sure the Spinneret is used to benefit all mankind. I'm sure your input will be considered extremely valuable; perhaps associate directorships of Spinneret operations for you and the other three would be the proper way to make your importance official."

"An interesting offer." Perez leaned forward to look past Carmen at Meredith. "I must apologize to Colonel Meredith though—I don't believe he had finished his discussion with you and President Allerton. Colonel?—the floor is yours."

Meredith gazed at Perez's face for a heartbeat before turning back to Allerton. *What is he up to? He's got Msuya's offer—why turn the conversation back to me? Just to see if I'll go ahead and hang myself?*

"Actually, we were about finished," Allerton said. He, too, was looking at Meredith . . . and his intense expression was nearly a duplicate of Perez's. "The colonel will be turning over Spinneret operations to Mr. Msuya immediately."

Meredith braced himself. *All right, you ghouls, here I go. Watch me twist in the wind.* "No, sir, I will not," he said. "I don't feel Mr. Msuya or any other UN official can handle the Spinneret under the current conditions as well as we of Astra can, and I can't in good conscience relinquish my command to him."

"Then you're relieved of all duty," Msuya said, the satisfaction in his voice unmistakable. "General Sandoval can be down in an hour; until then—"

"One moment, sir," Perez interrupted mildly. "I don't believe the Council's been consulted on whether General Sandoval would be an acceptable replacement for Colonel Meredith."

Msuya stared at him. "What are you talking about? Who the UN appoints to oversee its territory is its own business."

Perez looked at Carmen. "Miss Olivero, I submit such an attitude toward a duly elected assembly indicates the UN's unfitness to properly manage the Spinneret."

"I agree," she said, a slight tremolo in her voice betraying her tension. "Mr. President; Mr. Msuya—pending an official vote, the Astran Council tentatively rejects Colonel Meredith's replacement."

"What sort of nonsense is this?" Msuya snorted. "Meredith is leaving Astra and that's final. If you don't like it you can send a protest to General Sandoval through one of his troops."

"'Troops'?" Hafner asked. "So now you're bringing in occupation—"

Meredith silenced him with a gesture. "Miss Olivero is right," he said quietly. "I'm not leaving Astra."

The silence from the other end of the table was thick enough to drive tent stakes into. "You will leave," Msuya said at last, "or you will be guilty of treason, both to your own country and to the UN. Your own troops will turn on you rather than share in your crime."

"Possibly. But you may overestimate their loyalty to the UN. Most of us remember your lack of genuine interest in Astra before the cables began appearing."

"You have a paltry four hundred men," Msuya barked, his control snapping at last. "I can rent a cargo cruiser from the Ctencri and have four times that many here in ten days. Do you want to see your people ground like vermin into the dust?"

Meredith lifted his left arm, tapped the phone strapped to his wrist. "In less time than it takes for your sixteen hundred men to board their shuttles, I can be in contact with the chief Rooshrike representative out there. What do you think he'd do if I told him I was being invaded and asked for his help?"

"I'd simply explain you were no longer in charge—"

"He knows me. He doesn't know you."

"The Ctencri would support our demand."

"The Ctencri have no warships here . . . and the Rooshrike aren't disposed toward doing them favors."

Msuya spat something venemous-sounding, the tightness of his jaw visible through his cheeks.

Allerton cleared his throat. "You realize, though, that Mr. Msuya is right about the legal consequences here," he said. "By disobeying my direct order you automatically draw a court-martial. All of you, in fact, will almost certainly be found in violation of various federal laws, up to and possibly including treason."

Meredith focused on him. "All Astrans who'd rather not stay under the new conditions will be allowed to leave on the next ship," he said, wishing he knew what the other was thinking. Allerton's words were harsh enough and his tone only marginally less so; but his expression was relaxed almost to the point of contentment. *Is this what he really wants?* he wondered. *Open rebellion that'll draw the UN's fire away from the U.S.? In that case he's got a real treat in store.* "For the rest of us, I expect you'll have to try us *in absentia*. But I'm not sure American laws will apply to citizens of a foreign nation."

The words hung in the air for a good three seconds before anyone else caught on. "A *what?*" Hafner whispered as Carmen and Perez turned to look at him.

Allerton's expression never changed. "You're seceding from the union, then?" he asked.

"Not really, sir—Astra never was technically U.S. territory. We *are* declaring independence, however."

Msuya slammed both fists onto the table. "This has gone far enough. Guards!—all four of these people are under arrest."

The two men to the right of the door stepped forward, small guns magically appearing in their hands. "Allerton—your men, too," Msuya snapped.

The other two guards took tentative steps forward, stopped at Allerton's signal. "The Secret Service doesn't follow your orders," the President said coolly. "They have no authority to act in a case like this and therefore will not do so."

Msuya flashed him a look of pure hatred . . . and Meredith raised his phone and flipped its speaker to nondirectional mode. "Major, did you get all of that?" he asked.

"Yes, sir," Brown's voice came back, loud enough to be heard at the far end of the table. "The Rooshrike have been alerted. A landing party is standing by."

Msuya was the first one to speak. "You're bluffing."

Meredith shook his head. "They'll come if we ask them to," he said calmly. "The last thing you're equipped for is full-scale combat."

"I could kill you and your fellow scorpions first," he spat.

"You could," Meredith acknowledged. "But you'd be killing three of the five people who have access to the Spinneret control room. If something should happen to the others you'd be locked out forever."

For a long moment Msuya sat there, frozen. Then, slowly, he stood up and gestured to his guards, who put their weapons away. "As I said once before, Colonel," he said, his voice quiet as a graveyard, "you can throw me off Astra now . . . but you *will* live to regret it. The goods shipment you've contracted for with the Rooshrike will not leave Earth; the UN and the Ctencri will see to that. The embargo against you will be vacuum-tight, and will not be lifted until Astra starves to death or you're brought to New York in chains. Think about that when you're reduced to eating sand."

Turning, he strode to the door, yanked it open, and disappeared into the night air, followed by his guards. Allerton stood up and nodded, his face carefully neutral. "I'm sure, Colonel, that you haven't heard the last of this," he said quietly. "But—unofficially, of course—I wish you luck." Without waiting for a reply, he turned and left.

"Well," Hafner breathed as the Secret Service men closed the door behind them. "He must still be in shock."

Perez pushed his chair back and let his own straight-backed posture dissolve into a tired slouch. "Not at all," he said with a sigh. "Allerton's delighted at the way things have turned out. By declaring independence we've gotten him off the hook with the UN—he's not responsible for our actions, so Saleh can't legitimately stick the U.S. with a trade embargo or whatever."

"So we get hit by it instead," Carmen murmured.

"We were going to get embargoed anyway," Perez shrugged. "At least this way the U.S. doesn't suffer."

Meredith cocked an eyebrow at him. "I was under the impression you didn't think much of the U.S.," he said.

"Not liking the government but caring about the people aren't incompatible attitudes," Perez replied.

"You just like the UN less?"

"I like the idea of UN control of Astra less," he corrected. "Like you, I believe all of us here can do a better job of administering the Spinneret than any big government. And with the Ctencri trade locked up, the UN is fast becoming a form of big government." Wearily, he got to his feet. "Colonel, if you don't need us anymore, I'd like to get back to bed."

"Of course," Meredith nodded. "You might as well all go. I'll need you alert by midmorning when I announce our new independence. I've got a feeling it's not going to go over very well."

"Don't worry, Colonel," Hafner said, yawning prodigiously as he levered himself out of his chair. "We'll probably even have a national anthem written by dinnertime."

Meredith sat quietly for a few moments after they were gone, his own eyelids feeling like stone tablets. *National anthem, indeed,* he thought. *You can tell right away how much experience he's had working with people.*

His phone buzzed: Major Brown. "The UN shuttle's ready to lift, Colonel," he reported. "Shall I let 'em go?"

"Sure." He paused, waiting. A moment later the roar of repulsers filled the room, oddly deadened by the soundproofing they'd packed into the walls. The sound faded slowly, finally reaching the point where normal conversation was possible. "Major? You still there?"

"Yes, sir," Brown growled. "Damn dizzy yahoo took it low and slow; probably trying to wake up as many people in Unie as he could."

"More likely trying to pick out the Spinneret entrance. Msuya's not going to give up that easily." He thought for a moment. "You still have a connection through to the Rooshrike?"

"Yes, sir."

"I want you to invite Beaeki nul Dies na down here for a meeting the day after tomorrow—well, tomorrow, actually, since it's already Thursday morning. Then contact all the other aliens with the same message. Set it for, oh, sixteen hundred hours."

"Friday at sixteen hundred; right," Brown said. "What do I give as the purpose of the meeting?"

"To discuss our marketing plans for the Spinneret cable . . . and to settle on a security arrangement for Astra."

Brown was silent for a moment. "You don't seriously think Saleh would send troops here, do you?"

"I don't know, but if I were him I'd take some kind of action pretty damn fast. You see, as a sovereign nation, we can make trade deals with other countries without going through the UN bureaucracy—and if that trade includes Rooshrike-supplied technology, we'll be bypassing the UN's monopoly. Saleh'll go from master of the universe back to chief referee at the world's biggest nursery school, and I can guarantee he's not going to go quietly."

"Mm. So you're meeting the aliens here to keep Msuya from eavesdropping?"

"More or less. Also to underline our new independence—I doubt that the aliens much care where we talk, but it's a symbol of authority on Earth to have people come to you instead of vice versa."

"If you don't mind my saying so, Colonel, I think we have more important things to worry about than taking symbolic pot shots at Msuya's backside. How in the world are you going to sell this to the troops and civilians, good U.S. citizens all?"

"I don't know," Meredith said frankly. "I'm sure we would have come to this point eventually—we couldn't stay UN territory forever—so it's not like the idea will be totally unimaginable. It *is* going to be a mess, though. I just hope we can keep people from going off half-cocked one way or the other before they've thought about all the pros and cons."

"We'll have to keep an eye on the troops, especially," Brown pointed out. "Leading a 'loyalist coup' might be some ambitious lieutenant's idea of a shortcut to captain."

"A lieutenant or someone higher," Meredith grimaced. "Maybe you'd better try and sound out the other area commanders before the announcement. Barner, I think, will be okay, but Gregory and Dunlop could conceivably be trouble."

"Especially Dunlop, given all the friction you've had," Brown said. "Maybe we'll be lucky and he'll decide to go back to Earth."

"Don't I wish," Meredith said sourly. "But chances are he'll stay. After all the pride he had to swallow to keep his Ceres post we probably couldn't get him out of there without a crowbar."

"Um. Well, maybe we can persuade him he's too patriotic to continue breathing this freshly sullied Astran air." Brown snorted. "Sorry—he still gets to me sometimes. One other thing I thought of, Colonel: do you think we should ask the Rooshrike to jam any attempts at broadcast communication from the UN ship?"

"Keep our propaganda unsullied by theirs?"

"Well-l-l . . . I know it sounds totalitarian, but I still think it would be a good idea. At least until you've had a chance to present our case."

"I don't really like it . . . but go ahead. Besides, Astra can't possibly qualify as a dictatorship as long as Perez is running around loose."

Brown chuckled. "He'd be almost funny if he wasn't so good at charming the brains out of people."

"Well, for once that talent's going to come in handy. Perez helped dig us into this position, and he's damn well going to help us sell it."

"I hope he can do it. Frankly, I don't know myself whether or not we're making too much of a fuss over the Spinneret."

Meredith smiled wanly. *Right again, Carmen; it* does *make a difference*. "Remind me to take you down to the Spinner cavern some day, Major. You'll see we've got something worth fighting over—and I'd just as soon keep the battles confined to words."

"Yeah." Brown paused. "Colonel, did you read how the Rooshrike went about testing their Spinneret cable's strength?"

Meredith frowned. "No, I never got to that section of their report. Why?—is it important?"

"Oh, not really. They attached a couple of five-ton asteroids to the ends and started the whole thing spinning. They had it going nearly twelve turns a minute when the gee forces tore the asteroids apart. It just occurred to me that if that's how they do their science, I don't think I'd care to see their approach to warfare."

And the Rooshrike are supposed to be technologically behind the other races, Meredith reminded himself. "Me, too," he told Brown. "Let's hope we can avoid a private demonstration. Get those messages off; I'll talk to you again after I've had some sleep."

"Yes, sir. Pleasant dreams."

Chapter 22

The roar of descending alien shuttles had long since faded away by the time Perez brought his motorboat to a stop by the Martello Base dock. "Cristobal Perez; Council member," he identified himself to the two soldiers guarding the boats. Like those at the Unie docks, they looked skeptical; but, also like the others, they called in for instructions, and a minute later Perez was walking toward the conference room. *Only forty hours since Astra became its own master—at least on paper,* he thought, his head aching with too little sleep and too much conversation. *Feels more like a week.*

Meredith had made his broadcast at ten o'clock that first morning; and while he hadn't done a bad job of describing Astra's new status, he'd left out the answers to several popular questions, and Perez had spent a great deal of the time since then giving those selfsame answers to various individuals and small groups. The worries generally revolved around the Astrans' status with the U.S. or the possible reprisals that could be taken against families and friends back on Earth. It was those conversations that lay behind most of his headache. The rest had come from the project that had kept him up most of the night.

The guards at the conference room door were a bit more stubborn, but in the end they too passed him through . . . and though Perez knew what to expect, the scene was still something of a shock. He'd seen photos of all five alien races, but there was nothing like seeing them up close and in person to drive home how alien they really were. The Ctencri, with his loose skin and batwing head crest, sat stiffly in his chair, his darting head movements vaguely reminiscent of a chicken pecking. The Whist beside him, by contrast, looked almost Buddha-like in its motionlessness . . . at least, insofar as a creature shaped like a fat mushroom with lobster claws and antennae *could* look Buddha-like. The M'zarch, resplendent in what looked like formal-wear body armor, was a hulking nightmare out of the Middle Ages, his physical presence matched only by the bear-sized Orsphis sitting across from him. Their rivalry, Perez had heard, was ancient and intense, and even without knowing either race's body language, he could sense the tension between them. He shivered involuntarily, glad he wouldn't have to approach either one of *them*. The space-suited Rooshrike was seated next to a large, torpedo-shaped tank; focusing on the latter, Perez was startled to see a tentacled dolphin floating behind the dark glass. Meredith's announcement hadn't mentioned that a Pom would be coming to the meeting; apparently they'd decided their physical representation here was worth the cost of running a water-filled shuttle down and back up. *How in the world do they launch even a shuttle-sized ship?* he wondered abruptly. *Water is* heavy.

Meredith and Carmen, seated together at the head of the table, had apparently just finished their presentation, and the air was filled with quiet chirps, hisses, and grunts as the aliens conferred with each other. Sidling around the chairs, Perez exchanged polite nods with Meredith and leaned over Carmen's shoulder. "How's it going?" he whispered, glancing over the papers scattered on the table in front of her.

"Fine, so far," she replied. "Everyone seems happy with our

proposed cable price, and they're now apparently discussing whether or not Colonel Meredith's security plan is acceptable.''

"And that is . . . ?"

"We'll allow two warships each by the Whissst and Orspham to stay in geosynch orbit, which will also be the normal parking orbit for unarmed trading ships. The Poms and Rooshrike can patrol further out, and of course will keep an eye on the approaches through their respective territories."

"The M'zarch and Ctencri don't get in on this?"

"Not for now. The M'zarch are being punished for their earlier takeover try; the Ctencri apparently don't even like admitting they *have* warships, let alone showing them around."

"Um. So if the Orspham or Whist—"

"Whissst. Longer S-sound for plural."

"Excuse me. If the Orspham or Whissst try to grab something and run they've got the whole Rooshrike space force to get through on the way out. And if anyone else gets cute, we get enough warning while they're fighting to do . . . something. Any idea what?"

"I think we're still working on that."

"Ah." Perez glanced down the table as the Rooshrike rose to his feet. "It is acceptable," his translator box said.

"Good," Meredith nodded, also standing. "Then—"

He was interrupted by a squelch sound from the direction of the Pom's tank. "It is acceptable," a more resonant voice said.

This time Meredith just nodded and waited. One by one, the M'zarch, Orsphis, Whist, and Ctencri rose to voice agreement of their own. "Thank you for your time and cooperation," Meredith said when all but the Pom were standing. "As before, all trade questions or orders should be addressed to the human Carmen Olivero, using the channels already discussed." He paused, glancing at the silent aliens. "This meeting is now over."

He turned toward Perez; and as if that was the signal they'd been waiting for, the aliens finally moved, stepping away from the table and moving generally toward the door that opened onto the landing field. "Well, at least that's settled," Perez commented, hoping to deflect Meredith from awkward questions about what he was doing here. The Ctencri, he noted, had paused to touch fingers to the Orsphis's pine cone–shaped tusks and to speak for a moment with the Whist. "And we gained another drop of social information in the bargain: the aliens' pecking order."

"You mean the order in which they accepted the agreement?" Carmen asked, collecting her papers together. "Hardly. My guess is that that was simply in order of increasing distance between Astra and their capitals."

"Oh." Across the room, the Ctencri was following the M'zarch outside. "Well, I suppose I'd better get back to the mainland. See you both later."

He caught up with the Ctencri a few meters past the door. "I'd like to speak to you for a moment, sir, if I may," he said, falling into step beside the alien.

The Ctencri stopped abruptly, twittering. "Certainly," the disk around his neck said.

Perez swallowed. Standing there together, in full view of a dozen soldiers, he felt painfully conspicuous. "I would like to ask a favor of you and your people," he told the alien. "I have some messages I would like to have quietly delivered to various people on Earth—that is, delivered without knowledge of the UN authorities."

"You wish for us to perform messenger service for you?"

"I doubt it'll be all that much work," Perez said dryly. "By now you must have built up a network of human informants in various parts of the world. My envelopes are sorted by nation; you need merely to distribute them to your agents, who can stamp and mail them."

The Ctencri seemed to be considering that. "And what payment do you offer for this service?" he asked.

"I'm sure we'll be able to work that out later," Perez told him. "A certain quantity of Spinneret cable, most likely."

"A valuable payment for so small a task."

So the Ctencri were good enough businessmen to be suspicious of something-for-nothing deals. "Not really . . . because there's a bit more to this. A number of these people—perhaps all of them—will be wanting to come here to Astra, something the Earth governments would probably try to stop if they knew about it. I'm counting on you to provide quiet transport for them."

The alien's facial features shifted, his crest simultaneously stiffening. Perez felt his leg muscles tighten in automatic response, wondering if he'd said something wrong. "You ask a great deal," the Ctencri said at last. "Have you the authority to guarantee payment?"

Perez began breathing again. "Yes, I believe I do. I am a member of the Astran Council, and am influential in other ways, as well. If you carry out your end properly, you will be adequately paid."

"Give me the messages."

Reaching under his coat, Perez dug out the fat envelope and handed it over. "You should be prepared to hear from these people within a few days after you mail the letters. I presume there are channels they can go through to get to you?"

"There are; and we will record their names for reference before the messages are delivered."

"Good. I'll expect to see the first of them here within a couple of weeks. And remember: this *must* be kept secret from the authorities."

"I remember. Is that all?"

"Uh . . . yes."

"Good-bye." Without any parting gesture Perez could detect, the Ctencri turned and continued on his way. Perez watched him a moment, then started back toward the docks. *Well, that's that,* he thought, feeling strangely nervous about the whole transaction. *In a few weeks I'll either present Meredith with a* fait accompli, *or be up to my neck in trouble. Or both.*

* * *

"A package?" Meredith asked quietly, holding his phone close to his mouth. "What sort of package?"

"About twenty centimeters by ten by maybe five," the soldier said. "Looked soft, like paper or wrapped disks instead of some kind of hardware. They talked for a couple of minutes, but we weren't able to get an eavesdropper lined up on them in time. Do you want Perez picked up, or the Ctencri shuttle barred from launching?"

Meredith pursed his lips, glancing past the phone. Beaeki nul Dies na and the Pom representative had, by prearrangement, stayed behind the general exodus for a short talk, and he didn't really want to keep them waiting. Especially not to haul the Ctencri in for some sort of questioning. Besides, at the moment neither Perez nor anyone else on Astra had any information that could possibly be considered classifiable. Once they figured out some of the Spinneret's controls . . . but that was still months or longer in the future. "No," he told the soldier. "Let them both go. I'll have someone check on Perez's recent movements and computer usage later. You're sure nothing passed the other way?"

"Positive, sir. Perez's hand wasn't in position to even palm something small."

"All right. Let me know if Perez goes anywhere but the docks; otherwise just go back to normal duty. And that was a nice bit of observation, Sergeant; expect to find a commendation logged on your record for it."

"Thank you, Colonel," the other said, pleasure clearly evident in his voice. "Just doing my job, sir."

"Carry on, then. Out."

He clicked off the phone, his irritation at Perez somewhat mollified. *For everyone like Perez, there's at least one more like Sergeant Wynsma*, he decided . . . and for the moment, at least, Astra's military force seemed pretty solidly on his side.

Of course, if things started getting tight, some of that loyalty could wear a little thin.

Carmen, sitting by the two aliens, must have been keeping at least half an eye on him, and as he lowered his arm she nodded. "All set, sir," she said. "Beaeki nul Dies na can get the tanks to us by the day after tomorrow—their mining base on the inner planet has a complete set of spares. And Waywisher says they can have a full-sized ship for our use within a month."

"Excellent." Meredith looked at Beaeki. "You've considered the fact that our plants will be very different chemically from yours?"

"We have dealt extensively with carbon-based life," the Rooshrike said. "The tanks will be perfectly compatible with your flora, especially as the lower temperatures here will make the tank materials even more inert."

Meredith nodded and turned his attention to the glass-enclosed Pom. "Waywisher, we're under no illusions as to how much rental of your ship will cost. Are you aware we can offer payment only in Spinneret cable?"

"We have need for vast amounts of your cable," the Pom's deep-voiced translator said. "We are happy to assist you in this matter as a way to defray the costs we will soon be incurring."

"I see," Meredith said, feeling a brief flicker of uneasiness. Aside from their spacecraft, the Poms supposedly built little if anything requiring great structural strength. Were they embarking on some large-scale space project, such as an orbiting habitat? Or were they planning something else—a fleet of indestructible ships, perhaps?

He put it out of his mind. The Rooshrike had thus far proven themselves to be accurate sources of information, and they'd never given any hint that the Poms were anything but peaceful. "Well, then," he said to both aliens, "we'll be ready with our end of the project by the time you deliver on yours. I believe, Beaeki nul Dies na, that your first load of metal will be delivered about the same time as the tanks?"

"Yes," the Rooshrike said. "One hundred ten metric tons, for a cable fifty kilometers in length. I trust you can make one that long?"

"I'm sure we can," Meredith said, trying to sound confident. *Well, Spinneret Incorporated is now in business,* he thought. *I hope to hell none of the equipment decides to go on strike.*

Chapter 23

The Rooshrike hydroponics tanks actually wound up arriving a day late, but as Astra's microbiologists took that long to get their cultures of gene-tailored algae going anyway, Carmen wasn't inclined to press the point. The Rooshrike ship captain, apparently used to stricter insistence on contractual fine print, seemed greatly relieved at Carmen's leniency. She accepted his thanks gracefully, but made a mental note to learn more about normal interstellar business practices as soon as possible. She didn't mind getting a reputation for fairness, but she didn't want anyone thinking they could get away with murder, either.

The metal delivery was another matter entirely, and clearly under the command of someone who knew what he was doing. The heavy-duty shuttles dropped out of the sky with clockwork precision, each gliding down on its swing-wings to the new landing region north of Mt. Olympus, discharging its cargo of scrap metal, and lifting on repulsers in time for the next shuttle to take its place. The pile of boxes grew; and as it did so, Carmen worried alternately about what would happen if the leecher kicked in prematurely, and what they'd do if it didn't kick in at all.

Fortunately, the need to explain either never arose. The last shuttle was climbing into the sky, and workers were beginning to spread the piles of boxes for better ground contact, when the leecher worked its quiet magic. Carmen was standing next to the Rooshrike project manager as the metal began sinking into the ground; and though his startled comment came out untouched by the translator, she found herself nodding in full agreement.

There were some things that were universal.

In the Spinneret control tower the mood was considerably less philosophical, hovering as it did between excitement and frustration. "It's starting," Major Barner reported, holding his headphone tight against his ear. "Leecher's gone on."

Hafner nodded, his eyes sweeping the garish control board and trying to follow the changes in the pattern of lights. It was an unnecessary exercise, of course; the cameras that had been painstakingly set up were recording every square millimeter of the tower's controls, as well as synching their data with a hundred other monitors both above and below ground. But Hafner felt useless enough here as it was, and studying the indicator lights was better than doing nothing.

The short-range radio crackled in his ear. "Got something on level ten," one of the other observers reported. "Whole bank suddenly lit up. Anything happening to correlate?"

"Hang on, I'll check." Hafner relayed the message to Barner, then stood chafing as the other checked his own comm net. The most painful part of this, Hafner knew, was that he had originally agreed with Meredith's insistence that only a single long-range radio be allowed at each observation point. From a security standpoint it still made sense; but Hafner hadn't counted on the frustration such an awkward setup would generate. *First a den mother, now an organic telephone relay*, he groused inwardly, staring at the vigilant Gorgon's Heads flanking the doorway. *Why should we really care if someone gets a peek at the controls, anyway? How would they get in to do anything—bribe one of the Gorgon's Heads?*

"The long coil's starting up," Barner announced.

Hafner's mind snapped out of its reverie. "You mean that solenoid that knocks flyers out of the sky?"

"That's the one." Barner listened a moment longer. "Hope it's all right—it's got a hum they can hear right through the wall, and the pitch has changed twice already."

Hafner frowned, raised his radio. "Stimmons? Have those lights changed at all?"

"Yeah: two of 'em have gone out. And listen—I just figured out what the light pattern reminds me of. It's almost like a periodic table with the top right-hand section chopped out—"

"All the nonmetals?" Hafner interjected.

"Yeah. But there's also three more rows of lights underneath where the actinide series usually goes."

Barner had moved close enough to hear both sides of the conversation. "I thought there were only a hundred and seven elements."

"Maybe the Spinners found some new ones," Hafner suggested. "The cable's made out of *something* we don't know about."

"So what is the coil doing, sorting out the metal that's coming in by element?"

"That'd be my guess," Hafner said, a little surprised at Barner's quickness. "They could be running the solenoid like a giant linear accelerator, where the frequency of the driving electric fields will depend on both the mass and charge of the ions being accelerated. Either it's keyed to go through each element in sequence, or else the stuff that's coming in determines what goes through first."

"Mm. You know, this whole place is using up one hell of a lot of power. You had any indication yet where it's coming from?"

"Probably put their generator at the end of a tunnel somewhere. That's sure where *I*—" He broke off as Barner's face abruptly changed. "What's wrong?"

"Doctor," the major said slowly, "that coil down there. If it can knock out a flyer's repulsers a thousand meters up . . . what's it doing to the men in the tunnel with it?"

"Why . . ." Hafner felt his mouth go dry. The medical people *had* okayed all of the observer positions . . . hadn't they? "But weren't you just talking to them?"

"No—it was the men in the outside hall." Barner was tapping the call signal. "Edmonds, are you in contact with the men inside? . . . No, I mean since the humming started? . . . Damn. Get that door open and—"

"Wait a second," Hafner interrupted. "Ask them to test first for electric field strength in the hallway where they are. If there's no reading, the wall may be acting as a shield, and they'd better not breech it."

"It doesn't matter," Barner said quietly. "The door won't open anyway. It seems to have locked itself."

Hafner stared at him, then let out a quiet sigh and turned away.

The solenoid ran for another two hours before finally shutting both itself and the door safety interlocks off. The two men who'd been inside were found in contorted positions against the door, dead.

And at sundown, in full mechanical indifference, the Spinneret sent its cable out toward the equally uncaring stars.

Two more men, Meredith thought wearily, his eyes fogging slightly as he read the report. *Two more men*.

Sighing, he leaned back in his chair and stared out the open window into the darkness outside. It was late, and he knew he'd pay for that the next day, but his mind was far too keyed up to sleep. The whole event had come off virtually without a hitch: they'd successfully produced a cable to order, had taken disks and disks' worth of data on the Spinneret's operation, had obtained their first clues as to what boards in the tower controlled which activity.

And the deaths of two men had turned it all to ashes.

There was a tap at his open door, and Meredith looked up to see Carmen standing there. "Up late, aren't you?" he asked, waving her to a chair and flipping his terminal to standby.

"I saw your light and thought I'd drop in on my way home," she said, sitting down and handing him a disk. "You might be interested to know we now have an official balance with the Rooshrike of just over one point eight billion dollars."

"Which makes us either a fair-sized corporation or a small country," he grunted, plugging in the disk and scanning the financial data recorded there. "That's, what, two billion minus the hydroponics tanks?"

She nodded. "And we've got several hundred million in other stuff on order, so this won't last very long. But for the moment, at least, we're rich."

"Um." Ejecting the disk, he handed it back. "I trust the Rooshrike are happy with their new plaything?"

"Delighted. Last I knew they'd caught one end of it and were starting a long, leisurely turn toward the proper shift direction."

"I hope the cable shifts with them."

"It should. Sileacs tal Mors kith indicated they've done some tests with normal cables trailing behind starships. Besides, the Spinners obviously got the stuff out of the system." She paused, her eyes searching his face. "I understand we lost a couple of men today."

Meredith nodded grimly. "Burned-out brains or something— none of our doctors are really sure of the exact mechanism."

"I didn't realize electric fields could kill."

"Neither did I. Neither, apparently, did anyone else." He sighed. "Looks like Perez is going to turn out right again. We're simply not going to be able to handle everything here by ourselves. The colony population was designed for geological studies and farming—period. Dr. Hafner and the others have made some damn good guesses all the way down the line, but none of us really knows what we're doing down there. It's a wonder more people haven't gotten themselves killed."

"So what's the answer?" Carmen asked after a moment. "Import experts from Earth?"

"It's that or let the aliens in on it. The real question is whether Saleh will be hard-nosed about it and lump people in with everything else he's embargoing."

"You're going to be making a list of people you'd like to invite?"

He raised an eyebrow. "You've been talking to Perez, have you? Ah" —he added as the light dawned—"it was *you* who pulled the *Scientific Directory* out of cold storage for him to give to the Ctencri, wasn't it?"

She blushed violently, but almost instantly the color vanished into a look of surprise. "He did *what*? But—he said he only wanted to make up his own list for the scientists to vote on."

"Apparently he decided to skip the procedural details," Meredith said dryly. "He must have given the Ctencri a stack of invitations to deliver. I wonder how he expects them to get the UN to provide transport."

Carmen still looked confused. "But how did you know—I mean—"

"We checked his computer usage after he gave a packet to the Ctencri at the security meeting. He hadn't gotten around yet to clearing the file you dumped the *Scientific Directory* into." He smiled briefly as she suddenly looked stricken again. "Don't worry; I'm not mad at you for doing it—he would have gotten in one way or another. There's probably no real harm done, though I'm going to wring his tail for bypassing me like that."

"Only if I don't get to him first," Carmen growled. "That smooth-talking—"

"Save your anger," Meredith advised. "Consider him as now owing you a big favor, and make sure he knows it. It may help keep him in line."

"I doubt it." Carmen shook her head. "I just can't figure him out, Colonel. One minute he's on our side, and the next minute he's pulling something underhanded like this."

Meredith shrugged. "He's *never* been on our side; we've just occasionally been on *his*. He has a vision for Astra and has been pushing us toward it ever since he got here."

Carmen's lip twitched. "Yes—his paradise for the poor of Earth. Probably want to put a duplicate of the Statue of Liberty in orbit somewhere."

"Actually, as matters stand now, his huddling masses are probably the only new colonists we're likely to get. Permission to leave Earth lies with individual nations and, ultimately, the UN, and Saleh's not likely to let us lure away the brightest and best."

"Which means," Carmen said slowly, "that unless the Ctencri are personally bringing Cris's scientists here, they're probably not coming."

"Probably." Meredith glanced at his watch. "Well, I'd better let you get home. You're bound to be busy taking orders tomorrow after the way today's operation went."

"Yes." Carmen sighed and got to her feet. "Are we going to have a proper funeral, or are you going to keep the deaths secret from the aliens by giving them a private burial somewhere?"

"We'll have a funeral. We don't have to advertise how they died." Hitching his chair closer to the desk, he reactivated his terminal. Taking the cue, Carmen left.

For a moment Meredith stared through the terminal, wondering for the millionth time why this burden had fallen to him. *I never asked for this*, he reminded the universe resentfully. *I wanted to make Astra a modest success, collect my brigadier's star, and go home. Why the hell couldn't the Spinners have turned off their damned voodoo machine when they left?*

The terminal had no answer for him. Shaking his head, Meredith cleared his mind of questions and got back to work. At least, he told himself, he'd soon have some experts here to help share the load—presuming, of course, that the Ctencri came through on their end of Perez's deal.

* * *

Loretta Williams was just putting the vegetables on the stove when the doorbell rang. "Kirk, can you get that?" she called, grabbing the potholders. "I've got to get the roast out."

"Sure, Mom," the teen's laconic voice came from their tiny living room.

Preoccupied with the roast, Loretta didn't hear the door open; but the next thing she knew, Kirk was standing in the kitchen doorway. "Couple of guys to see you," he announced. "They say they're from the government."

Her first thought was that it had something to do with her latest grant request; but even as it occurred to her that National Science Foundation officials worked a strict nine-to-four day, she turned and got her first look at the men behind her son . . . and all thoughts of science evaporated. Attired in common business suits, they could have been bureaucrats from anywhere in Washington . . . until you saw their faces. . . .

"Dr. Williams?" the taller of the two asked.

"Yes," Loretta acknowledged, stepping forward and handing Kirk the potholders. *IRS?* she wondered. *Or even FBI?* The second man looked vaguely Iranian; could this be about that pottery fragment she'd brought back from the Dasht-i-Kavir?

The tall man already had his wallet open. "I'm Stryker; CIA. This is Mr. Taraki from the UN. We'd like to talk to you for a few minutes."

"All right," Loretta said through dry lips.. The *CIA?* "Kirk, please finish getting dinner ready; you and Lissa can start eating without me."

Closing the kitchen door behind her, she led the men to the farthest corner of the living room. It wasn't until they were all seated that she noticed they'd subtly maneuvered her into the corner chair, putting themselves between her and any exit. Consciously relaxing her jaw, she waited for the axe to fall.

"Dr. Williams, I have a letter here for you," Taraki said, his English good but with a strong accent—Farsi or one of its dialects, she tentatively identified it. Pulling an envelope from his pocket, he handed it to her.

The seal was already broken, she noticed as she withdrew the paper. The letter was short, but its message left her with the feeling of having been out in the desert sun too long. She read it twice, hoping that would help. It didn't.

Finally, she looked up. "I really don't know what to say," she murmured. When neither man spoke, she went on, "I mean, I recognize that Astra is a trouble spot right now, but it's still flattering to be invited to go work on translating the Spinner language."

"Would you like to go?" Stryker asked.

She hesitated, wishing she'd kept more up to date on the flap going on out there. "I'd *like* to, yes. But I thought the UN had banned travel to Astra for the time being."

"It has," Taraki said. "Your letter was brought to Earth aboard a Ctencri ship. You were supposed to sneak out the same way."

So that's what the business about contacting the Ctencri was all about, she thought, her eyes flicking to that part of the letter. "Oh. That sounds . . . rather illegal."

"It depends," Stryker shrugged. "How good an American do you consider yourself to be?"

"Why, I—pretty good, I suppose," she managed, taken somewhat aback by the question.

"And what do you think of the UN?" the CIA man continued.

Loretta shot a glance at Taraki's impassive face. "The tirades against America annoy me sometimes, but they've done a lot of good in the poorer nations. I guess that, on the whole, I support them."

The two men exchanged looks, and Loretta caught Taraki's shrug and fractional nod. "In that case," Stryker said, turning back to Loretta, "we'd like you to accept the invitation . . . on one condition." He paused. "That you agree to turn over all your findings directly to the UN."

She looked at them for a half-dozen heartbeats, shifting her eyes back and forth between their faces. "You want me to be a spy," she said at last, trying hard to keep the distaste out of her voice.

Taraki apparently heard it anyway. "You seem to think that working against traitors to humanity is somehow wrong," he said. "The colonists are attempting to keep the Spinneret for themselves, in violation of orders from both Secretary-General Saleh and your own President Allerton. If a group of terrorists were planning to mine the Strait of Hormuz or reconstruct the smallpox virus, would your conscience also act irrationally?"

"I—well, no, probably not. But the Astran colonists aren't terrorists—they're just normal American citizens, most of them—"

"Not anymore," Stryker interrupted quietly. "They've declared total independence from Earth."

She sat for a moment in silence, trying to digest that. Surely something *that* newsworthy would have penetrated even her normal inattention to such things. Which meant the government was keeping the news a secret. Which meant . . . what? "I'm very sorry, Mr. Stryker; Mr. Taraki," she said. "But I really don't think I could do what you're asking."

Stryker pursed his lips. "Actually, Dr. Williams, I'm afraid you really don't have a choice. You're the only linguist on the Astran list who possesses both the skill and the—ah, other qualities—that we're looking for. If you won't go voluntarily, the President has prepared a special executive order drafting you into the armed forces."

Loretta licked her lips. Two thoughts—*that's a pretty totalitarian thing to do* and *things on Astra must really have them worried*—chased each other around her mind. But it was all simply mental gymnastics. Confronted with an order like that, she knew she'd give in. It was far too late in her life to learn how to buck that kind of authority. "I'll need a few days to make arrangements with the university," she said. "Also, to have someone look after my children—"

"All taken care of," Stryker said as he and Taraki stood up.

"A car will pick you and your children up at nine tomorrow morning."

"Wait a minute," she put in as they turned toward the door. "Why do Kirk and Lissa have to come, too?"

"We'll be announcing Astra's rebellion sometime in the next week," Stryker told her. "At some point your supposed collaboration may leak out, and of course we won't be able to explain your true role anytime soon. There could conceivably be violence, and we'd rather your kids be where we can protect them."

"Oh." Loretta's throat felt tight. That was an aspect to this that hadn't occurred to her. "But . . . what about school and—"

"It'll all be taken care of, Doctor; trust us," the CIA man told her soothingly. "They'll be fine—and when you come home they'll get to share in the honor you'll have earned. Now, don't worry about anything, and be ready to leave at nine tomorrow. And thank you."

She saw them out, then walked slowly back to the kitchen. Kirk and Lissa were nearly finished, their usual bickering subdued by the knowledge that something unusual was going on. She broke the news as best she could, which they fortunately took without argument or complaint. *It's something that has to be done,* Loretta thought as she dished out her own food, *and it's now up to me to do it. Who knows?—maybe I'll find out being a spy queen is a lot of fun.*

But despite the pep talk, the expensive roast still tasted like so much warm cardboard . . . and she was long falling asleep that night.

Chapter 24

Carmen had done a fair amount of scuba diving back on Earth, and during the long trip to Astra she'd had several chances to experience weightlessness. The combination of the two, though, was something that took getting used to.

Floating in the center of the Pom ship, flapping her hands slowly against the gentle sternward currents, she focused her attention away from her rebellious stomach and onto the circle of huge windows set into the hull around her. Through one of them Astra's sun was visible, its light filling the chamber and turning the water into a brilliant green fog. "Impressive," she said carefully, keeping her facial movements to a minimum. The full-face mask wasn't supposed to leak unless mishandled, but she had only Lieutenant Andrews's word for that, and she had no wish to have any of this gunk inside with her.

"Thank you," said a deep voice in her ear. The Pom had been drifting toward the windows; with a powerful flip of his tail he rolled over and returned to Carmen's side. She caught just a glimpse of a small black cube in his tentacle as it was slipped back into a pocket on the alien's harness. "Light intensities seem to be within a few percent of optimal," the translator voice continued. "It's still too early to get a good growth curve for the algae, but that should only take another few hours."

"Good." A second Pom swooped in out of the murk, his wake catching Carmen and starting her spinning. She flailed a bit, managed to stop herself. *Like being in the porpoise tank at the aquarium,* the thought struck her. *At feeding time,* she added as a third Pom brushed casually between her legs to join the party. For a moment the three aliens drifted together like spokes of a wheel, their noses almost touching as they conferred. Then they broke formation and her earphone came alive again.

"The flow speed is now properly adjusted," the Pom leader informed her. "The algae will have the proper light and dark periods for maximum growth."

"Good. Will your extractors be able to handle the output?"

"Certainly. The usual crop for this design of ship grows nearly twice as quickly as yours will."

"Interesting. We might like to purchase a sample for study. If it proves compatible with our chemistry we might try switching products."

"You would do better, in all honesty, to rent a second ship. The expense and difficulty of cleaning a ship this size is prohibitive."

"Oh. Still, you've done it at least once."

"With this ship? Not true. It was a new craft, water-filled but not yet seeded. We were all fortunate the timing worked out so well."

"Indeed," Carmen nodded. Textured algae foods wouldn't be the ultimate solution to Astra's supply problems, but for the time being they would enable the colony to stretch out its stockpile well into the next growing season. *As soon as the output and delivery system stabilize,* she decided, *we can switch the Rooshrike's ground tanks to normal vegetable production. I*

*wonder if we could support any livestock yet . . . or how we'd
get hold of them, for that matter.*

"If you're finished with your inspection," the Pom said, "I
believe Waywisher would like to speak with you in private in
the control area."

"All right." *Probably wants to discuss rental fees,* she
decided, kicking herself toward the hull where the currents
would make noseward motion easier. Two of the three Poms fell
into formation beside her, the third disappearing somewhere
back toward the stern. A half-dozen openings led forward from
the central room; picking one at random, she swam through it,
flicking on her light as the sunlight faded behind her. The
"darkroom," as she'd privately dubbed it, was nearly as big as
the area they'd just left and just as full of algae. Fortunately, the
exit hatch was rimmed with red-orange lights, and she was able
to find it without assistance. The lock was big enough for all
three of them, a definite plus for visitors who didn't have the
sort of manipulative equipment the mechanism had been
designed for. After the warmth of the algae tank the clean water
flooding in felt like the North Atlantic, and she was glad when
the inner door finally opened and she could get her arms and
legs moving again.

If the algae tanks had reminded her of an aquarium, the
forward part of the ship was nothing less than a 3-D mouse
maze lined with Christmas lights and sunk in water. She
assumed that the sudden twists and turns in the corridors made
some kind of sense, but on the basis of a single visit she couldn't
figure out exactly how. *Must have an interesting room layout,*
she thought as they negotiated two right-angle turns in less than
four meters. *I'd hate to be on a landing party assigned to take
this ship.* The thought reminded her of the question Meredith
had wanted her to ask while she was here, and she spent the rest
of the swim trying to come up with a polite way to phrase it.

They emerged from the maze into a control room whose
impressiveness lay less in lights and gadgetry than in the quiet

competence she could sense in the Poms on duty there. Off to one side, floating next to a porthole, was the alien she recognized as Waywisher. As she turned in his direction he flipped his tail, timing his movement to meet her exactly halfway.

"Good day, Miss Olivero," the translator said as Waywisher swam around her in a brief pattern she took for a Pom welcome dance. Possibly a sign of responsibility as well, she decided, noting that her escort withdrew to the other side of the room as it ended. "I trust the ship has been set up to your satisfaction?"

"It seems to be, so far," she said. "We'll know in a few days or weeks, after the whole system reaches equilibrium. You wished to talk privately with me?"

"Yes." There was a brief hum on the circuit, and when the translator voice began again it had changed subtly in tone. "We are now cut off from communication with either of our species. I would like to offer you a barter: information for credit against Spinneret cable."

"Indeed?" Carmen asked, trying to dislodge the tight knot that had abruptly formed in her stomach. "What sort of information?"

"We have formulated self-consistent hypotheses concerning both the cable material itself and the 'glue,' as you call it, with which it is coated. We will trade this information for a credit of one trillion dollars."

"That's a lot of money," Carmen said. "What makes you think the information is that valuable?"

"It is unlikely your science will be able to provide you with these insights in the foreseeable future. However, once you have been put on the right track, your progress toward understanding and control of the Spinneret will undoubtedly be greatly enhanced."

"What makes you think we don't have control and understanding now?"

"Two of your fellows died during or shortly after the first Rooshrike cable operation. The conclusion is obvious."

Carmen pursed her lips tightly. "All right. Then as long as we're on the subject anyway, some of us would like to know why you want so much cable. It seems to us that, living under water, the possible uses for something this strong would be extremely limited."

If Waywisher was annoyed by the question, neither his manner nor his words showed it. "It's precisely *because* of our habitat that we need the cable so desperately. Tell me, how do you think we launch our ships into space?"

"Why—" She fumbled at the sudden change of subject. "I assume you do like everyone else: build the ships in orbit with material brought up in shuttles."

"No. For us it turns out to be more economical to build them on the planet surface"—*under water,* Carmen's mind edited in—"and then launch them essentially empty, with only the control areas flooded and most of the crew packed into small boxes under artificial hibernation. A skeleton crew then guides the ship to the nearest ringed gas giant planet—or asteroid belt, if the system is fortunate enough to have one—and spends up to a year mining enough ice to fill the ship. Only then can the crew be revived and the ship made fully functional."

"Complicated," Carmen murmured.

"And very costly," the Pom said. "One of every twenty-eight who undergo hibernation does not survive the revival procedure."

Carmen swallowed. "You must want very badly to go into space."

"The oceans of our home are wide and unbounded; we have always been a people who swam freely wherever we chose. Should we now be bound to the surface of a single world?" The Pom's fins rippled restlessly for a moment, and Carmen had the sudden feeling she'd been granted a brief glimpse into the innermost workings of the Pom psyche. *Odd,* she thought, *how*

*the translators tend to mask how really alien we are to each
other. I wonder whether that's a strength or a weakness of the
whole technique*? An interesting thought; but before she had
time to follow it any further, Waywisher had composed himself.
"It's for this reason we desire your cable," he said. "With it we
will build a device with which we may bring our ships directly
to space."

And suddenly Carmen understood. "You're going to build a
skyhook, aren't you? Run a Spinneret cable from orbit to the
surface and use it like an elevator."

The Pom's tentacles rippled. "You're familiar with such
devices? Astonishing!"

"Only the theory," Carmen admitted, dredging her memory
for any details she may have squirreled away. "We worked that
out—oh, at least half a century ago, I think. I don't know if we
never came up with anything strong enough to build it or if
someone found a flaw in the theory or what."

"There are no theoretical flaws, but we've found no material
strong enough for our needs. Until now."

"Yes, the cable would be ideal, wouldn't it?" Was that what
the Spinners had used it for? "A trillion dollars is still a lot of
money, though. For good, *hard* data we might be willing. But I
want an overview first, some idea of what exactly we'd be
paying for."

"I suppose that's not unreasonable," Waywisher said after a
short pause. "Very well. Our first clues came from the
Rooshrike heat tests on their first cable. As you know, it
becomes superconducting at relatively low temperatures, dis-
tributing the applied heat evenly through its mass. What you
may *not* know is that at higher temperatures it begins to show an
almost black-body radiation spectrum, but with gaps that
resemble absorption lines for various metals. At higher temperatures still the lines disappear."

"Yes, the Rooshrike report mentioned all that. There were
some lines like those of simple molecules, too—titanium oxide,

I think, and one or two others. I didn't know they'd given the data to anyone but us."

"They didn't. But they did their tests in space, and we had a probe nearby."

"Ah." It was becoming increasingly hard for Carmen to maintain her old image of the Poms as gentle, guileless creatures. "They seemed to think it indicated the presence of nontransmuted metals in the cable skin."

"Not true. The strength of the cable indicates it to be a perfectly homogeneous material."

"Why? A lot of alloys are stronger than their constituent metals."

"True. But alloys cannot be internally bonded by enhanced nuclear force."

Carmen's skin prickled. The Poms' mastery of nuclear forces was supposed to be what had allowed them to develop an underwater technology in the first place, and it was a secret they'd guarded jealously from other races. If *that* was what they were offering. . . . "You've done that kind of bonding yourselves?" she asked, as casually as possible.

"Yes." Waywisher's fins and tentacles ripped restlessly, a mute indication of how much this revelation was costing him. "The theory is quite straightforward, though application can be difficult, and under it the 'glue' can also be partially explained as a stepwise-enhanced edge effect. The absorptionlike spectrum lines would then be due to weak force-electromagnetic coupling between nuclear fluctuations and the electron shell response. Is all of this translating properly?"

"I think so," Carmen said, the taste of irony in her mouth. All the talk on Astra of protecting the Spinneret's secrets—and here the Poms had been using those same secrets for centuries. "I'm not a scientist, but all the words sound familiar. So why are you bothering to buy *our* cable when you can make your own?"

Waywisher barked, an almost seal-like sound the translator

didn't touch. "We've mastered the technique only for the lightest metals; the difficulty, as well as the material's final strength, increases rapidly with atomic weight. If our theory is correct, the Spinneret cable is composed of an entirely new element with weight approximately three hundred seventy times that of hydrogen . . . and its actual tensile strength around ten to the twelfth pounds per square inch."

Which was, Carmen realized with a shiver, a thousand times as strong as the lower limit the Rooshrike had established for it. "I don't *believe* it," she murmured.

"The numbers are accurate to within ten percent."

"No, I didn't mean that—I was just talking to myself." She took a moment to get her brain back on its rails. "You've got the whole thing—theory, numbers, speculations—all written out for us?"

"I have it with me now. It's on a disk compatible with the reader we delivered to Colonel Meredith four days ago."

"All right, then," Carmen nodded. "A trillion dollars in cable for the disk. You still have to supply however many tons of metal that'll come to, I'm afraid."

"That will be acceptable." Waywisher's left tentacle probed into his harness, emerged with a flat package. "I don't suppose I have to warn you that this information is a great secret of the Pom people, and that its contents are not to be given to any other people."

"Of course," Carmen nodded, taking the package gingerly. "The very fact we've got it at all will only be known by a few select people. We, uh, are honored by your trust."

"We have little choice." Waywisher's fins were undulating gently, and Carmen suddenly realized the two of them had begun drifting toward the outer lock and her waiting shuttle. "You have something we need; it isn't trust to offer something of equal value in exchange for it. Besides, your military weakness prevents you from the casual betrayal an empire might consider. Should you do so, your destruction would follow quickly."

Carmen swallowed. "And we value *your* friendship, too," she murmured.

With a flip of his tail Waywisher drove them the last meter to lock, steadying Carmen with one tentacle as he worked the mechanism with the other. "Good-bye, Miss Olivero. We look forward to a long and harmonious relationship between our peoples."

"As do we," Carmen nodded, kicking backward into the lock. "Good-bye, Waywisher."

Especially, she added to herself as the lock door slid shut, *a long one.*

Lieutenant Andrews was looking more than a little worried when she finally emerged from the lock's air dryer into the shuttle passenger bay. "You all right?" he asked, helping her maneuver the weightless but massive oxygen tanks into their jury-rigged latches.

"Sure," she said, exchanging her fins and mask for a pair of soft boots. "Why do you ask? Just because you lose your monitor for a few—"

"So you knew about that, did you?" His eyes probed her face, flicked to the package Waywisher had given her. "It wasn't equipment failure, then, I take it. Waywisher really meant it when he asked for a private chat?"

"Something like that. I'm not at liberty to discuss it with anyone but Colonel Meredith. I'm sorry."

Andrews shrugged. "It's okay by me—secrets I can't tell anyone else just add frustration to my life, anyway. You might as well go back and change, though," he added as she headed for one of the crash chairs. "We're going to be up here for another orbit."

She frowned. "Why?"

He grinned. "Because there's a Ctencri shuttle making its

approach now and Major Brown wants it to have lots of room. As befits incoming VIPs."

"VIPs? You mean . . . ?"

"Yep. Perez's little gamble paid off. The scientific cavalry has arrived."

Chapter 25

Loretta Williams would hardly have thought of herself as part of a cavalry, given both the number and loyalty of the group sitting together along one side of the conference table. A five-person guerrilla force, perhaps; a team dedicated to the ultimate overthrow of a depraved dictator and his gang of traitors. It was a noble and—she had to admit it—rather romantic image, one which had been so strongly emphasized during both their training and the voyage to Astra that she'd almost come to believe it.

Except that Colonel Meredith didn't strike her as the depraved dictator type.

It wasn't simply a matter of appearances, either. Loretta had ranged over sizable portions of the world in her fieldwork days, and she'd developed a knack for judging people by speech patterns and body language. Standing at the end of the table, describing the Spinneret cavern and the somewhat Spartan life that was all Astra currently had to offer, he seemed much more like an earnest if misguided department head than a power- or profit-hungry despot. Maybe, though, he was simply an excellent actor. She hoped that was it; and unless and until events proved otherwise it would be the only safe assumption to make.

The meeting took about an hour, and afterward they were taken by flyer to what looked like an army camp next to the lake Meredith had called the Dead Sea. Only a handful of permanent structures were yet in evidence, but each of the five scientists was assigned to one of them. From the outside they looked rather repulsive, enough so that the homey interior Loretta walked into was a pleasant surprise. Her luggage was stacked neatly by her bed—*probably searched during the meeting,* she decided—and after a quick tour through the house's four rooms she began to unpack.

She was interrupted halfway through the second suitcase by a quiet knock at the door. Opening it, she found a pleasant-looking young man in civilian clothing. "Yes?" she asked.

"Dr. Williams? I'm Al Nichols, one of the people who'll be working with you here. I trust I'm not butting into anything important—like sleep?"

"Oh, no," she assured him. "Please come in, Dr. Nichols."

"Al," he corrected, stepping past her and glancing around the room. "Not bad—I didn't know they'd gotten these places fixed up this nicely. I just dropped by to meet you and welcome you on behalf of Astra's scientific community. I trust you had a good trip?"

"It was all right—not much to do, though. Uh—can I get you something to drink? Though I'm not sure yet what exactly I've got."

He grinned. "No, thanks. And your selection's not going to overwhelm you by its diversity, I'm afraid. For the moment, anyway, we've got lots of money and nothing very interesting to spend it on. Sort of like being a millionaire in Idaho."

She smiled, some of his cheerfulness penetrating her mental shield. "Why don't we sit down, then, and you can tell me all about the Spinneret."

"By and large, it's a great alien machine that generates

indestructible cables and nervous ulcers," he said, sitting down at one end of the couch as Loretta took the chair opposite. "The *Scientific Directory* lists you as one of the best paleographers around, but I think you're going to have the challenge of your life in there." He jerked his thumb toward the picture window, where the tunnel doors Meredith had mentioned were just visible beyond the rows of tents.

"I'm looking forward to it," she said. "Are you a linguist, too?"

He snorted. "Hardly. By training I'm a geologist, but since I was stuck with Spinneret duty anyway it was either change specialties or go nuts with boredom. Luckily, I didn't have to start the whole field from scratch—we've got a very nice translation computer system the Rooshrike bought from the Ctencri for us. I've been busy transcribing the Spinner control and indicator labels into it, but so far we haven't got anything but hints as to what any of it means."

"I see," she nodded, wondering why he'd been stuck with the job. No one else with any more experience? "Well, I have some practice in figuring out unknown languages. Together we ought to be able to crack it."

"I hope so." Nichols glanced at his watch. "Oops—duty calls. I've got to escort the next shift into the tower." He got to his feet. "Maybe when you're settled in you could give me a call and I could show you what I've been doing," he suggested as Loretta walked him to the door. "My number'll be in your directory, and if I'm in the cavern someone'll take a message."

"I'll do that," she promised. "Thanks for dropping by."

"Sure. See you later."

She closed the door behind him and went back to the living room, where she watched for a moment as he jogged toward the tunnel. Then, with a sigh, she turned back to the bedroom and her unpacking. For a few moments things had been normal again; she'd just been one normal scientist conferring with another on a project of mutual interest. But that warm, comfortable feeling was fading quickly now. *This whole thing would be a lot easier,* she though bleakly, *if the people at least felt a little phony. Maybe the facade will crack after we've been here for a few days. I sure hope so.*

But, somehow, she didn't think it would.

"One more good squirt should do it," the young chemist said, his voice muffled by both his filter mask and the natural damping within the cramped tunnel. Perez nodded silently, wishing he hadn't volunteered for this job and simultaneously glad he didn't have to be the one to drip hydrofluoric acid onto the stone blocking the Spinner digging machine's tread. From the shuffling of feet behind him, he gathered he wasn't the only one glad of it.

It had been a dead-dull day all around. Meredith had decided he wanted the diggers looked at, and the four-man group had accordingly been sent out on a grand tour of the Spinneret's outer tunnel network. They'd spent six hours and located eight machines . . . and in the end only this one—the one Meredith had found on that very first trip—had a hope in hell of being restored without a complete maintenance manual. Perez's part had consisted mainly of standing around watching for Gorgon's Heads that were ranging more and more widely as human activity in the cavern increased. No one knew whether the digging machines were on the Gorgon's Heads' restricted list or not, but it wasn't a smart chance to take. Their single experience with Gorgon's Head enforcement to date indicated the machines were programmed to simply hold potential intruders for questioning; what was still needed was a way to explain the sensitivity of the human neck to them.

"She's moving!" the chemist barked, scrambling a hasty couple of steps backward. "Come *on* . . . there!"

And with a loud *crack,* the remains of the offending stone were kicked free. A low hum was almost instantly drowned out by a raucous grinding noise as the machine hit the tunnel face and began boring into it. "Just like it'd never quit," the chemist shouted over the noise. "Figured we'd at least have to find a reset switch."

"Probably been monitoring itself, waiting for someone to take the stone out," Perez shouted back. The digger was a good couple of centimeters into the rock now, and though Perez couldn't see where the fragments were going, it was clear they weren't simply being scattered around. "Let's get back to the cavern."

They made their way back to their car, parked outside the digger's tunnel, and headed inward toward the main entrance gallery. There was little conversation—everyone seemed equally tired—and Perez took advantage of the quiet to just sit and think. The scientists he'd invited to Astra could be here any time now, and he still had to figure out what he was going to tell Meredith when they suddenly showed up.

An operations center had been set up just inside the Spinner cavern, a sort of open-air office that clashed badly with the alien scenery beyond it. Perez turned in their car, was told Meredith wanted him in the tower, and checked the vehicle back out again with a sigh. Driving to the nearest gap in the Great Wall, as it was now generally called, he headed across the open area around the tower on foot. The twenty-minute round trip was an annoying waste of time, but none of the wall's gaps was big enough for a car to fit through. Carmen had ordered some golf cart-style vehicles from the Ctencri, but they'd been hung up by the need for major modifications, and until they arrived, there was nothing to do but put up with the forced exercise.

Meredith, as he expected, was in the tower's main control room, along with Major Barner, whose shift it was. What he *hadn't* anticipated was that the two of them would have guests . . . or who those guests could be.

"Ah, Perez," Meredith nodded. "I have a couple of people here I'd like you to meet. Dr. Bhartkumar Udani, Dr. Victor Ermakov; this is Councillor Cristobal Perez. Doubtless you'll recognize him as the gentleman who wrote you about coming here."

Seldom had Perez run into such a test of his poise, and he would later remember virtually nothing about the next few minutes except that no one seemed to notice anything odd about his behavior. By the time his brain began working again, Meredith had turned the scientists over to Barner and the three of them had left the room.

"Well?" Meredith asked when they were alone. "Not even a simple 'golly, Colonel, what a surprise'?"

Perez cleared his throat; it seemed to help. "I was expecting you to call me while all of them were still in orbit," he said.

"To find out what they were doing here?" Meredith shrugged. "We figured that out a long time ago. You were observed giving that package to the Ctencri, you know."

Perez swallowed. "Oh. I, uh, wasn't expecting you to take it so calmly."

Meredith's expression didn't change . . . but suddenly there was a look in his eyes that made Perez shiver. "Don't mistake control for calm, Perez," the colonel said coldly. "You didn't like the way I was running Astra, so you forced a new set of rules down my throat—and now you've shown you can't even live by *them*. By all rights you should be under house arrest right now, or at the very least Astra's first ex-councillor."

"So why aren't I? Because it worked?"

"You think it worked, do you? How many scientists did you send letters to?"

"About a hundred fifty. I wasn't sure all would be able—"

"Only five came."

Perez stared at him. *"Five? That's all?"*

"Five. Francisco Arias of Brazil, Slobodan Curcic from Yugoslavia, Loretta Williams from the U.S., and the two you just met. I hope you didn't offer anything like a blank check to the Ctencri for this."

Perez shook his head. "The agreement was for an unspecified

amount of cable. Carmen can take the low turnout into account when she hammers out the details." He cocked an eyebrow. "So again: why aren't I being punished?"

"Because I'd rather make you pay your debts in sweat than in blood," Meredith said. "Algae ship or not, we're likely to be facing some lean times; and I'm going to hold *you* personally responsible for the behavior of the Hispanics here. I've heard grumblings about profit-sharing or lack of it, and it's going to be your job to make it clear that all 'profits' from the Spinneret are currently going directly into their stomachs."

"You don't have to spell it out, Colonel," Perez told him stiffly. "As long as everyone is treated fairly there won't be any trouble. Credit me—*and* the other Hispanics—with that much sense."

"All right. Then tell me how the digger search went. Any of them in working condition?"

"Just the one with the stone in its tread," Perez said, relieved by the change of topic. "We got it out, and last we saw it was tunneling cheerfully into the rock. I left word at the op cent for a round-the-clock watch on it."

"Good. We'll want to see where it goes when it's full." He frowned. "You have any estimate on the horsepower of the thing?"

Perez shrugged. "Not really. Between fifty and a hundred, I'd guess. Why?"

"Because the ability to idle or whatever for a hundred millennia *and* also put out that kind of power means that the digger's either got one hell of a battery pack or else is running off some kind of broadcast power. Either way, it's just one more goody to tempt potential invaders."

Perez shook his head. "You worry far too much about that, Colonel, in my opinion. After the M'zarch fiasco no one's going to be brash enough to launch an invasion. *Especially* when they don't know exactly what we've got down here that might serve as weapons."

"Maybe," Meredith sighed. "But maybe not. The longer they hesitate, the more entrenched we become. And I'm sure they realize that."

"Let 'em realize it," Perez said, stepping toward the elevator. "In my humble and untrained opinion it's already too late for a successful invasion. Well. If that's all you wanted, my duty's up for the day and I'm going home. You coming?"

"Not yet," Meredith said, his eyes drifting to the windows and the Spinner village below. "I think I'll stick around and see if anything happens when the digger goes to dump its load."

Secretary-General Saleh—leader of the UN, chief trade representative to alien races, and arguably the most powerful man on Earth—laid down the last sheet of paper with the bitter taste of helplessness on his tongue. "What you're asking is essentially a carte blanche for whatever you want to do on Astra," he said wearily. "You know I can't give you that."

"Why not?" Ashur Msuya asked. "The people want action—or haven't you been watching the newscasts lately?"

Saleh snorted. "Surely you don't expect me to take all those carefully staged demonstrations seriously?"

"The rest of the world does. And as for my proposal, it's clearly spelled out that you have the final word on anything I do."

"Oh, of course—except that the eight-day round trip renders that effectively meaningless."

"Only if you're looking for true veto power," Msuya said quietly. "*And* true responsibility."

For a long time Saleh stared into Msuya's unblinking eyes, knowing deep within him there was no way the man would be stopped. Saleh had originally chosen him to lead the mission to Astra because of his intensely pro-Third World stance, a bias Saleh had hoped would act as a bulwark against the West's usual ability to get more than its fair share of things. But the plan had backfired. Whatever motivations of justice Msuya may once

have had were gone, submerged beneath his utter hatred for
Colonel Meredith. With or without Saleh's permission he would
find a way to destroy the colonel . . . and if Saleh stood in his
way he might well precipitate a power struggle within the
Secretariat itself, a battle that could cost Saleh his position and
simultaneously wreck any chance the world might have for
international peace and unity.

But if Saleh officially backed his proposal, the Secretary-
General was covered. A success in reclaiming Astra would
reflect favorably on him; a failure would be Msuya's responsibility alone. The inherent communications time lag would give
Msuya effective autonomy. If he chose to act on something their
new Astran spies reported, there would be no chance for Saleh
to exercise his supposed veto power.

And Msuya knew it. He was offering his political future
against a chance for vengeance.

Dropping his gaze to the papers before him, Saleh sighed.
"All right," he said, picking up a pen. "You'll take the *Trygve
Lie* and go to Astra, sending the *Hammarskjöld* home when you
get there. You *will* keep within the boundaries set in this paper,
observing and collecting information *only*. No action of *any*
kind without my written permission first."

"I understand," Msuya nodded.

Sure you do. The meaningless words still tingling on his
tongue, Saleh signed the page and tossed the batch of them
across the desk. "Have my secretary give you a copy," he
growled. "I'll arrange for the *Hammarskjöld* to rendezvous
with you periodically to deliver supplies and bring back any
information you gather. In an emergency the Ctencri could
probably be persuaded to deliver a message."

Msuya smiled tightly as he stood up. "Don't worry. I'm sure
there will be no emergencies." Turning, he left the room.

My new frontier, Saleh thought dully, staring at the closed
door. *My quixotic hope for the restless and hopeless; the world I
personally helped begin . . . and now I must simply sit by and*

watch while you live or die. For the first time in his life, he began to understand the permanent melancholy in his grandmother's face that had always bothered and frightened him as a child.

His grandmother had been a midwife in a small Southern Yemeni village . . . a village with a fifteen percent infant mortality rate.

Chapter 26

Suddenly, it seemed, it was autumn.

Not like autumn in Pennsylvania, of course, Hafner thought as he climbed up one of the hillocks bordering the Dead Sea; not even like autumn in southern California. Here there were no maples or oaks to scatter colored leaves around like God's own currency thrown freely to rich and poor alike. On Astra the only signs of fall were a drop in air temperature and a gradual reduction in the number of daylight hours. Turning, Hafner squinted at the cone of Mt. Olympus in the near distance. *Odd,* he thought. *I can't even force myself to see it as a natural formation anymore. I wonder why I couldn't see it as anything else before.*

Carmen's voice drifting up from below interrupted his idle reverie. "Aren't you supposed to plant a flag or something when you get to the summit?"

Turning back, he grinned at her. "You come up with an Astran flag I can live with and I'd be pleased to plant it," he called. "Most of the designs I've seen so far would be more suitable for burial."

"You're an aesthetic snob," she said, laughing. "Come on down; lunch is ready."

He scrambled back down the gentle slope and joined her on the spread-out blanket. "At least we won't have any problem with ants," Carmen commented, handing him a sandwich. "Eat hearty; it's the first batch of processed algae from the Flying Hothouse."

Cautiously, Hafner took a bite. It was pretty good, actually, though not quite up to normal California standards. The texture was about right, and it took no real effort to believe he was eating actual ham. "Not bad," he nodded, the words coming out mushy around the food. "Especially with, what, only a week of work?"

"Closer to two—you've been spending too much time underground lately. Of course, the processing'll go much faster now that all the bugs are out of the system."

"Yeah." Hafner took another bite. "Speaking of being underground, you haven't told me yet what you thought of the Spinner cavern."

She shook her head. "I wish I had the words to do it properly. It's the most fantastic thing I've ever seen. Does that artificial sun actually track across the sky?"

"Sure does," he nodded. "Gives us a cycle of twenty hours of daylight to ten of night, presumably matching that of the Spinners' home world. And the sun isn't a hologram, or at least they don't think so—the light intensity is too great and matches a G3 star spectrum too closely. No one knows yet what it is or how they get it to move. Ditto for the clouds and stars, by the way."

She shook her head again. "I see now why you and Cris and the colonel were so dead-set on keeping the place out of the wrong hands—human or otherwise. I've been thinking—well, never mind."

"You've been thinking we were all going megalomaniac?" he prompted.

"Well . . . maybe a little. But I think I understand now."

"Good. Maybe it'll help you in your trade negotiations. How are they going, by the way?"

"Oh, business is booming. I've got six contracts in the stack, just waiting on the raw metal deliveries. I calculate that in a couple of years we'll have a shot at passing the U.S.'s GNP."

"And with a fraction of its population. The old oil barons will turn over in their graves."

Carmen was silent for a moment. "Maybe we should start figuring out how we're going to share all that wealth."

He frowned at her, trying to place that tone of voice. "You've been talking to Perez, haven't you?" he asked. "All that stuff about the *New Mayflower*."

"The who?"

"Oh, he hasn't sprung that one on you yet? He wants us to buy the *Aurora* or *Pathfinder* and outfit it for shuttling immigrants here from Earth."

She sighed. "That sounds like him: great with people but no head at all for economics. We could probably rent M'zarch troop carriers a lot cheaper than buying one of our own."

Hafner made a face. "Well, I hope *one* of you experts is thinking about where we'd put this flood of fo—flood of people," he corrected himself hastily.

"We recognize the problems," Carmen said, giving him an odd look. "We're not going to rush into anything half-cocked. What kind of flood were you going to call it?"

Silently, Hafner cursed his tongue. "A flood of foreigners," he admitted reluctantly. "Perez wants to recruit people mostly from the poorer Third World nations."

"And?" Carmen prompted, her voice studiously neutral.

"Well, face it—if that happens we original Astrans are going to wind up as a pretty small minority here. Those of us who came here because we wanted to are going to be flooded out by people looking for the ticket window to the galaxy's gravy train."

"Yeah. Maybe." For a moment Carmen gazed out at the waters of the Dead Sea, her forehead furrowed in thought. "I don't know what to say," she sighed at last. "It *will* change Astra—there's no doubt about that. We're four small villages that are going to become huge cities, and those of us who've sweated through the rough times are likely to get lost in the crowd, But we can't simply live here alone like—well, like the oil barons you mentioned. After all, it's not like this is profit from something we've done ourselves."

"Why do we have to bring all of them *here,* though?" Hafner grumbled. "Why not just give the money to them right where they are or something? Hey—that may be it."

"May be what?" Carmen asked, eyeing him suspiciously.

"The answer to our dilemma." The thoughts were coming thick and fast now, and Hafner fumbled a bit as he tried to keep up with them. "It'll be like foreign aid—better yet, like a new Marshall Plan. We can funnel a portion of our profit to the poorer countries, probably in the form of credit with the Ctencri, maybe tie the amount to inverse GNP per capita so that it goes to the countries who need it most—"

"And how do you guarantee it goes to the *people* who need it most?"

"—with a clause to prevent—um? Oh." The grand scheme seemed to explode into soap suds in front of him. "Yeah. Well . . . we could write something into the agreements, I suppose."

Carmen smiled sadly. "Half the countries that need that sort of aid already reject help that has any strings attached. Besides, the contract hasn't been written yet that someone couldn't find a loophole in."

Hafner pursed his lips tightly. She had indeed been talking to Perez, he decided; talking *and* listening. "It'd still be better than trying to bring the starving millions here," he growled. "Most of them don't have any skill except farming, and they sure as potholes aren't going to continue that line of work here."

"I know," Carmen sighed. "And I don't know how we're going to get around that. All we can do is keep working on it."

"Yeah." Hafner looked down at the half sandwich still clutched in his hand. "So much for our nice, quiet lunch away from the universe," he said, shaking his head. "Look, why don't we sort of back out and come in again, okay? Let's just enjoy our algae and the lovely gray-brown scenery and forget about politics for a while."

"Sure. I'm sorry I brought up the subject." Carmen smiled wanly and took a bite of her own sandwich. "So . . . what sort of gossip do you hear lately?"

They talked about people, the rate of progress of the Earth scientists, and other relatively innocuous subjects for the next hour; and when Hafner escorted Carmen back to the Spinneret camp and her waiting vehicle, she professed herself satisfied with the break from the pressures of her work.

He pretended to believe her . . . but as she drove off toward Unie he felt his own cheerful expression sag into a grimace. *Just too dedicated to her job,* he thought, shaking his head as he trudged toward his crackerbox apartment to await his early-evening shift. *Probably won't be able to really relax until this whole immigrant thing is resolved. Perez will see to that, I'm sure.* The thought of the Hispanic infecting her with his own excessively liberal philosophy was more than a little annoying, but there wasn't a lot he could do about it.

Except perhaps to offer an alternative to his grand immigration scheme. So far, Hafner had heard nothing that corresponded to his Marshall Plan idea being tossed around during mealtime discussions; and if it truly *hadn't* occurred to anyone, he really ought to point it out to Colonel Meredith. Despite Carmen's skepticism, it seemed to him the plan had potential merit.

Changing his direction, Hafner headed toward the tunnel entrance. Meredith, he knew, was currently in the tower . . . and Hafner suspected he'd welcome someone to talk to.

The same three-squiggle pattern showed up over eighty times in the main control room alone . . . and the pattern of lights and switches associated with it was more than a little suggestive. *All right,* Loretta thought, tapping at the fist-sized walkabout terminal of the Ctencri translator humming quietly off to one side. *Call this "on" or "active" or "functioning." Correlate . . . ?*

She pushed the proper button and watched the translator screen list eight more combinations involving the three-letter pattern and their possible meanings. *Activate, standby—off? Ah—then that tilde would indicate inversion of meaning. Let's see where else the tilde shows up.* . . . Punching in the order, she was rewarded a moment later with an overhead schematic of the semicircular control panel, the tilded labels flashing in red. Referring occasionally to the picture, she walked slowly around the room, looking closely at each of the switches and indicators so identified. The next step would be to choose one or two of them and play through the data file of the last cable production again, watching for anything that might give a clue as to their function. Loretta hadn't done too well so far with that particular method; all the obvious correlations had long since been tabulated, and she lacked the engineers' knack of pulling seemingly unrelated sounds and activities into a coherent whole.

From underneath the control panel came a dribble of muttered Russian. A moment later, Victor Ermakov crawled stiffly out and unfolded into a standing position. "It is thoroughly ridiculous," he grumbled, waving a multimeter for emphasis. "Half the circuits are inert, with no current flow and infinite resistance—and the other half show an absolutely *steady* current, with no discernible modulation. How do you control something with unchanging current?" He turned to Meredith, sitting quietly next to one of the Gorgon's Heads. "Colonel, the digger *is* still at work, isn't it?"

"It was as of five minutes ago," the other said. "That's when it dumped its last load into the hopper." He pointed to the blue section of the control panel beneath which Ermakov had been working. "I saw the pattern change."

The Russian scowled at the board. "I'm beginning to think

Arias is right, that the Spinners aren't using conventional electronics here at all."

Loretta shrugged. Francisco Arias had tried to explain his theory to her, but his mastery of the more arcane branches of physics didn't include the ability to translate them into laymen's terms. All she'd taken away from the session had been a headache and the fact that too much of the Spinneret equipment was superconducting cable material for it to function along normal electronic lines. He'd then launched into something about subatomic forces and field waveguides that had lost her completely. "He *did* seem very sure of himself," she commented.

"He always does." Ermakov shook his head and turned again to Meredith. "Colonel, it's becoming clear that I'm going to have to literally invent the tools I need to study this equipment. Have you any data at all on the subatomic structure of the cable material, or on any general nuclear theory about the forces that may be involved?"

A thoughtful frown creased Meredith's forehead. "Possibly," he said slowly. "But I'm not sure what kind of access I can let you have to it."

For a scientist, Ermakov was an uncommonly good spy; Loretta had to give him that. His ears seemed to prick up at the mention of classified information, but his next comment was as casual and ingenuous as could be. "Well, it's your decision, of course," he shrugged. "But the more insight I can get into the Spinners' science, the faster I'll be able to understand their engineering."

"I'm aware of that." From the ceiling came the hum of the elevator motor. Loretta glanced at her watch, noted that it was still an hour before the next supervisor was due to relieve Meredith. She looked back up to see the colonel get to his feet and walk around the elevator cylinder to where the door would appear. Unconsciously, her muscles tensed . . . but it was only the geologist/supervisor Dr. Hafner.

"Colonel," Hafner greeted the other, nodding in turn to

Loretta and Ermakov. "I wonder if I could talk to you for a moment? It's about a possible alternative to mass immigration."

Meredith shrugged. "Sure."

Hafner launched into a description of something he was calling the new Marshall Plan; tuning him out, Loretta turned back to the control board. *All right: tilde means negation. Then on the digger board this might mean "empty hopper"; then— let's see: does this sequence show up anywhere else—?*

"I trust you're doing better than I am," Ermakov murmured from beside her. He had his multimeter on the edge of the control panel and was busily switching around the probe leads. "Incidentally, I wonder if I could borrow your tape player and some of your tapes this evening."

Lorettra's throat tightened, and she had to consciously force the muscles to relax. The tape player was her clandestine radio link to the UN ship overhead, the necessary electronics for transmission and scrambling concealed inside the plastic covers of two of the cassettes. "I suppose so," she said, trying to match his casual tone and wondering what had happened to his own radio.

"Thank you. I've been talking about music lately with Major Dunlop and he expressed a wish to listen to some Tchaikovsky and Rachmaninoff. I'll come by your apartment when we're through here and pick it up for delivery to him."

"Fine," she said through stiff lips. Dunlop. The officer the UN people said had fired stunners at a group of workers in Ceres and been severely reprimanded by Meredith for his actions. A man she remembered being described as a vain, hard-nosed type who preferred gunboat to all other forms of diplomacy.

And Ermakov was about to lend him her radio.

The Russian completed his adjustments and disappeared again beneath the control panel. Loretta moved away, staring at the gaudy Spinner colors without really seeing them. She hadn't even realized Ermakov and Dunlop had been talking together, let alone planning . . . what? What could the two of them have cooked up that Dunlop needed to talk to the UN ship about? The scientists' mission here was supposed to be the strictly passive acquisition of Spinneret data . . . unless Ermakov had special instructions she was unaware of. A sudden dread hit her between the shoulder blades and she glanced behind her, half expecting to see that Meredith had put such an obvious two and two together and was summoning soldiers to arrest her for espionage.

But the colonel was still talking with Hafner, apparently oblivious to both Ermakov's scheming and her own associated guilt. Weak-kneed with relief, she turned back and resumed punching in computer commands with shaky fingers.

Ermakov didn't bring up the subject again, and as they were leaving the cavern four hours later, she permitted herself to hope that he'd either forgottten his request or changed his plans. But as she walked past the tunnel guards and out into the early-evening gloom he quietly fell into step with her; and a few minutes later he left her apartment with the player tucked under his arm.

Loretta watched him go, then closed and locked her door behind him. She considered dinner, decided she'd lost her appetite, and lay down on the couch with a book instead. But her mind refused to concentrate, and eventually she gave up and went to bed. Two or three hours later, she managed to fall asleep.

And five hours after that, a group of soldiers led by Major Dunlop overpowered the guards at the tunnel entrance and took control of the Spinner cavern.

Chapter 27

". . . call on all loyal citizens of the United States of America to join us in reversing this clear and heinous act of treason that Colonel Meredith has committed," Dunlop's voice came through the phone speaker, its imperious tone masked somewhat by the dull roar of vehicles behind it. "Those who do not will share the massive guilt and the punishment—"

"Enough," Meredith barked, slipping on his jacket and sitting down on his bed to fasten his boots.

At the other end of the connection Lieutenant Andrews shut off the recording, and Dunlop's harangue vanished in midadjective. "Went out over the whole PA system, you said?" Meredith growled.

"Plus the civilian phone net," Andrews said. "Apparently decided he already had all the soldiers that were on his side."

"I hope so—I like having all my enemies bunched together in one place. Any idea how many there are?"

"The guards on duty at the time were all stunned, but I saw at least one truck go in after the dead-man alarm went off, so there could be forty or more of them plus a fair supply of materiel. They're only about ten minutes ahead of us, though, and I've got a team ready to go after them as soon as the demolitions men can get the other truck out of the way.''

"Tell them to go easy on that thing," Meredith snapped. "I doubt even a nuke could bother the tunnel, but if Dunlop wasn't lying about the size of the bomb in there it'll kill everyone in the area if it goes off.''

"I know, sir." Andrews sounded simultaneously miserable and furious. "We're getting people clear as fast as we can, but—well, there are a lot of civilians among them."

Who move slowly and ask unnecessary questions and otherwise waste time, Meredith thought bitterly. "Well . . . don't let it get to you. There's not a lot Dunlop can do in there except dig in and prepare for a siege. There isn't anyone at the op cent or in the tower, is there?"

"We don't think so, sir, but we don't know for sure. Again, the guards are unconscious, and they could have passed someone through—"

He was interrupted by the high-pitched squeal of the emergency breaker. "Colonel, this is Major Barner. Dr. Hafner's not in his quarters. No evidence of any struggle, but his phone is still here.''

Meredith felt something icy trickle down his spine. "Check on Perez and Nichols immediately," he told Barner. If Dunlop had barricaded himself in there with three of the Spinneret's five supervisors—

But it wasn't quite that bad. "They've already reported in," Barner said. "Heard Dunlop's broadcast and called to find out what was going on. I told them both to stay put till I could get them escorts.''

"Good." Not as bad as he'd feared, but bad enough. With Hafner as a hostage, Dunlop's options were no longer limited to digging in near the cavern entrance. The entire cavern, tower included, was open to him now. "Major, I want you to take charge of clearing out the area around the tunnel and then stay clear yourself. Andrews, start a full ID check—I want to know exactly who Dunlop's got in there with him. Feed the list through to Carmen Olivero at the admin complex here—I'll let her know it's coming. Also, have the demolitions crew slow down. We're not going to catch Dunlop before he's had time to deploy his men anyway, and I don't want them cutting corners and blowing themselves into orbit."

"Yes, sir."

"Keep me informed; I'll be there in a while." Breaking the connection, Meredith snatched up his gunbelt and hurried outside. The eastern sky was showing a faint glow now; stopping momentarily, he punched Carmen's number onto his phone before continuing his jog toward his office.

She answered on the first ring. "I heard the announcement," she said after Meredith had identified himself. "I figured it'd be better to wait until you called instead of bothering you with questions."

"Good thinking. How fast can you get to your office?"

"Thirty seconds; I just came through the front door. You want me to alert the Whissst and Orspham?"

Silently, Meredith blessed her quick mind. "Yes, but don't tell them anything except that the UN ship is not to launch any shuttles or come in closer itself. I don't have any proof yet, but this stinks of collusion and I don't want Msuya's people available to reinforce Dunlop's play. Then run a check of our military personnel and see if anyone's had counterterrorist or hostage-rescue training or experience."

"Hostage rescue?"

He grimaced. "Yes. We think they took Dr. Hafner in with them."

There was no startled gasp or exclamation . . . but when Carmen spoke again, her words were packed in ice. "Understood, Colonel. How many commando teams will you want formed?"

"Two, possibly three. I'll be there before you get that far, though." He hesitated. "Don't worry; Hafner's worth an incredible amount to them alive and nothing at all dead. Even Dunlop wouldn't be stupid enough to hurt him."

"Yes, sir," she replied in that same cold voice. "I'll expect you soon, then."

Breaking the connection, Meredith increased his pace, swearing gently under his breath. *If you're behind this, Msuya,* he thought toward the sky, *you and the whole UN are going to pay a heavy price. Count on it.*

What Hafner didn't know about Ctencri stunners would have filled several volumes . . . but as he lay limply on the ground with his eyes closed he concluded his captors didn't know a whole lot more. Whether they'd misjudged the setting or merely grazed him with the beam he didn't know; but from his lack of restraints it seemed clear they thought he should still be unconscious. All around him he could hear footsteps and muttered commands and the clink of metal on metal as they rushed around building something. *Where* he was was no problem to figure out—only the Spinner cavern had that particular combination of odors and shifting winds. Probably near the op cent, he tentatively concluded, as occasional echoes from the entrance tunnel reached his ears.

It was the events occurring a bare meter away, though, that he found the most interesting.

It had started as a technical discussion regarding the boosting of power to some instrument in order to get past the effects of all the cable material in the area. But within a few minutes the problem was solved . . . and Hafner listened with growing astonishment as two voices—one unknown, one all too familiar—held a brief conversation.

"The Spinner cavern is now in our hands," the unknown voice said without preamble once the connection was made. "We have both the tunnel entrance and the cavern entrance booby-trapped and are setting up gun emplacements from which we'll be able to fire at anyone approaching us."

"Excellent." Msuya's voice was faint and tinny, but nonetheless recognizable. "The *Hammarskjöld* joined us twelve hours ago; together we have fifty UN troops we can land to reinforce you—"

"Negative," the other interrupted. "Your troops will stay right where they are."

"Come now, Major—you can't hold out forever there by yourselves."

"I know that. That's why the *Hammarskjöld*'s going to head back to Earth and bring me a contingent of American soldiers. I'll turn the cavern over to a properly authorized officer of the United States Army—no one else."

There was a short pause. "So you're unilaterally scrapping our agreement, are you?" Msuya said. To Hafner's ears he didn't sound all that surprised. "Suppose I refuse to send the *Hammarskjöld* back? What then?"

"Oh, you won't refuse," the major said confidently. "As matters stand now you have no leverage at all on Astra; with the planet under U.S. control you'll at least have a chance to get what you want here by putting on the pressure back home."

"I don't trust America farther than I can shift the Zambezi," Msuya told him. "Allerton is as good at weaseling as any other Western politician, and I have no interest in turning legitimate UN interests over to his charity. No, Major—right now we have our best chance to reestablish UN control of the Spinneret, and I'm going to take it. You can cooperate or else."

"Or else what?" the major shot back. "You going to sit back and let Meredith get back in when our supplies give out? Don't be silly. You'll do as I say and be satisfied with the crumbs the U.S. gives you."

"I see I underestimated your ambitions," Msuya said coldly. "I assumed you'd be satisfied with the heartfelt thanks of the people of the world; but you apparently think you can become the Hero of Astra to the next generation of American schoolchildren."

"Your sarcasm is wasted, Msuya—your only miscalculation was in thinking Americans weren't patriotic anymore. You assumed I could be bought like some petty Third World dictator if you dangled enough empty promises in front of me. I trust you've learned differently now."

"I've learned you can't be trusted, but that's no great revelation. What now keeps me from offering aid to Meredith in taking the cavern back from you?"

"What for, the hope that our noble colonel will be grateful to you for abandoning your own coup?" the major snorted.

"It would be your word against mine," Msuya said. "From here I can destroy all traces of the transceiver you're using; you'd never be able to prove you'd been in contact with me. And as for Meredith's thanks, I think we could manage something more substantial once my troops were on the ground."

"I doubt it. You see, I brought a little insurance in here with me: Dr. Peter Hafner, one of the five people who has access to the main Spinneret machinery. Still think you're going to charge in here with blazing semi-auts?" He paused, but Msuya remained silent. "On the flip side, with Hafner as part of the bargain a peaceful takeover is now more important to you than ever—and the only way you're going to do that is with U.S. troops. So why not quit wasting time and get the *Hammarskjöld* burning up space back to Earth?"

"You seem to leave me without a reasonable choice," Msuya spat. "Very well, you'll get your American troops. But the matter will not end there."

"Maybe not—but it won't be you and me handling it, and I'd put President Allerton up against Saleh any day of the week. Good-bye, Msuya; let me know when my relief arrives."

There was a click and the scraping of a chair as the major got up and walked toward a sort of hammering sound in the near distance. His step seemed springy, and Hafner got the impression he was satisfied with the way the confrontation had gone.

Idiot, Hafner thought. *Msuya'll just bring back UN troops in U.S. uniforms or something.*

But that wouldn't happen for at least a week. Meredith had until then to take the cavern back . . . and his chances would be greatly enhanced if the major's prize hostage could arrange to disappear.

Concentrating on keeping his breathing slow and steady, Hafner listened to the sounds around him and tried to come up with a plan.

"He appears to have fifty-two men in there with him," Carmen said, gesturing to the listing on the computer display they'd set up in the temporary command center half a kilometer from the tunnel entrance. "Thirty-five are from his Ceres contingent; none seems to have any special terrorist or siege training, so we won't have to worry about them anticipating anything clever our teams come up with. I've found you eight men with hostage experience, and at last count two hundred others had volunteered for the assault squads."

Meredith nodded with grim satisfaction. In the two hours since Dunlop's broadcast not a single Astran had publicly voiced support for the major's attempted coup. Even among those who were planning to leave with the next U.S. ship the mood was reportedly one of anger. Whether out of respect for him or contempt for Dunlop, Meredith didn't know, but either way he was grateful for both their active and passive support. Having to split his attention between commando preparation and civilian crowd control would have badly diminished his ability to handle either. "Good. What news from the Whissst?"

"One of the two UN ships that were in orbit as of this morning left about half an hour ago, heading in the direction of Earth. The other hasn't made any moves at all, and there hasn't been any more activity on that superhigh band since the Orspham picked up the one set of transmissions."

"Um." So whatever Dunlop and Msuya had had to say to

each other, they'd apparently said it all and shut up. Meredith glanced out the tent flap at the double rank of armed guards facing the tunnel entrance, then looked back at the small group of people seated around the table. "Well. Suggestions? Major?"

Major Barner shrugged. "No way around it: a direct assault is all we've got. There's no way to pump in enough sleeper gas—even if we could get hold of it—to do any good, and the stunners don't have the range we'd need. We might be able to approach the cavern entrance from the side if the solenoid chamber or outer tunnels connect into the main passageway properly, but at that point we'll still just have to put our heads down and charge."

"What if they've booby-trapped the cavern entrance?" Perez asked from beside Carmen. "Your first line of men won't have a chance."

"I know," Barner grimaced. "But I don't see any other way."

"We have enough sets of body armor to outfit a five-man team," Andrews spoke up. "If necessary, we could send two or three men in first to deliberately trigger any traps and hope Dunlop went easy on the explosives."

"Dangerous, and possibly unnecessary." Perez turned to Meredith. "Colonel, I'd like to volunteer to go in and talk to Dunlop."

"And say what?" Barner snorted. "Appeal to his better judgment?"

"Hardly," Perez said coolly. "You forget my early experience with his better judgment. No, I thought I'd try pointing out the impossibility of any UN supplies or reinforcements getting through to him and the disadvantages of either starving to death or getting his head blown off."

"You won't change his mind," Barner shook his head.

"I don't expect to. But there would be other soldiers listening in; and some of *them* might reconsider their position." He shrugged. "You have to admit that fomenting discontent is something I do rather well."

"A good idea, but risky," Meredith said. "Unless you stay out of range and communicate by bullhorn he might be tempted to double his haul of hostages. But we may not have to go with the frontal assault, either. There's a chance we can sneak in the back door."

"Back door?" Barner asked. "You mean the volcano cone?"

"Exactly." Meredith indicated spots on the cavern diagram spread out before them. "We haven't gotten very far along either of the two tunnels that lead off from the tower side of the Great Wall. One of them has *got* to wind up somewhere under the volcano."

"But Peter tried to find an entrance through the volcano," Carmen objected.

"That was before he was an official Spinner supervisor," Meredith pointed out. "I think it'll be worth taking another look up there now." He nodded to Barner. "Major, you and Andrews get busy and organize those assault teams; if I find a way in we'll want to move quickly. Carmen, keep tabs on the UN ship and field any questions the aliens might throw at us. Perez, you'll stay here and assist Carmen."

"What about my idea of talking to them?" Perez asked. "As long as I stay back or with an armed escort—"

"If we find another entrance there won't be any need for sowing dissension," Barner told him gruffly. "Come on, Lieutenant."

"I know. But you might be able to use a diversion."

Barner and Andrews paused halfway to the tent entrance, turning to look at Perez. Meredith didn't share their surprise; he'd seen where the Hispanic's line of thought was leading. From the look on Carmen's face she'd expected the offer, too . . . and didn't like it at all.

But this decision, at least, could be put off. "We'll discuss it *after* we've found a way in," he told Perez. "I'm heading to the cone; let me know immediately if there's any change in the situation."

The flyer that had ferried Meredith and Carmen in from Unie was parked a hundred meters away, out of any possible line of fire from the tunnel. Meredith jogged over to find Nichols and the four assistants he'd requested already aboard. Giving the pilot landing instructions, he spent the short flight conferring with Nichols on the methods he and Hafner had used on their previous attempts to find a way in. It was a brief talk, and didn't tell him very much.

The cone steepened fairly rapidly at the very summit, but the original searchers had left behind a piton-secured ropeladder/bridge over the rim, and within a few minutes the six men were assembled together at the edge of three hundred square meters of unmarked floor.

Meredith glanced around, noting the TV monitors still pointed down at them from the volcano rim. "Did you ever get the shots of the last cable operation clear enough to show where the floor opened up?" he asked Nichols.

"No," the other shook his head. "None of the enhancement techniques could do anything with them. We think whatever produces the zero-gee fouled up either the camera or film. Or both."

"All right, then, I guess we do it the hard way." He pointed to his left. "I want you and two of the others to work that direction around the circle. Run your hands over the wall, poke at any crevices you find, and otherwise try to spark some kind of reaction. I'll go around the other way. Observers, you're to watch for anything Nichols or I might miss. Everyone understand? All right. Take it slow and don't miss anything."

Slow it certainly was; slow and frustrating. Half a dozen times in the first twenty minutes Meredith found himself wondering if he was giving in to wishful thinking in his old age. Certainly nothing in the Spinner cavern had suggested that their "supervisor" status extended any farther than the Gorgon's Head network, and whatever security system was hiding the entrance he was counting on finding was likely to be independent of the snake-topped machines. But giving up the search would lead directly to Barner's frontal assault, and he wasn't yet ready to concede the inevitability of that approach.

And then, with nearly two thirds of the wall covered, Nichols hit pay dirt.

"If you rest your hand right here for a second or two you get a faint scraping noise from behind the wall," the geologist told Meredith, indicating a section of wall pocked with tiny fissures. "We never noticed anything significant about these cracks before, but I wonder now if it could be an air intake of some kind."

"With a Gorgon's Head on the other side?" Gingerly, Meredith placed his palm over the spot. Sure enough, the scratching was just barely audible. Gorgon's Head snakes against the wall?

"Wouldn't an air vent show a more regular pattern?" one of the others objected.

"You haven't seen the Spinners' love of squiggles," Meredith told him, testing various sections of wall immediately around the vent. "Seems pretty solid. Let's check around, see if the door is offset or something."

A search of the five meters to either side proved fruitless. "If there's a door here it looks like we're going to have to persuade it to open," Nichols said at last. "I've got some hydrofluoric acid; we could try it in the air vent."

"Go ahead, but I doubt it'll do any good," Meredith said, eyeing the wall thoughtfully. "So far we've never come upon a Gorgon's Head that couldn't get out of its cubbyhole when it wanted to. I suspect the door's not jammed but locked, and we're expected to know how to open it."

"I don't see anything that looks like the buttons of a digital lock," Nichols said slowly. "An ID card in one of the slots?"

"More likely a verbal command—you wouldn't want some worker to get trapped in the cone with no way out." An extremely foolish idea was beginning to take shape in the back of his mind. "On the other hand, you may also not want the average Spinner who has no business up here just wandering in and out like they can with the Dead Sea entrance."

"Well, then, what are we going to do? We're a long way from deciphering the written language, let alone the spoken one."

"Let's try the acid and then maybe firing a few explosive shells around—just in case it *is* stuck. After that . . . well, we'll talk about it then."

Neither the acid nor explosions seemed to make any difference to either the door or the hidden Gorgon's Head . . . and eventually Meredith was forced to climb out of the crater, make contact with Carmen in the command center, and lay out his plan.

She didn't like it. Neither, when consulted, did Nichols, Perez, Barner, and Andrews.

"Ridiculous," was Carmen's immediate response. "Ridiculous and suicidal and you're not going to do it."

"Out of the question," Barner seconded. "It's too long a shot to gamble your life over."

"I'll be in no danger," Meredith assured them.

"What do you mean, 'no danger'?" Barner retorted. "You *know* half the safety interlocks in this mechanized anthill are gone—look at what happened to the men in the solenoid tunnel."

"There weren't any Gorgon's Heads present then, and the men weren't supervisors," Meredith pointed out. "Besides, even if it doesn't work I ought to be safe enough against the wall. Safer than the first troops through the main entrance would be, anyway."

"If it's so safe," Perez said suddenly, "then let *me* do it instead of you."

"No. It's *my* idea, and I'm going to do it. Period. Carmen, you'll make the proper arrangements immediately."

"Yes, sir." Carmen's voice was sullen; but she clearly recognized an order when she heard one.

Or maybe she, too, recognized that they had no other choice.

They'd been inside for nearly a day when Hafner was abruptly shaken out of a deep sleep. "What's going on?" Major Dunlop's voice demanded.

Squinting in the light streaming through the open tent flap, Hafner tried to chase the cobwebs out of his brain. "Going—what do you mean—?"

"That rumbling—can't you hear it? What's Meredith up to?"

Frowning, Hafner listened for a moment. The sound, though, wasn't hard to place. "He's not up to anything. That's just the Spinneret starting into its production cycle."

His eyes had adjusted enough now to see Dunlop's face . . . and the expression on that face was one of tense suspicion. "What do you mean, production cycle? He's making a cable? *Now?*"

"Why not? Probably demonstrating to the aliens out there that Astra's still in business . . . that you aren't really in control of anything except a few square kilometers of underground real estate."

The last dig may have been a mistake. Dunlop's brow darkened and the fingers clenching his holstered pistol butt tightened noticeably. "Perhaps we should prove otherwise," he ground out. "What do you say we go out to the tower and start pushing buttons until it shuts off?"

Hafner felt his mouth go dry. "I say that if you mess up the settings or erase some program in the process, Colonel Meredith will make a fortune selling tickets to your disemboweling," he said as casually as he could. "You'd probably have everyone from the Rooshrike to the M'zarch offering suggestions on technique, too."

Dunlop glowered at him for a moment, then turned on his heel and stalked away, letting the tent flap close behind him.

With a relieved sigh, Hafner checked his watch and settled back to try and catch another hour of sleep. *I wonder,* he thought as the darkness closed in, *just what the colonel is up to*.

Chapter 28

The last glint of sunlight had vanished from the inner lip of the volcano cone when the gravimeter fastened to the edge of Meredith's helmet began to change. "It's started," he announced quietly into his microphone. "Two percent down and picking up steam."

"Your restraints set?" Barner asked, his voice barely discernible over the static that was beginning to fill the radio bands.

"Yes," Meredith told him, trying to sound more confident than he felt. The lines and bracing bars fastening him to the inner cone wall near the air vent weren't nearly as secure as he'd hoped to make them——unlike the Spinneret cable itself, which stuck to other things with a vengeance, the flat panels with which the volcano cone and cavern structures had been built were made of a very inert substance. Depending on the gradient of the zero-gee field, it was conceivable Meredith would wind up being shot into space along with the latest batch of cable.

With a conscious effort, he put the thought out of his mind and reached out to press his bare hand against the air vent again. The gentle breeze that was starting to spring up kept him from hearing any scratching, but he was sure the Gorgon's Head behind the wall had detected and identified him. What it would do with that knowledge, though, was still an unknown.

The gravity was dropping rapidly now, and the local atmospheric pressure was beginning to follow. Cool air hissed behind Meredith's head, filling the pressure suit that covered all of the colonel except his hands. The general medical consensus was that such a limited exposure to vacuum would be safe enough for a reasonable length of time, but no one on Astra really knew what the limits actually were. Keeping one eye on the air vent and the other on his gravimeter, Meredith gritted his teeth and waited.

Brought up on a diet of American cliff-hanger drama, he was rather expecting the Gorgon's Head to wait until the last second before taking action . . . and it was therefore almost anti-climactic when, with the gravity only down to point four gee, a section of wall suddenly slid back and down, exposing the short-tunnel-and-elevator-shaft arrangement that had also been used in the cavern control tower. Meredith hit his harness release with one hand, reaching out with the other to try and get a grip on the edge of the opening. He needn't have bothered; from an alcove just off the tunnel a tentacle snaked out to wrap itself around his neck, and before he could do more than get his hands up to grip the metal hose he'd been pulled inside the tunnel and released. Massaging his throat, he watched the door slide shut again and, giving silent thanks to the Gorgon's Heads' programmer, set to work locating the inside controls.

Half an hour later the static cleared and he was able to reassure the anxious listeners that the gamble had worked. Twenty minutes after that, Andrews and the ten-man commando team had joined him. Together they crowded into the elevator and started down.

It was a long trip. Meredith hadn't until that moment had a real feeling for how far below Astra's surface the Spinner cavern was—the gentle slope of the entrance tunnel had effectively masked that fact—and he was beginning to get fidgety by the time the elevator finally stopped. Moving quietly, the men fanned out, weapons ready.

They were, as Meredith had anticipated, in an unexplored area of the cavern complex. The room they'd entered was as large as the storerooms leading off the main entrance tunnel, but without the curlicue floor designs and with a much higher ceiling. At either end of the room were huge doors; and linking them—

"Railroad tracks," Andrews muttered, poking carefully at one with the muzzle of his Stoner 5.56. "Heavy-duty, from the look of them."

Meredith looked back and forth between the two doors. One led directly under the volcano cone, he estimated. The other was flanked by two very familiar-looking bulges. . . ."Let's backtrack it," he said, starting toward that door.

The Gorgon's Heads emerged from their alcoves before the group was within fifteen meters, walking on their spider legs to stand in front of the door release. "It's all right," Meredith told them soothingly, speaking—he realized belatedly—as if they were a pair of pet Dobermans. Stepping forward, he ran a hand over the top of each, then reached between them to poke the release. The doors slid open . . . and Meredith found himself facing what could only be a spaceship.

A *big* ship, too; nothing like the *Aurora* or *Pathfinder*, of course, but certainly comparable to the UN's Ctencri-built courier ships. It rested on a transport cradle which, in turn, squatted across the tracks in the floor; and despite their age, Meredith had the feeling that, like the Spinneret itself, both would prove perfectly functional.

"At least," Andrews murmured from beside him, "we know now why they needed to make the volcano crater so big. Should we take a look inside, Colonel?"

Meredith swept the room quickly with his eyes, noting the quantities of support gear stacked around the walls. "Not right now," he told the other. "I doubt there's anything here that would help us with Dunlop, and even if there were it'd take us too long to find it. We'll mark the door and bring the experts in later." Stepping back, he looked around for another way out of the first room. "Back to the elevator," he decided. "We must have come down one level too many."

The guess turned out to be right, and a minute later they were moving silently down a corridor in what Meredith hoped was the direction of the cavern. Assuming they didn't get lost, they should be in range of Dunlop's rebels in a couple of hours.

There had been a long and—or so it had seemed to Hafner—heated debate going on over by the barrier for nearly half an hour now. Digging his spoon into the self-heating can of field ration stew, Hafner strained to pick out as much of it as he could. The topic itself wasn't hard to guess: Perez's latest message, delivered via bullhorn from down the tunnel, had succeeded beautifully in its obvious goal of undermining morale. If he'd been telling the truth—if Astra really *was* rallying unanimously behind Meredith—then Dunlop's cabal was indeed facing ultimate defeat and possible death besides. Apparently, the argument centered around whether the rebels should continue to maintain what was being increasingly seen as an indefensible position or whether they should withdraw to the cavern control tower. Hafner couldn't tell which side Dunlop himself was on . . . but when the major strode up to him a few minutes later, his lips were tightly compressed with anger.

"On your feet, Doctor—if you don't mind," he added in a token effort at courtesy. "We're moving deeper in."

"Oh?" Deliberately, Hafner scraped one last spoonful out of the can and ate it before leisurely getting up. "I'd have thought the other direction would be smarter."

Dunlop apparently had too much on his mind already for Hafner's pinpricks to have any effect. "We're moving you to the tower," he growled. "From the top we'll have a clear line of fire at anyone who tries to approach—and as you've already pointed out, Meredith won't dare shoot back at us there. Get in that car—we'll be leaving in a few minutes."

Hafner did as he was told, his mind spinning with unanswerable questions. Had Meredith pushed Dunlop into this move in the hope that he, Hafner, would find a way to escape in all the activity? Should he try and make such a opportunity? Or was the colonel expecting him to still be in custody when he made his counterstroke? *A pity we never planned for this kind of thing*, he thought, watching the soldiers breaking camp around him. *We could have set up contingencies, code words—something. I don't know how to play this by ear.*

But whatever move Meredith had planned, it didn't come before the cars began to move through the Spinner village. Looking out the window, Hafner noted with a growing tightness in his stomach that fourteen men—a quarter of Dunlop's force— had been left as rear guard at the tunnel barricade. *He's split up his people,* Hafner thought. *Somewhere on this trip the attack will come.*

It didn't come as they drove down the winding streets; nor did a squad roar up from behind as they piled out of the cars by the Great Wall. Unreasonably, Hafner tensed as the first four men slipped through the narrow opening—unreasonably, since no one could have slipped past the tunnel guards to set up any such trap by the wall. Sure enough, a moment later they called an all-clear, and when Hafner and his knot of guards squeezed through, he saw the terrain was indeed as empty as ever. Nothing moved but the usual number of Gorgon's Heads—

Moving Gorgon's Heads? Hafner felt his teeth clamp together as the anomaly hit him like a slap across the face. Ever since his first visit here he'd invariably found the Gorgon's Heads grouped with patient vigilance around the tower's base. Now, though, nearly half of them were clumping *toward* the tower from the rear section of the cavern . . . as if they'd gone to one of the exit tunnels back there to investigate intruders. . . .

Hafner's heart thudded in his ears as the rest of the details fell into place. Meredith had found a second entrance to the complex; he or Barner had led a team in through it; they had run ahead of the slower Gorgon's Heads and were waiting with stunners ready just inside the tower door. In five minutes it would all be over. . . .

And a hundred meters from the tower, Dunlop abruptly signaled a halt. "Smith, Corcoran; go check out the tower entrance," he ordered two of the soldiers.

"They can't get in without me," Hafner spoke up, a shade too quickly. "The Gorgon's Heads will stop them."

Dunlop eyed him for a long moment. "All right, then," the major said, "stand back from the machines and lob a couple of grenades through the opening. That shouldn't hurt anything, should it?"

Wordlessly, Hafner shook his head, his eyes on the soldiers moving toward the tower. They were barely five paces from the opening when, without warning, three khaki-clad men appeared in the doorway, the stunners in their hands sweeping the group of rebels. Even as he dived toward the ground Hafner felt a tingle ripple across his skin . . . and he'd barely hit the alien soil when the thunder of automatic weapons fire exploded into the air around him.

His ears were still ringing from the burst when a hand grabbed his collar and roughly yanked him to his knees. Peripherally, he saw Dunlop's men stretched out on their bellies, rifles pointed toward the tower . . . but his main attention was focused on the pistol Dunlop held against his temple. A pistol gripped by a white-knuckled hand.

"Meredith!" the major yelled toward the tower and directly

in Hafner's ear. "I've got Hafner here—you hear me? Surrender or I'll kill him. I mean it!"

He paused for breath or an answer . . . and in the silence Hafner heard, dimly, the sound of distant gunfire. Dunlop's hand twitched; but before he could do or say anything, Meredith's voice drifted faintly from the tower. "Give it up, Dunlop. You haven't got a chance."

"I've got Hafner!" the major shouted again. "You want to see him die?"

"Don't be a fool," Meredith called. "You can't get into the tower, your rear guard at the tunnel's been taken—you've got no supplies and nowhere to run. What the hell is a hostage going to buy you? You *or* your men?"

"Just shut up!" Dunlop yelled.

"Major," a sergeant spoke up tentatively, "maybe we *ought* to surrender—"

"Talk of surrender will be treated as desertion," Dunlop cut him off harshly. "Meredith! I'll make you a deal. You call the UN ship and have them send down a shuttle for us. Then have your people pull back and let us leave here."

"What about Dr. Hafner?"

"I'll ask Msuya to send him back down once we're aboard."

"Forget it," Meredith called. "However, I'll make you a counterproposal. If you turn Hafner loose right now, I'll guarantee you all safe passage to the UN ship."

"You think I'm stupid enough to trust you? We're leaving, Meredith—you'd better call your people off." Cautiously, Dunlop stood up, hauling Hafner to his feet. "All right; everybody get up and fall back to the cars."

Slowly, even reluctantly, the soldiers complied—and because he was watching them, Hafner saw the shocked expressions as they began turning to leave. "Oh, bloody hell," someone muttered.

Preoccupied with the gunfire and shouted negotiations,

Hafner had completely forgotten about the Gorgon's Heads. But the machines had obviously not forgotten them . . . and as he gazed at the six Gorgon's Heads standing motionlessly between them and the Great Wall, Hafner had the eerie feeling he was seeing a new level of programming being brought into play. With their tentacles poised like angry rattlesnakes, they seemed unnaturally alert, almost as if they sensed the tension and danger and were preparing to do something about it. Even Hafner, who was used to the things, felt uneasy; the effect on Dunlop's soldiers was an order of magnitude higher. The shocked expletives were punctuated by the clicks of rifles being put on full automatic.

"Take it easy," Dunlop snapped, pushing Hafner a step closer to the wall. "As long as we've got the doc here they won't touch us."

"Maybe, maybe not," Hafner put in, thinking quickly. "They're armed, you know, and I doubt they like having a supervisor as a prisoner." If he could get just a few steps ahead of the soldiers, on the pretext of calming the machines, and then duck behind one of them . . .

"They're not armed, and they wouldn't understand what 'prisoner' means if you drew them a picture," Dunlop countered. "Come on, men."

"Hell with *that*," someone behind Dunlop muttered. "Meredith! I'm accepting your deal!"

Dunlop swung around, releasing Hafner's shirt as he brought his pistol to bear. "Back in ranks, you!" the major snarled— and Hafner leaped for the Gorgon's Heads.

He'd covered less than half the distance when something that felt and sounded like a small bomb blasted into his thigh, slamming him hard into the ground. A scream of pain welled up in his throat . . . but even as his clenched teeth blocked the escape he was deafened by a second thunderclap. He tensed for a new wave of agony, but it never came; and as the smell of ozone finally penetrated his pain-fogged consciousness he realized something else entirely had just happened. Raising his head with an effort, he looked back over his shoulder.

Where Dunlop had been standing a charred figure now lay sprawled on the ground. Around it the rebel soldiers stood frozen, their weapons sagging in their hands. From the tower a new group of soldiers was running toward them. "Well, what do you know?" Hafner heard his own voice say, as if from a great distance. "I guess they *are* still armed."

And then, thankfully, the darkness took him.

Chapter 29

Busy with the task of straightening things out in the Spinner cavern, Meredith wasn't able to get to the Unie hospital until nearly an hour after Hafner had been flown there. He arrived to find Andrews and Carmen sitting together in the tiny waiting room. "Any news?" he asked, sinking into a chair across from them.

"It doesn't look like he's going to die," Andrews said. "They're not sure yet whether they'll be able to save his leg—the thighbone was pretty badly damaged."

Meredith nodded tiredly. "Yeah. Carmen . . . I'm sorry."

"Wasn't your fault, Colonel." Her voice was under control, despite the strain lines in her face. "Dunlop had to be stopped."

"Stopped and a half." He shifted his eyes to Andrews again. "You tell her?"

The other nodded. "Any idea yet what that flash was?"

"Simple old-fashioned high voltage, apparently. Probably grounded through a cable-material base or grid underlying the cavern soil."

"So now the supervisors have been raised to demigod status," Carmen murmured. "Able to call lightning down on their attackers." She sighed. "I don't think I like the idea of Gorgon's Heads equipped with offensive weaponry."

Andrews shrugged. "It'll sure slow down any more would-be rebels."

"Oh, it's fine *now*. But what about twenty years from now?"

"We'll have the whole system figured out by then," Meredith assured her. "I've already made the supervisor/security programming a high-priority project. We'll be able to make new supervisors long before we need them."

"That wasn't what I meant," Carmen shook her head. "I mean it's just one more way the Spinneret's resources can be applied directly to warfare. Is that what the Spinners originally planned for this place, or is it just our human viciousness that's turning everything in sight to weapons?"

"There aren't a lot of things in this universe that can't be used for both good and evil," Andrews said. "If the Spinners were so morally pure that they couldn't see the negative uses of their stuff, they would've been wiped out pretty quickly by the first group that did."

"Or enslaved." An idea was beginning to brush the back of Meredith's mind. "Maybe the Spinneret was built by slave labor."

Carmen shuddered. "That's a horrible thought. To be living on a slave planet. . . ."

"You make it sound like living in Auschwitz," Andrews said. "Remember, whatever happened here it was all over a hundred thousand years ago."

"Besides which," Meredith said, "I doubt that the overseers they would need to run this place would have needed a lifeboat as big as the one we found."

Carmen blinked at him. "A *what*? Where is it?"

"It's stashed away in a room just off of the volcano cone," Meredith told her. "For the moment its existence is classified information—which is why Andrews is giving me such an odd look right now."

Andrews reddened slightly. "Sorry, Colonel, but I thought you weren't going to tell anyone else about the ship."

"I wasn't. I've decided, though, that we might want to try flying it . . . and for that we'll need a pilot."

Carmen's jaw dropped. "You don't mean . . . you mean *me*?"

"That's right. I want you to start figuring out the controls first thing tomorrow. You'll need the list of tentative translations that linguist—Dr. Williams—has worked out; I'll see she makes you a copy."

"But why me?" Carmen protested. "You've got lots of pilots who're better than I am."

"True," Meredith said frankly. "But after Dunlop's move, there aren't hell of a lot of people on Astra I can implicitly trust. You're the only one besides me with any flight experience; ergo, it's your baby."

Carmen shook her head in disbelief. "Lieutenant, will you kindly explain to Colonel Meredith that the chances of my figuring out an alien ship from scratch are about the same as swimming the Dead Sea underwater?"

"Actually, it shouldn't be as bad as you think," Andrews said. "If it *is* a lifeboat, it'll be designed to be as easy as possible to fly, with a lot being done automatically. Though"—he added with a glance toward Meredith—"I don't know what exactly we'd want to use it for."

"We'll figure something out once we know more about it," Meredith said, deliberately vague. "Incidentally, did the Whissst make their cable pickup okay?"

"Yes," Carmen nodded. "And I didn't get a chance to tell you: the whole cable came out nonsticky."

Meredith's heart skipped a beat. "*Non*sticky? Uh-oh."

"Oh, there's nothing wrong," she hastened to add. "It's just that the cable's coated with about a millimeter's thickness of a rubbery material that seems to absorb or redirect the surface attraction. They tried peeling some from one end; it comes off quite easily and the cable underneath is like every other the Spinneret's turned out."

Meredith felt his tense muscles go limp with relief. "You had me worried for a minute. How are the Whissst taking it?"

"Oh, you know the Whissst outlook on life—they think the whole thing's a priceless joke. Do you suppose Dunlop's people changed some tower settings?"

"According to them, no one ever got up there," Meredith shook his head. "We can confirm that with Dr. Hafner later, but I suspect we're just seeing the result of getting that digging machine back on the job."

"Oh, right—I'd forgotten that." Carmen shook her head tiredly. "Brain's shut down for the night, I guess."

"Then you ought to take your body home and let it do likewise," Meredith said.

"I want to wait here until they know for sure about Peter's leg." She hesitated, as if casting around for a less painful topic of conversation.

Andrews saved her the trouble. "Colonel, what are we going to do about Msuya? Even if we can't prove it, it's pretty obvious the UN was backing Dunlop's power play. Can we get the Rooshrike to throw him out of the system?"

"Probably, but I don't know if it'd be worth it. Whatever we decide about immigration or direct aid to poor countries, we'll need at least halfway peaceful relations with the UN to make it work. Besides, Saleh's suspicious enough of what we're doing out here."

"But what if they try to stir up more trouble?" Carmen asked.

"How? With Dunlop gone, who's left for Msuya to work through?"

"How about the five scientists Cris brought in? Surely they've been missed by now. What if Saleh threatens their families if they don't cooperate?"

"Again, how? Even a threat needs to be delivered, and our friends upstairs have no way of contacting them."

"They got to Dunlop," Andrews reminded him. "Remember those high-band transmissions? Msuya got that radio to him *some*how."

Meredith grunted. "I'd forgotten that," he admitted. "We'll have to figure out how that was done and shut down the pipeline." An obvious possibility occurred to him, but he decided not to mention it. "We can ask the Orspham to monitor that band, too, see if anything else shows up on it."

A motion through the swinging door's window caught Meredith's eye, and he turned as Astra's chief surgeon came quietly into the room, his pastel green coveralls stained with dried blood. "Well?" the colonel asked, tensing up again.

"I'd say he's got an eighty percent chance of keeping the leg," the doctor said with tired satisfaction. "A bad blood-flow interruption down there, but I think we got it restored in time. If so, the bone itself shouldn't be a problem; we can build a porous ceramic implant the remaining pieces can grow into." His eyes had drifted to Carmen. "He'll be under sedation for at least another ten hours—longer if we decide he's stable enough for an implant operation—so you might as well go home."

"Thank you, Doctor; good job," Meredith said, getting to his feet. "Andrews, you may escort Carmen home and then hit the sack yourself. Good night, all."

Five minutes later, he was in his office. From the corner, his spare cot beckoned temptingly; turning his mind away from it, he sat down at his desk and punched for the Martello duty officer. "I want to talk to the Orspham officer-in-charge," he told the other. "Get him for me on the secure radio channel. After that, see if you can locate a Rooshrike ship; I have a special equipment order that I need right away."

"Yes, Colonel."

Leaning back in his chair, Meredith checked his watch. The

first contact would take several minutes to establish and perhaps triple that to get sufficiently deep into the Orspham hierarchy for what he wanted. And as long as he was waiting anyway . . . "Get me the UN ship, too," he instructed the officer.

There were several very salty things he wanted to say to Msuya.

Chapter 30

It took three weeks for Hafner's leg to recover sufficiently for him to begin taking short trips without a wheelchair—and, coincidentally, it was after the same three weeks that Carmen finally threw in the towel on her own project. "I'm just not getting anywhere," she told Meredith, slapping her notebook in frustration. "Loretta's translations make sense enough when I read them, but I just can't apply it all to the squiggles on the control boards."

"It's not a different language, is it?" he asked her.

She shrugged helplessly. "I can't even tell *that*. The same forty-six symbols are used, but that's all I know. If you want that ship figured out, you're going to *have* to let Loretta come and work directly on the ship with me."

Meredith stared out across the cavern, and Carmen held her breath. If he turned her down she'd likely spend the rest of her life aboard that stupid lifeboat. "As a small inducement," she said, "I can let you have Major Barner back for normal tower duty. Peter's told me he wants to start picking up his share of the load again, and while he obviously can't go running up and

302

down the tower all day, he could certainly walk Loretta and me past the Gorgon's Heads and sit in the boat while we work."

Meredith turned back to her with a wry smile. "I think you've been our trade rep too long—you're getting entirely too good at this sort of bargaining." He pursed his lips. "All right," he said slowly. "As a matter of fact . . . yes, let's do it. We'll take them in to see it tomorrow morning; no word to either until then, understand?"

"Yes, sir—and thank you. I know you wanted to keep the ship secret, but I really think this is the only solution."

For a moment an odd look passed across his face . . . and then he again smiled faintly. "Yes. I think you're right."

Nodding, he turned and left. *Strange sort of comment,* Carmen thought as she headed toward the cavern exit. But she quickly put it out of her mind. So far, certainly, Meredith had proved he generally knew what he was doing.

"A Spinner spaceship."

Msuya made no attempt to hide his satisfaction as he repeated Ermakov's words aloud. At last—at long last—he had the key that would bring him the political power he desired even as he crushed Meredith down into final humiliation and defeat. "Is it operational?"

"Williams didn't know, but it's obvious Meredith thinks so," the Russian's voice came from the speaker on the control panel. "She was shown the craft for the first time only two days ago."

"And she'll be working with the others until all the systems are deciphered?"

"She didn't say." Ermakov hesitated. "I think it would be wise to provide her with a new radio, if that can be arranged. She's been rather cool toward me ever since Dunlop's fiasco."

"Did you explain the radio in her tape player had been autovaporized and that there was no way Meredith could connect her with the revolt?"

"As a matter of fact," the other said dryly, "I believe it's the revolt itself that has annoyed her. Perhaps a small talk with her would remind her of her responsibility to the UN.''

Msuya smiled to himself. Ermakov probably saw his own duty on Astra as furthering the goals of Mother Russia, with his UN allegiance a convenient facade. *Old habits die slowly,* he thought, *but the Soviets too will learn not to trifle with us.* "You may inform Dr. Williams that there is a backup radio built into her hair dryer," he told Ermakov. "Assembly and use are as she learned in her training. I will expect her to resume her normal contacts with me."

There was a short silence from the other end: Ermakov, Msuya decided, wondering if a second radio had also been planted on *him* . . . and wondering perhaps what else might be in his belongings. Msuya's smile widened; these operations always ran more smoothly when the carrot of greed was accompanied by the stick of fear. "I'll tell her," the Russian said at last.

"Good. Then let me hear your own report."

He listened with half an ear as Ermakov plunged into the arcane language of electronics, knowing the recorder would save the details for later scrutiny by the *Trygve Lie*'s experts. Little was new; that much even his layman's ear could tell. Still, a breakthrough could always occur, so when the Russian had finished he avoided criticizing the lack of progress. Instead, he merely thanked the other and signed off.

Afterward, he gazed for several moments out the porthole, watching Astra and the stars tumble by and savoring the news. At last—a piece of the alien technology that was self-contained and movable. A better chance to break Meredith's monopoly would be hard to find . . . and Msuya had no intention of letting the opportunity pass. As soon as Williams learned how the lifeboat worked, he would find a way to steal it.

Glancing at the room's clock, he rang the galley and ordered another pot of tea. It would be ten more minutes before the Indian computer man—Udani—was due to report in.

Chapter 31

Meredith read the report through twice, feeling the tightening of his stomach muscles that had become almost as common as inhaling for him. The bombshell he'd known was coming had done so . . . and at the worst time he could have imagined. Flicking the page from his screen back to the secure file, he muttered a curse and leaned back, gazing at the snow outside his window.

The timing was ultimately his own fault, of course, which was probably what rankled the most. Carmen had originally suggested Council terms of one year; it had been his idea to cut that to six months. At the time it had seemed harmless enough . . . but at the time there'd been no Spinneret and no Spinneret profits. Or hot debate as to what to do with them.

The real problem was that both of the main factions had reasonable positions, a fact that made Meredith's job as ultimate decision maker all the stickier. Perez, as usual, was pushing for immediate—if somewhat selective—immigration, arguing that while trapped in unfair sociopolitical systems the poor of Earth had no chance to improve themselves, no matter how much aid was given them. On the other hand, the group adopting Hafner's

"*In Loco* option" pointed out the vulnerability of the Spinneret to takeover and possibly sabotage, and claimed to have developed a method by which unfair Third World governments could be successfully bypassed in giving assistance to their people. With Hafner on his crutches as their symbol and most credible spokesman, they were successfully cultivating the xenophobia that had simmered at a low level ever since the UN had tried to take over back in August. With only three weeks left before the election, the campaigning was beginning to get uncomfortably warm . . . and relationships between the five supervisors increasingly strained.

And now this.

Raising his wrist, Meredith punched Carmen's number into his phone. There was no answer; disconnecting, he keyed for the Spinner cavern duty officer and left a message. Then, pulling his chair up to the desk again, he called up the main supply inventory and started to assemble the equipment he half hoped he wouldn't be needing.

He'd finished that job and was busy typing in a detailed interim instruction list when Carmen arrived. "You wanted to see me?" she asked, closing the door behind her.

"Yes." Meredith waved to a seat. "I need the lifeboat ready to fly before morning. Can it be done?"

Carmen froze halfway down to the chair seat, her eyes widening. "By *morning*?"

"Yes. You know how to handle it yet?"

Slowly, she sank the rest of the way to the chair, expelling a breath through pursed lips. "I don't know what to say. Yes, we've got all the controls relabeled, and the operating manual we found on the computer makes the thing sound absurdly easy to run. But there's no way to check the engines or other gear until we understand how they work, and that's a *long* way in the future."

Meredith nodded. "It's a risk we'll have to take—though given the Spinneret's performance record I think it's a pretty safe one. All right. I want you, Dr. Hafner, and Dr. Williams to go back in there immediately, do all the checking you can and try to figure out the launch sequence. You said once that the navigation system was designed for children—does that still hold?"

She nodded. "The computer displays your choices on a map and all you have to do is indicate which one you want. The selection's sort of odd; it includes only a few of the stars shown, but all of them are listed as being only five to fifteen days' flight away."

"Maybe it only lists the places emergency facilities were available," Meredith grunted. "All right. I'll be there sometime tonight with the supplies we'll need and our other passenger."

"Yes, sir." Her tongue flicked across her lips. "Uh . . . may I ask . . . what's going on?"

Meredith sighed. "What's going on is the collision of three major events: the upcoming elections, the discovery of that Spinner lifeboat"—he hesitated—"and the cracking of the Gorgon's Head security system this morning."

Carmen's jaw dropped. "You mean the supervisor programming? I didn't realize Udani and Ermakov were that close."

"Apparently they were," Meredith said, sliding over the details. There were some things he didn't yet want Carmen to know. "You see the potential crisis, I'm sure. The five of us supervisors no longer have exclusive power over control tower access. We can now give everyone on Astra the ability to walk into restricted areas if we want to."

"Or anyone from the UN," she added quietly. "Is that what you're afraid of, that someone will leak that information to Msuya and bring down an attack?"

"That, and the nasty political games that could be played with it right here. Dunlop's coup failed largely because his only access to the tower was an untrustworthy hostage. What would happen if Perez, say, sneaked a dozen of his allies in there and made them supervisors?"

"Cris wouldn't do a thing like that," Carmen defended the other. But she nevertheless looked uncomfortable.

"Then those dozen fanatics haul him bodily into the tower and do the job themselves," Meredith shrugged. "The end result's the same."

Carmen nodded reluctantly. "I don't suppose we could classify the details or something."

Not hardly. "It wouldn't stay classified long enough," he said aloud. "In fact, as soon as it becomes public that we've got the code there's likely to be a political struggle for control of it."

"So how is taking a trip in the Spinner ship going to help?"

"It may allow us to buy some time by defusing the current battle over what we're going to do with our money. I'd rather not say any more about it just now."

Slowly, Carmen got to her feet. "I hope you know what you're doing," she said. "I'll get Peter and Loretta back to work right away. I presume I can tell them what we're doing once we're back aboard?"

"I suppose you'll have to." Meredith hesitated, then opened his middle desk drawer and withdrew a small stunner. "Neither of them is to return to the cavern once they know," he added quietly, handing her the weapon.

Her face was tight as she accepted it, holding it for a moment before slipping it into her side coat pocket. Then, without a word, she left.

Meredith waited until the door was again closed before exhaling loudly with frustration and relief. He could count on Carmen to do the job he'd given her . . . but he wished mightily he hadn't had to drop this on her shoulders. But there were so few people on Astra he could really trust.

And in the next hour he made calls to all of them, giving orders and alerting them to the special files he was setting up. After that he stretched out on his office cot and took a nap in anticipation of the long evening ahead.

It was pitch dark by the time he arrived at the security fence that now surrounded the tunnel entrance and the buildings grouped around it. The sentries passed his car through, and a few minutes later he was driving down the long tunnel, doffing his coat one-handedly as the winter outside gradually changed to the constant late spring of the cavern climate control.

Major Barner was waiting for him at the operations center, and together they drove to the Great Wall. There they transferred the supplies Meredith had brought from Unie into two of the open-roofed golf carts and drove to the tower. Parking next to the two carts already there, they rode the elevator to the top.

"Hello, Colonel; Major," Perez nodded as they walked into the main control room. "I thought mine was the last shift in here today."

"Something special's come up," Meredith told him, casually eyeing the three scientists working at the control boards. Only Ermakov was able to manage the proper idle interest in the conversation; Udani and the Brazilian physicist, Arias, were several shades too alert. "I need your help with some things downstairs." he told Perez. "Major Barner'll take over your job here for whatever time's left."

Perez shrugged. "Fine with me. Lead on."

"Carmen and Hafner've been doing some work in one of the far chambers," Meredith explained as the elevator returned them to ground level. "We're taking a couple of carts of special equipment to them."

"I noticed them heading off in that direction once," Perez said, nodding. "Neither will say anything about what they're doing. Though with the doctor's new interest in isolationist politics, he doesn't talk to me about much of anything."

"You'll find out all about it soon," Meredith promised.

It was no more than a ten-minute drive from the edge of the cavern to the elevator connecting with the lifeboat bay. Loading the boxes into the elevator, they rode down.

"Welcome to Martello Spaceport East," Meredith said as they passed the Gorgon's Heads and triggered the door release.

Perez's reaction was a whispered Spanish oath. "A *Spinner ship*?" he murmured. "Incredible!"

"That's what it is, all right. Come on—we've got to get these boxes inside."

The only entrance Meredith knew of was halfway up the curved side, accessible via a narrow accommodation ladder. Together he and Perez manhandled the supplies aboard, stacking them just inside the hatchway. Then, mentally crossing his fingers, he led the way forward.

Carmen, Loretta, and Hafner were waiting in the control room, their expressions tight. "We heard you come in," Carmen said quietly. "Everthing's ready, as far as I can tell."

"Ready for what?" Perez asked suspiciously, his eyes flicking over the room.

"We're taking a short trip," Meredith said, gesturing to a row of seats well away from any of the control boards. "If you three will strap yourselves—"

"A trip where?" Perez interrupted.

"To the Spinners' home world."

Even Carmen's eyes widened at that. "You're not serious," Perez growled. "I, for one, am far too busy to take any trips— certainly in an untested alien craft."

"I'm sure Major Barner and Dr. Nichols can handle cavern duties until we get back," Merdith told him, drawing a stunner from his pocket. "Let's avoid the need for force, shall we? I'd like everyone to be on speaking terms during the voyage."

Perez sent a hard, accusatory look at Hafner and Carmen. "What about the election?" he asked, turning back to Meredith. "Or is this simply an elaborate way of eliminating my influence on Astra?"

"You'll note Dr. Hafner is also going with us," Meredith pointed out. "If you don't consider that being evenhanded, I'll simply mention that Major Barner has instructions to postpone the elections until we return."

"So what are you trying to prove? That you're still the man with all the power on Astra?"

"I've got no more power than anyone in this room," Meredith said flatly. Turning the stunner around, he tossed it to

Perez. "What I've got is curiosity and a hell of a lot of unanswered questions. We've got the chance now to go see what the Spinners did with all the cable they took from Astra; maybe even find out what ultimately happened to them. It seems to me that anyone who's really interested in Astra's future should be interested in knowing whether the simple fact of owning the cable contributed in some way to their destruction. Doesn't it seem that way to you?"

For a long moment Perez stared at him. Then, without a word, he walked over to the seats Meredith had indicated and sat down, dropping the stunner almost contemptuously on the seat beside him. Meredith stepped past him, retrieving the weapon and putting it away as he joined Carmen by the forward viewport and wraparound control board. "Let's go," he told her.

Turning back to the board, she pressed a handful of buttons. Beneath them, the deck vibrated momentarily; and then they were moving along the tracks toward the double doors. Carmen consulted a screenful of Spinner characters and a translator display that had been set up beside it and adjusted another set of controls. "It appears to be automatic now until we're off the planet," she told Meredith, her voice tight. "After that I just need to indicate where we're going on the map I told you about."

"Right." They were into the next room now and approaching the second set of double doors. Sliding into the seat next to Carmen, Meredith took a minute to puzzle out the alien restraining straps. By the time he looked up again, they were slowing down in a machinery-packed room that seemed to have no ceiling. "Under the volcano cone," he grunted, eyes probing the jungle of oddly shaped devices and cables surrounding them. "Um—up ahead, by the wall: isn't that a duplicate of the transport cradle we're riding on?"

"Looks like it," Carmen agreed. "Maybe the empty room we passed through originally held a second lifeboat."

"That might explain why this one was never used," Hafner

put in quietly behind him. "By the time they left, there weren't enough of them still here to need two ships."

Meredith craned his neck to look at the other. Seated next to Loretta, his injured leg sticking awkwardly out from the ill-fitting Spinner seat, the scientist had the look of someone trying hard not to pass judgment prematurely; and it occurred to Meredith that whether or not he succeeded in holding Astra together he stood a fair chance of losing whatever respect and trust he'd built up with these people. But it was far too late to regret his decision. "You think there may have been a plague or something?" he asked Hafner.

"Or else they were running with a skeleton crew at the end. I suppose that's one of the things we're hoping to find out, isn't it?"

Meredith nodded and turned back. The lifeboat had stopped now, and a slight movement among the thinner cables outside caught his eye. "Evacuating the air," he muttered. "Must be going to launch us with the gravity nullifier."

The words were barely out of his mouth when the room seemed to tilt away in front of him and, simultaneously, the viewports blackened. "What—?"

"We must be starting up the shaft," Carmen said. "The windows opaque when the boat turns nose up, probably to protect them."

"Nose up?" The deck felt perfectly normal beneath him. "—Ah. So the Spinners could create gravity as well as eliminate it."

"In a craft this size?" Amazement momentarily pulled Perez out of his tight-lipped silence. "Incredible."

"Yeah." Just one more item, Meredith thought grimly, to add to Astra's list of militarily useful hardware.

He hoped to hell the Spinners, whatever had happened to them, had left behind some answers when they went.

"It was pure luck we spotted them," the *Trygve Lie*'s captain told Msuya, his tone indicating he still wasn't sure he should have awakened his superior. "As per instructions we had a telescope trained on Olympus—"

"Yes, yes," Msuya interrupted him, struggling into a robe as his feet searched the floor for his slippers. "Have they shifted yet?"

"No, sir," the other said. "Actually, they seem more like they're heading somewhere in Astra's outer system."

"Or else are trying to get far enough out that we won't be able to get their direction vector when they go," Msuya snarled. It was the sort of precaution he'd expect Meredith to take. "After them, Captain—I want to be right next to them when they shift."

"Yes, sir. We'll leave orbit in five minutes."

Nice try, Colonel, Msuya thought, smiling with grim satisfaction as the alarms sounded their warning of the upcoming activity. *But you can't get that ship away from me. It'll be mine . . . or it'll be no one's.*

Lurching a bit as the *Trygve Lie*'s rotation slowed, he headed for the bridge.

Chapter 32

"So why haven't we shifted?" Perez demanded.

"Keep your RAM cool," Meredith shot back over his shoulder, trying to hold his own fears in check. "Well?" he added as Carmen blanked the screen and leaned back in her chair.

She waved her hands helplessly. "Every diagnostic I can find says nothing's wrong," she said. "The course we're on seems deliberate, as opposed to being random, so I can only conclude the boat knows what it's doing. Or at least thinks it does."

"Great." Meredith pondered. "You said the computer indicated four days to Spinnerhome?"

"Spinner days, yes. About a hundred twenty hours total."

"Does our course indicate anything that far ahead that could be our destination? A larger preprogrammed ship, say, that has the necessary star drive?"

Carmen shook her head. "There's no way to tell at this range."

"This is ridiculous," Perez snorted. "Something's obviously gone wrong. Let's give up and go back to Astra."

"I don't think that would be a good idea," Meredith said.

"There's a repulser flare moving on what looks like an interception course off our starboard side."

"What?" Perez moved to the side viewport to look. "Who is it?"

"Does it matter? Whoever it is would probably be willing to risk even a Spinneret cable embargo in exchange for this one ship."

"But how did they spot us? Carmen—you said we were using a gravity drive of some sort, right? So *we're* not putting out a flare of our own—"

"Msuya will have been watching from the UN ship," Loretta put in quietly. "He knew about the lifeboat."

Carmen twisted around. "He *what*? How could he?"

"Because she told him," Meredith said calmly. "Don't look so surprised; it's been obvious ever since Dunlop's coup attempt that Dr. Williams and her friends were spies planted on us."

"But the Ctencri . . ." Perez trailed off as cold anger replaced the shock on his face. "*Damn* them. They probably went straight to Saleh with my letters." He turned to Loretta. "So they hired you to come here and learn the Spinner language for them."

"They pressured me into doing it," she corrected tiredly. "And now they have my two children. That's the pressure Msuya's been using on me lately."

Perez snorted, looking back at Meredith. "*You* seem remarkably phlegmatic about all this. If you knew she was a spy, why did you let her aboard?"

"What choice was there?" Meredith countered. There were other reasons, but if the UN ship had a chance of overtaking them, he'd best keep his hole card private. "We needed her to decipher the controls, and we'll probably need her at Spinnerhome even more."

"If it helps, I don't really want Msuya to win out here," Loretta said. She looked at Hafner. "Especially after . . . what he tried to do through Major Dunlop. If I'd known he was going to use violence . . ."

"Well, he hasn't won anything yet," Meredith told her. "Why don't you come up here and double-check Carmen's translations, make sure we're not missing some warning light or something."

Loretta nodded and moved to the control board. Meredith took one last look at the distant repulser flare and walked over to Hafner. "You're very quiet, Doctor," he said, sitting down next to him. "Still mad at me for shanghaiing you like this?"

Hafner smiled. "All you had to do was ask, you know—I wouldn't have missed seeing Spinnerhome for the world. No, actually, I was just sitting here trying to figure out what kind of star drive can take us anywhere from a dozen light-years to several hundred in the same few days."

Meredith frowned. "Is *that* the scale Carmen's nav map shows?"

"I don't see it making sense any other way. What we've got here, it seems to me, is that old standby of science fiction, the instantaneous-jump drive."

"Um." Meredith chewed on his lower lip. "Then the five or six days between planets is just the insystem travel time between port and . . . what?"

"A safe distance from large masses, perhaps, or a low dust density," Hafner suggested. "Hard to tell what they came up with. The immediate question, then, is whether Msuya will see anything we don't want him to see when we go."

"Before that comes the question of his capturing us," Meredith said dryly.

"Won't he run out of fuel first? A couple-three days of constant acceleration—"

"Won't bother him. The Rooshrike gave me the specs to Ctencri courier ships a few months back; it turns out they're designed for long-range insystem work as well as interstellar."

"Oh." Hafner pursed his lips. "I don't suppose we're armed or anything."

"I doubt it. Maybe Carmen can program a little more speed for us." He stood up, paused as Hafner touched his arm.

"Did you know Msuya could follow us?" the scientist asked quietly. "In other words, do you have a plan?"

"Afraid not," Meredith shook his head. "I thought he'd see us emerge from Olympus, but I expected to be long gone into hyperspace before he could do anything about it. We'll just have to hope it takes him long enough to figure out how to perform deep-space piracy for us to reach our jump point."

"If not, we break out the cutlasses?"

Meredith gave him a reassuring smile and moved off.

"You're just making this harder on yourselves," Msuya growled, the distortions caused by the Spinner speaker not quite masking the other's rage. "You obviously can't control your ship well enough to escape, and it's clear your star drive's broken. I assure you I'm quite willing to disable you if I have to."

"If you really wanted to shoot us down, you could have done so anytime in the past eight hours," Meredith reminded him. Their talk had been going on sporadically for nearly that long now, and he, for one, was getting sick of hashing over the same territory. But as long as Msuya was reluctant to damage his prize—and as long as the odd gravitational effects from the lifeboat's drive continued to make a boarding dangerous for both ships—the impasse was a remarkably stable entity. "As I've said before, if you can't offer suitable guarantees for our safety, we'd just as soon go down with the ship."

"You talk very casually of throwing your lives away," the UN official spat out. He, apparently, was getting impatient as well. "Let me tell you a secret: sacrificing yourselves will no longer protect the Spinneret's secrets. We—*I*—know everything you do about the operation of your precious machine."

"Yes, Dr. Williams has been telling us about your little spy network. Not a particularly clever setup, you know—I'm sure the CIA or KGB could have designed something better for you."

There was a moment of silence, and in the gap Carmen

snapped her fingers twice. Meredith looked at her; she pointed urgently to his seat belts and then to the screen. Against the navigation grid had appeared two spots that flickered back and forth from red to orange; directly between them sat the Lorraine-cross course indicator. Meredith raised his eyebrows questioningly, got an uneasy shrug in return, and began strapping in.

"So you know about that, do you?" Msuya said at last. "Well, it'll do you no good. Arrest them—execute them if it makes you feel any better—but understand that all I need to control the Spinneret is already in my hands."

In front of Meredith, the viewport opaqued. "This must be it," Carmen muttered tightly.

"Good-bye, Msuya," Meredith said. "We'll look for you when we get back."

"Meredith—!"

From somewhere aft came a shriek like a parrot being smothered in cotton; an instant later Msuya's voice was cut off as a brief wave of vertigo threatened to turn Meredith's stomach. The nausea subsided . . . and when the viewports cleared again a dull red sun the size of a basketball sat directly in their path.

"Well," Meredith said, letting out a breath he hadn't known he was holding. "I think we're here."

"Wherever 'here' is," Perez said, climbing stiffly out of his seat and coming forward to peer over Carmen's shoulder. "What was that scream just before the gravity jumped? It sounded like we were losing the whole tail section."

"I don't know." Carmen indicated a readout. "But the local-grav indicator went crazy right then."

"How crazy?" Hafner asked. "Like we'd skimmed the edge of a small black hole?"

"Is *that* what those two spots on the screen were?" Carmen asked.

"Two?" Hafner frowned.

"Wait a minute," Perez growled. "Are you saying we just flew *through* a black hole?"

"The course marker went *between* the two spots," Meredith told him, "so we probably didn't hit either one. Though why we had to get even that close, I don't know."

"Possibly the high gravity gradient's needed to trigger their star drive mechanism," Hafner suggested thoughtfully. "And if that's true, it would explain why there are so few jump points listed on the boat's map."

"It does?" Carmen frowned. ". . . Oh. There aren't going to be many systems with even a single black hole nearby, let alone a pair. So Astra was picked for the Spinneret for no better reason than its accessibility?"

"With maybe a minor point being its proximity to an asteroid belt. They may have brought down some of the bigger asteroids themselves." Hafner craned his head to see out the viewport. "Any idea where Spinnerhome is out there?"

"It doesn't show on the displays yet. But the boat seems to know where it's going."

"Then it may be confused," Perez said softly. "This isn't the Spinners' system."

Meredith spun to look at him. "What?"

Perez gestured toward the viewport. "The sun in the cavern is yellow."

For a long minute there was dead silence in the room. "Maybe it's a double star system," Loretta offered at last. "With a yellow star behind, where we can't see it."

"In that case we should be veering to go around the red one," Perez pointed out.

"Maybe we will, once we build up more speed," Carmen said.

"Maybe," Perez said darkly. "Maybe not."

Meredith broke the silence that followed. "There's no point in worrying about it now. We're all dog-tired; let's go aft and find somewhere to sleep. In a few hours we'll have a better idea what the boat's got in mind."

* * *

The main passenger section consisted of three airline-type cabins, each with twenty tall, thin chairs that flattened out into beds. By unspoken agreement they all stayed together, stretching out in the five beds closest to the forward door. One by one, with little conversation, they went to sleep.

Meredith was the first to wake, six hours later, and when he padded to the control room he found Carmen's hunch had been correct. The red sun, noticeably larger, was now sitting off their port bow, while the screen indicated a course that would come perilously close to the edge but clearly miss it. Bringing forward one of the supply boxes, he improvised a table and was setting out five field-ration breakfasts when the others drifted in.

"So Dr. Williams was right after all," Perez said grudgingly after surveying the situation. "Any sign of the other sun yet?"

"Not that I could see," Meredith said, waving Loretta to the seat beside him. He didn't blame the others for being cool toward her, but it was about time to put a stop to that nonsense. He was opening his mouth to do so when Perez suddenly yelped.

"Hey! What was that?"

"What?" Carmen asked, joining him.

"A flash of yellow near the middle of the sun," he said, pointing. "Just for a second."

"A solar flare?" Meredith ventured.

"Doesn't sound like it," Hafner grunted, struggling to get out of his seat. Loretta moved to help him. "Flares are hot spots, all right, but a yellow burst from a red sun seems pretty excessive. Whereabouts was it?"

"A little below the center—there! There goes another one!"

This one lasted several seconds before winking out as abruptly as it had appeared. "That *is* damned odd," Meredith agreed uneasily. "Carmen, is there some way you can get spectrum or intensity data on those?"

Carmen was peering at the translator screen. "I don't know. I don't remember seeing anything like that in the manual. Of course, I wasn't looking for it either."

"Dr. Williams, help her," Meredith ordered. "The rest of you keep an eye on the sun."

They counted twelve more of the brief flashes before Carmen and Loretta found a spectrometer program for the boat's sensors. It was, unfortunately, useless for their purposes, lacking any fine-directional capability.

"Could there be a ring of asteroids grazing the surface?" Perez suggested. "Maybe the flares occur when one of them impacts."

"They're still too short-lived for that," Hafner shook his head. "Besides, there's no real 'surface' to a star; just a steadily thinning atmosphere."

"Sure there's a surface," Perez retorted. "I can see it."

"You *what*?"

"Sure. Watch the edge—the stars disappear right behind it."

Closing one eye, Meredith held his hand up to cut out as much of the sun's glare as he could. Sure enough, the stars disappeared behind the edge with no preliminary dimming that he could detect. Shifting his gaze, he found himself looking into Hafner's eyes. "Are you thinking the same thing I am?" the geologist asked carefully.

Meredith's mouth felt a little dry. "It's impossible," he said. "The size alone—no, it can't possibly be."

"What can't be?" Carmen demanded.

Hafner waved at the viewport. "That's not a star," he said quietly. "It's a gigantic artifact. A sphere, enclosing the Spinner sun . . . and probably Spinnerhome, as well."

Chapter 33

"It's called a Dyson sphere," Hafner explained, the dull throbbing in his head and leg forming an odd counterpoint to the giddy feeling of unreality seeping into his brain. After the Spinneret he'd thought he could handle anything. But *this*— "It was supposed to be a way for a civilization to trap all the energy from its sun. Odds are that thing's made of sheets of cable material, supported by a framework of the cables themselves."

"I'll be damned," Meredith murmured. "That *would* explain what they needed a planetworth of cable for, wouldn't it?"

"Possibly," Carmen said slowly. "But it doesn't explain why they left the Spinneret running."

"We're back to them assuming they'd be coming back when they left," Hafner agreed. Something was gnawing at the back of his brain, something about that huge artifact that seemed wrong. But he couldn't place it. "I gather the boat's heading for a passage through the sphere. Colonel, you mentioned last night you brought a telescope along?"

"A small one, yes." Meredith turned away from the viewport. "Perez, give me a hand and we'll set it up in here."

The two men left, and Carmen and Loretta resumed their

examination of the boat's manual. Easing into the seat beside Carmen, Hafner stretched out his leg and tried to nail down what was bothering him.

He hadn't succeeded by the time Meredith and Perez had the telescope set up between the two control panel seats . . . but an hour later, as Carmen was calling attention to a curious flattening of the sphere's limb, he got at least a piece of it.

"Best guess is that the sphere wasn't finished and that we're coming up on the uncompleted edge," Meredith was suggesting as Hafner limped over from the side viewport to the group huddled by the telescope.

"Seems silly to start a project that size and then not finish it," Carmen said.

"Their Congress must've cut the funding," Meredith said dryly, eliciting a snort from Perez.

"Or maybe they discovered it wasn't working," Hafner offered. "A superconductor like cable material would be great for collecting light and particle energies, but I'm not at all sure how you'd then turn the heat into something useful."

"What's wrong with thermocouples?" Perez asked.

"You need a temperature difference somewhere for those to work," Meredith said. "As a matter of fact, it seems to me that almost *all* energy-extraction schemes require an energy differential."

"Maybe they know a method that doesn't," Loretta suggested. "After all, they built at least half the sphere before they quit."

"The Poms told me the radiation spectrum from cable material lacks some lines," Carmen said doubtfully. "Could something like that be the 'cool' part of the extraction cycle?"

Meredith shrugged. "That's as good a guess as any. Maybe we'll know better when we get a look at the inner surface."

"There's something else, though," Hafner muttered. "Something else that's not right. . . ."

"Well, when you think of it, let us know," Meredith said,

peering through the telescope. "Carmen, is there anything like an emergency beacon aboard that we ought to trigger?"

"It's already on," Loretta told him, pointing to one of the indicators. "I believe it's been going since we got here."

"And no response. Doesn't look very promising."

Unnoticed, Hafner returned to the side port and his thoughts . . . and as he stared at the bright red sphere a disturbing idea slowly began to take shape. An interpretation so wildly improbable, in fact, that he spent the next two hours searching his memory for something—anything—with which to refute it. Instead, everything he knew about the Spinners and their cable merely strengthened the theory. *But there's still so much I don't know,* he told himself when he finally gave up the effort. *Better not to tell anyone else. Not just yet. . . .*

He spent the rest of the day struggling to hide his feelings from the others. Fortunately, everyone was so busy discussing and observing the sphere that they didn't seem to notice his silence. When, during dinner, Carmen did, he passed it off as temporary discomfort in his leg. She didn't press the point then; but when they all returned to the passenger cabin that evening she casually took the bed next to his, and a few minutes after Meredith turned down the lights he sensed her lean over the narrow gap separating them.

"You all right, Peter?" she whispered. "You're quieter than I've ever seen you."

In the darkness he shook his head. "There's nothing you can do," he whispered back. "If I'm right . . . and we'll know in a day or two."

"Want to talk about it?"

"No. Not until I know for sure."

She didn't say any more, but a moment later her hand reached across to touch his. He gripped it tightly . . . and, eventually, fell asleep.

By morning the sphere filled nearly half the sky, giving a bright red glow to everything within range of a viewport and triggering a low hum that Carmen finally identified as the boat's cooling system. The light was too intense for telescopic viewing to be safe, but Perez discovered that by using a piece of cardboard with a small piece cut out, enough of the glare could be eliminated to see the holes through which glimpses of the true sun had earlier been visible. In all he located twenty-eight gaps of various sizes, their positioning on the surface following no pattern anyone could detect. For a while there was a lively discussion of their possible function, but it eventually died from lack of data. Hafner stayed out of the discussion; for him, the gaps merely added to his gloom.

And two hours after lunch the lifeboat rounded the ragged edge and entered the sphere.

"You know," Carmen said, shaking her head slowly, "I don't think I really believed Peter was right . . . until now."

There were murmurs of agreement; and even Hafner found his depression lifted temporarily by the sheer grandeur of the sight. This side glowed, too, but its intensity was considerably muted, as if the Spinners had coated their superconducting material with something to send the light outward. Attached to the sphere they could see clumps of rock spaced at regular intervals in all directions; on the very closest the telescope was just able to pick out spiderweb-thin lines leading outward like latitude-longitude markings on a globe.

"Asteroids," Meredith identified the rocks, shading his eyes as he peered farther away down the vast curved surface. "Held in place by a framework of Spinneret cable. So *that's* why they needed something that strong—they've got to support umpteen tons of rock against the sphere's rotation."

"Ideal for the job, too," Perez murmured. "Flexible enough that you don't need to smooth out the asteroid much to make good contact."

"What are they for?" Loretta breathed. "The asteroids, I mean."

"Customs ports, maybe," Perez suggested. "Those holes

must have been how ships were going to get in and out when the sphere was finished."

"More likely they were where the antigrav stabilizers were located," Hafner spoke up. "Even rotating, the sphere's position isn't really stable; they'd need some way to make periodic corrections." He hesitated. "And they must also be where the sphere's heaters are set up."

They all turned to face him. "The *what*?" Perez asked.

Hafner took a deep breath. "We were wrong about the sphere's purpose. Even if it collected and radiated every bit of the interior sun's light, it couldn't possibly get any hotter than about three hundred degrees absolute—room temperature, essentially. But in fact it's at least ten times that hot. There's no way that could happen without a massive input of energy."

"That's ridiculous," Perez snorted. "You must have made some order-of-magnitude error."

Hafner shook his head. "I almost wish I had. But it's a perfectly straightforward Stefan-Boltzmann calculation."

"All right, then, let's assume you're right," Meredith said. "Can you give a reason why they'd go to that kind of trouble?"

"It wasn't just to heat their planet up," Hafner said. It was odd, a small observer in his brain noted, how even now he avoided simply coming out and saying it. "Orbiting reflectors could have done that. A smaller sphere would have done if they'd decided they wanted a red sky. It wasn't built to live on; they wouldn't have needed to heat it like that and I suspect we'll find the main shell is too thin to support much weight." He paused. "Colonel Meredith . . . what would you do if you knew there was an enemy looking for your position and you didn't have the strength to fight him?"

Meredith's eyes gazed unblinkingly into his. *He's figured it out,* Hafner thought. *I was right, then: it* does *make sense. God help them . . . and us.* "I would retreat," the colonel said quietly. "Or else try and camouflage myself. Is that it?"

"No," Carmen whispered. "You don't mean—they built the sphere to make themselves look like a red giant star system?"

Hafner nodded. "It fits, doesn't it? The superconducting shell to spread the heat out evenly; the missing spectral lines you mentioned undoubtedly corresponding to those of a real red giant. The hard edge wouldn't be noticed at any real distance, even if they thought to look for it."

Perez stirred. "And the lack of completion. . . ." He left the sentence unfinished. "The holes aren't entrance ports, then, are they?"

"Blast damage," Meredith murmured. "Whoever they were afraid of found them too soon."

For a long moment there was silence. The edge of the sphere was slowly receding, and looking ahead Hafner thought he could see a small dot of reflected light a few degrees from the sun. Spinnerhome, undoubtedly. He wondered how much of the devastation of that long-past war would be visible from orbit. He wasn't looking forward to finding out.

"But *why*?" Loretta finally voiced the question Hafner knew they were all thinking. "Why did they sit here and let themselves get blown up? Surely they knew these enemies were coming—they had to be *centuries* building this thing. Why didn't they use the time to build up their armaments, or even just pick up and leave?"

"Maybe they had nowhere else they could go," Carmen said. "Their star drive only allows them limited choices, remember."

"What about Astra?" Loretta countered. "It must have been habitable before they drained all the metals out of it."

"I think Carmen's essentially correct," Hafner said, "except that it may not have been a matter of conscious choice. I think they were so tied to their own world that they simply *couldn't* relocate elsewhere."

"Ridiculous," Loretta snorted.

"You're forgetting the Spinner cavern," Meredith said, shaking his head slowly. "You're right, Dr. Williams; they *could* have lived on the surface while building and operating the Spinneret. But they chose instead to spend enormous time and effort in duplicating their home planet's environment, from the sunlight down to even the proper odors. If they could take the time from the defense of their race to do that, I can well believe they considered it something they couldn't live without. You shake your head; but remember we're not talking about human beings but about aliens. They're under no obligation to think and react like we do."

"Or vice versa?" Perez's smile was bitter. "You're too kind to our species, Colonel. How many wars have been fought, do you suppose, because two groups of people each considered the same little plot of land to be theirs? How many people have died in battle or withered in refugee camps because they would not move over to a new place that was often every bit as good as the one their ancestors had lived on? You have an affluent, mobile American's view of land, I think. The rest of the world differs from the Spinners more in degree than in substance."

"Point," Meredith admitted. "But you're too kind in turn to modern Americans. I might not be willing to die for any given acre of land, but I *would* do so for my country as a whole. And when my car was stolen once I genuinely wanted to machine-gun the guy who did it." He looked out at the sphere.

"You see what that means, of course," Hafner said, the words trying to stick in his throat. "We can't allow humanity to get stuck in a single spot like the Spinners did." He looked at Carmen. "You remember—once—I said the Spinneret cable might have been used to make a giant cage for something. I was right; but it was a cage for their whole race." He shook his head. "And the only way to make sure that doesn't happen to us is to open immigration to Astra."

The others all looked at him. "You mean that?" Perez asked, frowning. "You're changing sides?"

"Don't flatter yourself," Hafner snapped. "I still think bringing a bunch of people into what's essentially a make-work situation is stupid. But putting our eggs in two baskets is at least a little better than leaving them in one. So go ahead: bring in your spies and parasites. I don't care anymore."

"*I* care," Perez shot back, glancing once at Loretta. "I was the one who originally worried about spies stealing our secrets, remember. And I don't want to bring people to Astra just for the sole purpose of having warm bodies lying around. If we can't get useful jobs for them—"

"Ease up, both of you," Meredith interrupted. "You'll wind up adopting each other's basic politics in a minute. I brought you here to end this battle, not to start it over again backward."

Perez cocked a suspicious eyebrow. "I thought we came to learn about the Spinners and the cable."

"We did; but since all the information I wanted probably got blown up with the rest of the planet, I'm going to have to try something else. Let's start with the problem and go from there."

Briefly, he outlined how possession of the Gorgon's Head security code opened up the possibility for terrorist attack. Hafner felt a shiver climb his spine; he hadn't realized they were that close to solving the code, and he certainly hadn't thought through all the implications. "As long as we don't know how to correct any sabotage that gets done to the control settings, we're extremely vulnerable to a Dunlop-style attack," Meredith concluded. "And the stronger the political tensions on Astra, the more likely that kind of operation becomes. What we have to do is drastically tone down the disharmony, at least past the election and probably a year or so beyond; and what *that* means is eliminating these budding political parties."

"And how do you intend to do that?" Perez asked. "A ban by royal decree?"

"No, I'm simply going to knock the props out from under them. Since they're both single-issue groups, all we need is for their leaders to publicly come out for a compromise. That'll take the wind out of everyone's rhetoric, at least until the new Council is elected."

Perez snorted. "So you dragged us all the way out here to talk about a compromise? We could have done all this back in your office."

Meredith gazed at him. "No," he said quietly. "I brought you here to tell you that you *will* accept a compromise—either mine or whatever else we can all come up with. One way or another, we're going to be in agreement before we leave this ship."

"Or else?" Perez prompted coolly.

"Or else you, Perez, will be arrested for treason. It was *your* actions that brought Dr. Williams and her fellow spies from Earth and ultimately resulted in Dunlop's coup attempt—and, yes, I *can* prove all of that in court. I think even your most avid supporters would fade back into the woodwork at that point."

"Blackmail," Perez nodded. "Do you have something similar to hold over Hafner's head, or am I a special case?"

"Dr. Hafner doesn't have your talent for influencing crowds," the colonel said. "Besides, I expect him to be reasonable on this."

Perez sighed. "You know, it gets very tiring after a while to *always* be misunderstood," he said, shaking his head. "Did it never occur to you that I might *jump* at the opportunity to find some middle ground; that I might possibly prefer to lose half of my wish list in exchange for not making a long-term enemy?"

"It did," Meredith nodded. "But I didn't want to rely on it. You're very good at getting things done your way; this time, we're damn well going to do things *my* way. So you want to be a statesman? Here's your chance to get in some practice."

And with that he began to outline his plan.

The discussion lasted the better part of that day and the next, and through it all Perez indeed proved himself able to compromise. By the time the boat went into orbit around Spinnerhome and clicked itself back to manual control, most of the details had been satisfactorily worked out, leaving all aboard free to perform what studies they could on the shattered world below them.

It was as depressing a sight as Meredith had ever seen. Even after thousands of years the huge icecaps that must have formed after the saturation bombing still covered nearly a quarter of the planet. Elsewhere, a few patches of green and yellow could be seen through the clouds, but most of the land seemed to be desert hues of brown and gray-red. Nothing but solar noise existed on any band the radio could pick up; nowhere were any lights visible. By the fifth orbit Meredith called it quits. "Whoever they were, they were apparently very thorough," he said grimly. "If any of the Spinners had survived, they should have been able to recover at least some of their technology by now."

"That could be us someday," Carmen said with a shudder.

"Maybe we've got a chance to avoid it now," Perez said. "At least total extermination. . . ." He looked at Meredith. "Have we seen enough? It seems to me we ought to be getting back."

Meredith nodded, doing a rapid calculation. Four Spinner days each way, another one in orbit at Spinnerhome—eleven Earth days total. Plenty of time for Msuya to have made the necessary arrangements with Saleh and made it back to Astra. "Yes," he nodded. "Let's go home."

The return trip was uneventful but subdued. Meredith spent a great deal of time with the lifeboat's operating manual, taking advantage of the rare leisure time to learn as much as he could about the craft and the Spinner language generally. The others, too, seemed to keep to themselves, as if each needed to sort out privately the revelations of the past few days. At times Meredith found himself staring out a side viewport at the Spinner's grand failure, wondering if his own plans would crumble as theirs had, and wishing he could discuss them with someone. But he resisted the temptation. It was too late to change anything now, and there was no point in everyone else losing sleep as well.

And at last the twin black holes appeared on their screen; and when the nausea of the jump had passed and the viewports cleared again, they were indeed home. Astra, marginally closer to the jump point than when they'd left, was a bright spot with an almost discernible disk. Surrounding it were smaller flecks of light that resolved in the telescope as spaceships.

A *lot* of spaceships.

"Wonder what's happening," Carmen said uneasily as Perez sat at the telescope counting the ships for a third time.

Meredith, in the seat beside her, adjusted the radio to what he hoped was the right frequency. "If I've read Msuya right," he said, "what we're seeing is a UN military attack."

"*What*?" Carmen gasped. "But—"

"The security code," Hafner said abruptly. "The other spies—he's got the code to make new supervisors, doesn't he?" He snapped his fingers. "*That's* why you wanted to take this trip right away, isn't it? To get the lifeboat out of his reach."

"You mean you deliberately left Astra open to that—" Perez began.

Holding up his hand for silence, Meredith mentally crossed his fingers and flipped the Send switch. "This is Colonel Meredith," he said into his mike. "Please patch me through to Major Barner."

Chapter 34

Secretary-General Saleh was seated alone at the far end of the conference room table when Meredith and Carmen entered. Passing up his usual seat at the table's head, the colonel moved down to sit directly across from their visitor. The usual unspoken conventions of position and relative power could be ignored in such an informal meeting. "Good day, Mr. Saleh," he nodded as Carmen sat down beside him. "May I present Miss Carmen Olivero, head of the Astran Council."

Saleh nodded with tight-lipped courtesy and looked back at Meredith. "Before we go any farther, Colonel, I must officially insist that the bodies of the UN commando squad be returned to us."

"You're not in much of a bargaining position, but we have every intention of sending the bodies back. Whether or not the Rooshrike will let you leave the system is, of course, another matter entirely."

"Indeed. Their spokesman informs me that decision is up to you."

"Ah," Meredith nodded. He'd already heard that from Beaeki nul Dies na, but he'd wanted to make sure Saleh knew it, too. "Well, you can't blame them for being touchy. As our supply partners and sort-of sales agents, they have a vested interest in making sure the Spinneret stays in Astran hands. You, on the other hand, are seen as allies of the Ctencri, whom they have no special affection for."

"You need not spell out all the details," Saleh said coldly. "I'm quite aware Msuya's attempted raid has stirred up a great deal of antagonism toward Earth."

Msuya's raid, Meredith thought. The phrase was as subtle as a public hand washing—and almost certainly proclaimed Msuya's political demise. *Goal one; check.* "All right, then. The races that provide the wonderful gadgets on which your power is based are mad at you. How would you like it if I broke your stranglehold on Earth for good?"

Saleh's face remained impassive. "How would you do that?"

"By opening up direct trade with individual nations, of course. After this fiasco the Ctencri couldn't lift a finger to protect their monopoly with you, and with our cable income we could undercut any price you or they could offer. In no time you'd be back to being the overgrown debating society you were a couple of years ago. I presume you would find that distasteful?"

"Of course—as would you," Saleh said. "Surely you recognize from history that Earth has a better chance for international peace under the sort of economic empire the UN now represents." He waved a hand. "You didn't ask me down here simply to gloat over my impending destruction, Colonel; you're not the sort of man who does. I conclude you wish to make a deal. May we get down to it?"

"Fine. Basically, we want to open up Astra for immediate immigration."

"I see. And the prospective settlers will come predominantly from North America, I expect."

"You expect wrong. We want mostly poor and dispossessed from the Third World countries."

For just a second Saleh's impassive expression cracked with

surprise before settling into place again. "The people you speak of are mostly farmers," he pointed out. "What would they do here?"

"Work their butts off, for starters. Don't misunderstand me— I don't want Bangladesh or whoever dumping its street bums and criminals on us. We want people who haven't got much chance where they are but still have the ambition and hope to grab a new opportunity when it presents itself." He leveled a finger at Saleh. "That'll be *your* job: to make sure this offer gets to those people and to provide information to us for screening purposes. Miss Olivero has a file with all the details."

Beside him, Carmen pulled a cassette from her shoulder pouch and handed it over. Saleh hesitated a fraction of a second before taking it. He fingered it for a moment, frowning as if he suspected it might explode. "I . . . appreciate what I believe you're trying to do," he said at last, looking up at Meredith. "But do you think you can truly give vast numbers of people a better life here?"

"No—but most of them won't actually be here for long. Once their education and training are completed they'll be sent out to the neighboring empires to monitor the installation and use of Spinneret cables."

Saleh frowned. "They'll *what*?"

"Don't look so surprised. One of the major worries we've had all along has been the ease with which the cables can be applied to warfare. I don't want the stuff used that way, and neither do any of the races I've talked to—or at least that's what they say. So okay; from now on each cable is going to be accompanied by a small group of monitors, who'll go with it to the installation site and certify it winds up doing what it was supposed to. Other teams will routinely look at old installations, both to make sure the cable hasn't been moved and to perform long-term studies of strength degradation and such. Sure, there won't be all that much to do for now, but it'll take a while to train the monitors anyway. And we *do* plan to sell *lots* of cables."

Slowly, Saleh nodded. "It may work—for a limited number, at least. Very well; you may count on my complete cooperation in this project." He hesitated. "In fact, you would have had my help even without resorting to threats. It appears your vision for Astra is not so different from mine, after all."

"Glad to hear it." _Goal two; check_. "Then there's just one more thing." Meredith let his gaze harden. "Do you know how your commandos died?"

Saleh grimaced slightly. "I understand they were electrocuted by your Gorgon's Head machines in the Spinner cavern control tower. I don't know how Major Barner managed it."

"Major Barner didn't do a thing. One of the commandos, keying in what he _thought_ was the sequence for authorizing new supervisors, actually typed something that translates roughly as 'supervisor in danger.' The rest followed automatically." He paused, but Saleh remained silent. "I'm sure you see what that means, but I'll spell it out anyway. With the best transmission equipment and most elaborate scramblers the Ctencri could provide your spies, we still could not only monitor their communication with Msuya, but could even inject our own information into their data transfers. That first of all means you can't trust _anything_ Ermakov and company gave you; and it second of all means you'll be wasting your time if you try this sort of trick again. Clear?"

"Clear." Saleh's voice was calm. "Will the scientists be executed?"

"I'm tempted; but no. Instead, I'll trade them to you for Dr. Loretta Williams's two children, whom you've got in protective custody somewhere. Dr. Williams is staying with us, and it would be nice if her family could be here with her."

A dozen questions flickered across Saleh's face, but he merely nodded. "They'll be brought here as soon as possible."

"Good. Well, then, I think that wraps things up for now." Meredith rose and extended his hand. "Read Miss Olivero's proposals carefully and contact us with any questions or comments."

Saleh reached across the table to grip Meredith's hand. "I'll do so . . . and whether you believe it or not, Colonel, I look forward to working on this with you." He nodded gravely to Carmen, then turned and opened the outside door. There was a brief gust of icy air, and then he was gone.

"Goal three and game," Meredith muttered, feeling the tension draining out of him. If Saleh was even half as sincere as he'd seemed, the whole thing might just work. Taking a deep breath, he looked at Carmen. "Well. I don't know about you, but I still have a mountain of work waiting for me back at Unie. Shall we go?"

Carmen snorted as they headed for the door leading to the rest of Martello Base. "You make it sound like I have nothing to do."

"It's got to be easier than it was before all the campaign rhetoric started cooling down." He glanced at her as he opened the door for them. "You're still troubled about something, aren't you?"

She nodded. "Loretta Williams. How are you so sure she's really on our side now? If it's not a secret, that is."

"No secret—I just never got around to telling all of you on our little excursion. You know how we tapped the spy comm net, don't you?"

"Major Barner said you installed Rooshrike gadgets in the radios that let you receive the signals before they went through the scramblers."

"Right. And since the Orspham could give us copies of the corresponding scrambled conversations, we could break the scrambler code itself, which is why we were able to substitute our own computer sequence at this end when Udani tried to send the supervisor data."

"If you knew they were spies, though, why didn't you arrest them right away?"

"Because we still needed their help to decipher the Spinneret equipment." Meredith smiled. "Besides which, it was handy to have Msuya thinking he knew more about the Spinneret than we did. You see, Ermakov and his gang were editing out crucial bits of information in their reports to us, bits they naturally passed on to Msuya. With the bugs in place we actually got everything, of course, but as far as Msuya knew we shouldn't have had the means to even look for the supervisor-danger code, let alone find it. So it never occurred to him to plan for such a contingency."

Carmen seemed to digest that. "I take it, then, that Loretta's reports to us *were* complete?"

"Better than that, actually. After Dunlop's move she started shaving data going the *other* direction. Msuya never knew the lifeboat's full size, for example, and the location she gave him was down an entirely different tunnel system."

"Odd she never mentioned that."

"Not really. As far as she knew, it would be an unprovable and all-too-convenient-sounding excuse."

They'd reached the door that looked out over Martello's docks now. Glancing out the small windows as they pulled their coats from the nearby rack, Meredith saw that it was beginning to flurry again. He hoped the major storm the satellites had spotted would miss the area as predicted; the Rooshrike were due to start landing two hundred tons of iron and aluminum early in the morning. Pushing the door open, he squinted against the wind and led the way to the nearest hovercraft.

It wasn't until they were out in the open water that Carmen spoke again. "It won't work, you know. I've run the numbers, and there's no way this cable monitor program can absorb enough people to do any real good. Even with the teachers and community setup people we'll need to support the whole thing, we're not going to be able to give genuine jobs to more than a couple hundred thousand people at the most. Even the embassies we'll be setting up everywhere in sight won't absorb that many more." She shook her head tiredly. "There are more than a hundred thousand unemployed beggars in Calcutta alone."

"True," Meredith nodded. "But on the other hand we aren't limited to Astra and Earth anymore, either."

Carmen frowned . . . and, slowly, a look of astonishment spread across her face. "You mean . . . Spinnerhome?"

"Why not? Surely the Spinners' enemies are long gone by now, and it seems unlikely that the basic soil fertility could have been destroyed. Of course, we'll need to check the place out thoroughly first, and we'll have to learn enough about that black hole drive to build bigger ships. But that's one of the reasons I want to concentrate so hard on educating our immigrants. By the time we're ready to open up Spinnerhome, we'll need a cadre of capable people available to spearhead the effort."

"And what if Spinnerhome *is* uninhabitable?" she persisted. "What'll we do then?—start checking the other systems on the lifeboat map until we find something?"

"We could," he nodded. "Or we could search the region around Spinnerhome using our own star drive. Between the two of them we've got access to practically the whole damn galaxy." He shrugged. "And in the meantime we'll have spread mankind out as far as we can and have set up on Astra the first crack at a genuine melting pot that anyone's seen since 1776. On the whole, I think the human race is in better shape now than any time in the past century."

Behind them came the roar of the repulsers, and Meredith looked out the hovercraft window as the UN shuttle arced overhead. Going back to Earth . . . and Meredith chuckled.

"What's funny?" Carmen asked.

He shook his head. "I'd almost forgotten . . . but one of my most hopeful goals for the whole Astra project was that it would earn me a brigadier general's star. I guess, instead, I'll have to settle for a few of the real thing."

*Here is an excerpt from Book I of THE KING OF YS,
Poul and Karen Anderson's epic new fantasy, coming from
Baen Books in December 1986:*

THE KING OF YS: ROMA MATER
POUL AND KAREN ANDERSON

The parties met nearer the shaw than the city.
They halted a few feet apart. For a space there was
stillness, save for the wind.

The man in front was a Gaul, Gratillonius judged.
He was huge, would stand a head above the centurion when they were both on the ground, with a
breadth of shoulder and thickness of chest that
made him look squat. His paunch simply added to
the sense of bear strength. His face was broad,
ruddy, veins broken in the flattish nose, a scar
zigzagging across the brow ridges that shelved small
ice-blue eyes. Hair knotted into a queue, beard
abristle to the shaggy breast, were brown, and had
not been washed for a long while. His loose-fitting
shirt and close-fitting breeches were equally soiled.
At his hip he kept a knife, and slung across his
back was a sword more than a yard in length. A
fine golden chain hung around his neck, but what
it bore lay hidden beneath the shirt.

"Romans," he rumbled in Osismian. "What the
pox brings you mucking around here?"

The centurion replied carefully, as best he was
able in the same language: "Greeting. I hight Gaius
Valerius Gratillonius, come in peace and good

will as the new prefect of Rome in Ys. Fain would I meet with your leaders."

Meanwhile he surveyed those behind. Half a dozen were men of varying ages, in neat and clean versions of the same garb, unarmed. Nearest the Gaul stood one who differed. He was ponderous of body and countenance. Black beard and receding hair were flecked with white, though he did not seem old. He wore a crimson robe patterned with gold thread, a miter of the same stuff, a talisman hanging on his bosom that was in the form of a wheel, cast in precious metal and set with jewels. Rings sparkled on both hands. In his right he bore a staff as high as himself, topped by a silver representation of a boar's head.

The woman numbered three. They were in ankle-length gowns with loose sleeves to the wrists, of rich material and subtle hues, ornately belted at the waist.

The Gaul's voice yanked him from his inspection: "What? You'd strut in out of nowhere and fart your orders at *me*—you who can talk no better than a frog? Go back before I step on the lot of you."

"I think you are drunk," Gratillonius said truthfully.

"Not too full of wine to piss you out, Roman!" the other bawled.

Gratillonius forced coolness upon himself. "Who here is civilized?" he asked in Latin.

The man in the red robe stepped forward. "Sir, we request you to kindly overlook the mood of the King," he responded in the same tongue, accented but fairly fluent. "His vigil ended at dawn today, but these his Queens sent word for us to wait. I formally attended him to and from the Wood, you see. Only in this past hour was I bidden to come."

The man shrugged and smiled. My name is Soren Cartagi, Speaker for Taranis."

The Gaul turned on him, grabbed him by his garment and shook him. "You'd undercut me, plotting in Roman, would you?" he grated. A fist drew back. "Well, I've not forgotten all of it. I know when a scheme's afoot against me. And I know you think Colconor is stupid, but you've a nasty surprise coming to you, potgut!"

The male attendants showed horror. One of the woman hurried forth. "Are you possessed, Colconor?" she demanded. "Soren's person when he speaks for the God is sacred. Let him go ere Taranis blasts you to a cinder!"

The language she used was neither Latin nor Osismian. Melodious, it seemed essentially Celtic, but full of words and constructions Gratillonius had never encountered before. It must be the language of Ys. By listening hard and straining his wits, he got the drift if not the full meaning.

The Gaul released the Speaker, who stumbled back, and rounded on the woman. She stood defiant— tall, lean, her hatchet features haggard but her eyes like great, lustrous pools of darkness. The cowl, fallen down in her hasty movement, revealed a mane of black hair, loosely gathered under a fillet, through the middle of which ran a white streak. Gratillonius sensed implacable hatred as she went on: "Five years have we endured you, Colconor, and weary years they were. If now you'd fain bring your doom on yourself, oh, be very welcome."

Rage reddened him the more. "Ah, so that's your game, Vindilis, my pet?" His own Ysan was easier for Gratillonius to follow, being heavily Osismianized. " 'Twas sweet enough you were this threenight agone, and today. But inwardly—Ah, I should have known. You were ever more man than woman, Vindilis, and hex more than either."

He swung on Gratillonius. "Go, Roman!" he roared. "I am the King! By the iron rod of Taranis, I'll not take Roman orders! Go or stay; but if you stay, 'twill be on the dungheap where I'll toss your carcass!"

Gratillonius fought for self-control. Despite Colconor's behavior, he was dimly surprised at his instant, lightning-sharp hatred for the man. "I have prior orders," he answered, as steadily as he could. To Soren, in Latin: "Sir, can't you stay this madman so we can talk in quiet?"

Colconor understood. "Madman, be I?" he shrieked. "Why, *you* were shit out of your harlot mother's arse, where your donkey father begot you ere they gelded him. Back to your swinesty of a Rome!"

It flared in Gratillonius. His vinestaff was tucked at his saddlebow. He snatched it forth, leaned down, and gave Colconor a cut across the lips. Blood jumped from the wound.

Colconor leaped back and grabbed at his sword. The Ysan men flung themselves around him. Gratillonius heard Soren's resonant voice: "Nay, not here. It must be in the Wood, the Wood." He sounded almost happy. The women stood aside. Vindilis put hands on hips, threw back her head, and laughed aloud.

Eppillus stepped to his centurion's shin, glanced up, and said anxiously, "Looks like a brawl, sir. We can handle it. Give the word, and we'll make sausage meat of that bastard."

Gratillonius shook his head. A presentiment was eldritch upon him. "No," he replied softly. "I think this is something I must do myself, or else lose the respect we'll need in Ys."

Colconor stopped struggling, left the group of men, and spat on the horse. "Well, will you challenge me?" he said. "I'll enjoy letting out your white blood."

"You'd fight me next!" yelled Adminius. He too had been quick in picking up something of the Gallic languages.

Colconor grinned. "Aye, aye. The lot of you. One at a time, though. Your chieftain first. And afterward I've a right to rest between bouts." He stared at the woman. "I'll spend those whiles with you three bitches, and you'll not like it, what I'll make you do." Turning, he swaggered back toward the grove.

Soren approached. "We are deeply sorry about

this," he said in Latin. "Far better that you be received as befits the envoy of Rome." A smile of sorts passed through his beard. "Well, later you shall be. I think Taranis wearies at last of this incarnation of His, and—the King of the Wood has powers, if he chooses to exercise them, beyond those of even a Roman prefect."

"I am to fight Colconor, then?" Gratillonius asked slowly.

Soren nodded. "In the Wood. To the death. On foot, though you may choose your weapons. There is an arsenal at the Lodge."

"I'm well supplied already." Gratillonius felt no fear. He had a task before him which he would carry out, or die; he did not expect to die.

He glanced back at the troubled faces of his men, briefly explained what was happening, and finished: "Keep discipline, boys. But don't worry. We'll still sleep in Ys tonight. Forward march!". . .

It was but a few minutes to the site. A slate-flagged courtyard stood open along the road, flanked by three buildings. They were clearly ancient, long and low, of squared timbers and with shingle roofs. The two on the sides were painted black, one a stable, the other a storehouse. The third, at the end, was larger, and blood-red. It had a porch with intricately carven pillars.

In the middle of the court grew a giant oak. From the lowest of its newly leafing branches hung a brazen circular shield and a sledgehammer. Though the shield was much too big and heavy for combat, dents surrounded the boss, which showed a wildly bearded and maned human face. Behind the house, more oaks made a grove about seven hundred feet across and equally deep.

"Behold the Sacred Precinct," Soren intoned. "Dismount, stranger, and ring your challenge." After a moment he added quietly, "We need not lose time waiting for the marines and hounds. Neither of you will flee, nor let his opponent escape."

Gratillonius comprehended. He sprang to earth,

took hold of the hammer, smote the shield with his full strength. It rang, a bass note which sent echoes flying. Mute now, Eppillus gave him his military shield and took his cloak and crest before marshalling the soldiers in a meadow across the road.

Vindilis laid a hand on Gratillonius's arm. Never had he met so intense a gaze, out of such pallor, as from her. In a voice that shook, she whispered, "Avenge us, man. Set us free. Oh, rich shall be your reward."

It came to him, like a chill from the wind that soughed among the oaks, that his coming had been awaited. Yet how could she have known?